FIRST KISS

Her brown eyes looked directly into his. "You're awfully sure of yourself, aren't you, Bart Montgomery?"

Bart could not resist reaching out to pull her next to him and bending down to kiss her sensuous lips. His kiss was demanding, and Tawny was helpless to refuse.

She felt so tiny in his arms! When he finally sought to release her, Tawny felt herself gasp. His arms still held her, gently, and his eyes beamed down upon her. She was glad he was still holding her, for her legs felt so weak that she would surely have sunk to the ground.

"Sweetest lips I've ever kissed, Tawny Blair!"

She gazed up at him, wondering what else he would say . . . what else he would do.

"One kiss is not enough," he whispered. His head bent down so his lips could capture hers again. She knew that she shouldn't allow such liberties, but with his heated lips on hers, she was powerless to deny herself the pleasure.

She felt his arms pressing her closer and the warmth of his body against hers. His kisses became more ardent and she gasped as she felt his hand slipping up the loosened tunic she wore.

"Tawny," he moaned. "Oh, Tawny, love! I want to make love to you. I must make love to you!"

PASSIONATE NIGHTS FROM ZEBRA BOOKS

ANGEL'S CARESS   (2675, $4.50)
by Deanna James

Ellie Crain was a young, inexperienced and beautiful Southern belle. Cash Gillard was the battle-weary Yankee corporal who turned her into a woman filled with hungry passion. He planned to love and leave her; she vowed to keep him forever with her *Angel's Caress*.

COMMANCHE BRIDE   (2549, $3.95)
by Emma Merritt

Beautiful Dr. Zoe Randolph headed to Mexico to halt a cholera epidemic. She never dreamed her caravan would be attacked by a band of savages. Later, she refused to believe that she could love and desire her captor, the handsome half-breed Matt Chandler. Captor and slave find unending love and tender passion in the rugged Commanche hills.

CAPTIVE ANGEL   (2524, $4.50)
by Deanna James

When handsome Hunter Gillard left the routine existence of his South Carolina plantation for endless adventures on the high seas, beautiful and indulged Caroline Gillard learned to manage her home and business affairs in her husband's sudden absence. Caroline resolved not to crumble and vowed to make Hunter beg to be taken back. He was determined to make her once again his unquestioning and forgiving wife.

SWEET, WILD LOVE   (2834, $3.95)
by Emma Merritt

Chicago lawyer Eleanor Hunt was determined to earn the respect of the Kansas cowboys who openly leered at her as she was working to try a cattle-rustling case. The worse offender was Bradley Smith—even though he worked for Eleanor's father! She was determined not to mistake passion for love; he was determined to break through her icy exterior and possess the passion woman who lurked beneath her.

Available wherever paperbacks are sold, or order direct from the Publisher. Send cover price plus 50¢ per copy for mailing and handling to Zebra Books, Dept. 3091, 475 Park Avenue South, New York, N.Y. 10016. Residents of New York, New Jersey and Pennsylvania must include sales tax. DO NOT SEND CASH.

KISS OF FIRE

WANDA OWEN

ZEBRA BOOKS
KENSINGTON PUBLISHING CORP.

ZEBRA BOOKS

are published by

Kensington Publishing Corp.
475 Park Avenue South
New York, NY 10016

First printing: August, 1990

Printed in the United States of America

This book is dedicated to my dear uncle Earl. I was lucky, for I had not one, but two fathers when I was growing up. This is my way of saying that I love you very much, Uncle Earl.

Part One

A Girl Named Tawny

Prologue

Villagers of Longcreek warmed to the adorable Tabitha Blair even though they did not hold her promiscuous mother in high esteem. The child could not help what her mother did but all the settlers in the village knew how Maybelle Blair earned the extra money that her wages at the local tavern did not provide.

Tabitha was a beautiful child with thick, curly dark-brown hair and big doelike eyes of the same color. By the time she was six years old and began to walk around town on her own she became known as little Tawny.

No one was more protective of Tawny than a neighbor, Roberta Thacher. She felt a deep resentment that she could not have a child while a whore like Maybelle was blessed with a little angel. It didn't seem fair to Roberta.

The middle-aged Mrs. Thacher was convinced, as Tawny grew, that it was her duty to do what she could for this child. As often as she could, she gave the little girl her fresh-baked cookies and pretty ribbons for her glossy chocolate-brown hair.

When her neighbor, Samantha Towers, dared to criticize Tawny for running wild, Roberta came to her defense by saying, "Now, you wait just a minute, Samantha—what would that brood of yours do if they were left on their own to do as they pleased? Tawny has no one to lay down the law to her! The child can't be blamed."

Samantha never dared say another harsh word about Tawny in the presence of Mrs. Thacher. Most of the people of Longcreek felt as Roberta Thacher did and sought to watch over Tawny and give her the attention she didn't get from her mother.

Amazingly, Tawny Blair was not a lonely child as she grew up in the small village a few miles from the coastline of Virginia. And she had no inkling that the same people who were so kind to her held her mother in utter contempt.

Nothing about Tawny resembled her mother. Maybelle's hair was a brassy blond and her complexion was not the light olive hue of Tawny's. Tawny's doelike dark-brown eyes flecked with gold were spellbinding. Maybelle's blue eyes were usually bloodshot.

There was much speculation about who could have sired the magnificent little girl, but no one in Longcreek knew who the father was—no one but Maybelle Blair!

A gamut of rumors had cropped up over the years about this issue. The man had to have been a handsome rogue, whoever he might have been. Tawny was too beautiful to have been fathered by some ordinary fellow.

The day Roberta Thacher was convinced just how much the six-year-old child had captured her heart was when she fell and skinned her knee and Roberta gathered her up in her arms to take her into her house to doctor it. Tawny looked up at her with those warm brown eyes and declared, "Oh, Mrs. Thacher, I don't know what I'd do without you!"

Roberta decided there and then that Tawny would never have to! She kept Tawny at her house the next couple of days and Maybelle Blair voiced no objections. Roberta felt a terrible void when the girl returned to her mother's cottage a few days later.

Many miles away, on his father's country estate an English lad of seventeen had also injured his leg while riding one of the prized Thoroughbred mares. He'd been riding with his friend, Jason Hamilton.

Bartholomew Montgomery, however, was favored with the attentions of a doting mother and father. Lord and Lady Montgomery were concerned about their only son's accident until the doctor assured them that young Bart would be just fine.

Only then did they relax and breathe easy. Bart was their pride and joy. Their whole life revolved around this son, their only child.

Jason Hamilton found it amusing what a difference it made when you had brothers and sisters. All the doting attention had not gone to him—nor would he have wanted it.

Jason and Bart shared a common interest, and that was their love of fine horse flesh and ships. These interests held them together for the next ten years.

When Bart's father suddenly died, he found himself handed the responsibility of becoming the man of the house, though he was only twenty.

By now, Jason Hamilton was involved in his wealthy father's shipping lines. When his grandfather died, he had inherited a fine sleek-lined ship, the *Sea Princess*.

The two handsome young Englishmen were the most sought-after bachelors in London. They were a dashing, adventurous pair as they attended the grand social affairs and horse races or sailed out for a spree on the *Sea Princess*. All the beautiful young women were eager to be their companions on these escapades.

Both of them led a jolly good life as carefree, devil-may-care bachelors.

When Bart Montgomery heard about a rare black Arabian stallion across the ocean in Virginia, it was only natural that he suggest to his friend Jason that they sail across the Atlantic together so that Bart could purchase the fine beast for the Montgomery Stables. Bart could not imagine anything grander than accomplishing this feat. It became his obsession!

Jason finally agreed to take him there in the *Sea Princess*. But neither of them knew when they left the shores of England that another obsession would consume the two of them and would test and threaten their long, devoted friendship.

11

Chapter 1

Tawny Blair was nature's child. She loved to roam the country lanes unhampered by shoes. She loved the pleasure of going barefoot on the dirt roads and grassy grounds around the small cabin where she and her mother lived.

By the time she was sixteen she didn't have to curl her thick, long hair, for there was a natural curl to her brown tresses. She didn't fret about the blazing summer sun harming her complexion as some of the young girls in the town did; Tawny's golden skin glowed like rich satin.

The few frocks she possessed were much mended because she was constantly snagging them on the underbrush when she wandered in the woods to feed the small animals and birds. They were Tawny's companions and friends. The wildflowers flourished there and she could pick them as often as she wished.

Maybelle's earnings at the local tavern were meager, and her gentlemen friends came around less frequently now than they had when Tawny was just a tot. Maybelle's once voluptuous figure was no longer so alluring to them. She had never possessed a beautiful face, and age had taken its toll.

It was Tawny who kept their little cottage clean and their meals prepared because Maybelle slept for hours to prepare herself to go to the tavern to put in her shift at work.

Once she did finally crawl out of the bed, she would eat the meal Tawny had prepare and then drink many cups of black coffee to get herself awake. She spent a long time before her mirror attempting to do something with her blond hair and painting her face in hopes of covering the wrinkles.

Although Tawny never voiced her opinion to her mother, she had decided that her mother was too overpainted to be attractive. Many other things about Maybelle had begun to disturb Tawny. It was established long ago that Tawny stay in her bedroom when her mother came home after work long after midnight. Even now that she was sixteen, she still did not venture through her mother's door, though she'd been tempted to do it for the last year when she'd heard the drunken laughter of her mother and some man in the next room. Lately, she'd found herself sickening with disgust at the sounds she'd heard.

At times, she wanted to rush out of her room and scream at her mother, asking her why she couldn't be a decent lady like Mrs. Thacher. But she never did. Whatever Maybelle was, she was her mother, Tawny told herself.

Tawny was also curious about her father. Who was he and where was he, she wondered? The other girls had fathers, and they lived with the mothers. She'd not been so bold to question her mother about this as yet, but she had decided that she was going to. She had a right to know.

Never had she been anything but the obedient, submissive daughter to Maybelle Blair until the night she heard her mother stumble through the front door as dawn was breaking. Her moans of agony woke Tawny up and she rushed through her door. "Dear Lord, Mama! What in the world happened to you?"

"Lock the door, Tawny!" Maybelle gasped. "The crazy sonofabitch might decide to come back."

"Who, Mama? Who did this to you?" she asked as she bent down to the floor to help her mother who was lying there with blood flowing from her nose and angry red marks on her cheeks.

"Doesn't matter, kid. You wouldn't know him," Maybelle moaned as she struggled to rise with the support of Tawny's help.

Once she'd helped her mother get to the old settee and

left to get a cloth to clean the blood from her face, Tawny called back to her, "I ask you who it was, Mama. I expect you to tell me!" There was a tone in her daughter's voice that Maybelle had never heard before. Watching Tawny move around the cabin to get the things to tend to her injuries, Maybelle suddenly noticed the sensuous curves of her sixteen-year-old daughter's body that she'd paid no attention to before.

"Don't you ever let Jeb Turner through this door. You hear me, kid? He's the one." Maybelle pushed her frizzy blond hair away from her face.

"Turner did this to you? May I ask why?" Tawny came back to the settee to sit down with the pan of water and towels she'd brought from the kitchen.

"Who knows why a man goes crazy sometimes," Maybelle said with a shrug of her shoulders.

But that was not enough to satisfy Tawny. "The tavern's been closed a long time, Mama. Have you and this Jeb been together all those hours?"

Maybelle's blue eyes darted up at her daughter standing over her, staring down at her with those big brown eyes and searching her face.

"What's the matter with you tonight, Tawny? Yeah, Jeb and me spent some time together after I left work."

"And the two of you obviously drank some whiskey 'cause I sure smell it on your breath," she told her mother as she finished cleaning the blood from her face and wet the cloth again to place it across her mother's nose.

"Now, you wait just a minute, kid—who are you to lecture me, eh? I'm the mother," Maybelle declared indignantly as she watched her daughter raise up from the settee.

Maybelle was hardly prepared to hear her daughter's next remark. With her lovely head held high, Tawny retorted, "Then, Mama—I think you should start acting like a mother."

Maybelle watched her walk into the kitchen to take the pan and cloth. She absorbed the sting of Tawny's words,

15

realizing Tawny was no babe anymore. No longer would she be able to conceal from her what she'd been doing all these years to earn the extra money.

She sat there in silence, for she could say nothing right now. She was glad that Tawny said no more, either. When her daughter came out of the kitchen, she asked if she was all right and Maybelle told her she was just fine. "Go on to bed, Tawny. I'm going, too, in just a minute."

"I think I will, Mama. I am tired," Tawny declared as she marched on into her room without coming over to Maybelle to plant a kiss on her cheek as she usually did.

Maybelle sat there in the silence of her small cabin. Tawny could not know the devastating impact she'd had on her. For the longest time Maybelle sat there thinking about her miserable life and the man she had to thank for it. She could thank him for making a whore out of her. How else was a woman like her to make a living when she had no folks to turn to when she found herself pregnant? It had not been a pleasant life and she had nothing to show for it except her beautiful Tawny.

But the way she was looking at her tonight, Maybelle realized that she was losing the respect of her daughter. She should have known that the time would come when what she was doing would become known to Tawny. It had just come sooner than she'd expected. It seemed to Maybelle that her darling little Tawny had blossomed overnight. But something else sparked a greater fear in her now. Some of the gents she'd brought to her house would surely be driven by the wildest, untamed desire if they spotted her beautiful daughter. She could not chance this. None of that scum was going to taint her beautiful Tawny!

How they'd ever make it on her meager earnings at the tavern she did not know, but she vowed to herself that she'd never sell herself to any of the fellows she met at the tavern. Never again would she bring another one of them to her cabin after tonight.

* * *

The next day when Tawny woke up and started her usual routine, she could not know that this day was to change her life forever. Maybelle slept peacefully while Tawny brewed a pot of coffee and fixed her breakfast. It never took her long to get the small cottage in order. But Tawny's motions were swift and fast as was her fiesty walk when she wandered down the country lane.

The beautiful spring day outside the cottage windows beckoned her to go for a stroll along the lanes and by the woods.

She knew that Maybelle would be sleeping for hours after the ordeal she'd endured last night. However, Tawny was still out of sorts with her mother and she was glad she had spoken her mind. She had noticed the stunned look on Maybelle's haggard face.

In her bare feet Tawny left the cottage with her wicker basket swung over her arm to gather the usual bunches of wildflowers she might find as she roamed along the lanes. The sun was bright and its rays gleamed down on her as she strolled along the dirt road. She had not gone too far before she came upon a cluster of wild verbena and she paused to pluck them.

On down the road she came across some lovely golden buttercups and she stopped once again to help herself to the generous clusters growing there. But as she was raising up from the ground a sudden shriek made her freeze. She stood there, wondering where it had come from.

Once again, she heard the cry of someone in pain. With the basket flung around her arm, she began to run in that direction. She did not have to go very far before she came upon a lady lying on the dirt road. She was magnificently dressed in a fine-tailored riding ensemble of deep green. Her fancy hat was sitting to the side of her head. Tawny heard the galloping hooves of the horse that had obviously thrown her.

Tawny rushed up and bent down to help her up to a sitting position. "Ma'am, here let me help you. You got a nasty scratch on your face." Tanwy's nimble fingers

17

brushed the tousled hair from the woman's face and set her bonnet straight.

Reba Cameron looked up into the prettiest face she'd seen around these parts in many a day. "I thank you, young lady, for coming to help me." By now, the middle-aged matron was sitting up, but she felt the arm of the young lady supporting her back. Her warm brown eyes reflected concern when they searched Reba's face.

"I'm all right, dear. I just had a high-spirited stallion that got spooked by a rabbit running across the road," Reba assured her.

"Are you sure? You got a nasty scratch across your face," Tawny declared. She'd never seen such a fancy lady before. She was like the regal ladies in the stories Mrs. Thacher had read to her when she was little. To Tawny, this lady was the image she envisioned as a queen.

Reba smiled. "Well, this face has had a scratch or two before so I guess I can consider myself lucky. By the way, I'm Reba Cameron. What is your name, dear?"

"Tawny Blair, ma'am."

"Tawny Blair, is it. Well, that is the perfect name for you," Reba Cameron declared as she looked at the girl's lovely face with that glorious crown of deep brown hair. With the sun shining down on them, Reba thought that her expensive sable cape was no more exquisite than this lovely little creature's glossy mane of thick, dark brown hair.

"It's a pleasure to meet you, Mrs. Cameron. Let me take you to my home to doctor the scratch on your face. You're going to have to wait somewhere anyway, aren't you?"

The young girl was right, Reba Cameron realized. That wild, crazy stallion was God knows where, and her husband Bill was going to have a fit when he heard about this because he had tried to persuade her not to take the horse out today. She had stubbornly ignored his warning that she might not be able to control the high-spirited Arabian. Reba considered herself to be a very capable rider, but Diablo was no ordinary horse.

Bill had told her the Arabian was the purest of all the

18

equine breeds and a very proud beast. Their bloodlines went back thousands of years. Reba had never seen a more beautiful animal than this one and they'd bred their fine Thoroughbreds for years.

She accepted Tawny's offer to go to her cottage, for she knew that any of the people of the town would recognize the fine stallion and take him back to their farm. Then Bill would have to come looking for her.

But as Tawny was helping Mrs. Cameron up and they were starting to walk down the road toward Tawny's home, a local gentleman was approaching them from behind with the stallion in tow. Obviously, he was not brave enough to try to mount the spirited horse so he was leading the animal by the reins.

When Reba turned to see that her husband's prized Arabian was safe, she gave him her heartfelt thanks.

Tawny helped her secure the reins tightly to the trunk of a tree close to the cottage. Reba laughed. "We'll just pray this will hold that rambunctious critter."

Tawny laughed and agreed that she hoped so, too, for he was a beauty. "I can see why your husband prizes him so highly. He takes my breath away, he is so handsome!"

When Reba Cameron left the cottage an hour later after Tawny had doctored the angry scratch and she'd enjoyed a refreshing cup of coffee, she had decided that she liked this little Tawny Blair very much. Tawny was glad that Maybelle had slept through the visit and had not come through the bedroom door.

"Tawny, I am most grateful to you for your kindness to me and I'd like to invite you to come to Cameron Farms to visit us. Will you, dear, if I send our driver to pick you up? It would be a pleasure for you to come and meet my Bill," Reba told her as she prepared to mount the stallion to leave.

Tawny's brown eyes twinkled as she declared, "Oh, I'd love to! Yes, ma'am. I surely would!"

Reba patted her hand and told her, "Well, then shall we say that I send my driver for you a week from today about

19

eleven and you can have lunch with me and Bill?"

"Oh, Mrs. Cameron—I . . . I'll look forward to that."

Reba smiled and gave her a nod of her head as she mounted the prancing stallion. "I'll look forward to seeing you." Tawny stood and watched the magnificent stallion galloping away. She gave out a silent prayer that Mrs. Cameron would arrive home safely. She found herself wishing that she could ride that magnificent black beast as Reba Cameron was riding him.

As she strolled back to the door of the cabin, her bare feet kicking at the ground, a wave of guilt swept over her as she realized she would have been embarrassed if she had been forced to introduce her mother Maybelle to the genteel lady she'd just met.

What Tawny could not know was that the destiny of her young life was set in motion from this moment on now that she'd encountered Reba Cameron. Nothing could possibly change that.

Tawny was about to enter a strange new world!

Chapter 2

It was a perfect day to be sailing on the high seas. Bart Montgomery was not the sailor his good friend Jason was, but he did admire the *Sea Princess* very much. He knew that Jason considered her his prized possession.

They were sailing across the ocean for Bart to claim what he hoped would be his—the black Arabian that was going up for sale. If the horse was anything like the description and report he'd had a few weeks ago from a friend of his father's who had just returned from Virginia, then Bart was prepared to pay the price.

Jason had quizzed him as to why the owner of such a rare Arabian would want to sell it. He would never want to part with that grand an animal.

"The owner is ill, but his wife doesn't suspect or know it yet," Bart had told him. "He figures the Arabian can bring him enough to keep his wife comfortable for the rest of her life. They are both past middle age. At least this is what Jeffers told me."

"So we're to go to this place, Longcreek, and you will make him the offer?" his friend Jason asked.

"Yes, Jason. That is exactly what I will do. If he accepts, we will celebrate as we've never celebrated before," he laughed. Over the years the two of them had put in a generous amount of time reveling around London.

Jason observed the excitement in Bart's bright blue eyes and he taunted him, "Damned if I don't think you can get more excited over some horse than you can over a woman, Bart."

"Indeed I can."

21

Jason shrugged his shoulders and laughed, "Not me! No four-legged animal could possibly thrill me like those pretty two-legged fillies. Sorry, fellow, but I can't see it. The fact is I left one very unhappy lady to make this long voyage with you. Lady Barbara is very put out with me, I'll have you know. When I get back to London I shall pay a very heavy price for my wandering with you."

The two of them broke into a gale of laughter, for Bart knew that Jason was not the least bit serious about Lady Barbara. Both of them were reckless rogues where the ladies were concerned.

Bart Montgomery was a tall, fair-haired young man with flashing bright blue eyes. His trim, firm-muscled body was the result of the active life he led as a sportsman.

In contrast to Bart, Jason Hamilton was a mixture of breeding from his English father and his Irish mother. He had inherited his mother's black Irish eyes and hair. He was not a tall, towering figure like his friend Bart, but he was just as firm-muscled and strong. Because he strolled around his ship barechested, his face and body were tanned by the sun and sea breeze. The ladies found him just as appealing as Bart when the two of them were together.

Jason was not the serious young man Bart was nor did he strive for the wealth and glory that seemed to drive his friend. This attitude of his did not always please his father, Lord Addison Hamilton. However, Jason was always in the good graces of his adoring mother, Sheila Hamilton. She had three daughters, but only one son so Jason was most dear to her.

Bart's mother doted on him and had depended on him completely since Lord Edward Montgomery died. As head of the prestigious Montgomery family, Bart had quite an image to live up to, for his father had been a revered, respected gentleman throughout England. The Montgomery Stables and their prized horses were sought by people all over the world.

Bart was determined that he would be as successful as his father had been. That was why he had become so determined to own the fine black Arabian in Virginia. In fact he'd thought about nothing else since Jeffers had told him about the stallion.

He was determined to own him!

For the next week, Tawny's whole world changed with the anticipation she was feeling about the visit to Cameron Farms. Eagerly, she told Roberta Thacher about the invitation. The first thought racing through Roberta's mind was what the poor child could wear that would look nice.

She searched through her closet to see if one of her dresses could be cut down and some fluffs and frills could be added to make it more suitable for Tawny.

None of her frocks were colorful and most had long sleeves, but the one that gave the most promise was a brown calico sprinkled with colorful flowers. If she lined the sleeves and neck with some of the pretty ecru lace she had, it might just work out. Of course she would certainly have to cut some inches out of the waistline.

That same afternoon Mrs. Thacher got busy on the adjustments to transform the dress for Tawny, but she had no answer to the problem of slippers, for hers were too large for Tawny and she did not have the money to purchase new ones. But she would suggest to Tawny that she wear the little moccasins she'd seen her wear on rare occasions. This was one time when she should deny herself the pleasure of going barefoot.

Roberta was more than pleased with the little brown-flowered dress after she'd finished sewing the ecru ruffling on the neckline and sleeves. Tawny would look so pretty in it with her dark-brown hair flowing around her shoulders.

With the dress draped across her arm she dashed out of her cottage to go over to the Blairs' house.

Excitement sparked in Tawny's brown eyes when Mrs. Thacher handed her the dress. "It's yours, honey," she told her. "Thought you might like to wear it when you go to see Mrs. Cameron."

"Oh, you can't imagine how I've been fretting about what I would wear to Cameron Farms! They must be awfully rich people, Mrs. Thacher," Tawny declared as her fingers played with the pretty lace around the sleeves.

"Well, you're going to look rather fancy yourself when you put this on." Roberta said.

"Guess I should wear my brown moccasins and some of Mama's stockings," Tawny suggested.

Roberta had to suppress a smile because she sensed that the stockings and shoes were not a pleasant thought to Tawny. "Yes, dear, I believe I would wear them."

Tawny gave an agreeing nod. "I will."

Mrs. Thacher told Tawny she must get back to her house to see about the pie in her oven. She knew Maybelle would be getting up shortly, and she had no desire to be there when the woman came out of her bedroom.

Roberta Thacher could not know that Maybelle Blair recently had mended what Mrs. Thacher considered her wicked, wanton ways. Since the night Jeb had beat her up, Maybelle had come home directly from her tavern every night. This had pleased Tawny, but she wasn't convinced about how long it would last. She hoped her mother would not start bringing men to the house again. It was nice to enjoy peaceful nights of sleep. It was also nice to see that her mother's battered face had finally healed.

Tawny thought she'd never looked so grand as she did when she had finishing dressing and combing her hair. With her pretty new dress on, the restraining moccasins and stockings did not bother her. Yesterday she'd washed her hair in the rainwater they'd caught during the last rainshower and it looked like shimmering deep-brown silk falling around her shoulders.

When the Camerons' driver knocked on her door she leaped to her feet to rush to the door. "Are you Miss Tawny Blair, ma'am?" a lanky-hired hand inquired.

"I am," she declared.

"Well, Mrs. Cameron sent me to bring you to the farm."

"I'm ready," she told him. As she marched out the door of the cottage, she felt like a princess going to a grand ball.

Tawny couldn't believe how brief the buggy ride was from her home to the Camerons' farm. A long rail fence extended as far as Tawny could see as the driver guided the buggy off the main dirt road onto the Cameron property.

The driver heard the young girl exclaim as they neared the sprawling white-framed house. Tawny felt that she had stepped into a fairyland. The buggy was her carriage and she was a princess being taken to some magnificent palace. The driver glanced back to see her awestruck face. She was certainly a pretty little thing, he had to admit. He had confess to himself that he was curious about Miss Reba's connection with this little miss, but then no one about the farm ever questioned Miss Reba. They just carried out her orders.

Around Cameron Farms, Miss Reba was considered their boss as much as her husband, Bill. Most of them addressed her, as her devoted husband affectionately called her — Miss Reba.

When the driver pulled up to the front of the house, Tawny saw Miss Reba, waiting to greet her.

By the time the buggy came to a halt, Reba had come through the gate and was waiting beside the buggy to offer Tawny her hand to get down.

"My goodness — what a pretty sight you are, Tawny. It is so good to see you again, dear."

"And it's good to see you too, Mrs. Cameron. I've . . . I've been so excited about coming. It's so beautiful here!" Tawny declared to her.

Reba locked her arm with Tawny's as the two of them walked down the stone walkway toward the house. Reba told her how happy she was to have her here and how anxious she was to have her meet her husband, Bill. "I've bragged about you all week and how you helped me when I needed it. He's eager to express his special thanks to you, Tawny."

"Oh, I didn't do that much, Mrs. Cameron — not really." Tawny smiled at her.

Tawny had never seen a more beautiful house. Why, her mother's cottage was not as large as Reba Cameron's parlor!

She felt uneasy when she sat on the pretty chair and she could not help comparing the furnishings here to the dull, drab furnishings back home. A lot of thoughts were parading through Tawny's pretty head as she sat there listening to Reba. Someday she was going to have a house like this and someday she was going to wear clothes just as pretty as Reba Cameron's. She didn't care how hard she had to work to accomplish it, but it would not be as a tavern maid, she silently vowed. There had to be other ways a lady could earn money.

Suddenly a huge shadow engulfed the archway of the parlor and Tawny glanced up to see a gigantic black woman with a white apron tied around her middle and her head bound in a white kerchief. She addressed Reba, "Miss Reba, Mr. Bill told me to tell you he'll join you in about five minutes out on the east veranda. Everything is ready when you wish me to serve it."

"Thank you, Aurelia," Reba told the servant. She turned her attention back to Tawny and urged her to follow her as she guided her out of the parlor and across the long hallway. Tawny followed her through the elegant dining room and out the double doors onto the veranda.

Once again, Tawny found herself entranced by the beauty of this setting of white wicker settees and chairs with brightly colored floral cushions. Over on one side of the veranda was a table and four chairs and Tawny noticed immediately that the table was arranged with three china place settings. She remembered that Mrs. Cameron had mentioned, when she invited her out to the farm, that she must come early enough to have lunch, but Tawny had forgotten about that, and suddenly she was nervous about dining with such fine, elegant people. She prayed she'd do nothing wrong to embarrass herself.

When she noticed the colorful floral arrangement in vivid shades of purple, red, and white in the center of the table, she had to conclude that Mrs. Cameron loved flowers as much as she did. Huge pots of blooming flowers were placed everywhere around the veranda.

In her simple, straightforward way, Tawny expressed the thoughts rushing through her mind to Reba. "You must love flowers as I do, Mrs. Cameron."

But Reba Cameron did not have a chance to reply to Tawny. A deep male voice gave a friendly chuckle to answer Tawny. "She certainly does!"

Tawny turned to see a gentleman standing in the doorway, smiling at her with warm, friendly eyes. No one had to tell her that this was Mr. Bill Cameron. As she looked at the man with his snow-white hair and warm brown eyes, she was amazed to see that he was much older than his wife.

Reba rushed to take his hand and led him to the table where she and Tawny had already taken a seat. "This is Tawny Blair, Bill. Tawny, I want you to meet my husband, Bill."

Tawny did not know whether she should rise or not, but she did, and gave him a bow. "It's a pleasure to meet you, Mr. Cameron."

"Well now, young lady—I see why I've heard so much about Miss Tawny Blair for so many days. It's my pleasure to meet you, too!" He urged her to have a seat as he helped Reba into her chair and took the chair between his wife and Tawny.

Tawny was to realize a short time later that she had no cause to feel ill at ease. The meal was a simple but very tasty bean soup with generous chunks of ham in it. After the three of them had enjoyed the huge bowl of bean soup, Aurelia served a generous slice of egg custard pie sprinkled with nutmeg.

Tawny was not accustomed to eating such a hearty, delicious lunch, and she gave out a sigh as she finished the last bit of the pie. "It was delicious!"

Reba gave a pleased laugh. "I'm so glad you liked it, Tawny. We shall do this again."

Bill agreed with his wife that she must join them again and Tawny quickly accepted their invitation. "I have Diablo to thank for meeting you nice people. By the way, how is that rascal?"

Bill quickly noticed the twinkle in her eyes when she inquired about his prized stallion. "You like horses, Tawny?"

"I love them. I think Diablo is the most wonderful horse I've ever seen!"

"Well, then you must visit us so you can see him and the three of us shall take some rides over the country. Would you like that?"

"Oh, Mr. Cameron I—I would love that!"

Reba smiled lovingly at her husband, for she knew that he now knew why she was so taken by this young girl.

The Camerons exchanged smiles of understanding. Bill Cameron extended the invitation that he knew his wife approved of when he told Tawny that she must visit them next week.

"Oh, I shall be here!" Tawny accepted his invitation. For her, it seemed her life had been changed by this glorious day she'd shared with Bill and Reba Cameron. By the time she boarded the buggy to go back to her humble cottage she knew she had stepped into a different world here at the Camerons.

She'd been given two fine tailored riding ensembles that Reba swore she could no longer get into due to the extra weight she'd put on and she was also given a pair of fine leather brown boots that Reba insisted cramped her feet.

It was a very happy young lady who left Cameron Farms late that afternoon. Bill told his wife that she had the biggest heart of anyone he knew.

"Well, Bill Cameron—you didn't fool me for a minute. I think your heart went out to Tawny, too!"

She knew him so well that he dared not try to lie to her. "It did! She is a most unusual young girl!" What he did not say was that he wished he and Reba could have had a daughter like Tawny. What was to keep them from doing for Tawny what they would have done for a daughter of their own?

To enrich this young girl's life could be most rewarding, Bill Cameron was convinced. He knew Reba would agree with him.

Tawny Blair could be the daughter they'd never had.

Chapter 3

Tawny could not believe how different her world had suddenly become during that wonderful month of June. True to their word, the Camerons sent their buggy to the Blair cottage every week to bring Tawny out to their farms. Each trip she made endeared her to Bill and Reba Cameron and each time Tawny went back to her own home she was given a huge basket of fresh vegetables and fruits or a fine cured ham and slab of bacon.

But Tawny was hardly prepared for the gift that Bill Cameron presented to her on her fourth visit to the farm. They had enjoyed their ride around the farm as they'd been doing the last three visits and then they'd gone into the house to enjoy Aurelia's hearty lunch. But after lunch Bill had given Reba a wink. "Reba," he suggested, "shall we take Tawny to the corral to show her our newest little mare whose glossy coat reminds us of Tawny's pretty hair?"

Reba gave out a lighthearted laugh, for she knew what Bill's plans were. "I certainly think we should. Shall we join my husband, Tawny?"

"Oh, yes, ma'am. You bought a new horse?" Tawny asked as she raised up from the chair.

"You just wait until you see her, Tawny." Reba excitedly took her arm as they left the veranda to walk across the grounds. When they reached the fence of the corral, Bill gave out a yell. "Hey, George — bring out that new filly!"

Very soon, Tawny saw the hired hand leading the most beautiful young mare out of the barn. Her mane and tail were thick and glossy, the deep dark brown color of her own hair. Tawny gasped, "Oh, she's beautiful! I never saw any horse more beautiful except Diablo!"

Reba and Bill exchanged pleased smiles and knew that the mare was worth the money they'd spent to get her for Tawny.

"So you like Coco, eh?" Bill quizzed her.

"Oh, I love her!"

"Well, honey—that's all Bill and I need to hear because she's yours," Reba told her. Bill quickly added that they would keep the mare here and tend to her until arrangements could be made to properly keep the mare at Tawny's home.

"Nevertheless, Tawny, this is your own horse."

For a moment Tawny could not speak. She was too overcome with emotion. Tears welled in her brown eyes as she finally managed to stammer, "I . . . I just can't believe this. My own horse!"

Bill Cameron had experienced many gratifying moments in his life, but this was a very special one for him. He knew that he'd never forget this spring afternoon of 1856, and he rather suspected that Reba would feel the same way. This young lady had brought such joy to their life. Bill was especially happy about these last four weeks, for he was not too sure how Reba was going to take his announcement that a wealthy young Englishman was arriving soon to look at his prized Arabian. He knew the first question she was going to throw his way was why he would want to sell the stallion. He could not bear to tell her the truth, for he did not want her to worry, but his practical side urged him to do so before his health took a turn for the worse. He was the horse trader of the family. He'd had the joy of owning the magnificent Diablo the last year, but after many hours of thinking about selling him, he knew it was the wise thing for him to do—for Reba's sake.

Long after Tawny had left the farm and they were alone, both of the Camerons were still feeling the warmth of the splendid afternoon. It was a wonderful memory for the two of them to share for the rest of their life, Bill knew.

Whatever fate had in store for him, Bill Cameron knew

31

that he could surely die a happy man. He'd been blessed with a loving, doting wife for the last twenty years of his life. She was much younger than he and when they'd married there had been speculation that the marriage would not last, but it had. Reba had been a good tonic for him and settled him down from the rowdy fellow he had been as a younger man.

The advent of Tawny Blair into their life had been a miracle that he could not explain to himself. He knew that destiny had led Tawny to them that day she'd rescued Reba there on the lane when Diablo had thrown her.

It was meant to be that they met! He was firmly convinced of that.

The minute the Camerons' driver halted the buggy for Tawny to get out, she leapt down before he could get down to assist her.

She gave him a wave of her hand and told him goodbye. She was in a rush to get over to Roberta Thacher's cottage to tell her the exciting news that she was now the owner of a horse.

When Roberta went to open her door she wondered who was so urgently rapping, but when she saw Tawny standing there, with her lovely face so flushed with excitement and brown eyes sparkling so brightly, she knew that she was going to hear about another generous gesture by the Camerons. Each time Tawny had gone out there she'd come back to tell her about the grand time she'd had and what Reba Cameron had given her to bring home.

"Well, Tawny—it's you! I wondered who in the world was knocking on my door so frantically. Come on in, child."

"Can you believe that I . . . I have my own horse?" she declared breathlessly to Mrs. Thacher. "They gave me a beautiful little brown mare!"

This was a little startling to Roberta, and for a moment she couldn't find her tongue. Tawny giggled. "They really did—honest!"

"Oh, I believe you, child. It just took me aback for a moment. My, they must think the world of you. Not every day someone gets a gift like that, Tawny."

"I think they must be about the nicest people in the whole wide world except for you, Mrs. Thacher," Tawny told the middle-aged lady.

"Well, thank you, Tawny dear. You're a sweet girl and you make people want to be nice to you."

"And everyone *is* nice to me," she declared as she turned to leave. "I must get on home so I can tell Mama my good news. She'll be as surprised as you were, I bet."

Roberta Thacher stood in her doorway to watch the girl scamper across the ground dividing her property from the Blair front yard.

It had been a perfect crossing for the *Sea Princess* and its captain, Jason Hamilton. He and Bart Montgomery had shared another great adventure! They'd enjoyed fair weather all the way and smooth sailing, so by the time they docked in the coastal port of Chesapeake in Virginia, they were both in a jovial mood.

The first night they sought to celebrate their swift, pleasant voyage by going out on the town. But the next day Jason's mood suddenly changed when Bart announced that they must travel to a small inland village called Longcreek.

"Now wait a minute, Bart—I'm not going there. You can go on your own, my friend."

"What's the matter, Jason? Got no faith in the first mate you hired? A day or two away from your ship isn't going to kill you. It will be here when we get back." Bart sought to tease Jason, knowing how he felt about his ship.

"It's strange country to me. Back in England I wouldn't feel this way," Jason shot back at him.

For an hour they argued about Jason accompanying him before Bart finally convinced him to go. "I value your

33

opinion when we see this stallion," he said. "You know the kind of Thoroughbreds we have in our stables. You'll help me make the right decision."

"Oh, all right, I'll go, but damned if I'll stay away more than a couple of days. We have an understanding on that, don't we?"

Bart's blue eyes twinkled with amusement. He'd known that before it was over he'd be able to talk his friend into coming along. Jason wasn't the stubborn, unyielding cuss he himself was; there were times when Bart wished he were more like his easygoing friend.

Jason took each day and lived it to the fullest, but Bart's nature would not permit this. He supposed he inherited his character from his father, Lord Montgomery. He was certainly his father's son in the way he thought and also in his looks.

As soon as he had Jason's agreement to accompany him, Bart left the *Sea Princess* to seek out the livery to hire a buggy so they might travel to Suffolk where he'd been advised to seek lodging before going on to Longcreek, for the small village had no decent accommodations.

When Bart returned to the dock, he announced to Jason that he was ready to travel. "How about you, Jase?"

"Well, I will be after I throw some things together. Give me a half hour."

"Takes you as long as it does a woman, Jason," Bart remarked.

By early afternoon the two young Englishmen were on their way to the inland town of Suffolk and by the time the sun was setting, they were comfortably settled in at the Backbay Inn.

Bart Montgomery's excitement was beginning to mount now that he was so close to seeing the magnificent black stallion that had been described to him as a prince of Arabians. His friend saw the anxiety mounting after they'd arrived in Suffolk. As the evening wore on, Jason took sweet revenge in taunting Montgomery. "Damn, you'd think it was a woman you were pursuing. If you ever set

34

your cap for some particular lady, I'll wager that you'd go after her with as much fervor."

"Jason, you have no appreciation for fine horseflesh. This stallion could be one of a kind. You can imagine what that could mean to the person who owned him?"

"I suppose so, but then I'm not a horseman, I'm a sailor. Maybe that's why I love the sea; because no one can lay claim to it. It belongs to any man who wants to sail its waters."

"But Jason, isn't it important to you to own something?"

Jason's black eyes gleamed as they locked into his friend's blue ones. "I have my *Sea Princess*. She gives me pleasure, but I guess she owns me more than I own her. To answer your question, Bart, I truly don't know. Right now, I'd have to tell you no."

"Known you for a lot of years, but I guess I'll never figure you out," Bart smiled and shook his head.

"That's probably why we're good friends. If you figured me out you might not like me," he laughed.

Bart suggested that they turn in, for he wanted to get an early start to this place called Longcreek. He'd have to also make some inquiries about directions to the Cameron Farms, located just outside the village.

When Bart was dimming the lamp, Jason could not resist one last jest. "Maybe I'll spot myself some pretty little two-legged filly while you're inspecting your four-legged beast."

"Shut up, Jason, and go to sleep." Bart admonished his friend and they both gave way to lighthearted laughter.

The Virginia countryside was beautiful and green this time of the year. Neat, well-kept white frame houses dotted the dirt road Bart and Jason were traveling as they left the small hamlet of Longcreek. It had been no problem to get directions to Cameron Farms. The first fellow Bart stopped to ask about the farm knew the way.

"England doesn't have a monopoly on beautiful coun-

35

tryside," Jason remarked as he took in the picturesque scene. This was the first time he had crossed the Atlantic and seen this part of the world.

Bart didn't answer him, for he had caught sight of a huge archway and impressive gateway. The long strip of property adjoining the roadway was enclosed by a fence which set it apart from the smaller farms they'd just gone by. He knew that he was approaching Cameron Farms.

Jason took no notice of any of this; his dark eyes had spied a breathtaking vision riding through the pastureland. Her gorgeous warm brown hair was flowing back from her face as she galloped along on the horse whose coat was the same color of her hair.

"God, she's beautiful! I just saw a princess, Bart! Did you see her?"

"What are you babbling about, Jason, for God's sake?" Bart glanced over at his friend.

"That girl riding that horse across the way! Most beautiful creature I ever laid my eyes on," Jason told him.

"Sorry, my friend, I missed that sight, but here is where we turn in," he said as he guided the buggy through the archway.

"I'm not lying, Bart. I saw a beautiful girl riding through the pasture over there. Right over there."

Giving a shrug of his broad shoulders, Bart casually replied, "Well, she will have to wait, Jason."

"You sure know how to spoil a fellow's fun, Bart."

Bart did not bother to reply. He only gave his friend a broad grin as he looked back at the road leading up to the white frame house.

Bill Cameron was out on the veranda with his wife Reba when he spotted the buggy coming up the long drive. He knew instinctively that this was the Englishman, Montgomery, who was interested in buying his magnificent Diablo.

He was glad he'd discussed his intentions with Reba last night. He had procrastinated about it long enough, he realized.

Although she was trying not to show it, Reba was disturbed. She knew Bill Cameron well, and she knew he had a definite reason for wanting to sell the stallion. He was keeping something from her and that disturbed her very much. Bill had never kept secrets from her before.

She couldn't bring herself to believe that something was wrong with his health. Why, he looked as fit as a fiddle! She'd never known him to have been happier than he'd been the last month.

Little Tawny was visiting again today. She'd just left the veranda a few minutes ago to take her horse for a jaunt around the pastureland. Reba knew that she'd soon return to join them, her pretty face glowing radiantly after her ride on Coco.

Nothing could happen to Bill now when their life was so happy! She'd kept trying to reassure herself since last night.

Like Bill, Reba knew that this was the Englishman. His appearance made shadows of doubts cross her mind. She didn't welcome the sight of the Englishman and his companion.

The idea of selling the Arabian did not appeal to her at all. She couldn't believe Bill would part with the stallion unless something very serious was urging him to do it for the money Diablo would bring. And Reba knew they had plenty of money. She should know, for she kept the books for the farm.

Chapter 4

Bill Cameron was waiting by the gate to greet the two gentlemen as they leaped down from the buggy. After a cordial reception, he guided them around the side of the house to join Reba on the veranda.

Reba gave her guests a warm, friendly smile as the trio approached. As they walked up the steps and across the veranda, Bill announced, "Reba, honey—I'd like you to meet Lord Bart Montgomery and his friend, Jason Hamilton. Gentlemen, my wife."

"A pleasure to meet you, Mrs. Cameron," Bart addressed her.

"My pleasure, too, Mrs. Cameron. You have a beautiful place here. My first time in Virginia," Jason said.

"Nice to meet you, and please have a seat. If you'll excuse me I'll go fetch Aurelia to bring you some refreshments."

She returned shortly with the huge black woman following her with a tray. Bill was already discussing Diablo. "So you are interested in my Diablo, eh, Lord Montgomery?"

"Yes, sir. I certainly am. I've heard that he is one fine animal," Bart replied.

"He is more than fine, young man. He is a king!" Bill boasted. Reba found herself wanting to cry out to him—why did he want to sell the stallion?

Instead she turned her attention on the handsome black-haired young man. It was obvious to her that he was not particularly interested in the discussion between his friend and Bill about the horse, so she spoke with him as they enjoyed the refreshments Aurelia had served.

But their conversation was interrupted by the sound of galloping hooves moving up the long drive. Tawny was returning from her ride. Reba sat there admiring the vision of her in the golden-colored riding outfit she'd given her. She looked very attractive in that shade with her dark complexion and hair. She sat a horse so well, Reba thought, being an expert horsewoman herself. Tawny had no idea that she was the center of attention and that four pairs of eyes were ogling her.

Impulsive person that he was, Jason exclaimed, "God, she's beautiful!"

Reba laughed. "You speak of the horse or the young lady?"

His black eyes had a devilish twinkle as he looked at Reba Cameron. "Both of them. Your daughter, Mrs. Cameron?"

Reba wasn't fooled for a minute about what had caught Jason Hamilton's eye, but she replied, "No—she is our dear little friend, Tawny Blair."

"Tawny Blair," Jason mumbled after her as though he wanted to be sure he remembered the name, for it was an unusual one and it fit her perfectly.

For a few brief moments, the sight of Tawny galloping toward the corrals distracted Bart Montgomery. She was a fetching little filly, he had to admit, but he didn't allow himself to be distracted. He turned his attention back to Bill Cameron.

Reba saw that the two of them were engrossed in conversation so she suggested that she and Jason go to the corral to meet Tawny and escort her back to the veranda.

"She might be a little shy about joining us if she saw that we had guests. Tawny is very young," she told Jason.

She noticed the look in Jason's eyes as she said that, but she had her reasons for making the remark. Tawny's blossoming figure would lead one to believe that she was older than she was. There was a sultry look in Tawny's doelike brown eyes that could make a man like young Jason Hamilton think things that were not true.

She'd seen the exciting sparkle in Hamilton's eyes when he'd been watching her ride up the drive. She'd recalled something that Bill had told her many years ago when they were first married. He'd told her how she'd excited him when he'd watched her riding astride her horse. Most ladies rode sidesaddle, but Reba had preferred to straddle a horse when she rode and Tawny felt the same way.

Jason thought he'd seen many a beautiful lady in his life and he'd wooed several, but he had never seen one quite like Tawny Blair as she came walking toward them, her body swaying, her moccasins in her hand, her dainty feet bare.

Tawny had not seen the young man with Mrs. Cameron as she walked hastily to meet her. She had left the barn carrying her shoes and now it was too late to try to slip into them so she made no effort to do so.

It mattered not to Jason, for this little barefoot princess was the prettiest thing his eyes had ever beheld. He watched her young body move with uninhibited grace. Her face was flushed from her ride and her long brown hair had been blown and flowed around her face. She was breathtakingly lovely!

Reba could not help smiling, remembering the expensive leather boots she'd given Tawny. Tawny had not thought to wear them today with her nice riding ensemble, but then that was what made her so special.

"Honey, I'd like you to meet Jason Hamilton. Jason, this is Tawny Blair."

"Good day to you, Mr. Hamilton," Tawny greeted him and extended her small hand for a friendly handshake.

Jason eagerly obliged her unexpected gesture by taking her hand in his. "My great pleasure to know you, Miss Tawny Blair!"

The intensity of Jason Hamilton's piercing black eyes had a hypnotic effect on Tawny. She also liked the feel of his hand holding hers so tight. When she thought about it, she'd never had a young, handsome man hold her hand before. It was a pleasing feeling.

Reba Cameron observed all this and realized that young Tawny was ready to fall in love for the first time in her life.

But Tawny was due for another new experience when she was introduced to the handsome young fair-haired Lord Bart Montgomery. Never had she expected to meet a real lord.

He was as dashing and handsome as his friend, Jason Hamilton. Tawny could not believe that she was actually sitting at the table with such people. She was thoroughly enjoying herself until she realized that the handsome Bart Montgomery was here to buy Diablo.

Her brown eyes darted over to Reba Cameron and Reba saw the disbelief reflected there. She felt sorry for the young girl and it also endeared her to Reba.

"Diablo will be leaving here and we'll never see him again?" she stammered as though she was crushed by the news.

Her serious intensity about the stallion impressed Bart Montgomery. "You will always be welcome to see Diablo if I buy him, and so will the Camerons," Bart told her, hoping to soothe her. It was obvious she was enamored of the black Arabian.

His words did not soothe her at all. How easy it was for him to say that. How could she travel all the way to England just to see the black stallion? Perhaps the Camerons could, but she couldn't.

She did not like Bart Montgomery and she didn't care if he was a wealthy lord. He didn't deserve to own such a special horse as Diablo.

She was close to tears at the thought of the Englishman taking Diablo away. She wanted to leave here just as soon as she could, but she was sure her voice would crack if she tried to tell Mrs. Cameron that she should be getting home. Finally, she gained the courage to speak. Reba realized that she was upset about the startling news she'd heard and she wasted no time getting up to summon their driver.

But Jason Hamilton quickly suggested that she not

41

bother. "I'll be most happy to see Miss Blair home if she'll tell me the way, Mrs. Cameron."

"Is that all right with you, Tawny?" Reba asked her.

"That is fine with me if Mr. Hamilton is sure that it won't put him to too much trouble," Tawny replied.

"No trouble at all. That will give Bart a chance to look at the horse. My interest is not in horses. I merely brought him here on my ship."

"Well, I shall trust you to see our Tawny home then, Mr. Hamilton. She is very dear to us," Reba Cameron declared.

Jason understood exactly what Reba Cameron was implying. "She will get home safely, Mrs. Cameron," he assured her.

Tawny rose from her chair and reached over to plant a warm kiss on the cheek of Reba Cameron. She made the same gesture when she walked over to Bill Cameron. To Bart Montgomery, she bid a curt farewell before joining Jason.

When she finally came to stand by his side, Jason asked, "Shall we go, Tawny?"

"I'm ready if you are," she told him and took the arm he offered.

Jason could not have been happier to be escorting this beautiful young lady, for he was absolutely bored by all the talk of horses. The breathtaking beauty beside him in the buggy excited him.

By the time he'd taken her to the humble cottage she called home, he'd told her about his fine ship, the *Sea Princess* and he'd seen the excitement in her brown eyes.

He could not resist telling her, before he finally said good-bye, that he found her a most entrancing young lady. "I never met anyone like you before, Tawny. I honestly haven't."

"I like you, too, Jason," she declared in that candid way of hers. "But I . . . I can't say that I feel the same way about your friend, this Lord Montgomery."

Jason laughed. "Well, I'm happy to hear that you like me, Miss Tawny Blair."

She had the most inviting rosy lips! Jason wanted desperately to have one kiss before he told her good-bye, for he knew that he might never see this little beauty again. His black head bent closer to her as he asked her, "May I kiss you good-bye, Tawny?"

"I suppose so," she said impulsively. She felt Jason's arm press her closer as his lips met hers in a gentle kiss. Such honeyed sweetness he'd never tasted before.

He sensed immediately that it might have been the first time she had ever been kissed. Just thinking this pleased Jason Hamilton.

Those big brown eyes of hers looked up at him with such innocence that a tenderness for this lovely girl engulfed him.

When he released her lips from his most tender kiss, he looked down at her lovely face. He knew it had affected her as he had hoped it would. "There are many kisses a man can give a woman, but I want you to know that mine was from the heart."

Her trusting brown eyes looked up at him as she murmured softly, "I know it was, Jason. I trust you and I can't say why because I just met you a few hours ago." She meant what she said, for she'd felt completely at ease with Jason from the first moment they'd met. That was why she'd been bold enough to let him kiss her. She would never had been so daring with his friend, Bart Montgomery. Something about Bart made her feel ill at ease.

"Thank you for saying that, Tawny. I'm glad you feel you can trust me," Jason told her. He was hardly satisfied with the one kiss, but something told him that he should not be greedy. After all, Reba Cameron's words were ringing in his ears and he didn't wish to chance anything that would put him in the Camerons' disfavor while Bart was negotiating for the horse.

After the transaction was complete and they were ready to leave Virginia, he wouldn't say what he might be tempted to do where the pretty Tawny was concerned.

So he bid her farewell when she leaped down from the

buggy after she'd insisted that there was no reason for him to walk to the cottage door with her. Besides, she did not wish an appearance by Maybelle to spoil this wonderful day.

By the time Jason returned to Cameron Farms, he found the veranda deserted, so he figured Bart and Bill Cameron had gone to the barn to see the stallion.

Reba had seen Jason Hamilton returning so she rushed down the hall to greet him. "Come in, Jason. As you've probably guessed, my husband is showing Lord Montgomery Diablo. Oh, by the way, it has been decided that the two of you will stay overnight instead of returning to Suffolk."

"Oh, we are?"

"Yes, it is growing so late now and Lord Montgomery would like to take the stallion out for a run in the morning before he makes a decision."

Reba told him she would be happy to have him join her in the parlor. Before dinner, she would have Aurelia show him to the room. "Perhaps you'd like me to take you to the barn?"

"Oh, no, ma'am—I think I'll just go to the room to freshen up before dinner." Jason was in no hurry to view the black horse. He'd see more of him than he cared to by the time he got Bart and Diablo back to the shores of England, he figured.

By the time Aurelia had guided him to the upstairs bedroom and Jason had closed the door behind him, he noticed that the sun was quickly setting. He ambled to the west window and saw Bart and Cameron coming out of the corral.

He wondered if Montgomery was pleased or disappointed about the stallion he'd just seen. Nothing about the expression on his face or his manner told Jason anything as he watched the two of them coming toward the house.

But Jason knew Bart could wear a mask and no one would know what was going on behind it. Whatever

44

thoughts were whirling around in that fair-haired head of his were known only to him. As close as the two of them were, there were times Bart could be like a stranger to Jason.

A short time later, Jason heard Bart's footsteps climbing the stairs to his room. He heard the door slam directly across the hall from his own room, but he figured if Bart wanted to talk to him, he'd come across the hall. He took off his coat, flung it over the chair, and pulled off his boots to pad around the room in his stocking feet.

Bart was doing the same thing in his room, but as soon as he unfastened the buttons of his shirt after he'd removed his coat and boots, he knew he had to tell Jason about the black stallion. The Arabian was everything Cameron had boasted that he was!

When Jason opened the door, he saw the bright sparkle in Bart's blue eyes. This was one time Bart could not conceal his feelings. "You liked him!"

"He is more than a prince. He is a king! I'd pay Cameron whatever he asked, but he doesn't know that. Told him I had to sleep on it tonight and that I wanted to take him out in the morning before I decided."

"He's actually that great, eh?"

"Tomorrow at this time, Jason, we'll be taking him away from here and back to Suffolk or maybe back to Chesapeake," Bart declared to his friend. "I won't rest until I have him aboard the ship so no idiots can try to steal him from us. I have no intention of putting him in a livery at Suffolk. We will go on to Chesapeake."

"Sounds fine to me. Sooner I get back to the *Sea Princess* the happier I'll be," Jason replied.

"On that I'll agree with you for once," Bart smiled at his friend.

"I trust you saw Miss Tawny Blair safely home?" he quizzed his friend just before he turned to leave Jason's room.

Jason was surprised that Bart had even remembered her name. He would have been surprised to know just how

45

distracting Tawny had been to Bart Montgomery.

Tawny had reminded Bart of a high spirited Thorough-bred as he'd watched her prance up on the veranda with her head held high. He'd seen the fire in those brown eyes when she'd found out that he intended to buy Diablo, and he sensed her instant disapproval.

But there was a regal grace about Tawny Blair just like the black Arabian he'd viewed in the Camerons' stable. That kind of young lady he'd never met before!

He found her breathtakingly beautiful!

Chapter 5

There was something untamed and untarnished about Tawny Blair that excited Bart Montgomery in a way that he'd never experienced before. When he looked into her eyes, he saw sweet innocence, but when he saw her nostrils flare at the news that he intended to buy Diablo, he saw a woman of spirit and fire. He liked this!

She did not blink her thick dark lashes when he was introduced as Lord Bart Montgomery, as a lot of young ladies did. That had not impressed Tawny at all. Always, he'd detested young ladies fawning over him just because he was a wealthy young lord and could usher them into a certain social circle.

He resented Jason taking her home, for he'd seen the way Jason was looking at her and he knew the look he saw in Jason's eyes.

He certainly had a winning way with the ladies, Bart knew. It was probably a good thing that he would not be lingering long in Longcreek. Tawny Blair would certainly lose her sweet innocence hastily with Jason around.

The evening spent with the Camerons was very pleasant. When Bart retired he knew that sleep was not going to come easily; he could not wait for dawn to break because he was going to be up and on his way to the barn to saddle up Diablo.

He'd heard of nervous bridegrooms from some of his bachelor friends and he was having similar feelings tonight. If he and Diablo did not get along, that would influence his decision to buy the Arabian.

He welcomed the first rays of sun that came streaming through his window. Instantly, he leaped out of bed, pulled on his black pants, and slipped into his white shirt. He took no time to button it all the way. When he had yanked on his black boots, he was ready to dash from the room. He cared not that his hair was tousled.

Bill Cameron was downstairs waiting for him when he came bouncing down the steps. He knew exactly how Bart Montgomery was feeling, for he recalled how he had felt the night before he purchased Diablo. He hadn't slept a wink.

"Ready, young man, to try that stallion out?"

Bart laughed. "Yes, Mr. Cameron—I'm more than ready!"

"Thought you just might be. Well, let's go and get Fred to saddle him up for you," Cameron suggested to his guest.

At the barn Bart stood watching the prancing, fiery Diablo. How proud and majestic he was as he jerked his head up and down and swished his thick, glossy tail. Bart took in all the details of his perfectly proportioned legs and the power of his haunches. But his face, with the broad forehead and flaring nostrils, was a study to Bart. It seemed to Bart that the Arabian was scrutinizing him!

Soon Bart was going to find out if he was going to be the master, and if he was, then Diablo would be his, for he would certainly pay any price to own him.

As soon as Bart mounted and flung his muscled leg over to fit his booted foot into the stirrup, he sensed that he and Diablo were going to be fine together.

Cameron knew that Bart Montgomery was the right man to own his fine Arabian. He felt no regrets now that he was going to be selling him to the Englishman. Montgomery was a fine horseman; he had only to watch him ride off on Diablo to know that.

Cameron left the corral to go back into the house, for he expected that it would be a while before Montgomery returned.

Reba had watched from her bedroom window as the two galloped out of the corral, and she also watched her husband as he returned to the house. Bill was happy; that was enough to make her happy, too.

She suddenly realized that over the years she'd forgotten that her husband was much older than she. He'd never seemed that way, but no longer could she forget it. Someday she would be left alone, without her beloved Bill to share the days and nights.

Bart gave Diablo the freedom to gallop at a fast, swift pace as they traveled down the dirt road. He knew not what direction he was going and he didn't care.

The road he was traveling led to the small village of Longcreek and he was soon to approach the area where the Blair cottage was situated. Any passing wagon or cart on the way to the village was like a blur to Bart as he swiftly passed them by.

But then there appeared the sight of a young vision moving off the dirt road to take a side lane into the woods. Over her arm was swung a wicker basket, Bart immediately recognized that shimmering hair as she pranced along. It had to be the beautiful Tawny Blair! No other girl had such beautiful hair.

He gave a hard jerk on the reins to slow up the pace of Diablo. The Arabian was reluctant to obey so Bart spoke firmly to the horse so he would know who was the master. He veered off the main dirt road to take the same trail leading into the woods that he'd seen Tawny take.

Tawny sensed that a rider was coming up behind her. Rarely did she encounter riders on the trail through the woods. Instant fear ignited in her, for the woods were thick and dense. The thought of an intruder disturbed her.

She quickened her pace down the trail, but the sound kept coming closer and closer so she darted through the brush and trees to conceal herself. But as she dashed through the bushes, her skirt caught on one of the branches and tore when she yanked it loose.

She bent low to the ground to wait to see who the intruder might be. When the rider and his horse came in view, she gasped when she saw that it was Diablo and Bart Montgomery.

Leaping up from her hiding place, she called out to him. "Bart Montgomery, you scared me to death!"

Bart quickly halted Diablo and turned to see the most divine sight. Tawny stood on the trail with her hands on her curvy hips, and in her bare feet. A most indignant look was on her lovely face, and her dark-brown eyes were flashing with fire and anger. Her calico skirt was torn; the yellow tunic she wore revealed a portion of her golden flesh.

Bart was fired with an untamed desire to make love to her. For a moment, he let his eyes devour the sight of her. She was like the wild creatures roaming this woods — untamed and unconquered. He decided he wanted to be the one to tame and conquer her.

"I'm sorry, Tawny, for it wasn't my intention to scare you," he said as he leaped down from the horse and moved up to where she was standing.

She made no reply as she turned her eyes from him toward Diablo. Her hand went up to rub the horse's silky mane. "Oh, you pretty thing, Diablo." The horse gave her an approving nod of his head.

Bart watched her with fascination as she talked to Diablo. With an amused smile, he remarked, "Damned if I couldn't be jealous of Diablo!" Actually he wasn't exactly teasing, now that he thought about it. He wasn't used to a lady ignoring him to talk to a horse as Miss Tawny Blair was doing.

Tawny gave way to laughter and turned around to look at Montgomery. "Now why would you be jealous of Diablo?"

"Because of the affectionate way you speak to him. Am I not to have any of your attention after I came seeking you out here in the woods?"

"You came seeking me?"

"I certainly did. I saw you taking this path when I was back there on the main road."

Suddenly Tawny became aware of how close to her he was standing. He was so tall that she had to lean her head back to look up at him. Her heart was pounding wildly and she wondered if her cheeks were flushing.

"I . . . I didn't know you were still at the Camerons," she finally managed to stammer.

"I spent the night there so I might take a ride on this fellow this morning. Couldn't make up my mind to buy him without doing that," he told her. He knew that Tawny was not pleased about him purchasing Diablo.

"And now I suppose that you've made up your mind, Lord Montgomery?" she said stiffly.

He smiled down at her. "I have. He's worth every penny Cameron is asking for him and I shall buy him, Tawny. In fact, I plan to tell him that as soon as I return to the farm. But now I must say I like you better when you were angry with me and called me Bart."

"And you don't think I am angry with you now?"

Bart shook his blond head and declared, "No, Tawny— you aren't angry at me. Not really!"

Her brown eyes looked directly into his as she saucily retorted, "You're awfully sure of yourself, aren't you?"

Her breathtaking loveliness was so tempting that Bart could not resist reaching out to pull her next to him, and his head bent down so he might kiss those sensuous lips of hers. His kiss was not like the gentle kiss Jason Hamilton had taken yesterday. It was a demanding one, insisting that Tawny respond to him, and she did, for she found herself helpless to refuse.

She felt so tiny in his huge arms! Bart felt he could have been holding a child, but this was no child. He felt the swell of her breasts pressing against his broad chest.

When he finally sought to release her lips, Tawny felt herself gasp. His arms still held her and his eyes were staring down at her. She was glad he was still holding her, for her legs felt so weak that she would surely have sunk down to the ground.

"Sweetest lips I've ever kissed, Tawny Blair!"

For a moment she said nothing and only stared up at him. He wondered what was going through her mind as she stood in silence. "Now don't tell me I scared you again, Tawny. You weren't frightened. I would have sensed it."

"No, you didn't frighten me, Bart Montgomery!" she mumbled. She was frightened by the way she'd so willingly surrendered to him, but she'd never let him know that.

"Good! It's nice to meet a truthful young lady. I have to be as honest with you. One kiss is not enough for me. I must have another." His head bent down so his lips could capture hers again. She knew that she should protest, for she'd barely met him and she shouldn't be allowing such liberties. But with his heated lips on hers, she was powerless to deny herself the pleasure.

She felt his arms pressing her closer to his chest and the warmth of his body against her. Before she was aware of how it had happened, the two of them were lying on a blanket of fallen leaves. One of his huge hands had moved from around her back to caress her breast. His kisses had also become more ardent as his tongue tantalized her lips and mouth.

She gasped as she felt his hand slipping up the loosened tunic she wore. His finger began to play an exciting magic around the tip of her breast and she arched against him in response. Huskily, he moaned, "Oh, Tawny, love! I want to make love to you. I must make love to you."

Her head was whirling. Such wild passion and consuming desire possessed her that she wanted Bart to make love to her. Eager impatience overwhelmed Bart as he hastily removed his pants and her skirt to burrow between the silken flesh of her legs. Knowing that she'd never been with a man he tried to be most tender as he gave the first deep thrust. Once that instant of discomfort was over, he tried to pleasure her as he'd never done before with any woman. Her soft sighs told him that he had.

That moment of ecstasy he shared with Tawny was like

nothing he'd ever experienced before. Long after it was over, he continued to hold her in his arms to plant featherlike kisses on her cheek. His finger removed her hair from her face.

She was the first to stir and wriggle free. Hastily, she moved to cover herself with her clothing to hide her naked body. Bart was not so modest, and he lay there giving her a lazy smile to declare how breathtakingly beautiful she was. But Tawny was now feeling guilty and embarrassed.

"I've got to go, Bart. I shouldn't have allowed this," she declared. "I guess you always have your way, don't you?"

"One way or the other I usually do, Tawny," he answered her. Before he could get up off the ground to grab her, she was dashing down the trail like a scared doe.

By the time he'd pulled on his pants and flung on his shirt, she was out of sight, so he mounted the Arabian and headed back toward Cameron Farms. It seemed the countryside had swallowed her up and he knew not what direction she'd run.

But he knew that beautiful face was going to haunt his dreams for many a night!

Chapter 6

Before Jason Hamilton had roused from the comfortable feather bed, Bart had returned to the farm and he and Bill Cameron had consummated their deal. Both men were happy. Bart Montgomery was taking back to England a prince of a horse. Arabians sired by Diablo would be highly prized by horsemen who purchased them in the years to come. The prestige of the Montgomery Stables would be greatly enhanced by his presence.

Bill Cameron was just as happy as Bart because he felt he had secured the future of his sweet wife, Reba. The price the young Englishman had paid him enriched his coffers tremendously. He was satisfied that he'd had the joy and pleasure of owning the Arabian for a while. This was enough to ease the parting from Diablo.

Diablo would be in good hands with Bart Montgomery. Bill was certain of this, or he would not have made the deal. Cameron always formed his opinions hastily and rarely changed his mind. He'd like Bart Montgomery after their brief meeting and conversation yesterday afternoon. By the time they'd shared the evening meal together last night, he found himself liking Montgomery even more.

After the deal was finished and the two of them had another cup of coffee in Bill's study, Bart rose from the chair. "Guess I better check in on that sleepyhead friend of mine or we'll never get started back to Suffolk," he announced. "It was a pleasure doing business with you. I'm going back to England with fond memories of gracious hospitality. Someday I'd like to revisit your beautiful Virginia," Bart told him.

"Well, Reba and I hope that you will," Cameron said. He added that he would certainly take Montgomery up on his invitation to visit him in England if they ever strayed that far from Virginia.

When the two of them emerged from the study, Jason was slowly ambling down the stairway. "Which shall it be for you, Jason—breakfast or lunch?" Cameron jested.

Goodnaturedly, Hamilton laughed. "Got to tell you that that bed was really soft and comfortable, sir."

Jason sat in the dining room alone while Aurelia served him a hearty meal, and Bart went upstairs to get his things.

Cameron had gone to the barn to say his final farewell to Diablo since Montgomery had told him they would be departing soon. Reba was tempted to accompany him, but she decided against and went downstairs to find Jason in the dining room, enjoying his meal.

"Well, young man, it would have been nice if the two of you could have stayed a few days longer," she said.

"That would have suited me just fine, Mrs. Cameron, but I doubt that you could have talked my friend Bart into lingering." Jason declared. He would have loved nothing more than having more time to spend in the company of the enchanting Tawny Blair.

"Now that he has the horse he is ready to get started back to England, eh?"

"That's Bart. I guess if I had to be honest I'd have to admit that an Arabian full of spirit aboard my ship is going to be a new experience for me and I'm not too sure about how that's going to go. Only for Bart would I undertake such a feat."

"Well, I shall pray for a safe crossing for you, Jason. Come back to Virginia again and see us."

An hour later the two young Englishman were on their way. In less than twenty-four hours, Bart Montgomery had accomplished exactly what he'd set out to do many weeks ago in England. It never ceased to amaze Jason how Bart never failed at anything he sought to do. He'd never known anyone like him.

All the time they rolled along the country road from Cameron Farms leading into the village of Longcreek, Jason was thinking about the beautiful brown-haired girl, Tawny. He gave one long lingering glance back at the small cottage where she lived as the buggy moved on down the road.

He knew it was foolhardy to let himself think he could take her away on his ship, carry her back to England with him. But it had been a divine thought for a brief moment or two yesterday.

As thrilled and elated as he was over having Diablo trotting behind the buggy as they moved down the dirt road, Bart was also having his private thoughts about Tawny.

His blue eyes spotted the trail he'd ridden down bright and early this morning when he'd chanced to see Tawny. He recalled the sweet taste of her lips and the supple softness of her body as he'd held her. He wondered where she lived; he was almost tempted to ask Jason. After all, he'd taken her home the day before.

Once they left Longcreek and headed toward Suffolk, Bart tried to sweep any thoughts of Tawny Blair out of his mind. He had his Arabian, and he could hardly have managed to woo and win a pretty girl's heart, too, in such a brief stay.

Seeing how high the sun was in the sky, he figured that he'd be able to go on to Chesapeake before dark. He'd not rest easy with the stallion in a livery stable.

He kept the bay pulling the buggy at a fast, even pace all the way to Suffolk. It was only after they left the outskirts of Suffolk that he relaxed. They'd make Chesapeake long before sunset now.

He had only to look over at Jason's face to see that he was anticipating the sight of his ship after being away for the last two days. One thing troubled Bart now, and that was the handling of the fiery stallion once they took him aboard the ship and attempted to lower him into the hold for the long journey homeward. He knew that it was going to be a tremendous task.

He had inspected the special stall Jason had built for the animal before they'd sailed from England. There were special hoists and lifts the two of them had worked together on and Jason's men had installed. But Bart knew he was not going to rest easy until he led that stallion out on the docks in England.

Once they got back to the *Sea Princess,* Bart would have the expertise of one of his own trainers, waiting to help. He had insisted that Harvey Green come along on this trip. No one was better with horses than Green, and Bart had been certain that he would be bringing this fine beast back with him. Never had he considered that the voyage across the ocean would be for naught.

They arrived at the wharf in Chesapeake at sunset. It was a grand sight for Jason to see his fine ship moored there, but Bart was not the only one having apprehensions about getting the spirited stallion safely in the hold. If that damned horse did any damage to his pride and joy, the *Sea Princess*, it might sever his friendship with Bart.

Jason was the first one to leap down from the buggy and rush across the wharf, leaving Bart to worry about his horse.

All day long Tawny could not dismiss the strange new sensations Bart Montgomery had stirred in her. As she'd rushed toward the cottage, the flaming heat of his body seemed to be still pressing against her. Once she was inside the cottage, she looked at herself in the mirror to see the rosy glow of her cheeks. She looked no different, but she *felt* different.

She planned to tell no one what had happened to her this early spring morning. She dared not tell anyone! It would be her secret.

For the longest time after she'd returned, her wildflowers remained in her basket and she ambled around the room absentmindedly, not caring that she hadn't even started her chores.

"What is the matter with you, Tawny Blair?" she mumbled to the empty room. She was glad that Maybelle would be sleeping for a few hours.

She did not make her usual trip to the Thacher cottage. In fact, she had not been over to Roberta's for two days. It suddenly dawned on Tawny that if Mrs. Thacher had seen her returning from the Camerons yesterday and saw Jason Hamilton kissing her, what would she be thinking? Could that be the reason she'd not been over to see Tawny the last two days? This bothered Tawny, for Mrs. Thacher's opinion of her was important.

Roberta Thacher had not seen her, but Tawny's mother happened to be looking out her window when her daughter had been escorted home by the handsome black-haired Englishman. Maybelle did not mention this to Tawny when she came out of her bedroom later and Tawny had not mentioned Jason, either. Maybelle figured he had to be a friend of those Camerons who seemed to have taken Tawny under their wing the last few weeks. She'd seen all the fancy things Tawny had brought home after her visits there.

She had to admit that the baskets of food they'd given to Tawny had been a great help in keeping them from going hungry. Her wages at the tavern were not enough to cover all their expenses.

Now she was so far behind in her rent on the small cottage that her landlord was threatening to throw them out next week if she didn't pay him what she owed.

She might not be able to keep the vow she'd made to herself and Tawny several weeks ago. Last night she had been tempted to break her word when a fellow approached her after the tavern closed. If he happened to come again tonight, she might just accept his offer.

Maybelle had been awake longer than Tawny realized when she came out of the bedroom door in her faded wrapper that late afternoon. Looking at her pretty daughter, she realized that Tawny deserved much more than she could ever give her. Yesterday she'd observed Tawny sitting there in the buggy with that elegant young man and she watched the gentle kiss he planted on her daughter's lips. Maybelle had never possessed the exquisite beauty to attract a fine-looking gentleman, but her daughter did.

Maybelle could only hope that some gentleman would come along and take Tawny away from this miserable existence. But until that happened, she would do whatever it took to keep a roof over her pretty head, for that was about all she could do.

"Your wildflowers are pretty, honey," she told Tawny as the girl came through the door and walked into the small kitchen to pour herself a cup of coffee.

"Thank you, Mama. I picked them early this morning when I went into the woods," Tawny said. She dared not confess what else had happened in the woods.

Maybelle helped herself to a generous bowl of the ham and beans Tawny had simmering in a big cast-iron pot on the stove. "Those Camerons are sure nice to you. This ham has a fine taste to it."

"Nicest people you'd ever want to meet, Mama," she told her mother.

"Well, if anything ever happens to me, I want you to go to them, Tawny. You hear me?"

"Nothing is going to happen to you, Mama. I won't listen to you talking that way."

Maybelle noticed the concerned look on Tawny's lovely face. "Ah, honey, don't look so serious! I just meant that if something did happen, I know they'd take care of you, and I know of no one else who would. I've no sisters or brothers to step in for me. Tawny, something can happen to someone when they least expect it. You're old enough for me to talk this way. I am no young woman anymore."

"But you're not as old as Mrs. Thacher, Mama."

"Well, honey — let's just say that Mrs. Thacher hasn't had to work as hard as I have and she had a husband to tend to her needs up to a few years ago."

Tawny had wanted to ask her mother one question for the longest time, and this seemed like the moment to do so.

"Mama, tell me about my father? Who was he?"

"Tawny, he was one fine man, but I am not going to lie to you; I was never married to him. He came into my life and he left just as quick as he'd appeared." She got up quickly from the chair and excused herself. "Got to get myself dressed to go to work, honey. We'll talk about this later." But Maybelle knew she would never tell Tawny who her father was, and she had only one thing in her possession that would ever reveal his identity — a simple gold ring with his initial on it. She'd cherished it throughout the years. He'd given it to her the night Tawny was conceived.

How young and trusting she'd been, and she'd truly believed this man loved her. Back then she was as sweet and innocent as Tawny was now. She'd been overwhelmed when this older man declared that he adored her, for she'd never considered herself to be a ravishing beauty.

One day, her parents, who were farmers, had been stricken by a violent illness and died within three months. She was left all alone and pregnant. The farm was taken from her for debts owed by her father and she was left penniless.

Some kind-hearted neighbors took her in, and she stayed with them until after Tawny was born. Shortly after that, she started working at the tavern where she was still working now, some sixteen years later. It had been the one night of pleasure she had surrendered to years ago that led to a miserable, unhappy life for Maybelle. At first, she was too proud to go to the man. Then just as she was at the point of telling him he had a three-year-old daughter, he married another lady.

Maybelle accepted that she was doomed to raise her daughter alone. She should have gone to the man the minute she realized she was expecting his child, but she was so young and naive. The next thirteen years had been a constant struggle to raise Tanwy. Her beautiful daughter was the only happiness she'd enjoyed. Maybelle wasn't proud of how she'd lived and she knew what the village thought about her, but that pain and hurt had quit bothering her a long time ago.

Most of the ladies who snubbed her would have been mortified to know the tales she'd listened to from their husbands when they'd been well into their cups and had slept in her bed. Often, when she'd gone down the street and passed by them, she'd smiled when she recalled the stories she'd heard about them.

This last year had been particularly painful as Maybelle had noticed the change in Tawny and how her daughter had looked at her. She didn't blame Tawny for comparing her to ladies like Reba Cameron and Roberta Thacher. It was only natural.

The day of reckoning had come, Maybelle realized. It didn't matter to Maybelle what other people thought about her, but it did matter what Tawny thought.

Chapter 7

Maybelle had been gone for over an hour when Tawny decided to go sit on the front step of the cottage. It was oppressively warm this evening, so she'd slipped into her short batiste gown and washed her face in cool water.

She'd glanced out the window to see nothing but the blackest of nights, for there were no stars in the sky. With such vast darkness just outside the front door of the cottage, she saw nothing wrong about going out there in her gown. Who was there to see her, she reasoned?

But she understood why the night was so dark after she'd been sitting there for a while. In the distance she heard the distant rumble of thunder and the flash of lightning. She watched the storm moving closer and closer, but when the drops of rain began to fall she leaped up from the step to get inside.

She scurried around the house to shut the windows, then went back to the small parlor and brightened the kerosene lamp. It had never bothered her to be at the cottage alone at night when Maybelle worked, but stormy nights had made her uneasy for as long as she could remember.

Less than a half hour later the full fury of the thunderstorm was overhead. Tawny paced the floor to look out the windows, only to jump back when the fierce flashes of lightning darted through the window.

But as quickly as the storm had brewed, it had also gone on to the north, and she heaved a sigh of relief. To soothe her churning stomach, she went to the kitchen and poured herself a glass of milk and grabbed a handful of the cookies she'd baked this afternoon.

Now that everything was quiet outside and she was relaxed, Tawny sought the comfort of her bed.

Once she sank down on the bed and her head rested on the pillow, she fell asleep.

Maybelle thought about Tawny as she worked her tables down at the tavern, for she knew she was scared of storms. There was so much loud laughter and noise inside she could not tell if the storm had ended.

It was a busy night and Maybelle's feet were killing her as she worked that last hour. She'd seen fellows in the tavern tonight who she hadn't seen for weeks. Joe Sawyer hadn't been here for months, but he was here now and she'd stopped by his table to have a friendly chat with him. Maybelle found him a likable sort who just liked to take a night away from his farm to enjoy a little folly every so often.

Before closing time, Pete Farrell, one of Sawyer's neighbors, joined him. Maybelle served him a whiskey and shared a little chatter with him as she had with Joe. But it was the sight of Jeb Turner ambling in at the end of the evening that made the hardened Maybelle nervous. The man was mean and ornery.

She felt his eyes following her around the room everywhere she moved. She began counting the minutes until the door would close and all of them would have to leave.

When that happened, Maybelle wasted no time cleaning off the tables. As the tavern owner was dimming the lamps and lanterns, Maybelle pleaded with him. "I'm dead on my butt tonight. I'll come in an hour early tomorrow to get all this mess cleaned up, Luke."

"Fine with me, Maybelle. I'm tired, too," he told her. Taking her nightly wages from his apron pocket, he told her good night.

Maybelle made a hasty exit out the back door and into the fresh air; it had a pleasant aroma after the rains. She was glad she wasn't going to be walking home in a storm and relieved she hadn't encountered the fierce-looking face of Jeb Turner the minute she stepped outside the door.

She walked around the back of the tavern and took the shortcut to the dirt road she walked down every night to return to her cottage.

Suddenly, Maybelle was startled when she heard someone call out to her. "Maybelle, honey—come on and we'll give you a ride home!" She saw that it was Joe Sawyer sitting there in his flatbed wagon. As she moved closer to the wagon, she realized that the other man on the seat with him was his friend, Pete.

"Come on, Maybelle. I'll help you up," Pete declared as he leaped out of the seat and gave her his arm. He got into the back of the wagon after he'd helped her on the seat.

But they'd not traveled too far down the road when she realized that this was not going to be a free ride home. The men were expecting a favor from her. Out of the corner of her eyes she saw that Pete was eagerly arranging the jute sacks stored on the bed of the wagon in anticipation that she was going to crawl back there with him.

She sought to tease Joe playfully to bid for some time since she recognized the familiar sights of the countryside and knew that her cottage was hardly a half mile away.

"Now, Joe, you need to be getting on home to your wife," she laughed.

"Don't concern yourself, honey, about Joe. Old Pete here needs some comforting. Come on back here with me and you can worry about Joe later," Pete Farrell huskily urged her as his hand took a firm hold on her arm. Maybelle was no small woman, but she felt herself being lifted off the seat of the wagon and flung back on the bed of the wagon before she was aware of what was happening. The man was ungodly stout and his heavy body was covering her as his busy hands were yanking and tearing away the bodice of her blouse.

A whore she might be, but this brute sickened her so Maybelle fought him as she'd not fought a man in a long time. But the harder she fought, the crueler Pete became.

His finger pinched her breast. His slobbering mouth bit her flesh.

All the time, Joe kept his eyes straight ahead because he knew that he was approaching Maybelle's cottage. He had no inkling that Maybelle was protesting Pete's crude advances all this time, for he knew she could give a man a lot of wild, wonderful pleasure when she bedded him. It would seem she and old Pete were having themselves a heck of a time in the back of his wagon.

But Pete was getting nowhere with this hellcat. His fierce, powerful hands reached for her throat as he muttered in her ear, "Lay still, bitch. I'm going to have you one way or the other. What are you trying to pull on me? Everyone knows that you lay with any man."

So heated was his passion that his hands clasped her throat in a frenzy. He was not even aware that Joe had stopped the wagon, for they'd arrived at Maybelle's cottage. When her body quit fighting him, Pete thought he had won his battle and released his hold, but Maybelle gave one long, agonizing scream and Pete's hands went around her throat again with even a firmer grip. She gasped again—and it was to be her last one.

"Wha—what the hell, Pete?" Joe jerked around to see what was going on. What he saw was enough to sober him up quickly, for Pete was already tugging Maybelle's limp body out of the wagonbed and tossing it to the ground.

The next few seconds were like a hellish eternity to Joe Sawyer as he watched the tiny figure of Tawny Blair rushing out of the cottage. He'd never forget the panic-stricken look on her face as she sank down beside her mother. Like most people in Longcreek, he'd known Tawny since she was a tot. He had daughters about her age.

He was like a man frozen in shock as he watched Pete grab the girl around the waist, fling her up in the wagon, and yell at Joe to get out of there. Only after he had the tiny miss secured in a couple of the jute sacks, kicking and screaming, did he move up on the seat with Joe.

"The girl could identify us, Joe. I'm going to have to kill

her, too. That whore is dead back there. You hear me, Joe," Pete whispered as he bent over toward Joe in hopes that Tawny wouldn't hear him.

"Oh, God! What are we going to do with her?" Joe asked Pete, adding that he was not going to allow her to be killed.

"We'll take her a far piece away so it'll take her a long time in getting back. You just keep this wagon going down the road until I tell you we've got the right distance between us and Longcreek."

The next hour and a half was spent in silence, broken only by the whimpering sounds Tawny was making in her prison of jute sacks in the bed of the wagon.

"Too close, Joe. Don't you know that?" Joe asked Pete when they came to the edge of Suffolk. "No, let's go on to Chesapeake. That's a busy port town." Pete pointed out to Joe Sawyer what could be at stake in this, and he had only to remind Joe what something like this could do to his family to make Joe agreeable to anything that Pete Farrell suggested.

So they journeyed on to Chesapeake, and when they arrived down around the wharf of the small port town, there was only one large ship docked there. Dawn was just breaking, but the dockhands were already milling around a load of cargo going onto the ship.

Pete leaped off the wagon and urged Joe to stay there. He ambled along the wharf and talked to some of the hands loading up crates and sacks to go aboard the ship. When he returned to the wagon, Pete did not tell Joe what he intended to do until after he'd carried out the act. He gave a mighty blow to the jute sack to render Tawny unconscious, and when Joe gave out a protest, Pete informed him that it was necessary to keep her silent so he could get her on the ship as part of the cargo.

"The ship is leaving for England. That should be far enough away to save our skin, Joe."

Flinging the limp form of Tawny covered in the jute sacks over his shoulder, he marched toward the dock. Joe

66

Sawyer sat there in the wagon knowing that the nightmare was never going to end for him.

There was a pleased smile on Pete's face when he returned to the wagon and announced to his friend that the ship would sail within the hour. "Let's go back home, Joe."

Joe did as he was told, but he knew that home would never be the same again.

But this night was to have its effects on more lives than just Joe Sawyer's. No one was to feel the shaking impact of it more than Bill and Reba Cameron.

Speculation and rumors ran rampant through the small village for the next week or two that Tawny was involved in the death of her mother, but Roberta Thacher's only concern was for the missing girl. Where in the world was Tawny?

The Camerons were distraught about Tawny, too. She could not possibly have killed anyone! Out of their great devotion to her, they took charge of the burial of her mother and the packing up of the few possessions in the cottage.

Only the boxes of personal belongings were taken to their farm, for the furnishings were not worth storing. Reba placed all the pretty clothes she'd given Tawny and her few personal possessions in one of her guest rooms.

But the things belonging to Tawny's mother, Reba dared not dispose of, because she was sure there would be a day when Tawny would return and want them. All the old, tattered clothing Reba packed neatly in a box to save for Tawny. There was only one article the woman possessed that was of any value and she took it out to show to her husband the night after they'd buried Maybelle.

"How sad it is, Bill! They had so little. It makes me so happy to know what we did for Tawny. How happy we must have made her when she visited us here at the farm. Oh, Bill!" Reba sighed, tears flowing down her lovely cheeks.

67

"I've never regretted anything we've done for Tawny. I know that she is innocent of this. I don't know where she is, but I do know we'll see that girl again as sure as I'm breathing."

"Look what I found among her mother's things, Bill. A ring! It's solid gold," Reba told him as she handed the ring to him.

For a minute he did not speak. "I'll hold on to this, honey," he finally said. "I'll put it in my safe here in the study." He gave her a warm smile and patted her hand. "You've had a long day, so why don't you go to bed and get some rest, eh?"

"I think I will, Bill. I am so tired." She bent down to give his forehead a gentle kiss before she turned to go out the door.

It was one of the rare times that Bill Cameron did not wish the company of his lovely Reba. Now he had to think in solitude. He had only to gaze on the ring to recognize it. It was his, and his father had given it to him on his eighteenth birthday, a long time before he'd met Reba.

Walking to his liquor chest, he poured himself a generous glass of whiskey, as he recalled a certain night long long ago when he'd encountered a voluptuous blonde who had wildly excited him. They'd shared one wild, reckless night of lovemaking and he'd walked away from her, giving no thought that he might have left her with a child. That child was Tawny. *Dear God, why hadn't she come to him?*

But now that he was older he had to be honest with himself. If the woman *had* come to him, he might not have been too understanding. Now he was filled with guilt that this poor woman's miserable life was due to him.

He knew one thing that he must do before he'd ever be rid of this guilt plaguing his soul, and that was that he must be honest with Reba. He had to cleanse his soul before he died.

The next day he sought to do this, and his dear Reba smiled at him, declaring after his revelation that she'd suspected the truth after finding his ring in Maybelle's belongings.

"I saw the look in your eyes, Bill, as I gave you the ring, and so much began to fall in place. Why, my goodness, Bill—the child looks like you and there is that same twinkle in her eyes when she laughs," Reba told him as she smiled at him. "I can't think of anything nicer than finding out that Tawny is your daughter," she declared as her hand affectionately patted his shoulder. "That makes her my stepdaughter."

Bill could only shake his head and sigh. "Oh, God, Reba Cameron, you are the most wonderful woman in this whole wide world and I have to be the luckiest sonofabitch I know!"

She bent down to kiss his cheek. "Well, I'll remind you of that from time to time. And Bill, we shall see our daughter one day. She will come to us. I feel so strongly that Tawny will come home." Bill had never loved her more than he did this day!

Chapter 8

As black as the night was, Tawny knew that she would forever remember the face of that horrible man who wrestled with her to slam the sack over her head and tied the rope around her waist. She fought him like a tiger with her feet and legs until he rendered her helpless by securing them in another jute sack and tying another rope to her small waist.

As she lay a prisoner, unable to move one way or the other, she surrendered to defeat and cried. She'd heard what that bastard had told Sawyer once the wagon started to roll away from the cottage. Her mother was dead. There was nothing she could do now, and perhaps this man would kill her, too. But if she lived, she vowed to do the same thing to him that he'd done to her mother.

She didn't even know the man's name, but she certainly recognized Joe Sawyer and she'd considered Mr. Sawyer a nice man. So how could he have had any part in this despicable act? She didn't understand it at all. All she knew was that he had, and that was all she needed to know when she sought her revenge on both of them.

She had no inkling of the hours as they passed. Each minute seemed endless, but she saw the futility of trying to free herself. It was impossible!

So all she could so was lie there and stare at the black enclosure. Finally, the wagon stopped and she heard the two men talking in slow tones, but she could not hear what they were saying. She prepared herself for the worst. Her keen ears did pick up strange sounds and there were other voices far away, it seemed to her. The air permeating the openings of the sack seemed to have a different smell to her.

As she lay there trying to figure all this out, she felt the fierce blow slamming across her face and side of her head and she gave way to the excruciating pain, losing consciousness.

She dwelled in this state with no awareness that Pete Farrell had carried her limp body from the wagon and that she'd been loaded aboard the *Sea Princess* by one of the dockhands who thought the sacks were part of the ship's cargo.

She knew nothing about the *Sea Princess*'s departure from the shore of Virginia. The ship was out of the bay area and plowing steadily through the Atlantic Ocean when Tawny finally began to come out of her haze and back to reality.

She heard the sound of a footstep nearby and there was nothing stopping her from calling out. "Help me! Someone — whoever you are — please help me," she whimpered.

Jason Hamilton, being a very nervous sea captain with Bart's prized cargo aboard, had come down in the hold to check the Arabian. It mattered not to him that he'd assigned one of his seamen to sit down there with the horse, he wanted to check out the situation himself now that the ship was on its way and everything was running in perfect order.

He turned to the young sailor. "Did you hear what I heard?" he asked.

"Sure did, Captain. Sounded like a woman crying to me."

"Stay here. I'll check this out," Jason said, then called out, "Where are you? Tell me. I heard your call." He moved slowly around the hold until the voice echoed across the hold again and Jason rushed in the direction. He had only to glance down to see the strange-looking bulk of jute sack and see the movement to know he had himself a stowaway.

He bent down quickly and reached for his knife to give a cut to the ropes tying the sacks. He had only to yank off the sack to see the tear-stained face of the lovely Tawny. "Good Goddamn! What the bloody hell are you doing like this, Tawny?"

The sight of Jason was enough to make her arms reach

71

out and go around his neck as she broke into grateful tears. Jason's arms enclosed and comforted her. "That's all right honey, you just get all your crying through and Jason will hold you. You're safe now!"

For the longest time the two of them sat there on the floor of the hold and Jason held her close in his arms. His lips gave soothing kisses to the side of her face. But as he was holding her, he suddenly noticed that she was clad only in her thin batiste nightgown and he pondered how he was going to take her back to his cabin like that.

When she had calmed enough for him to leave her for a moment he went over to Diablo's stall and urged the young sailor to toss him a blanket. "Everything is all right, Phil. I'll explain later. You keep an eye on that stallion and I'll attend to this."

When he walked the short distance to where Tawny was sitting like a frightened child, a wave of compassion washed over Jason. He never wanted to see that pretty face of hers looking this way again, he told himself.

"Come on, love — let's get this around you so I can get you to my cabin and then you can tell me everything. All right?"

Jason's arm supported her as she got up off the floor and let him drape the blanket around her. It still had not dawned on her that she was in her nightgown when she'd dashed out of the cottage to answer her mother's screams for help.

It was only after she was in Jason's comfortable cabin with the warm blanket still tucked around her and was enjoying a cup of hot chocolate that she became aware of her state of undress. But the kind-hearted Jason had not made her feel embarrassed.

He'd finally urged her to tell him what had happened. As it had been from the first moment they'd met, Tawny found Jason Hamilton easy to talk to. Something about those warm black eyes of his urged her to trust him, and she did.

She told him everything that had happened from the moment she'd rushed into the cottage when the rains had started to fall and the violent storm had broken out. Jason watched her lovely face as she told how she was awakened by

72

her mother's agonizing screams and rushed out of the cottage. Her mother was lying lifeless on the ground and the man grabbed her and flung her in the flatbed wagon, yelling to the other man to get going.

Jason listened to the rest of the sordid story. He couldn't change what had happened back in Longcreek now. They were heading for England and there was no turning back. But he had to give her some kind of consolation and comfort.

"Tawny, the Camerons love you very much and they'll do the things that you're not there to do. You must write them a letter so we can send it back to Virginia on the next ship after we make port in England so they will know that you are all right. They must be very concerned for your welfare."

"Oh, Jason, I . . . I never thought about that. I must do as you say. I'd not want them to worry about me." She sat there very quietly and thoughtful for a moment as though she was absorbing everything he had said.

"Are you all right now, Tawny?" Jason rose up from the chair. He had been so occupied with her that he'd not thought about the possibility of Bart coming through the cabin door unannounced to see Tawny sitting there in her little batiste gown and making some sly remark. He had to alert Montgomery about all this.

"I'm fine, Jason. Really I am. I'm just sorry I've put you to so much trouble," she told him.

Jason ambled over and kissed her on the top of her head. "You're no burden to me, Tawny. You never would be that, but I am going to leave you for a while to see to the ship. My sailors aren't used to such a pretty lady aboard my ship so I want you to lock the door after I leave and keep it locked until I return. Will you do that, honey?"

"I promise, Jason. I will open it to no one but you," she vowed, her big doelike eyes looking up at him.

"All right, you do just that. I may be gone for a long time, but my cabin is yours. Stretch out on the bed and get some sleep. You've just gone through a hell of a nightmare, but you will be safe now."

73

"I know that, Jason. I think that I will lie down," she said, smiling up at him as he turned to leave.

"But don't crawl under the covers until you come over here and turn this lock." He sought to tease her.

She moved to obey his command as he walked through the cabin door. But as soon as she'd done his bidding, she scampered back to the huge double bunk to crawl under the covers. At last she felt safe!

Jason wanted to talk with Bart and tell him how he found Tawny aboard the *Sea Princess*. Jason planned to share Montgomery's cabin so that Tawny could have his. He went directly to his friend's quarters figuring that this was where he'd find him. Bart was not exactly the best sailor so he didn't spend much time up on deck.

As he'd suspected, Bart answered his rapping and invited him in. It was a happy face Montgomery wore, for it had not been as difficult as he'd anticipated lowering Diablo into the hold. Jason's men had done a fine job.

"Think we'll do as good going home as we did crossing to get to Virginia, Jason?" Bart asked, strolling back over to the table where he'd been sitting and going over some papers laid out there. He picked up the cheroot he'd been smoking. "Want one, Jason?"

"Don't think so, Bart. Just wanted to find you to tell you some news."

"Diablo riding all right?" Bart's blue eyes flashed with concern that the stallion might be going a little wild in his strange surroundings.

"He's fine, Bart. No problem with him, and I've assigned one of my crew to stay there so we could be alerted immediately and you and that handler of yours could get down there to tend to him. No, it's something else you need to know."

"Well, sit down, Jason, and tell me what's on your mind," Bart urged him.

"Well, we've got a passenger aboard that I hadn't exactly

74

planned on. So I wanted you to know about it."

Bart broke into an amused laugh, "Jase, you got a woman in your cabin, eh?"

"I do."

"Well, you warned me that it was the two-legged fillies you were more interested in, but damned if I can figure how you managed that. You worked fast, I've got to say!"

"This isn't exactly a filly, Bart, and I didn't work this all out. It just happened. The young lady is Tawny." Bart lunged forward out of his chair with a stunned look on his face.

"Tawny Blair?"

"The same." Jason went on to tell him the bizarre story that Tawny had told him. For a brief moment Bart said nothing after Jason had finished talking, but he was having some very disturbing thoughts. The beautiful Tawny sharing Jason's cabin surely did not sit well with him, for he knew what a passionate little miss she was after he'd shared that brief, intimate interlude with her in the woods. Instant jealously flared in Bart Montgomery.

There was a tone of sarcasm in his deep voice as he remarked to Jason, "Well, it should be a most pleasant crossing for you, my friend." Bart ambled over to the small cabin window to stare out at the ocean.

Jason's black eyes were piercing his back, but there was no mistaking that he was angry. "If anyone else but you said that to me, Bart, I would have knocked hell out of them. Since we are friends, I'm going to pretend you didn't say it this time. I've no intention of sharing my cabin with Tawny. I plan to share yours. But then I might add that no one aboard this ship is going to share the quarters I assign to Tawny. Aboard this ship, I'm the boss!"

By the time Bart turned around, Jason was exiting the cabin. Bart was feeling like a cur. His friend had certainly put him in his place and he damned well deserved it, he realized. But such a surging jealousy had shot through him when Jason had told him Tawny was in his cabin! Yes, for the first time he was jealous of his good friend Jason!

75

For the next few minutes, he paced the floor of the cabin trying to figure out this thing gnawing away at him. He was the self-assured Bart Montgomery and no woman had ever been worth fretting about before. He and Jason had courted some of the loveliest ladies in London the past years, but nothing like this had ever come up between the two of them. Now this little backwoods girl from Virginia had managed to make him act the fool and Bart didn't like it! He didn't like it at all!

So he busied himself around the cabin making room for Jason's things. Then he left the cabin to seek out Hamilton to apologize to him and tell him he'd acted very stupidly.

He'd not allow some little slip of a girl to make him act like an idiot again!

Chapter 9

Nothing was more breathtakingly wonderful to Jason Hamilton than the sunset in the distant horizon when he was sailing the *Sea Princess*. While he was talking to his first mate, he glanced westward to see the glorious hues of gold mixing with the rose and purples. It was a magnificent sight!

His ship was sailing smoothly in the calm waters, and the first day of his voyage was going without incident. Jason was pleased that the stallion had not created any problems. He could not say the same thing for Diablo's master. Right now he was not too pleased with Bart and had decided to make a hasty exit from his cabin before he said something he would regret.

It was then that he happened to see his tall, fair-haired friend sauntering across the deck toward him. He just hoped that he had got his mouth under control, for Jason was in no mood for his sardonic remarks.

Bart Montgomery saw the coolness in Jason's black eyes as he walked up to him. He'd been privy to that exploding black Irish temper once before, so he said nothing until Jason had dismissed his first mate. As soon as only he and Jason were standing there on the deck, Bart wasted no time in saying what he'd intended to say. "I'm sorry, Jason. I had no right to speak as I did. Can't explain what got into me."

"Just like the rest of us mortals, Bart, we sometimes make fools of ourselves," Jason replied as his dark eyes locked into Bart's. But Bart sensed something about Jason's manner that told him he'd give him no quarter where

Tawny was concerned.

"Well, I will admit to that. So let's forget it. Move in when you like. I've made room for you." Bart started to turn to go, but Jason quickly stopped him by suggesting that the three of them dine in his cabin that evening. "We'll share the evening meal with Tawny and I'll get my things together to go to your cabin."

"Sounds fine to me, Jason. When should I come?"

"I'm through with my rounds. Shall we say in an hour?" Jason suggested as the two parted to go their separate ways.

Jason was troubled by what he was going to find for Tawny to wear in the next hour before Bart appeared at his cabin. He sought out the young cabin boy and asked if he might borrow a pair of his trousers since he was as short as Tawny.

With the faded blue pants flung over his arm, he figured he could provide one of his white linen shirts for her. Oh, it was going to swallow her, but she could roll up the sleeves. Under the circumstances, it was the best he could provide.

So deep was her sleep that he had to knock on the cabin door several times and call out to her before he was admitted to his cabin. He realized just how drained and exhausted she was as he ambled in the cabin.

"Tawny, I have a pair of trousers from my cabin boy and I'll get you one of my shirts to wear. Bart will be here in an hour to dine with us. I wish I had more to offer, but it's better than that nightgown and you can't eat with a blanket wrapped around you."

She pushed the tousled hair away from her face and took the trousers he offered her. "Oh, Jason—this will be fine and I know I've caused you trouble you didn't ask for. I'm sorry for that."

She felt Jason's hand clasp her arm. His black eyes were warm and tender. "Tawny, would you believe me if I told you that I'm not the least bit sorry you're here on my ship?" he told her. "I'm happy, but I wish it had not happened the way it did. Will you believe me?"

"I believe you, Jason." She gave him a warm smile. No one could be nicer or kinder than Jason Hamilton, she was convinced.

Jason smiled as he turned to go to the chest at the bottom of his bunk to get her one of his white linen shirts.

A teasing glint was in his eyes as he handed her the shirt. "Now, young lady—go make yourself presentable," he said. "I'll be back in a minute after I order our dinner. Got to have a talk with my cook."

Once she was alone, she wasted no time taking off the nightgown to slip into the cabin boy's pants and Jason's shirt. The length of the pants was fine, but the waist was a few inches too large and the sleeves of the shirt had to be rolled a few times. But as Jason had pointed out to her, they were much better than her flimsy nightgown.

She used Jason's hairbrush to comb her tangled long hair, which took more time than the changing of her clothes.

When Jason came back to the cabin to see her standing in this garb, he vowed someday he'd dress her in the finest silks and satins.

She reminded him of the little urchins roaming the streets of London. He looked down to see her dainty bare feet, then rushed over to pull out a pair of woolen stockings. "Here, honey, you need something to keep your feet warm."

She smiled and sat down on the bunk to slip them on her feet. "They are so pretty, Jason," she told him as she admired the blues and vivid scarlet trim of the yarn.

"Yes, they are. I have a sister who loves to knit so she keeps me well supplied," he told her.

Tawny found she had more stocking than she needed for her tiny feet and she laughed.

He laughed, too. "You are a wee little mite, aren't you, Tawny Blair." It was nice to see her able to laugh and forget the terrible experience she'd gone through, at least for a little while, though he knew it was going to come back to haunt her.

Other thoughts were haunting Jason. He recalled what he'd told Bart—that no one was going to bother Tawny while she was aboard his ship. But he wondered about himself. Could he keep his own desires under control during the days and nights they'd be at sea? Right now, he wasn't too sure of himself. Tawny was enough to drive any man crazy.

The sweet little innocent that she was, he'd wager that she had no inkling how she could stir a man's passion. To get his mind off Tawny, he decided it was a good time for him to gather some of his things together to take to Bart's cabin.

He explained that he was going to be sharing Bart's cabin, so she could have his. But he made a point of telling her that it was very important that she keep this door locked at all times.

"My first mate already knows that he can find me in Bart's cabin and my cabin boy will also know after this evening, but my other men will not know this, Tawny, so I'm going to have to depend on you to do as I ask in case one of them should come to the cabin."

"Oh, you can depend on me, Jason. But don't tell me that I'm not causing a mess of trouble." Her next words told Jason just how very naive she was. "You could remain here in your own cabin, Jason. I'd be very comfortable over there on that bench. As you said, I'm pretty small. It bothers me for you to give up your own cabin."

"It would bother me if I didn't," Jason told her, realizing that she wouldn't know what he was talking about.

"Well, I guess that I must do as the captain says," she smiled.

"That's right, young lady, and don't you forget it!"

There was a sharp rap on the cabin door and he knew that it was Bart. As Jason went to the door, Tawny took the opportunity to light the candle in the center of the small table where they would be dining.

The minute Bart Montgomery walked through the door, Tawny's relaxed, lighthearted air suddenly changed. The tall blond Englishman had such an imposing manner about him! She felt completely different around him than she did around Jason. Every fiber in her body seemed stimulated as she looked into his brilliant blue eyes. He was even more handsome than she'd remembered.

"Well, Tawny — I must say this is an unexpected pleasure. Jason's news was a little shocking. I'm sorry that your bad experience is what landed you aboard the *Sea Princess*. Nevertheless, it is nice to see you again," Bart declared as he came on into the cabin.

Jason appreciated how gallant Bart was behaving, for he was not too sure what to expect from his friend.

"Thank you, Bart, for your kind words." She took the opportunity to sink down into the nearby chair, for she felt like her legs were turning to jelly. Why was she this way around Bart Montgomery and not when she was around Jason Hamilton? Jason was just as handsome with his jet-black hair and warm black eyes. And he was a much kinder man.

Bart took the chair next to Tawny and turned to look up at Jason. "Jase, I think we should have a glass of that good wine to celebrate the beautiful Tawny being here with us tonight. We've got to be two of the luckiest fellows!"

Tawny wore a lovely smile on her face as her eyes darted over to Jason and back to Bart. Jason could hardly refuse his friend's request, but he also wondered just what was going on in that cunning head of Bart's. He was being too bloody nice to suit Jason.

When each of them were holding their glasses of wine, the towering Montgomery stood back up and presented a toast. "To Tawny Blair, the most beautiful sea siren of all!"

Jason's eyes were on Tawny, for he suspected that she'd never drunk wine before and he leaned over to whisper in her ear. "Sip it, honey. Sip it very slowly."

She smiled and gave him a nod of her head. Bart realized that Jason had appointed himself Tawny's protector. He found himself resenting this assumption on Jason's part.

There was another knock on the cabin door and the galley cook entered, bringing their meal to the cabin. Bart had to admit that Jason had a fine cook in his ship's galley.

Jason had requested a special meal for tonight. The beef roast and the fresh vegetables were delicious. Bart knew they were probably bought in Chesapeake only yesterday before they'd shipped out. It was near the end of the voyage that the fresh vegetables always ran low and the meals were not as good.

For a wee little thing, Bart noticed that Tawny had a hearty appetite. He wondered when she had last eaten a meal. Jason observed that Bart's eyes were constantly on the girl as she was devouring the food.

To top off the grand meal the cook had brought a juicy apple pie for dessert. Tawny had eaten so much of the roast and vegetables that she could not imagine eating a piece of pie, but neither could she resist it.

She understood what Jason was trying to warn her about the wine, so after the one glass of white wine, she refused the rich red Jason and Bart were drinking. A glass of milk was her request, and Jason gratefully obliged her by having the cook bring it.

Once the meal was over and the cook had cleared away all the dishes, he was more than pleased to hear the beautiful young lady tell the captain that it was the best meal she'd ever eaten. His chest swelled with pride.

"Tawny, would our smoking bother you, for if it does Bart and I will just take a stroll around the deck?" Jason asked her.

"It won't bother me, Jason. I've always enjoyed the smell of a man smoking a pipe. Mr. Cameron smoked a pipe, you know," she remarked. What she didn't say was that she had once tried one of the hand-rolled cigarettes left at her cottage by one of her mother's friends.

Bart and Jason lit their cheroots and the three of them sat there talking. Jason finally rose up from the table to tell Tawny that he and Bart were going to leave so she could get to bed. He moved around the cabin to gather up the belongings he intended to take with him, then he halted before starting for the door. "I'll send Rudy to the cabin with a breakfast tray, Tawny. But no one except Rudy is to be admitted through this door. All right?"

"All right, Jason."

Bart bid her good night. As he ambled out of the door, there was a sly smile on his handsome face.

As they were going down the passageway, Bart could not resist making a facetious remark to his friend. "Jason, I've got to say that I came to the conclusion tonight that you're going to make a damned good father." He broke into a booming explosion of laughter.

Jason's dancing black eyes looked straight at his friend and he suddenly realized that Bart Montgomery was jealous. He'd never known him to be this way before in all the time they'd spent together or at all the social affairs they'd attended in London.

Well, he was going to make old Bart more jealous, Jason decided. A devious grin on his face, he turned to his friend. "Bart, I hardly feel like a father where Tawny Blair is concerned," he declared. "Don't kid yourself for a minute on that!"

Jason noticed that there was no smile on Bart's face now! In fact, he became very silent and sober.

Chapter 10

Tawny had slipped back into her thin nightgown after Jason and Bart had left the cabin. But there seemed to be a chill to the air and she was about to drape the blanket around her when she noticed Jason's brown woolen robe hanging on a peg, so she helped herself to it. Then she felt cozy and warm.

There, in the night's quiet and all alone, she found herself exploring his cabin. She'd not noticed the pictures displayed on his desk that sat over in one corner of the cabin. There was a very distinguished-looking gentleman she knew had to be Jason's father, and beside it was a picture that must be of his mother. Jason was the image of his mother, with the same dark eyes and coloring. The pictures of the young ladies had to be the sisters he'd spoken about. What a grand family he had! It had to be nice to belong to such a family, Tawny thought to herself as she stood there looking at the pictures.

How she would have loved to have had a doting father and a nice home when she was growing up! How luck Jason was! She imagined that Bart had as nice a family, since they were good friends.

Dwelling on thoughts about family reminded her of the last time she'd looked at her mother, there on the ground, so lifeless and quiet. She moved away from Jason's desk and dimmed the lamps as she moved toward the bunk.

Once again she allowed herself to give way to the tears welling up in her. But when she'd shed all the tears and snuggled under the covers with Jason's robe still on her, she fell asleep.

* * *

Tawny's sleep was sound and deep and she did not wake up once during the night, but in the morning young Rudy knocking on her door to announce that he had her breakfast tray awakened her.

"Just . . . just a minute, Rudy. I'm coming," she called out as she leaped out of the bunk.

The bright-eyed youth came through the door with a broad smile on his face. "Good morning, Miss Tawny. Hope you rested well last night. Captain told me to bring you this tray. Hope everything is to your liking."

"Oh, I'm sure it will be. The coffee smells so good!" she told him, inhaling the steaming aroma.

The stocky, young boy set the tray on the table and told her that the captain had instructed him to bring her anything she wanted.

Surveying everything on the tray, Tawny laughed. "My goodness, Rudy—this is enough for two people. I will need nothing more. Thank the captain for me if you see him before I do."

"Yes, ma'am, I will. Enjoy your breakfast, Miss Tawny," he said as he turned to leave the cabin. Tawny did as Jason had insisted—she followed Rudy to the door and locked it before she returned to the table to pour herself a cup of the hot coffee.

She ate the eggs and slice of ham, but the portion was far too generous for her. One of the huge, fluffy biscuits was all she could eat. It was delicious and she was not used to such a huge breakfast back home. Rarely had they had fresh eggs or ham in their cupboard.

After she'd eaten all she could, she dressed back in the shirt and pants she'd worn the night before and neatly folded her little nightgown.

Once again, she used Jason's brush to stroke her tousled, thick hair. She thought about what would happen to her once they landed in England. She could not expect Jason to take on the responsibility for her when he got home; but

85

what was she to do if he didn't? She had no funds to buy herself the passage back to Virginia.

If she thought about her future right now, it looked hopeless. The only thing she could think of doing to get her mind off her dilemma was to sit down at Jason's table and write a long letter to the Camerons as Jason had suggested yesterday.

For the next hour this was what she did. She did not see Jason all morning, for he was occupied with his captain's duties and checking in on Bart and his trainer. It seemed the spirited stallion had been in a rambunctious mood. He was concerned about the horse breaking from the stall to do untold damage to his ship.

By midafternoon things had calmed and Jason finally made his way down the passageway to his cabin.

Tawny eagerly dashed to the door when she heard him calling out to her. She was beginning to feel very bored being in the cabin by herself. She was certainly not hungry, after such a huge breakfast, when Rudy had come by to see if she was ready to eat lunch. She smiled and thanked him. "I won't be needing anything, Rudy. That breakfast was more enough to hold me all day."

Jason was greeted by her smiling face. "I'm sorry that I didn't make it in time to share lunch with you. I had intended to, but things prevented it."

She laughed. "Well, I could not have eaten with you anyway, Jason. Rudy was too generous when he brought my breakfast."

"I know it isn't much fun, but I'm sure you can understand why I can't let you roam freely around the ship, Tawny. It could be dangerous for you. A pretty girl amid all my seamen could prove to be chancy."

She nodded her head. "Oh, I'd not do that, Jason. I'd certainly not want to cause you any more headaches."

"Well, my only concern is your welfare, Tawny." Jason got up from his chair. While he'd have liked to linger, he had things to attend to during the afternoon.

As he started out the door, he turned back. "Help yourself to any of the books over there in the shelf," he told her. "I read a lot when I have the time so you'll find quite a few to pick from. Maybe that would help you pass away the afternoon. See you as soon as I can, Tawny."

He disappeared through the door and Tawny was left alone. She took Jason's suggestion and strolled over to the shelves holding dozens of books. When she finally picked one, she thought about dear Mrs. Thacher, for she had been the one who'd spent endless hours teaching her to read and write. She could also count, thanks to Roberta Thacher.

Dear Mrs. Thacher — what was she thinking by now? Tomorrow she would also write her a letter as she had written to the Camerons today.

Curling up on the bunk, Tawny began to read. She became so engrossed in the story that the afternoon went by much faster than the morning.

The late afternoon ended on a very pleasant note for Jason when his redheaded cabin boy came rushing toward him on the deck with a bundle tucked under his arm. "Captain, may I have a moment with you?"

"Of course, Rudy. What is it?"

"Well, sir, when we were in Chesapeake a couple of days I took my salary to get my sister Amy a dress. You know, you've heard me talk about her. She was the one who raised me. Well, I thought if Miss Tawny could have this one then I'd have time once we dock in London to get Amy another dress."

Jason looked down at the smiling cabin boy. He could hardly refuse his gracious offer and Tawny could certainly use the dress. "Well, Rudy, I think this is very nice of you and I'll be happy to give it to her, but I must insist that you let me give you the money you spent on the dress so you can get your sister another one. Is that a deal?"

"Sounds fine to me, Captain."

Jason took the bundle and told the young lad to come to Bart's cabin in about an hour. Jason watched Rudy go. He'd never had such an energetic cabin boy as Rudy. The young lad had endured a tragic childhood with a brute of a father who was now in prison for beating his mother to death so Rudy had lived with his sister Amy until Jason hired him. He'd been on the *Sea Princess* for a year now.

With the bundle under his arm, Jason went to his cabin. He had to confess that he was curious about what kind of frock Rudy had picked for his sister.

He didn't get as quick a response as he had when he'd come by at midafternoon, so he knocked harder on the door and called out to Tawny. When she didn't open the door, Jason began to get nervous.

He turned the knob, but it was definitely locked, so once again he knocked on the door and called out to her. When it finally opened and he saw a sleepy-eyed Tawny standing before him, he heaved a deep sigh of relief. Her thick long lashes fluttered lazily and she mumbled, "Sorry, Jason— I . . . I fell asleep, I guess. I got to reading one of your books this afternoon."

"That's all right, honey. Did wonder for a minute or two if you were all right, though." He walked in and closed the door behind him, then handed her the bundle he was carrying and told her that Rudy had given this to him to give to her. "He bought it for his sister, but he will get her another when we get to England," he explained.

She opened the bundle to find the very pretty deep-green cotton frock trimmed with cream-colored braid around the scooped neckline and long sleeves. Tawny smiled up at Jason. "How sweet of that young man to do this for me. I'll have to admit that it will be nice to have this on after those pants and your large shirt."

"I have to applaud his selection. Rudy has good taste in ladies' clothing and I wasn't too sure of what he might have bought for his sister. Now I'll be anxious to see you in it, so I'll leave and let you do all the things a lady must do to get ready for dinner. Bart insisted that he play host to us tonight."

"We're—we're going to Bart's cabin?"

"That's all right with you, isn't it, Tawny?"

"Oh, of course it is, Jason. Please forgive me for still being so sleepy. You will be back to get me, did you say?"

"I will come to get you in an hour, Tawny. Will that give you enough time?"

"I will be ready."

Jason once again left the cabin, but he wondered what was behind the weak smile she gave him when he left the cabin. Did something about Bart disturb Tawny? Did she not like him, he wondered?

He pondered this possibility as he went down the passageway to Bart's cabin. Bart would be terribly wounded if this was the case, for most ladies found him devilishly attractive. But Tawny was not like most ladies!

Bart sat in the chair with his booted foot propped up on the table and smoked on his cheroot. "Well, is the captain calling it a day?"

"The captain is calling it a long day thanks to that fire-brand Arabian of yours. Got to tell you, Bart, I'll not ferry another damned horse in my ship as long as I live." Jason flung his cap on the bunk.

Bart laughed. "Ah, he's cooled down now. He'll do fine, Jase. Just take my word for it."

"We better hope he will, or we could all end up at the bottom of the ocean," Jason told him as he helped himself to one of his friend's expensive cheroots from the silver case on the table.

"Is the beautiful little Tawny joining us for dinner tonight or is it to be just us, Jase?"

"Tawny will join us. I'll go get her in a while." He made no mention of Rudy's gift so Bart was going to be in for a surprise when she returned with him to the cabin.

But Bart was not the only one to be surprised at Tawny dressed in her pretty new frock.

Jason Hamilton stood awestruck when he saw her in his cabin. She was the most beautiful thing his dark eyes had beheld in a long time!

In the oversize shirt and faded trousers she had looked almost childlike, but in this green dress, displaying the soft, sensual curves of her young body, she looked like a very enchanting young lady who he'd be delighted to squire anywhere in London.

There was one problem: there were no slippers for her to put on her dainty feet!

Chapter 11

Young Rudy had filled the bronze tub full of water and
Tawny had enjoyed a warm, luxurious bath. She'd lathered
herself with the sweet-smelling soap she'd found and had
helped herself to a bottle of lime tonic, the smell refreshing
and sweet. She'd dabbed some across her hand and at her
throat. She found it a nicer fragrance than the toilet water
her mother was always putting behind her ears and wrists.

When she slipped into the green dress she was more than
pleased with the way she looked. Rudy's sister must be
exactly the same size, for it was a perfect fit. She loved the
color; it reminded her of the trees in the woods where she
had spent so many hours wandering to gather her flowers
and feed the squirrels and birds.

When she had finished brushing her hair and looked at
her reflection in the mirror, she was quite pleased with
what she saw. *Tawny Blair,* she told herself, *you look pretty
tonight.* She was now eager to have Jason arrive to take her
to Bart's cabin, but her mood saddened when she happened to
look down at her bare feet. She had no slippers and the
stockings she'd worn the night before with the faded pants
and shirt looked awful with this pretty dress. She sat down
on the bunk and took them off. She'd go in her bare feet
before she'd wear them, she decided.

Jason knocked on the door. "Well, hello Princess! You
look absolutely beautiful tonight."

She gave him an uneasy smile as she thanked him for his
kind words. "Oh, Jason, the dress is so beautiful but the
blue socks are—"

"Wait a minute, honey," he interrupted her. He moved

91

around her to a chest and pulled out a drawer. In his hand he held a pair of stockings. "Told you my sister kept me well supplied, didn't I? You like these better? Try them on, for we want to get a happy smile back on that face of yours."

Once she'd put them on her feet, she looked up at Jason with a shy smile. "Do they look all right, Jason?"

"They look fine to me, Tawny!" His warm black eyes glowed tenderly down at her. His hands reached out to her and she took them. "Shall we go to dinner?"

With her arm locked with his, they went down the passageway toward Bart's cabin. Bart was hardly prepared for the glorious vision in deep green standing there with his friend when he opened the door. He'd expected that tiny miss in the faded pants and oversize shirt she'd worn the night before.

His usual cool demeanor was taken aback by the lovely image in the flowing, gathered skirt and scooped neckline displaying her golden flesh. His blue eyes trailed from the top of her head down the soft, curved body. He noticed for the first time how tiny her waistline was. What she wore or did not wear on her dainty feet were of no importance, for Bart's eyes did not focus there.

"Good evening, Tawny. May I say you certainly look beautiful! That color is most flattering on you," Bart told her as she and Jason came on into the cabin.

"You see, Tawny—both of us agree about how beautiful you look. You have two admirers tonight," Jason teased her. But Jason really wasn't teasing, for he'd seen how Bart had looked at her when they walked into the cabin—and he knew that look in his friend's eyes whether it was directed at a horse or a lady.

Tawny took a seat and Jason took the one next to her as Bart walked over to the small table in his cabin. He poured each of them a glass of wine from the decanter sitting on the table. "Last night you had Jason's favorite wine. Tonight you must try mine," Bart told her as he handed her the first glass. Tawny remembered what Jason had told her the night before so she took a very small sip.

She was conscious of Bart's piercing eyes on her. "Well, Tawny, love—which wine do you like the best?"

Her doelike eyes looked up at him as she confessed. "I'd find it hard to say, Bart. They have such different tastes. But then I'd never drunk any wine until last night."

An amused grin came to Jason's face as he looked from Tawny over to Bart. He would have wagered that Bart was figuring Tawny would say she liked the sweeter taste of his red wine.

The cook came to Bart's cabin with another one of his special meals. It was the pretty young lady he hoped to please tonight. He was already thinking of her as the captain's lady.

While they were moored in Chesapeake Bay, the cook had sent young Rudy out to get a supply of shellfish. This was a special fish dish he had prepared tonight with the oysters and crabs. The delicious concoction was poured over fluffy white rice. The cook hoped to hear her praise of the meal after she'd eaten it as he'd heard last night.

He was not to be disappointed, for Tawny had never tasted an oyster or a crab and she'd certainly never tasted such a delectable sauce.

She found herself wanting to know what the magnificent dish was and yet she was embarrassed to confess her ignorance.

Bart found her absolutely delightful as she ate with relish. "You like it, Tawny?"

"I love it!"

He noticed that she'd eaten almost all the food the cook had put on her plate. "I think Miss Tawny would enjoy some more, Tobias."

With a broad grin on his face, the cook gave Tawny another generous helping.

Jason spoke up. "The oysters and crab are really good, Tobias, but then no one can make this the way you do."

As he directed his conversation toward Tobias he noticed that Tawny was listening to him with much interest. He realized the young girl did not know what she was eating, but she was certainly enjoying every mouthful.

A moment later Jason knew what was so refreshing and delightful about Tawny. She looked up at Tobias to declare, as if she had been eating them her whole life: "Oh, Tobias, I've never ever ate better oysters or crab!"

"Well, I thank you, ma'am. I really thank you!" Tobias said, pleased that the captain's lady was so impressed by his special recipe.

But when the meal was over and Tobias had cleared away all the serving dishes, Bart was expecting the pleasure of the beautiful Tawny's company for a while longer. He was taken by surprise by Jason's abrupt announcement. "Bart, I promised Tawny a stroll around the deck tonight. She's been in the cabin all day. I'm sure you'll excuse us."

That son of a gun, Bart thought to himself! He wanted the bewitching little Tawny all to himself. Well, Jason had won this round tonight, but wait until tomorrow, he vowed to himself.

"Of course I will, Jason. A cabin can get damned boring all day long. Besides, I need to go check on Diablo before I turn in," he declared casually.

Tawny hesitated at the door for a minute as she looked back at Bart. "May I see Diablo some time, Bart?"

"Anytime you wish, love. He'd probably love seeing you," he said. But he also noted a puzzling look in Jason's eyes as the two of them went out the door.

As they left Bart's cabin and went up on deck, Jason was aware of the distraction Tawny caused among the sailors. All of them stopped to stare at her as they strolled along the railing of his ship. As the captain of the ship it made him aware that he had not one, but two very dangerous passengers aboard—a very alluring young lady who could make any of his sailors lose their reason and a high-spirited Arabian stallion that could cause all kinds of havoc.

The sight of the English shore could not come in sight soon enough to please him!

* * *

When Bart awakened the next morning, Jason was already gone from the cabin to attend to his captain's duties so that his first mate could have some time off.

When Rudy served Tawny breakfast the next morning she graciously thanked him for his gift. "I hope that I can do something as nice for you and your sister some time," she'd told him.

As she had done the day before, after eating the hefty breakfast Rudy had brought her, she sat at the table to write a long letter to Roberta Thacher. Later, she dressed in Jason's shirt and the faded blue pants that had belonged to Rudy.

Shortly after midday there was a rap on the cabin door and Tawny rushed to open it, thinking it was Jason coming to see about her. But it was not Jason; it was the imposing Bart Montgomery.

"Hello, Tawny." His blue eyes danced over her lovely face and down the neck of her oversize shirt.

"Hello, Bart. I . . . I thought you were Jason."

"I think Jason is having a busy day, but there's nothing wrong with me taking you for a stroll. You could use a little sunshine. Staying in a cabin all day must go completely against your nature. I remember a pretty little nymph who likes to roam the woods."

She found him hard to resist and she laughed. "I must confess that I love the woods much more than this desolate ocean. The sea does not interest me."

"Well, we agree on that, Tawny. Come on, we'll have a nice little walk in the sun."

"I guess it would be all right. I don't want Jason to be angry with me for leaving the cabin without him."

Bart took her arm to urge her out of the cabin. "Love, you're going to be with me. I'll see that everything is all right where Jason is concerned, Tawny, don't worry."

She could hardly argue with that, so she allowed Bart to lead her out of the cabin. Besides, she wanted to go for a walk with Bart. It seemed far more exciting than staying the whole afternoon in that lonely cabin.

For the free-spirited Tawny, the confining four walls of the cabin with only the small porthole to look out of with its view of that vast endless current of water was very depressing. Bart was offering her a wonderful escape and she was willing to accept it.

"You're right, Bart. Jason would not mind if I went for a stroll with you." Her trusting brown eyes looked up at him and Bart Montgomery suddenly found himself feeling very protective toward this tiny slip of a girl. She was like no other female he'd ever met. She had the power to make him forget everything that had ruled him all his life. His cool, calculating mind did not function when he was around Tawny Blair.

This bothered the arrogant young Englishman more than he cared to admit. He'd never known jealousy until Tawny Blair came into his life, but now he knew the full impact of it. It had gnawed away at him, making him utterly miserable.

Once they were on deck taking their leisurely stroll, he observed the sailors ogling Tawny. He gave them such a fierce look that they immediately turned their eyes away.

They'd had a leisurely, pleasant stroll for a half hour when Bart's trainer came rushing toward him. Diablo was tearing up his stall down below, Bart was informed.

"I'm going with you, Bart. Diablo always liked me," Tawny declared.

"All right, love! Let's go!" he declared anxiously, yanking her along with him as they ran across the deck to get to the opening of the hold.

Together, they ran across the deck with Bart's strong hand holding firmly onto hers. She did not hesitate for a minute to scamper down the extended rope ladder swinging down from the deck into the hold. She followed Bart down the ladder.

She saw the rampaging Diablo with his nostrils flaring and that proud head of his jerking in rebellion. His hooves were kicking frantically at the planks of the stall Jason had installed. The minute her feet hit the floor, she rushed ahead of Bart and climbed the stall. Her small hand reached out to pat his glossy mane as she softly talked to the stallion. "It's all right, Diablo. Tawny's here! Nothing is going to hurt you."

Bart and his trainer watched the young girl straddle the stall with no fear of the stallion whatsoever. She stood inside the stall where none of them had dared to tread. Bart watched her as the horse immediately responded to her gentle voice and touch. He was calmed instantly.

"You just don't like being in this small stall, do you, Diablo?" Tawny murmured to him. He seemed to understand exactly what she was saying. His head bent down to nuzzle her cheek.

"Can't we walk this horse, Bart? He's not used to being restrained like this. He'll go crazy before you get him to England." Tawny yelled back at Bart.

"Jason won't allow it," Bart told her, walking up to the stall. But he was hardly prepared for what he saw in the next few moments. Tawny had climbed up on the planks of the stall and flung her leg over his back. Her hands caressed his head and mane.

"Open the gate, Bart. Diablo and I are going for a ride," she demanded, and he obeyed. Without a saddle or reins, she and the black stallion paced the length of the hold back and forth. Bart Montgomery and his trainer stood and marveled at what they were watching.

Tawny allowed the Arabian to give way to his need to pace and roam the hold. Occasionally, she glanced in Bart's direction and smiled.

"She is quite something, Bart," the trainer gasped.

"I can't believe it! He's as docile as a pussycat," Bart stammered.

"He trusts her, Bart. I have learned something priceless today from this young lady," his trainer declared.

Tawny led the stallion inside the stall and leaped down from him. She stood there for an extra moment or two to pat his face and rub his mane. He seemed content when she left the stall and walked toward Bart.

"He was just scared, Bart. I think he'll be fine now. I'll come to see him every day, if you'll let me," she told him.

"Gladly, Tawny!" Bart exclaimed.

"Miss, I congratulate you! I have just told Bart I learned something from you this afternoon and I shall call on you in the future if I have any trouble with Diablo. You are a natural with horses, miss," the trainer told her.

"I just love Diablo, sir," she told him.

Her dark eyes were intense with feeling. Bart was amazed at this little girl from the backwoods of Virginia. "Diablo is a very special horse. I knew that the first time I saw him at Cameron Farms. He is the king of all horses!"

This was exactly Bart's feeling!

Chapter 12

Bart never expected to see Tawny Blair after he left the shores of Virginia. Oh, he'd taken her sweet kisses and made love to her but he'd done that with many women. Tawny's beautiful face had haunted him, and now he knew why.

He saw her in a different light this afternoon. His admiration for her had heightened and also his interest to know this young miss better.

Now, he knew why an overwhelming jealousy had consumed him when he saw her around Jason. The mere thought of some other man making love to her was enough to rile his temper. This was a strange, new feeling for Bart Montgomery, but he could no longer deny that the girl possessed a magic that drew him to her. He was powerless to resist it even if he tried.

After his trainer had left the two of them alone and it was just him and Tawny there by Diablo's stall, he was glad to have this moment alone with her.

He took her hand to lead her over to the stacked crates and urged her to sit down. "I'm beholden to you, Tawny, for what you did today. I don't think anyone else could have done it," he declared.

"It was nothing, Bart. I enjoyed being with Diablo again. It brought back fond memories of the Camerons and the wonderful times I shared with them. No one has ever been nicer to me than those two dear people."

Bart took in the expressive features of her face as she spoke. Usually he did not give way to speak impulsively but now he did. "You are beautiful, Tawny Blair! Do you

99

know that?" His deep voice was serious as he spoke, so Tawny knew he was not trying to tease her.

"Oh, Bart! You are going to embarrass me if you keep talking like that," Tawny told him with a shy grin on her face.

"I am just speaking the truth, and I mean every word. I'm not a man to waste my words or my time, Tawny. I guess you have already figured out that Jason and I are two different kind of men." Before she could make a reply she saw his blond head bending down and she knew he was going to kiss her. She knew the effect the kisses had on her!

She felt the heat of his mouth even before it met hers. The force of it rocked her. There was such a force in Bart Montgomery that it overwhelmed her. She felt herself submitting to him as his strong, powerful arms claimed her.

She heard his deep moans. "Oh, Tawny! Tawny, I can't resist you, damn it!" She felt him urging her down from the crate they had been sitting on to the floor of the hold. She could not fight him or protest as her body slid down to lie there with him towering over her.

She gave no protest as she felt his fingers unfastening Jason's shirt and his head bending lower to taunt and tease the tips of her breasts with featherlike caresses. Now she was the one giving out soft moans of pleasure and she felt his firm-muscled body swelling as his passion mounted.

A wild, untamed passion flamed in Tawny and she did not want him to stop the tantalizing pleasure he was giving her. Her supple body arched eagerly against him and Bart parted from her only long enough to fling aside his shirt and pants.

"God, Tawny, you are passion's woman. Come to me, and I will love you as you've never been loved before," he huskily swore to her.

He urged her close to him, and his muscled body covered her. She felt his strong thighs pressing her legs as he lowered himself down on her.

Bart swore that he'd never felt such satiny flesh as Tawny's as he burrowed himself in the velvet softness of her. His hands cupped her rounded hips, guiding them to the sensual tempo of his swaying body. She seemed to be joined to him as they moved together with their passions blazing like a wildfire out of control.

Tawny's soft, kittenlike moans and flushed body against him had him so fired that even his strong will could not control his desire to make this moment last.

His body gave way to a mighty shudder, and he heard her gasp as her tiny hands clasped his neck tighter. His hands pressed tighter against her back as his deep voice whispered in her ear. "Ah, Tawny, love! Tawny! I think I love you as I've never loved before."

For the longest time he held her until he heard footsteps moving across the floor of the hold. He came alive with a jerk as he cautioned her to be quiet. As he scrambled to get his clothes he only prayed that it wasn't Jason. Never would he remember dressing so hastily.

To his great relief, when he peered around the stacked, concealing crates, he saw it was one of the young sailors coming down in the hold to check on Diablo as Jason had ordered.

So he bent down to Tawny to tell her to get dressed so they could leave. "We don't want to get Jason riled at us," he whispered in her ear.

She gave him a sheepish smile and began to do as he said. But the mention of Jason's name put her in a quandary, and she wondered how she ever was going to face him after this afternoon.

What she felt for Jason was so completely different from the way she felt about Bart Montgomery. She could not imagine making wild, reckless love with Jason as she'd just done with Bart. Yet Jason held a special place in her heart.

Bart had led her nonchalantly around the crates and casually threw his hand up to greet the sailor standing guard over Diablo before he hoisted Tawny up on the rope ladder to climb up to the deck. He climbed up behind her, watching the tempting motions of her hips in the faded pants and found himself fired again to make love to her. But he

101

tried to sweep those thoughts away, as hard as it was.

When they arrived at the captain's cabin, they found a very sullen Jason. His black eyes glared at Bart as he walked in with Tawny. His glib greeting did not register with Jason. "Tawny helped settle down Diablo this afternoon, Jason."

"I know. I've already heard all about it. I congratulate you, Tawny. I've heard your praises sung all over the ship this afternoon. Bart should hire you as his trainer." There was a sardonic tone to his voice that Tawny found disturbing. She'd never seen Jason act this way before. His black eyes looked at her with such a chill she didn't know how to react or what to say, so she said nothing as she walked around the cabin. Sitting down on the bunk, she looked up at Bart as if to implore him to take charge.

"I didn't know when I sought to take Tawny for a stroll around the deck that things would go as they did, Jason. I told Tawny that I was very grateful for her help, for I doubt that things would have gone so smoothly without her."

"I understand, Bart," Jason mumbled. No one had to tell Montgomery that his friend was not feeling too kindly toward him tonight.

"Well, I'll say good-bye to the two of you," Bart said as he turned to go. He was well aware that Jason did not invite him to join the two of them for dinner.

"Thank you again, Tawny, for what you did this afternoon," Bart told her as he went out the cabin door.

She gave him her prettiest smile. "You let me know anytime you have trouble with Diablo," she replied, "and I will be there, Bart. Diablo and I get along fine."

"I will, Tawny. Good night." He went out, leaving the two of them in Jason's cabin.

When the door was closed and the imposing presence of Bart Montgomery was gone, Jason finally rose up from the chair to address Tawny. "I'm not going to be able to dine with you tonight, Tawny. I'm taking over the duties of my first mate. Rudy will bring you a dinner tray."

It disturbed Tawny to see Jason this way. She did not

know what was bothering him, but she quickly assured him that she would be fine. "After such an active afternoon with Diablo, I will be happy to have a dinner tray, Jason."

Jason raised a skeptical brow which Tawny didn't see, for his back was turned to her. He was wondering if it was Diablo or Bart who had given her such an active afternoon, for he could hardly have missed the rosy flush to Tawny's face when she'd entered the cabin with her hand on Bart's arm and he knew his amorous friend all too well.

Jason gave her a weak smile as he made a quick exit from his cabin. It was good that he was taking the watch tonight for his first mate, for he would not have been good company for Tawny or Bart. He was troubled by things that had never bothered him before, and there was nothing that acted more like a healing tonic to him than taking command of the *Sea Princess*.

The beautiful Tawny Blair was causing problems between him and Bart. He resented that Bart had taken the liberty to come to his cabin, when he knew Jason was on deck, to invite Tawny to take a stroll with him. Bart was a cunning devil and no one knew that better than Jason. But he was damned well not going to stand back and let him play her false! Tawny was so naive and trusting! He knew he could not protect her every minute of the night and day.

Long after he'd left the cabin, his thoughts were still on Tawny. However, an hour later when the smell of the sea air had permeated his nostrils and he stood on the deck of his ship to gaze up at the starlit night, his troubled mind was calmed. Jason knew then that the sea, and his ship, was the balm to ease his soul.

He enjoyed the rest of his watch and he was ready to collapse in the bunk when he went to Bart's cabin the next morning at seven. Bart was still asleep and didn't know when he'd come through the door.

How sweet the comfort of the bunk felt when he sank down in it! Nothing occupied his mind but sleep.

* * *

Tawny was glad she had not had to share the evening with Jason and Bart. It would have been a little strained after what had happened down in the hold. It was much more to her liking to be in the cabin all alone with the friendly Rudy serving her a tray. She enjoyed his light-hearted conversation.

Tawny had to examine the strange new thoughts she was having about Jason and Bart.

She found that her heart and feelings were involved where both of them were concerned. She loved each of them in a different way. She sat there in the cabin wishing the kind, understanding Reba Cameron were there with her. It would be so nice to have someone to talk to about her mixed-up emotions.

She recalled what Roberta Thacher was always saying—that time would take care of everything. Perhaps that was the answer for her.

It was late afternoon when Jason roused from his sleep, and by the time he dressed and shaved, Rudy was bringing him a tray. He was ready to eat a hearty meal while his cabin boy gave him a report on Tawny. Jason made no effort to go to his cabin to see her. He knew he had not been too nice to her when she'd returned to his cabin with Bart, but he was angry, an anger he could not control.

Jason did not like what was happening to him because of this pretty brown-haired girl. One tiny miss should not sever a long friendship like his and Bart's.

He figured that it might be best if he stayed away from Tawny before he took over the duty tonight. Rob could use another night off. But as he was about to leave Bart's cabin to assume the post, he wondered where Bart was. Were he and Tawny together this afternoon?

Time hung heavily on his hands as he took over for Rob. During the evening he left his post long enough to see if there was a light in his cabin and Bart's. Each time he slipped down the passageway, he found that the light gleamed from under the door. He could hear no voices coming from either of the cabins, so he felt rather foolish as he went back up on the deck to assume his captain's duties.

He realized that all his sensible words of advice to himself had failed. It was obvious to Jason that he could not control his jealousy where Tawny was concerned.

However, he came to a decision by the time his shift was over. He headed to Bart's cabin to get some sleep.

In the end, it would be Tawny who'd pick the man she wanted, and that was the way it would be! But he and Bart would never be the friends they once had been, he suspected.

Part Two

A Violent Tempest

Chapter 13

Tawny had no inkling of the tension she was causing between the two Englishmen during the following week. She was the only one of the three who was happy as she spent afternoons with Bart and went down for visits with Diablo in the hold. When she wasn't with Bart, she was with Jason, but she had noticed a change in Jason over the last week. He did not seem to be the happy-go-lucky fellow he had been and she wondered what was the matter with him.

After two weeks aboard the *Sea Princess*, Tawny had made many friends on the ship. Rudy was her slave and Tobias adored her. One of the sailors who was skilled in working with leather had made her a pair of moccasins and given them to his captain to give to her. She did not even know his name.

Reluctant as he was to admit it, Montgomery felt himself losing his heart to the little Virginia girl more and more every day, but he also knew that each day brought them closer to England. He asked himself what he was going to do. Was he going to claim her for his own or was he going to walk away to allow Jason to take her?

There was no doubt in Bart's mind by now that Jason was smitten with Tawny, but then so was he! It was one hell of a situation to exist between two lifelong friends. He didn't want to sever his friendship with Jason, but he wasn't sure he could give up Tawny now that he'd known the rapture he'd found in her arms.

But being a practical man, Bart knew that he had to make up his mind, and soon, because London was less than seven days away now. The voyage had been as smooth coming back home as it had been when he'd sailed for Virginia.

Suddenly, one afternoon after Tawny and Jason had taken a stroll around the sunny deck on the ship, she thought she knew the reason Jason had been acting so strangely. She had been in a very lighthearted mood and wearing her pretty new buff-colored moccasins and the dark-green dress Rudy had given her.

"How far away as we now from your country, Jason?" she'd asked him.

"A very few days, Tawny, if the weather holds, and it would seem that it will," he'd told her.

"It must be a good feeling for you to be getting back to see your family again after such a long time away"

"Oh, yes, I'm always glad to get home after I've been away this long. But I'll be ready to leave again after I've been there a few weeks. The sea always calls me back, Tawny."

Tawny did not share his enthusiasm for the sea. It was depressing to her to see nothing but the churning grayish-green water. She yearned for the feel of the ground under her feet, soft grass to walk on, and trees and flowers. Here there were no birds to see up in the skies or no smoke circling from the chimney of nearby cottages. She missed the sound of the rolling wagon wheels moving down the country road. Out here on the ocean she'd seen no other ships in the distance. It seemed to her that they were the only people in the whole world out here, completely alone.

No, the sea held no fascination for her. She would be delighted to see the sight of land!

"Tawny . . ." Jason began somewhat hesitantly. "I've something to ask you and I want you to be honest with me. You know that I want you to be happy. After we get to London, it would be no problem to get you passage on another ship back to Virginia. There are always ships going to America. But, Tawny, your mother is gone now, so who would you go back to? Wasn't she your only family back there?"

"Yes, she was my only family, but I had my good friend, Mrs. Thacher, and the Camerons. I think I must go back,

Jason," she declared with her head held as high and proud as that Arabian down in his hold. "I owe it to my mother to go back."

"Then I will see that you get back to your home, Tawny, if that is what you want," Jason told her. Jason was elated to know that Bart had not used his silken tongue to persuade her to stay in London. Oh, he knew that he would not have suggested that Tawny accompany him to the Montgomerys' country estate, for that was where his mother resided for most of the year. This was where the prestigious Montgomery Stables were, but Bart had a lavish little bachelor's townhouse in the city. Jason had wondered if he'd suggested she might live there and this had troubled him. He did not intend that Tawny be used as Bart's plaything.

Later, when Tawny was alone in Jason's cabin, she realized what a miserable burden she'd put on poor Jason. She had to make it easy for him, so the best thing she could do was leave England just as soon as he could book passage for her. This she would do even though the thought of getting back on a ship to sail for days on an ocean was the last thing she wanted to do.

There was nothing else she could do but accept Jason's generous offer to get her passage back to Virginia. She would be grateful forever, for all he'd done for her these weeks.

An idea had sparked when she was talking to Jason this afternoon and she was suddenly anxious to pursue it. Talking to him had brought back the painful memories of that night so many weeks ago when she'd seen her mother lying lifeless on the ground. She had to go back to Longcreek and seek out the two men who had killed her mother. Her soul would never rest until those two got what they deserved.

By the time her pretty head lay back on the pillow, Tawny had found the direction she wanted her life to go. No longer did she have to wonder what she was going to do when she got to England. She was going to mail her letters to the Camerons and Mrs. Thacher as soon as she arrived, and if Jason or Bart offered her lodgings while she waited for passage, she would accept either of their offers. She had one obsession taking over now and that was that she must return to Longcreek.

Bart was taken aback by Tawny's announcement that she was going to return to Virginia as soon as Jason could get her passage.

"You're going back, Tawny?" His blue eyes flashed and a frown creased his handsome face.

"Of course, Bart. I didn't choose to make this journey. I was thrust on the *Sea Princess* as a piece of cargo, if you'll remember. I had no plans to go to England!"

"But, love—your mother is dead, and who will take care of you?"

"I'm not exactly helpless, Bart, and who do I know in England except you and Jason? Besides, I've got friends in Longcreek and I've also got a mother buried there. There is another thing that I must do—I must see that the two men who murdered my mother get their just dues and I will, so help me!"

Bart saw the fire in her eyes and the tilt of her head. Never for a minute did he doubt that she would attempt to do just that. But he had grave doubts that one so young could accomplish this. He admired her spirit.

A broad grin came on his face as he looked at her. God, she was a little beauty! There was never a dull moment with Tawny Blair, for she was so different from any woman he'd ever met before. Since meeting her, Bart knew why he had been bored by the fancy maidens he and Jason had squired around London the last few years.

He'd had the urge to choke some of them when he'd endured their silly giggling for the whole evening. Others, who had fawned over him, were only impressed that he was a wealthy young man who could open doors for them. Oh, it wasn't hard to figure out those young women; that was why he'd never allowed himself to waste much time on them.

He knew Jason felt the way he did and that was probably

112

why both of them had been so enchanted by the brown-haired Tawny. She had bewitched both of them!

Bart could not dismiss the feelings for Tawny—she was like a fever in his blood. Like that unusual black stallion he'd just purchased, Tawny was that rare jewel that a man doesn't meet too often in a lifetime. Bart had no intentions of letting her walk out of his life.

He was tempted to offer her lodging at his townhouse for the time she was going to be staying in London but something stopped him. His good friend Jason could hardly object to the arrangement since his servants would be the only ones occupying the townhouse. He would be going directly to the family country estate to get Diablo settled as soon as the ship docked.

He decided that he should speak to Jason first before he would make such an offer to Tawny.

Later that same afternoon, he set out to see if he could find Jason on deck, for he was not in the cabin.

He quickly spotted his black-haired friend ambling along the railing of his ship looking toward the north. Somewhere to the north northeast lay their destination, Bart knew. He had to wonder if Jason was seeking out some telltale signs out there on the horizon. The sea had never fascinated him, but he did admire Jason's talent and skill. He was one of the best sea captains around and he knew that his sailors held him in high respect.

Jason was so engrossed in his thoughts that he did not hear Bart walking up behind him. It was only when Bart was standing right there at the railing that Jason turned to see him. "Well, Bart—I haven't seen you in a day or two. Diablo still behaving himself?"

"He's done fine ever since the day Tawny went down in the hold and calmed him. I give her the credit for making it easier on me and you, Jason."

Jason smiled. "Well, I'll have to remember to thank her myself. I wasn't too sure about that horse that first day or two."

"Well, the trip is just about over now, isn't it? I guess this is a good time for me to tell you, Jason, that I've a lot to thank you for as well. You took me to Virginia and I got the Arabian I'd dreamed of owning." Bart laughed. "Don't know about you, but I'm ready to get home. How about you, Jase? What's next for you?"

It had been a while since the two of them had talked. "I can't exactly say, Bart. Guess I'll moor the *Sea Princess* for about a month and give my men some leave. I'll spend some time with my father and mother."

Bart didn't know whether to say what was preying on his mind, but decided it was as good a time as any so he asked, "What about Tawny, Jason?"

"You mean, what am I to do about her?" Jason's black eyes twinkled with amusement.

"Guess that's what I mean."

"Well, Bart — Tawny became my responsibility the minute I found her on my ship, so I will take her to my home until I can book passage for her to go back to Virginia. This is her wish, so I will try to help her do this."

"I know she wants to go back. She told me this afternoon, but I wonder how wise that is, Jason. She has no family."

"Then do you have a better idea for her, Bart?"

"Well, I . . . I don't know. I thought maybe she would want to stay here. She . . . she can count on you and me to help her all we can," Bart stammered in a hesitating voice.

"But Tawny doesn't want to stay here. She wants to go home," Jason declared.

What he didn't say to his friend was that Tawny could not have both of them as her protectors. Their personal feelings were far too intense for such an arrangement.

"Well, that settles the question about Tawny, I guess," Bart said, trying to sound very nonchalant and casual. Giving a shrug of his broad shoulders, he bid Jason good-bye to go to his cabin.

But Jason knew Bart well enough to know that something was bothering him. He wasn't sure whether it was the fact that Tawny was going to be returning to Virginia or if it was because she was going home with him when they landed in

England.

Jason knew one thing for sure: as long as he'd known Bart Montgomery, he'd never known him to act so unsettled and unsure of himself.

He wasn't like the Bart Montgomery he'd known all his life!

Chapter 14

The next day Bart encountered a very excited Tawny when he went to Jason's cabin to take her for a walk around the deck. The morning had been cloudy and overcast, but the ship had moved into bright, sunny skies. Tawny's face was just as radiant as the sunshine. "Another day or two and we're going to be in England, Bart!" she exclaimed. "Jason said so this morning when he came to the cabin."

"So you're excited about getting to London, eh, love?" He gave her a broad grin.

"Oh, yes. I'm curious about this place you and Jason call home." Giving a shrug of her dainty shoulders, she candidly confessed to him. "To see land again will be so wonderful to me!"

"Oh Tawny, there is no one else like you in this whole wide world!" he declared.

She gave a lilting gale of laughter, and the sea breeze was blowing just enough to sweep her long hair away from her face. Bart thought she looked breathtakingly beautiful. What a gorgeous creature she would be if she was dressed in fancy gowns and jewels!

She noticed the strange look on Bart's fine-chiseled face and wondered what he was thinking as he gazed at her with adoration. She yearned to inquire, but she didn't.

"You know, Tawny, my family's home joins Jason's family's estate. That's how we got acquainted when we were just young lads," Bart told her. "You will not be that far away from me if you go with Jason when we dock in London."

"Oh, that will be nice, Bart," she said. She told him about seeing the pictures of Jason's family on his desk in the cabin. "It's a nice family he has."

"Only thing, he was plagued with a lot of pestering sisters all his life."

"And you? Do you any sisters?" she asked.

"No, I was an only child." He told her that his father had died and there was only his mother living on the country place where the Montgomery Stables were.

"And this is where you will take Diablo?"

"Yes, Tawny, this is where Diablo will be, and you will have to come over to see what a fine home he will have."

"Oh, I would like that, Bart," she told him as he guided her down the deck of the ship.

As Bart escorted her back to Jason's cabin, he thought about how hard it was going to be to be parted from her once they landed in London. He knew that she had no idea how she'd affected him these last few weeks.

He did not know when he told her good-bye at the door of Jason's cabin, that this was to be his last private moment with her before they docked in London. If he had, he would have taken an extra kiss or two of her sweet, sweet lips when he said good-bye.

A heavy, thick fog shrouded the ship the next morning as the *Sea Princess* plowed through the waters of the Channel.

Before the deck of the *Sea Princess* became a beehive of activity, as it always was when the ship sailed into a port, Jason made his way to his cabin to talk to Tawny. He wanted to advise her to stay in the cabin until he came for her because several things would require his attention before they could leave the ship.

Weighing heavily on his mind at the moment was the tedious procedure of hoisting Diablo out of the hold of the ship. He could only hope it would go smoothly.

When Tawny answered the door and he strolled inside, he saw that she'd been curled up on his bunk reading another of the books in his shelves. He had been happy to see that she had become an avid reader, but he was forced to accept the fact that she would never have any interest in the sea. At first he'd thought that before the voyage was over she might come to share the beauty he found there and it might intrigue her, but now he knew that would never be. Tawny abhorred the ocean.

"Reading again, I see, Tawny," he said, picking up the book from the bunk to see what she'd selected. "Tawny," he told her, laying it back down, "we will be landing very soon now, but I want you to stay below, for the deck will be bustling with my crew during that time. Stay in the cabin until I come to get you."

She said nothing, but she was wondering if she'd get to see Bart before he left. She had to see him, she thought to herself, one way or the other, even if it meant disobeying Jason's orders.

"You do understand why I'd not want you up there while my men were running back and forth, don't you, honey?" he asked her.

"Oh . . . oh, yes Jason. I could get in the way," she replied.

He playfully teased her. "You're so tiny that they could run right over you. You just be patient and I'll come for you as soon as I can."

"I will, Jason," she promised.

He turned to leave, and she followed him to the cabin door to lock it as she'd become accustomed to doing.

After he'd left, she took the book off the bunk to place it back in the shelf. This one she would not be finishing, she thought as she walked away. Knowing she would go to Jason's home and meet his family, she changed into the green frock Rudy had given her and brushed out her long hair until it was glossy and shining, them slipped into the moccasins. There were no articles for her to pack except her nightgown, which she folded neatly and put on the bunk.

When that was done she went over to the porthole to see if she could sight land, for she'd suddenly realized the ship was no longer swaying and plowing through the waters.

It was a wonderful sight for Tawny to see birds circling in the sky. It seemed like forever since she'd seen that glorious sight and she could also hear the echoes of voices. It must have been the sailors above on the deck.

Bursting with anticipation, she found herself impatient to rush out the cabin door to get her first glimpse of this strange new country, England. It seemed that a long time went by, and still Jason did not come for her. She sat there, yearning for Bart to come to the cabin to see her before he left. Surely he would not leave with Diablo without saying good-bye!

To calm her mounting nerves, she began to pace back and forth the length and width of the cabin. When she felt that she could not stand it another moment, she marched to the door and opened it. Just as she was about to dash out of the cabin, she found herself colliding with Bart.

His blue eyes twinkled as his arms reached to enclose her. "Well, my pretty—where are you off to?"

She looked up at him and laughed. "I was tired of waiting in this darn cabin as Jason told me to do. We're here, aren't we, Bart?"

"Yes, love—we're here. I'm glad that we have this little moment all to ourselves so I can say good-bye without Jason's eyes on us. I want to kiss those sweet lips before I have to part with you." His head bent down to take a long, lingering kiss. As his lips released hers, he whispered, "But I won't stay away from you too long, Tawny. I couldn't! Oh, Tawny! Tawny, I adore you."

Reluctantly, he urged her back to the cabin and told her to do as Jason had told her. "I've got to leave, Tawny. Two of Jason's men are holding Diablo out on the wharf, but I had to see you before I rode off. Jason will be coming soon now."

He stared down at her lovely face and forced himself to say a hasty farewell, but it wasn't easy to turn his back on her. He swore he saw a mist of tears gathering in those lovely brown eyes.

Tawny was glad that Jason did not appear until she'd wiped away the tears after Bart left her.

When Jason finally came to the cabin, she was sitting at the table waiting for him, but her thoughts were with Bart riding away on Diablo. She wished she was with him!

Jason told her that she was soon to put her dainty feet on the ground once more. "That will make you happy, won't it honey?"

"Oh, yes, Jason. I can hardly wait!"

After he'd gathered up some other articles to throw into his valise, they left the cabin together. As they walked across the deck of the ship, she surprised young Rudy by leaning over to plant a farewell kiss on his cheek. Jason smiled as he saw the blush on the youth's face.

Tobias grinned as he told her farewell. "Been my pleasure to serve you, ma'am. God go with you, Miss Tawny."

"And you, too, Tobias," she replied as she trailed a short distance behind Jason.

It was not until they were in the carriage traveling away from the wharf toward the outskirts of the city that Jason mentioned Bart and Diablo.

"He came by the cabin to say good-bye," Tawny told him.

Tawny was so engrossed in the wonderful green rolling countryside that she did not see the frown on Jason's face. "I was sure he would," Jason muttered. But she did not notice the displeased tone of his voice or the solemn look on his face.

"Your country is beautiful, Jason," she said. "I can't imagine why you'd ever want to leave it."

"I guess you'd call it wanderlust, Tawny. I like to sail to places I've never seen before. It's a big world out there."

"I suppose." But her curious eyes went back to the endless fields of flowers growing wild in the meadowlands. She could almost imagine that she was back in Longcreek.

Across the way, she spotted a huge two-story stone house set back on a slope. There were other stone buildings to the side of the spacious house. A tall fence enclosed the vast grounds. Jason heard her gasp with wonder at the impressive sight of the Montgomery Stables and the family home.

"That's where Bart lives, Tawny," he informed her.

Her next remark brought an amused smile to his face. "My goodness, Diablo will live like a king, won't he?"

"He'll live in a fine style," Jason assured her.

There were only a few more turns and bends in the road before they would be coming to his own home, which was just as grand as the Montgomery estate.

When they turned the final bend in the road that brought his home in view, she sighed again. "My goodness, everyone in England must be rich. Here is another castle. When I get back home I will tell Mrs. Thacher that I actually saw castles like the ones she read to me about when I was little."

"That is where I live, Tawny." He laughed lightheartedly.

"Oh, Jason." Tawny was awestruck. She suddenly felt ill at ease about going to Jason's home with him.

She was not the only one wondering how his family would react to the unexpected guest. Jason feared his father's reaction the most. Lord Addison Hamilton could be a very solemn, aloof individual.

He did not worry about his easygoing, warm Irish mother, Sheila, being nice to Tawny. She opened her heart and arms to everyone.

When the carriage stopped and Jason leaped down and extended his hands to Tawny, he saw the look of apprehension on her lovely face. "What's the matter, honey?"

"I'm . . . I'm scared, Jason. Your folks aren't expecting me to be coming home with you."

Jason's black eyes warmed as they assured her. "Everything will be fine, Tawny. You just believe me. I've got a mother who will adore you on sight. She loves to play the mother hen."

Tawny took his hands and moved to step down to the ground. Together they walked up the stone path to the front steps edged on either side by boxwoods.

The door was opened by a manservant Jason called Andrew. He'd been in service at the Hamiltons' since Jason was about four or five, and now he looked fondly at the young man and welcomed him back home. He tried to restrain a questioning look as he saw the young lady standing at Jason's side. Andrew wondered if Jason had brought home a bride. Nothing would please Lady Sheila more, but he wasn't too sure about how Lord Addison would take it.

"Andrew, this is my friend, Tawny Blair. She will be our guest for a while," Jason informed him.

"A pleasure to meet you, Miss Blair," Andrew greeted her. A pleased smile came to his face as he listened to Jason tell Tawny that he had practically raised him. "I'm probably the reason for all those gray hairs on Andrew's head."

Tawny laughed along with them as they crossed the spacious entranceway.

"Your father's in his study and I think your mother is in her garden room, as she usually is this time of day. Shall I take you there?"

"We'll go see mother, Andrew. I think I can still find my way." Jason laughed and Andrew left them to go down the long hallway.

Jason's mother was puttering around her favorite room when they entered through the double doors, but Tawny knew even before she turned around that she was going to look like that picture she'd spotted on Jason's desk in his cabin.

Her hair was as black as Jason's but lightly sprinkled with gray. She was a tiny little lady no taller than Tawny.

For a minute they stood there, listening to her sing one of her favorite Irish songs, for she had no idea that she was not the only one in the room. Jason looked over at Tawny and grinned.

When the song was finished, Jason applauded and Lady Sheila turned to see her son. She rushed across the room to be caught in his arms. As they embraced, her black eyes darted over in Tawny's direction.

Just as Andrew had wondered, Sheila also was wondering if her Jason had brought home a beautiful bride this time!

Chapter 15

Jason had no chance to explain why Tawny Blair would be their guest before the tall figure of his father stood in the doorway. He'd only finished introducing Tawny to his mother when Lord Addison sauntered into the garden room. The first thing Tawny noticed was his towering height; it reminded her of Bart Montgomery.

His deep bass voice seemed to roar like a lion when he spoke. "Well, Jason—you're home again. Montgomery get that Arabian the two of you went to Virginia for?"

"Yes, Father he did," Jason declared. But Jason saw his father's eyes were not directed at him but on the petite Tawny, so he wasted no time introducing her.

Tawny did not see any warmth in his stern face, so she immediately felt nervous as he addressed her. "Well, Miss Blair, am I to assume that you are from Virginia?"

"Yes, sir, I am." She felt her lips quivering as she answered him.

She noticed that his eyes darted back to Jason, and it never dawned on Tawny that he as well as his wife might be thinking about the possibility of her being Jason's bride.

Jason sensed this tension and knew that he must quickly dismiss this thought from both of their minds. But when he was about to tell them that Tawny would be staying for a while before she went back to Virginia, his youngest sister, Joy, came bouncing into the room.

Once again Jason went through the introductions while his parents were left to wonder if he might have married while he was in Virginia.

But Joy wasted no time getting right to the point. "Jase,

did you finally get yourself a bride? I can see why, now that you found someone as beautiful as Tawny, that you kept waiting so long!" she exclaimed.

"Joy! My goodness, where are your manners, young lady," her mother reprimanded her.

Jason laughed. "No, Joy. Tawny and I aren't married, but she will be staying here with us. That is, if she can put up with you."

Lady Sheila gave a gay laugh, for it seemed good to her to have her son home again, teasing his sister as he always did. But she also sensed that Jason was uncomfortable with his father's prodding eyes glaring at him and the young lady sitting by his side. At least Lord Addison knew now that Tawny was not Jason's wife.

"Joy, dear—I have a splendid idea. Why don't you take Tawny upstairs and introduce her to your sisters and help her get settled in the guest room across the hall from you. Would you like that, Tawny? I'm sure you've had a long day."

Tawny glanced over at Jason as if to get his approval. Jason gave her a nod of his head. "It has been a long day and a long journey. Now just one thing, Tawny—if you'd like to have some rest before dinner, then just ask my chatterbox sister to leave the room."

"Oh, Jason—you make me sound awful to Tawny." Joy gave a sigh.

Everyone in the room smiled except Lord Addison. But Tawny did not notice, for she'd got up from the settee to follow Joy out of the room.

"I'll see you at dinner, Tawny," Jason assured her.

When the two young ladies had left the room, Jason told them Tawny's story and how she had become his responsibility when he found her aboard his ship. "I had to bring her here. She would have had no place to go."

"Well, of course you did, dear," Sheila Hamilton quickly responded. "Poor, poor little darling! She's a lovely little thing, Jason."

Lord Addison sat silent, for he could hardly fault his son after the sad tale Jason had told them. While he would not voice it, he, too, admired the enchanting beauty the girl possessed.

"So you will book passage for her on a ship to take her back to Virginia?" his father asked him.

"Yes, Father, that is her wish, though I would prefer that she not go back there," Jason declared candidly.

"Does she have any family here in England?" Lord Addison inquired.

"No, but she has me."

Lord Addison and Lady Sheila exchanged looks, but neither of them said anything. Lord Addison did not have to hear any more from Jason to know what his son was saying. He asked the two of them to excuse him because he had some papers in his study that he wanted to go over before evening.

It was only when she was alone with her son that Lady Sheila asked Jason, "Are you in love with Tawny, Son?"

"I think so, Mother, but Tawny is very young and inexperienced. I've got to give her time to see if she feels the same way about me."

"How old is she, dear? She looks very young."

"Sixteen or seventeen, I think Mother. But I've never met a girl like her before—so sweet and innocent. You will see what I mean after you've been around her a while."

"I'm looking forward to getting to know her, Jason. I already find her fascinating and it would appear that Joy was quite taken with her."

Jason laughed. "I noticed that! Poor Tawny—Joy will not allow her any time to rest before dinner."

A twinkle was in his mother's black eyes as she told him, "You just leave that to me, my son. I will attend to Joy so that Tawny will be permitted to rest."

When Jason finally left the garden room and his mother, he had only to mount the stairs and start down the carpeted hallway to hear the lighthearted giggling of his three sisters and Tawny. Joy had obviously introduced Tawny to his other two sisters, Angela and Jane. A grin broke on his face as he shook his head and walked on down the hallway toward his own room.

Tawny was overwhelmed by the friendly warmth of the Hamilton family. All of Jason's sisters were so nice. Jane seemed to be the shyest and quietest. She was the one, Tawny found out, who had knitted those stockings for Jason. She was the first one to leave the gathering. Angela was the prettiest, with blond hair and bright blue eyes. She had an engagement for the evening so she left to start getting ready.

"Angela has a handsome new beau," Joy playfully teased her older sister as she left the room. Angela laughed, paying no attention to the girl's teasing.

Joy also excused herself, but she told Tawny that she'd be back in a moment. Like her kind-hearted brother, Joy had only to hear from Tawny that she'd landed in England with only one frock! She'd seen no reason not to tell his sisters how she'd happened to be aboard Jason's ship. But when she was finally alone she hoped that what she'd told the Hamilton girls was the same story he was going to tell his parents.

It would never have dawned on Tawny to tell anything but the truth. Her story filled Joy with compassion when she thought about her armoire stuffed with gowns and slippers that she never wore. Once in her room, she took a survey of her gowns and began tossing a half dozen on her bed. She picked two pairs of slippers to match the gowns. When she gathered everything in her arms and went back across the hallway, she had such a pile of clothing she could not see the door or the knob. "I don't have a free hand," she declared, giggling, as she yelled at Tawny to open the door.

Tawny could not see her face or head as she struggled into the room to fling the pile of clothing on the bed.

126

"There, take your pick or enjoy all of them. I've more than I can ever wear and I can't imagine having no change of undergarments. I think they'll fit you."

Tawny stood gaping at the array of silks and muslins in a rainbow of colors, along with the fancy lacy undergarments, the likes of which she'd never seen before. The dainty little leather slippers were the prettiest she'd ever seen.

"Goodness," Joy declared, "I guess I'd better get out of here and let you have a moment to relax before dinner or you'll be thinking Jason wasn't just teasing."

"I don't know what to say to you, Joy. But I do thank you for everything. You are so good to me," Tawny stammered.

Joy was about to leave when she remembered the bottle of toilet water she'd slipped in her pocket. "Oh, I almost forgot this. Jason brought me two of these when he went to Paris. Can't tell you the name, but it smells delicious. Just like gardenias. Here, Tawny."

She shook her head in disbelief and sighed. "Oh, Joy, you are as kind-hearted and generous as your brother."

"He is nice, isn't he?" She grinned and winked at Tawny.

After Joy left the room, Tawny picked up each of the lovely gowns to look at them before she carefully hung them in the empty armoire. She placed the slippers on the floor of the high chest. All the undergarments she placed neatly in the drawer of the dressing table. Atop the dressing table she set the bottle of toilet water. Joy was right, it did smell like gardenias. She recalled that Reba Cameron had a bush just outside her veranda and the delicate white blossoms smelled so sweet.

Tawny stretched out across the bed to rest. Her head was whirling, for it had been a very eventful day.

She had arrived in England and said a tearful good-bye to the handsome Bart Montgomery. Now she found herself in this palatial mansion and she'd actually met a lord and lady. She lay across the bed, staring at the gowns that Jason's sister had given to her. She had not closed the carved wooden doors because she wanted to decide which dress she would wear first.

Could she be dreaming all this, she wondered? She was Tawny Blair, the daughter of Maybelle, and she lived in a simple little cottage. Hanging from pegs in her bedroom were very few articles of clothing and one worn pair of moccasins.

It their cupboard there was never enough food for more than a day or two. One square meal a day was all they ever managed, if they were lucky.

It suddenly dawned on Tawny that she'd never known the pleasure of friends her own age. Her friends had been the creatures of the woods, the playful squirrels or the birds who sang their songs for her.

Roberta Thacher and the Camerons were friends, true, but they were older than she. That was why she'd found it so delightful this afternoon to enjoy the company of Jason's three sisters.

Tawny was to know yet another new experience before she joined the Hamilton family for dinner. The maid assigned to attend to her bath rapped on the door. Tawny was hardly prepared to have someone waiting on her, but she enjoyed the leisurely perfumed bath. The maid, Nellie, helped her into the lovely silk wrapper Lady Montgomery had sent up. Tawny sat on the velvet stool allowing Nellie to brush and fashion her thick brown hair.

It was a very pleasant experience to be so pampered. When Nellie inquired which of the gowns she wished to wear, Tawny chose the pale mauve gown with a high neck and long sleeves. Although it was a very basic gown, after the maid had helped Tawny into it, her alluring figure enhanced the soft, flowing material. She looked stunning even without any jewelry to display on the high neckline.

"Ah, miss—you certainly look beautiful!" Nellie declared as she stood back to look at Tawny.

"Why, thank you, Nellie!" Tawny replied.

It was at this moment that Jason's black-haired sister came bouncing into the room in her pretty daffodil-yellow gown and a yellow bow clasped at the back of her hair. Tawny thought she looked pretty and told her so.

"Oh, but not half as beautiful as you, Tawny." She quickly dashed out of the room to go back to her own room to fetch a cluster of mauve velvet flowers for Nellie to pin in Tawny's hair before the two of them went downstairs.

Tawny was impressed by her reflection in the full-length mirror. It was amazing what a lovely gown could do to instill confidence in a person, Tawny realized. She followed Joy out of the room and down the steps. The two of them chattered away as though they'd been friends forever. It was delightful to share the company of Jason's sister. She was so lighthearted and gay that Tawny found herself feeling the same way.

When they joined Lord and Lady Hamilton in their elegant parlor, Tawny was surprised that she found herself so much at ease.

Lady Sheila Hamilton's eyes flashed brightly when the two young ladies entered the parlor, for she immediately recognized the mauve gown and she felt very proud of Joy's generous nature. It looked stunning on the dark-haired Tawny, whose figure was so much fuller and more curvy than Joy's.

One by one the rest of the Hamilton family came into the parlor. Jason was the last one to appear. Sheila noticed where Jason's black eyes were directed, and she could hardly fault him for that.

He'd known back on the *Sea Princess* what a striking vision Tawny would be in a fancy gown like the ones his sisters wore. He found it hard to take his eyes off her, even to greet his parents.

He was saved from being embarrassed, for the servant came to the archway to announce that dinner was ready.

Chapter 16

Lady Laura Montgomery had no idea that her son Bart had returned, for he did not go to the house until he had the stallion settled in the stables and some very stern orders given to all the stablehands. Only then did he walk across the grounds toward the house. It was not the front entrance he used but the kitchen door, which was closer.

He first met their cook, Hattie, and she gave a scream of delight to see the young master back. She'd known Bart since he was a tot always falling down to skin a knee. Adoring the Montgomery's only son as she did and putting up with his boyish antics as she had, she'd developed a very bossy attitude with him. When it was just the two of them in each other's company she called him Scamp, and the name had stuck throughout the years.

"Well, Scamp — if you aren't a sight for sore eyes! Get yourself that horse you wanted?"

"Sure did, Hattie! He's out in the stables right now." He gave her a lovable pat on her hefty rump.

"Behave yourself or I'll take my rolling pin to you," she chuckled.

"Now, Hattie! Things been going all right around here while I've been gone?" Bart asked her, knowing that if anyone could tell him, Hattie would.

"As far as I know they have," Hattie replied. "I'm sure Lady Montgomery will be glad to have you back home. Your aunt came out here for a couple of days from London and stayed. She tried to get her ladyship to go back to her house for a few days while you were away, talked herself blue in the face, but Lady Montgomery wouldn't do it."

"I'm sure Aunt Augusta was fit as a fiddle?" Bart smiled.

"As sassy and saucy as always." Hattie giggled.

Bart bid her farewell, but didn't neglect to tell her that he was more than ready for one of her good dinners. She told him not to worry about that. "Along with your favorite pie, too, Scamp!" she called after him.

When Bart didn't find his mother in the parlor or her sitting room, he went on into his study. He almost wished he hadn't when he spied the mountain of papers awaiting his attention, but he went over to his desk to take a quick survey.

He saw right away that many household bills waited for him. He did not have much patience with paperwork and it always irritated him.

He found himself wondering what his mother did with her days, since she had a score of servants to run the house. When his father was alive, he gave more orders to the houseservants than his mother did. Bart considered that this should have been her task.

Now that his father was dead, and he was the head of the house, he realized that his mother was too old to change, so he gave up insisting that she play a more active role running the house. But Bart did not admire her helplessness. She was an incompetent woman.

When he turned away from the cluttered desk to go upstairs, he knew that he was going to hear whining from her when he sequestered himself in the study to catch up on all the bills that had piled up while he was away. But as in the past, he'd just turn a deaf ear to her complaints.

He walked up the steps and down the hall. At his mother's bedroom door he stopped and knocked on the door. The door opened and the tall, willowy lady smiled as she rushed to embrace her son.

"Oh, Bart! Thank goodness you're home. I missed you so!" she declared. Taking his hand in hers, she led him into the room.

"May I say you are looking grand, Mother," he told the aristocratic looking woman. He couldn't recall ever seeing his mother when she was not perfectly groomed and embellished with jewels.

"You think so, Bart? I had a few days of feeling poorly while you were away, dear."

"Well, you look fine. Hattie tells me Aunt Augusta was here. Is she fine?" Bart asked.

"Augusta has surely found some secret formula for remaining young forever. She exhausts me!"

Bart laughed. "Well, find out her secret, Mother."

They took a seat on the small settee by the windows. "And this Arabian that you traveled so far away to find, Bart dear—were you successful?"

"I found him, Mother, and I bought him. He is now the property of the Montgomery Stables, I'm happy to say."

"Oh, that's nice, Bart. Your father would have been very proud of you."

"I'm proud of myself, Mother, and that is what matters." He rose from the settee to leave, for he did not want to say something to hurt his mother on his first day home.

The mask Bart wore on his face did not reveal his feelings. He was an expert at hiding them. "I'll see you at dinner, Mother. I've some things to do before then."

"Yes, dear, it will be nice to have you at the table with me tonight."

Bart gave her a nod and silently left the room.

Two hours later, the two of them met again in the white-and-wedgwood-blue opulence of their dining room to dine by the twinkling splendor of candlelight reflecting against the cut-crystal glasses and candle holders. Bart thoroughly enjoyed the delectable meal Hattie had prepared for them. He lingered for a while after the meal chatting with his mother to appease her, but when he heard the striking of the clock in the hallway, he knew it was time to go to his study.

"Mother, you must excuse me. I've got some work to do tonight," he declared.

"Tonight, Bart? Your first night back home and you must work?" She glared up at him with disbelief.

"Someone has to, Mother. It doesn't get done if I don't do it."

"Well, dear—I think that you work too hard," she grumbled.

Bart sought not to answer her. She would not have understood. Instead he went directly to the study, and there he stayed until well after midnight. By the time he got to his bedroom, he realized the loyalty of their servants and his men attending his stables, for none of them had received their salaries during all the weeks he'd been gone. That was the first task he'd attended to, and in the morning he would make a point of distributing to them what they were due.

The next three days and nights were to follow in the same routine for Bart. He divided his time between the stables and his study. Lady Montgomery was feeling very neglected by the end of the third evening when Bart left her as soon as they'd dined.

The Montgomerys were not enjoying gala evenings as the Hamiltons were. The truth was that Jason was finding it impossible to find a moment alone with Tawny. His sisters kept her monopolized most of the time, and Tawny seemed to enjoy them. Never had he seen her more radiant.

He welcomed the fact that his sisters were keeping her entertained; he felt free to make trips back into London to work around the *Sea Princess*.

It was on one of these afternoons, as he was leaving his ship to walk down the wharf, that he encountered Captain Donald Crane whom he admired tremendously.

"How are you, Captain? Are you just coming in or going out?" Jason asked, extending his hand to the elderly captain who seemed hellbent to sail the seas until the day he died.

"Just came in, lad, but I'll be going out again in a week or ten days if I have my way about it," the white-haired gentleman declared.

If Tawny was determined to go back to Virginia, Jason could not put her in any safer hands than Captain Crane's. He knew that Crane would keep his eye out for her if he explained the circumstances to him. Crane had granddaughters about Tawny's age.

He explained to Captain Crane about Tawny Blair and that he wanted to make sure she was delivered safely back to Virginia. "I'll see that little girl back there, Jason," Captain Crane said. "I just must tell you that I'm glad she landed on your ship and the likes of you. The poor child could have been in for a horrible experience. She's a lucky miss!"

"Thank you, Captain. I would feel that she was in safe hands aboard your ship. Tawny Blair is a fine young lady and she's been through enough already."

Crane nodded his white head and smiled. "She's a lucky lady to have such a friend as you." The elderly sea captain knew that his young friend's feelings went deeper than he cared to express, so he was curious about this Tawny Blair!

Jason traveled back home feeling much happier about having to part with Tawny, knowing that she was in the care of the fatherly Crane. While he liked most of his seafaring buddies and captains, there were few he'd trust Tawny with. She was just too beautiful! Damned if he'd even trust his best friend Bart when Tawny was around. Never had he felt this way about him before. If he were to ask Bart if he was smitten by Tawny, he knew that Bart would deny it. But Jason knew he was.

Just before he reached his home, a wave of sadness washed over him when he realized how brief Tawny's visit was going to be. He decided that he'd delay the announcement to Tawny and his family. She seemed to be enjoying herself so much and his family seemed to be enjoying her. Lord Addison could not restrain a warm smile occasionally, and he was being much nicer than Jason had expected him to be. He was grateful for that. But who could possibly resist the charms of Tawny?

When he entered the front door, the first sounds he heard were the laughter of his sisters and his mother. As he walked into his mother's garden room, he found Tawny and Joy sitting on the floor with his mother and two other sisters on the settee. Tawny was telling them about the day she'd first met Jason and Bart Montgomery and how she was coming up to the veranda in her barefeet. "I'd just returned from a ride on Coco."

"In your bare feet, Tawny?" Joy giggled with a look of disbelief on her face.

"Oh, it was wonderful! I love to go barefoot." Tawny smiled.

Joy laughed. "Oh, Tawny—you're like no one I've ever known."

Lady Sheila Montgomery was reminded of herself as a young girl and she, too, had liked to go without shoes. "Tawny is like a refreshing breath of air. You just reminded me of something I'd not thought about for a long, long time. I liked to go barefoot when I was a young girl in Ireland, and my father was always scolding me, telling me I was going to get a thorn in my foot."

At that moment Jason made his entrance. "Did you tell them about wearing my stockings because that was the only thing we could find for you on the ship?"

His sister Jane spoke up. "That was what we were all laughing about just before you came in. Poor Tawny must have had a miserable time trying to walk in your big stockings."

"Oh, she managed very nicely, I think." Jason told them.

When the gathering finally broke up, Jason got a chance to be alone with Tawny for the first time since they'd arrived. He invited her to take a stroll with him in the gardens, for it was the loveliest time of day. A cool, gentle breeze always seemed to flow through the gardens in the late afternoon because the tall trees shaded the winding flagstone walkway.

Hand in hand they leisurely ambled along through glowing brilliant-colored flowers and shrubbery. Tawny had not felt so happy in a long, long time!

For a few brief moments the haunting, handsome face of Bart Montgomery faded as she strolled with Jason.

Chapter 17

"I love your family," Tawny told Jason. "You are so lucky to have such nice parents and sisters. I shall never forget how wonderful they've been to me, and I realize how sad I will be when I leave."

Jason held her hand tightly and looked down at her. "You don't have to leave, Tawny," he could not resist saying. "You could just forget about going back to Virginia."

"No, Jason, I can't forget about going back—not really." She smiled at him, her brown eyes twinkling. "But I'll not lie to you that I am tempted to stay."

"So you still want me to get passage for you?" he asked her.

"It seems I'm always asking a favor of you, Jason, but I do need to go back. It is just something I must do, so please try to understand. I'm most grateful that you ask me to stay on, but I will find no rest or satisfaction until I return to Longcreek."

Jason told her he did understand, but he remained silent about the passage he'd arranged this afternoon with Captain Crane. There was plenty of time yet, he convinced himself.

Perhaps it was the talk of Virginia that made Tawny suddenly grow quiet and thoughtful as they continued to walk in the gardens. It was obvious to Jason that the light-hearted, gay mood she'd been in when they began their walk had changed.

"Shall we turn around and start back toward the house? We've walked quite a long way," he told her.

Tawny looked up at him, for her thoughts had been elsewhere. "I . . . I suppose we should, Jason. I am enjoying our time together. I had not realized what huge grounds this garden covered."

When they got back to the house, he told her good-bye at the base of the stairway. "I've some business to discuss with my father, Tawny. I'll see you at dinner."

She bounced lightly up the steps to her room. She told herself she loved Jason as much as the rest of his family. Never would she ever meet anyone like him again, she was convinced. He was the kindest, sweetest man in the world.

But back there in the gardens, when they were talking about her return to Virginia, she had found herself feeling desolate about leaving another man. The fair-haired Bart Montgomery invaded her thoughts, and when she realized that she'd probably never see him again, she could feel tears wanting to flow. She was glad, as she walked down the hallway, that she had not encountered any of the Hamiltons. For the first time since she'd arrived here, she yearned for solitude in the quiet of her room.

She closed the door, hoping Joy would not hear her returning from her walk. She was just not in the mood to talk right now.

Jason's youngest sister was in her room, and she had heard Tawny going into her room. Right now she was sitting in the chair by her window, thinking about her brother and Tawny. Joy was convinced that her brother Jason was in love with Tawny Blair. She'd watched the two of them coming out of the gardens and she'd watched Jason's face as he'd been looking down at Tawny. She'd never seen such a look of adoration in his eyes before. She hoped he would marry Tawny, and she'd live here all the time. The days and nights had been such joy since she'd arrived. Why, even her father had seemed much less stern and gruff the last four days! That was really saying something for the magic Tawny Blair could create, Joy decided.

Joy was not the only one observing the young couple returning from their walk. Jane was sitting by her window, knitting a scarf for Tawny. A beautiful golden color was what she'd picked from her various yarns. Like Joy, she was also convinced that Jason loved the young girl from Virginia. And like Joy, she, too, could not think of any girl she'd rather see her dear brother take for a wife. Tawny was a sweet, unspoiled young lady and Jane appreciated her simple, honest ways.

Lord and Lady Hamilton had not observed the young couple as their daughters had, but they were discussing their young guest in the privacy of their bedroom. Lord Addison sat smoking his pipe as his wife looked in her armoire to choose which gown she would wear to dinner.

"I find her utterly charming, Addison, don't you?" she asked.

"I must say I do, Sheila." Addison saw the glow on his wife's face. It was her bubbling personality that had attracted him to her in the first place. He himself was restrained in expressing his true feelings, and reserved, but not his Sheila!

"A free spirit," she told her husband. "I found myself thinking this afternoon how much happier people could be if they were like Tawny Blair and did not allow convention and tradition to rule them."

Sheila confessed to her husband that she would be sad to see the girl leave. "I wish she would stay in England, Addison. In fact, I wish she and Jason would get married. I think she would be good for him."

"Now, Sheila — don't start interfering. That would never do."

She gave a dramatic gesture of her hand and sighed. "Oh, Addison I won't. I was just telling you what I wished. But I do think that Jason is very taken with her — much more serious than he's ever been before about a young lady."

"We'll see, Sheila dear. Now I guess it's time I remove myself to my own dressing room while you get yourself all pretty for dinner, eh?"

Addison smiled as she mumbled her reply, for he knew Sheila was preoccupied.

* * *

After five straight nights of working in his study, Bart was finding the mammoth pile of papers and bills slowly shrinking. Already he had received word from three breeders interested in Diablo siring a colt with their mare, so he was feeling very pleased with himself.

When he dimmed the lamp on his desk this evening, he knew that it was well worth that long trip to Virginia, to seek out Bill Cameron and purchase Diablo. Soon the Montgomery Stables would be known all over the world because of that rare black Arabian.

He sat there in the quiet to relive that journey and seeing Diablo for the first time, but suddenly there came the vision of a beautiful brown-haired, brown-eyed girl and thoughts about Diablo were swept away. He recalled the satiny softness of her skin and hair when his fingers caressed it. Those half-parted lips were recalled, their taste as sweet as the wine he was now sipping. He thought to himself that she had looked so fragile and tiny that she would be crushed if he put his strong, muscled arms around her to press her to his firm, male body, but that had not happened.

No, that wee Tawny Blair possessed more fire and passion than any other woman he'd made love to. All he had to do was remember how their bodies had sensuously swayed together to that tempo which had carried them to the height of rapture he'd never experienced before, and he was engulfed with overwhelming desire.

Two more nights would finish up all this work and then he was going to the Hamiltons to see Tawny, he promised himself. Whether it met with Jason's approval or not, he didn't give a damn!

The next morning before he left the house he informed his mother that he was going to be inviting a guest to dinner the next night.

"And who is this guest, may I ask, Bart?" she asked him.

"A young lady from Virginia, Mother," he told her be-

140

fore he made his abrupt departure. Lady Montgomery was left to ponder this for the rest of the day. She came to the conclusion that whoever this young lady was, it must be she who was causing Bart to act as he was, so she was determined not to like her when they met.

All day she fretted and fumed, so by the time they met for dinner she was barely cordial toward her son. What was more annoying to her was the fact that Bart did not seem to notice it.

In a sullen mood, she pushed aside the dessert the servant had placed before her. "If you will excuse me, Bart, I think I shall go upstairs. I am tired." He watched her tall, stately figure move out of the dining room. He suddenly wished that he had been like Jason, with some sisters so he would not have been an only child. He suddenly realized that his mother had doted on him and he could not meet all her demands.

He knew exactly what she was fidgeting about and he also knew why. He sat there alone at the dining table, thinking that exposure to Tawny Blair might be exactly what his mother needed.

Tomorrow night could be very interesting, for he was determined to protect Tawny should the occasion arise. He'd just hope that his mother would be gracious to Tawny.

He worked very effectively in his study, plotting how he would ride over to the Hamiltons the next morning to extend his invitation to Tawny for dinner and how that evening he would go to pick her up.

When he left his study, his desk was rid of all the papers and bills. Everything was cleared away, and Bart heaved a deep sigh of relief that it was all behind him.

When his head hit the pillow, he was instantly asleep, a sleep so deep that he did not even dream of Tawny.

Captain Crane sent word to Jason that the *Caprice* would be sailing the next morning. Jason dreaded relaying the news to Tawny and his family. He suspected that it was be a gloomy evening around the Hamilton home tonight.

Damned stubborn little imp, he thought as he sat in his room. He wished he could talk her out of going back, but he knew her mind was made up.

He left the room to go to a storage room on the second floor. Tawny was going to need some luggage to pack her things in tonight, for at dawn they'd leave for the harbor.

He encountered his mother in the hallway. "Don't tell me you're leaving us after only being home a week, Jason Hamilton!" she cried.

Jason urged her into his room and closed the door. "No, not me—Tawny," he told her. "But she doesn't know it yet. I just received word from Captain Crane that his ship is leaving in the morning. I've not had a chance to tell her yet, but I was hunting for some luggage for her to pack all the things Joy gave her."

Sheila Montgomery sank down on his bed with a crestfallen look on her face. "Oh, no! It seems she's just arrived. Oh, Jason—can't you persuade her to remain here with us? We all love her so."

"I've tried, Mother, but Tawny is a headstrong girl when she wants to be. I plan to try once more tonight, but don't get your hopes up."

As Sheila opened the door to leave, she winked at her son. "Use that Irish charm I know you possess, Jason, my son," she suggested.

Jason laughed as she closed the door behind her.

Lady Hamilton was very disappointed, for nothing was going as she'd hoped. She had become so genuinely fond of the girl the last few days. More than ever, she was hoping that Tawny and Jason would fall in love and get married.

Chapter 18

It was a bittersweet moment for Tawny. In a few brief days she'd become fond of the Hamilton family, and the thought of leaving was making her very sad. All the family lingered in the parlor later than usual after dinner. It was as though none of them wanted the evening to be over, and Tawny was feeling the same way.

When Tawny did finally mount the stairs with Joy clinging to her arm, Joy insisted that she promise to return someday.

"I swear it, Joy. I shall come back. You wait and see."

Tawny was carrying the beautiful gold scarf and gloves Jane had presented to her. Lady Montgomery gave her a lovely cape in the same shade. "You might find the nights a little chilly before you get back to Virginia, Tawny," Jason's mother had told her. Angela gave Tawny her gold velvet reticule to match her mother and Jane's gift.

Tawny had never had so many lovely things before! She was returning to Virginia dressed very elegantly, she thought to herself.

When they got to Tawny's room, the two young girls gave each other a fond embrace. They knew it would be their last one, for Jason had told them how early he and Tawny would have to leave the house.

"I'll . . . I'll write to you, Joy, when I get back to Longcreek, and you must write to me," Tawny said as she and Joy stood with tears streaming down their faces.

Good-byes were sad, and there was nothing else to be said. Joy knew that she was going to fling herself across her bed as soon as she went to her room and cry some more.

After Joy left, that was exactly what Tawny did, too. When she could cry no more tears, she got up from the bed to undress. She prayed that there would be no more good-byes in the morning and that she and Jason would just depart for London.

There was one person she would like to have seen just once more before she left, but she knew that she was not going to be granted that wish. But then, she had to ask herself why he'd not come to the Hamiltons during the last week as he'd promised her he would. It wasn't all that far away, she recalled.

The next morning she was granted her wish, the family did not gather to say good-bye when she and Jason left the house in the quiet of the early morning. Tawny could not bring herself to eat a thing. Jason only drank some tea before they climbed up in the buggy for the ride into the city.

But Joy was awake and looking out the window, weeping as she watched her brother and her new friend get into the buggy. Lady Sheila Montgomery sat in her dressing gown at her window and watched the young couple leave. What a handsome pair they made! She was tempted to rush down the steps when she heard Tawny walking down the hallway to go downstairs but decided not to.

Maybe Tawny would come back into their lives, she hoped.

When Jason's buggy rolled down the road, Tawny turned to glance at the spacious two-story stone house where Bart lived. He was so close, but she could not see him. Jason did not notice how her dark eyes stared in that direction for as long as the house was in view.

Bart was just stretching his long legs over the side of his bed to get up when Jason and Tawny passed his house on their way to London. In fact, he'd given himself the pleasure of a little extra sleep this morning since he'd worked late last night to clear off his desk.

The first thing on his schedule this morning was saddling up Diablo to ride over to the Hamiltons. The first thoughts he had were of the beautiful Tawny, and they were enough to send his spirits soaring as he got dressed. It seemed to whet a hearty appetite as well, Hattie noticed when she served him breakfast.

Immediately, he was off to the stables to order his young stableboy to saddle up Diablo. When they rode out of the gate, Bart noticed that the Arabian seemed ready to kick up his hooves and gallop swiftly down the road. Bart laughed as he allowed him to have his way. It did not take them long to arrive at the Hamiltons' drive.

It was Jason's seventeen-year-old sister Joy he first encountered as he dismounted. She was roaming aimlessly near the front entrance.

Of all of Jason's sisters, Joy was Bart's favorite and he always considered her a delightful little brat since she was the youngest. But he'd always felt that when she grew up she'd be the loveliest.

Seeing her now, he knew that indeed she was going to be the prettiest one. "Hello, brat!" he teased her. He'd expected one of her big, friendly smiles but he only got a weak, forced one.

"Oh, hello, Bart."

"Well, I'd expected a happier greeting than that, Joy, after you've not seen me for so long. I'm wounded!" He ambled up to her and she gave him a feeble apology.

"Well, since I can't get you to talk with me, I guess I'll let you go on with your walk and I'll go in to see Jason and Tawny."

Joy looked up at the tall Montgomery. "You're out of luck there, Bart. Jason and Tawny aren't here," she informed him.

"Oh, did they go into London this morning? They left awfully early," he remarked casually.

145

"They had to, for Tawny to board the ship," Joy told him.

"For Tawny to *what?*" Bart demanded to know with every muscle in his huge body tensed.

"Tawny caught a ship to leave England this morning to go back to Virginia." She could not hold back the tears as she talked to Bart. He was like her big brother, so she gave way to her need to cry. "That's . . . that's why I'm so sad, Bart. I didn't want to see her go. I came to love Tawny."

Bart embraced and comforted the young girl. "That's all right, honey. Now I understand why you were acting the way you were, Joy. I wish I had known it, damn it! I would have tried to stop her." Fury seethed in Bart at her brother for not telling him.

Without thinking about what he was saying, for he was so riled at Jason, he consoled Joy. "I know exactly how you feel, because I love Tawny, too. We'll get her back here, I promise you."

The petite black-haired girl gazed up at Bart. Her hand went up to wipe her eyes. "You mean that, Bart? You'll bring her back?"

"Joy, you and I will make a secret pact today, and you can believe me. I promise that I'll bring Tawny back." He patted her shoulders and told her that he had to leave now but she must remember what he'd said.

There was no reason for Bart to linger, he was in no mood to be cordial to the rest of the family. Besides, he had a score to settle with Jason.

He rode out of the drive, but as he swiftly galloped toward his home, he did not turn into the long drive of his property. He was not homeward bound. Bart was going into London to seek out Jason. Being a realistic man, he had no hope that her ship had not already sailed. Every mile he rode, his wrath mounted.

By the time he approached the harbor, he still could not believe that Jason could have betrayed him this way. But there was no doubt in his mind why he'd done it.

146

Jason didn't want him to know that Tawny was leaving. He'd find it hard ever to forgive him for this little trick.

There were dozens of ships in the harbor, and he didn't even know the name of the one Tawny was sailing aboard. He'd not thought to ask Joy that before he'd left. But he spotted the *Sea Princess* immediately, for he recalled the spot where Jason had moored it when they'd arrived here just seven or eight days ago.

Damn Jason. Why hadn't he tried to stop her from going back? Bart couldn't understand that!

Bart had no intention of leaving his fine stallion unattended on the docks, so he summoned a young lad. Handing him some coins, he asked him to go aboard the *Sea Princess* to get Jason if he was in his cabin.

The youth returned shortly to inform Bart that he'd delivered his message to Captain Hamilton, and he'd be there very soon. Soon, Bart spotted his black-haired friend coming across the deck of the *Sea Princess*. Jason had already figured out that it was not going to be a pleasant meeting when he told Bart that Tawny had left over two hours ago. After he'd given her a last warm embrace and left her in the care of Captain Crane, Jason had felt such a void that he'd sought the solitude of his cabin before returning home.

But he'd found no peace there, for in every corner of the cabin he could see the beautiful Tawny in the faded pants and his shirt, or that green gown. He picked up the two pairs of stockings lying on the bunk that she'd neatly folded and put them in the chest. He was already having regrets that he'd given in so easily to her request to return to Virginia. He should have delayed the journey, and he could have. But he also knew that the seas would not be as rough at this time of the year as they would be in a few more weeks.

It never dawned on Jason as he walked up to the spot on the wharf where Bart was sitting astride Diablo that he knew that Tawny was gone. Bart usually wore that self-assured, arrogant look on his face and there was no indication there to clue Jason to the fury seething behind that mask until he came up to him.

Jason greeted him in his usual friendly way. Maybe Bart's face did not give away his anger, but his deep voice did, the minute he spoke. "Why did you do it, Jason? Why did you let Tawny go back? She has no damned business traveling alone. She's too young and naive!"

Jason wondered how the devil he'd found out so soon. There was only one way he could have, and that was if he'd gone to his house this morning. "She wanted to go, Bart." Jason looked directly up at him. "I got her passage with the best captain around—Captain Crane. I felt I could trust him to look after her."

"And what happens to her after they land in Chesapeake, Jason? Had you thought about that?" he snarled at his friend.

"Look, Bart—I . . . I didn't know you were so concerned with Tawny Blair," Jason stammered. Bart made a good point. Once again, he could not argue with him.

Bart frowned and raised a skeptical brow. "Don't insult our friendship any more than you already have, Jason. You know and I know how we both felt about Tawny back there when we were crossing the ocean. Do you take me for a damned fool? I know why you didn't let me know she was leaving. So do you!" He gave a quick jerk on the reins and turned Diablo in the opposite direction. "You outfoxed me this time but I'll outsmart you yet!" he called back to Jason as he rode away.

Jason watched his former friend fade into the distance—for he knew that Bart was no longer his friend. Bart was not a forgiving man and what he'd said was true. He'd not wanted Bart to have the chance to see Tawny before she left. He'd had his own selfish reasons for that, he had to admit.

He strolled back to his ship, needing some more time to be alone. Overwhelming guilt was eating away at him.

Once he was back in his cabin, he made a decision.

He'd take that assignment for the Marlston Company to carry their goods to Virginia, and he'd seek out Tawny. He'd just pray that when he left in four weeks that he would not be too far behind her when she arrived back in Virginia.

When he finally left his cabin, it seemed some of the burden weighing on him was lifted. The next four weeks he would be busy getting the *Sea Princess* ready for another voyage.

Bart Montgomery had never possessed the easygoing, calm nature of Jason. He had no intention of waiting three or four weeks to go after the woman he found himself yearning for so desperately. It was not his nature to wait for anything he wanted. As he had been obsessed about the black Arabian, he was now obsessed about finding Tawny just as quick as some ship could get him there. Only this time, he would not ask Jason to sail him there.

Jason was no longer his friend!

Chapter 19

The ingenious Bart Montgomery had accomplished many things by the time he finally reined Diablo homeward. He'd booked passage aboard the *Moontide,* due to leave London in seven days. From the shipping office, he'd gone to pay a visit to his adored aunt Augusta in the city and she was overjoyed to see her handsome nephew at her door.

"What a pleasant surprise, Bart dear. Come in," she greeted him. She was as short a lady as his own mother was tall, but she was far more vivacious than his mother and he'd always admired her sharp, keen mind. He knew few ladies as clever as his aunt Augusta and he could have wished that his own mother shared some of these traits.

Bart always liked to tease her, and she adored every minute of it. If any lady had a reason to feel that life had cheated her, his aunt Augusta had reason to feel that way. She'd lost her beloved husband and only child in the same year a terrible epidemic swept the city of London twelve years ago. Bart and his family had escaped it, living on the outskirts of the city.

They spent a very pleasant hour in his aunt's small but cozy parlor before Bart approached the subject on his mind. "Aunt Augusta, I'm going to be leaving again in about a week. Do you think I could persuade you to come out there to look after things around the house for me while I'm gone? I came back from my last trip to a miserable task. I could be gone as long as a couple of months."

"Dear Lord, Bart, your mother is going to have a fit! You've only been home a little over a week now," Augusta sighed.

"I know, but something has come up."

"Have you said anything yet to her?"

"No, I wanted to talk to you first. I know you could handle everything pertaining to the running of the house. There would be a generous fee for you because God knows, Aunt Augusta, it would be worth it to me!"

"Oh, Bart—forget that!" she quickly assured him.

"No, I won't! But I can't get Mother to do what she would easily have the time to do, and I know you will."

She patted his hand and smiled. "Well, why not! I've nothing to hold me here, but I would want to come into London for a day or two to see about my little house here from time to time."

"That would be fine. But I could leave knowing that the servants and the bills would be paid while I was away and certain things demanding attention around the house would be done."

"You have my word, Bart. I will be happy to help you. All I can say to you about my sister is that your father spoiled her, and when he died you immediately stepped into his shoes. Maybe, just maybe I can do you a grand favor while you are gone this time," she told him, a twinkle of mischief coming into her blue eyes. "Maybe I can make her realize that it is long overdue that she become the mistress of her home."

Bart had to laugh at that. "I'll give you an extra bonus, Aunt Augusta, if you can accomplish that."

Augusta smiled at her handsome nephew who looked so much like his father, the distinguished Lord Edward Montgomery. She had never figured out what it was about her younger sister that had entranced Lord Montgomery. The only answer had to be that she was much younger when they'd met and married. He was thirty-six and she was sixteen, and that was why he'd indulged

151

and pampered her so much.

Augusta was already twenty and married when they'd married, but her husband was no lord and they did not enjoy the luxury or wealth of the Montgomerys.

When Bart finally took his leave, she went back into her parlor thinking that she did not envy him tonight if he told Laura that he'd be leaving again in another week. He never told her why he was leaving and she had not asked him. But she did know that he'd been successful in getting the Arabian he'd wanted so much. Now what was it this young, ambitious man was seeking?

Somehow, Augusta knew that it was not another Arabian. Augusta was wondering if it could possibly be a young lady. She knew how seriously he took the duties he'd inherited when his father had died. It had been a tremendous undertaking to run the Montgomery Stables the way Lord Edward had run them for many years. Augusta had a great admiration for the young man who'd taken over the helm at such an early age.

Ah, yes, she would be glad to run his house for him while he was away on whatever mission he was going on and she was quite sincere when she told him that she would try to inspire her sister, Laura, to assume her role, as she should have many years ago.

Bart rode back home with less fury smoldering in him than when he'd ridden into London. He'd had words with Jason and he knew that there could be no doubt in Jason's mind about how he felt. His aunt Augusta had once again agreed to give him support he needed and he'd booked passage to Virginia.

His only regret was that he would have to tell his mother that there would be no guest at dinner tonight. He also knew that she would be curious about where he had been all day, and he had no intention of telling her. All his well-laid plans were to be his secret for a while yet.

Any apprehensions Bart Montgomery or Jason Hamilton might have had about Tawny aboard Captain Crane's ship where for naught. The minute Jason introduced her to him he assumed a protective, fatherly attitude toward her. He made a point of instructing his cabin boy Jeff to look out for her at all times.

Each night the two of them dined together, and he took her on strolls around the deck of his ship each afternoon and evening. When they walked and talked, he found her to be a most engaging young lady and very smart, too. Captain Crane decided that there was no way that he was going to allow this young miss to leave his ship unescorted to her village of Longcreek. He was going to see her safely there. She was too sweet and nice to leave her on the docks of Chesapeake, and his sleep would have been haunted by what might happen to the girl as she traveled from the port to her village.

Tawny found that Captain Crane and Jason shared a lot in common. He loved the sea and his ship with the same fervor, and both of them were gallant gentlemen. She didn't have to be around Captain Crane very long to warm to him. He told her about his family back in England and that he had a granddaughter about her age. She felt safe and secure in her cabin next to his. His cabin boy seemed to be constantly nearby.

By the time they were three days out to sea, Tawny was finding that she was no longer fearful about the long journey she'd insisted on making. There had been a moment when Jason had embraced and kissed her that last time that she wanted to cry out to him to get her off the ship and take her back to his home. But now she was glad that she hadn't. She had a duty to return to Longcreek.

But she did start writing a letter to Jason the second day out and she also started a letter to dear, sweet Joy. She thought about the other two letters she'd written on Jason's ship, to the Camerons and Roberta Thacher. The letters would arrive only a short time before she arrived

153

back there. She had to confess that she had not expected Jason to book passage for her so quickly.

Tawny welcomed the woolen cape Lady Sheila Montgomery had given her. The nights seemed cooler now than when she was on the *Sea Princess,* when she recalled walking with Jason or Bart without anything around her shoulders.

Her thoughts seemed to keep roaming back to England and Bart Montgomery. She wondered if Jason had told him she was gone. She chided herself for foolishly thinking that he might be sad that she'd left. That was only her romantic heart wanting to think that this might be so. Over seven days went by while she was there and he had made no effort to ride the short distance to see her. That should tell her all she needed to know to be convinced that Bart Montgomery would not be losing any sleep over her leaving England.

By the time she'd spent a week aboard the *Caprice,* she found herself yearning for the simple garb of Jason's oversize shirt and Rudy's faded blue pants. Joy's billowing gowns were a problem when she was walking on the deck, and the loose pants would have been far more comfortable when she was spending the idle time there in her cabin.

The captain's cabin had no shelves lined with books as Jason's, so she had nothing to read to pass the long afternoons and evenings.

Captain Crane's cabin boy Jeff must have sensed that their pretty passenger was beginning to find time hanging heavily on her hands after so many days at sea and he was struck by the idea of bringing her the little kitten that had found his way on the ship before they'd sailed out of London. But there was another reason Jeff thought about bringing the kitten to the safety of Tawny's cabin—the galley cook was ready to take a knife to the kitten for jumping up on the table where he prepared the food.

With the little striped kitten tucked under his tunic,

he scurried down the passageway to Tawny's cabin. Giving a soft rap on the door, he called, "Miss Tawny, it's me, Jeff."

Tawny opened the door and invited him to enter. For a minute she was puzzled as to what he was about as he reached up under his tunic to pull out the kitten he'd named Calico. "Would you enjoy Calico's company, Miss Tawny? She's a playful little thing. Thought maybe you might get some laughs, for she's a real little clown."

"Well, now, isn't she cute! Where did you get her? Is she yours, Jeff?" Tawny asked, taking the tiny kitten in her hands.

"No, ma'am. I just found her here on the ship. She's a little stowaway and the cook's ready to kill her." Jeff laughed, for he could see that Tawny would certainly welcome the kitten to her cabin.

"Well, now, we can't have that, can we, Calico," she declared, rubbing her cheek against the kitten's head. "I'll keep Calico here with me, Jeff. She'll be safe and I'll enjoy her."

Jeff nodded his head and smiled as he turned to go out the door. "I'll bring an extra dish of milk when I bring your tray this evening. I think the captain's going to be on duty tonight."

The rest of the late afternoon and evening went by quickly for Tawny with Calico for company, and there was more than enough on the dinner tray for her and the kitten. With a full belly, the kitten curled up on Tawny's bunk and slept. Tawny wrote another page to each of the letters to Joy and Jason. Then she undressed and put on her gown. Before she dimmed the lamp, she moved Calico over so she could get into the bunk. So sound was the kitten's sleep that she didn't know that Tawny had picked her up.

Together, they both slept peacefully.

Bart Montgomery had said nothing to his mother

about his plans to leave in a few short days, nor did he intend to just yet. Nevertheless, he was making his plans each day.

He had a long session with Harvey Green about the Arabian, and gave the full responsibility of Diablo to Green for the time he was away. The responsibility of running the stables and his other Thoroughbreds he turned over to his other trainer, Ben Towers.

Finally, he decided that it was time to inform his mother about his plans to leave. This would give her two or three days to fuss and fume before he finally departed. Maybe his poor aunt Augusta would be spared the brunt of his mother's fury if she took it out on him for a day or two.

As they dined that night Bart found his mother in rare form. She was gay and talkative. "You're a hard-working young man, Bart. You are so much like your father. We are not exactly paupers, you know, Son," she laughed.

"I know that, Mother."

"I would have expected that you'd have brought that lovely Elaine Weatherford out here to dinner by now. She is quite charming, you know."

"Elaine is a beautiful lady, but I haven't wanted to invite her," Bart replied as he took another bite of Hattie's delicious pie.

"She seemed very taken with you when she was here for the dinner party we had last spring. I got the impression that you were attracted to her, too," his mother prodded him.

"That was last spring, Mother," Bart said, laughing. He knew that Elaine was the lady she had picked out for his future wife, but Bart had never considered that at all, not even back in the early spring. "It's late summer now, Mother."

"Oh, Bart—I think I must agree with Hattie. You are a scamp!" she laughed lightheartedly.

Bart knew that this festive air was about to change

soon. He decided it had to be done, so he finished the last bit of pie before he made his announcement.

To his amazement, Lady Montgomery said nothing. She rose from her chair and glared angrily at her son.

Chapter 20

Bart had no reason to go to his study after dinner, for his papers were all in order, so he went directly to his bedroom when he left the dining room. He got himself comfortable by unbuttoning the first three buttons of his white linen shirt and took a cheroot from the silver case on his nightstand. Strolling over to the liquor chest, he poured himself a glass of brandy and sat down in the chair by the small fireplace.

But he'd just had time to take two pleasant puffs on his cheroot when there was a rap on the door. When he opened it, the stately figure of his mother stood there in her elegant dressing gown.

"I have something to say to you, Bart, before I retire." She moved gracefully into the room to take a seat in the chair opposite Bart's.

"Bart," she told him, "I'm sending a message to Augusta tomorrow to come out here and stay with me while you are gone."

"Well, Mother, that won't be necessary. I went by to see Aunt Augusta myself when I was in London and she has agreed to come out here."

She stood up and he saw the indignant look on her face. She was very displeased with him as he had anticipated. "Well, there is nothing more I have to discuss with you, so I'll say good night, Bart. At least I will have my sister for company while you're away on your business trip."

"Well, I thought it would work out very nicely for both

of us, Mother. You'll enjoy her company and I'll have someone to keep my books up to date while I'm gone. I won't come back to a desk piled to the ceiling with paperwork. We both know Aunt Augusta is very good at that."

She said nothing more to him as she stiffly marched out of the room, and he knew that her foul mood would still be with her tomorrow. But he would be too busy to be affected by it.

Lady Montgomery had not been angry at her only son many times in her life, but this was one of those times. She'd always thought he was exactly like his father Edward, but after tonight she had changed her mind.

A deep resentment smouldered in her that he had taken the liberty of inviting Augusta here. This was her home, and Bart had better not forget that. She vowed to herself that by the time he got back from wherever he was going, she would show her son that she could run this house just as well as Augusta. Now that she was back in her own bedroom, it dawned on her that he had not mentioned where it was he was going this time.

Once Bart was gone, Lady Montgomery knew exactly what she was going to do. She would sit by the desk with Augusta and she would watch her attend to the household accounts. When she was sure that she could do them, she would send Augusta back to London. Whether her son liked it or not, she would do it!

Lady Montgomery blamed herself for being willing to allow Bart to take over so completely after Edward died. Tonight she'd decided that all this was going to change.

Finally, she was ready to dim the lamp by her bed and go to bed. Tomorrow was going to be a new day around this mansion, so she didn't intend to sleep as late as she usually did.

Bart might be in for a few surprises even before he left here.

As she had planned, Lady Montgomery was dressed and downstairs at least two hours earlier than usual. Hattie almost fainted when she saw her mistress at the dining table for breakfast, instead of eating on a tray in her room as she usually did.

Nevertheless, it pleased Hattie that she ate such a hearty meal — almost as much as her son ate. Hattie was due another surprise when Lady Montgomery asked what she planned for their dinner that night. When the cook brought her the list, Lady Montgomery suggested some changes for the evening. Hattie took back the list and told her she would see to them right away. It seemed the lady wished the leg of lamb, instead of the roast chicken. Hattie knew that this would meet with Bart's approval.

By the time Bart came strolling into the spacious dining room, Lady Montgomery had left to go for an early-morning stroll in her gardens. But Hattie was quick to tell him that his mother had beaten him down to breakfast this morning and Bart looked up with a quizzical expression on his face, wondering if he'd heard right.

"My mother has already had her breakfast? Is that what I heard you say, Hattie?"

"That's what you heard, Scamp. She's out in the gardens now."

By the time she had roamed around the garden for almost an hour, she had also given the two gardeners some instructions to thin out and divide some of the plants. She also told them to change the pair of iron benches so that she could see and watch birds feeding there in her gardens.

As she started back to the house, she thought to herself that she'd show that young son of hers whose house and garden this was. The stables could be his domain to run as he wished, but she was taking charge of the house and gardens as of today.

There was a chilling air in the elegant Montgomery dining room that night as the two of them dined together, but Bart ate so ravenously of the tender leg of lamb en-

160

hanced by the mint jelly and the roasted new potatoes that it didn't bother him that his mother made no effort to talk to him while they dined.

"Hattie outdid herself tonight," he declared when he could not eat another bite.

"It was delicious, wasn't it?" She smiled, making no mention that it was her idea.

Bart had made a point of going into the gardens on his way to the stables this morning and saw the gardeners going about the changes his mother had requested. When he inquired about where they were moving the benches and why they'd dug up the boxwood bushes, they'd informed him that Lady Montgomery had given them orders to do so. Bart shrugged his broad shoulders and casually went on his way. But he wondered why she'd had this sudden whim about the gardens.

The next day he was in the stables with his trainer Harvey Green when one of the stablehands started to prepare the carriage. When Bart asked him what he was doing, the young man told him, "Lady Montgomery had ordered the carriage, sir. She wishes to go to London."

"I see," Bart replied. What was she up to, he wondered? When he encountered her a short time later as she was preparing to board the carriage, he asked if she was going to pay a visit to Augusta.

"No, Bart. I'll be seeing her tomorrow, remember? You've invited her to come out here. No, I've other business to attend to in the city." With that said, she took a seat and instructed the driver to be on his way.

Bart was left to stand and wonder about this sudden change in her. It was late in the afternoon when she returned, but she had no packages, so Bart had to conclude that she'd not been into the city to shop.

But Lady Montgomery *had* shopped, and very expensively. She had purchased an entire new roomful of furnishings for her sitting room.

Just as Bart was departing to go to the docks to leave London to travel to Virginia, Lady Montgomery was summoning the four strong men who worked in the stables to move out all the old furnishings to the barn storage room so the room would be ready to accommodate her new things.

Before her sister Augusta arrived at midday, all the new furniture was in her sitting room and Lady Montgomery was feeling pleasantly smug about the changes she'd made. The pale pastels had now been changed to very bright and vivid colors. She was curious to see what Augusta's reaction would be when she stepped through the door.

As she'd expected, Augusta was slightly stunned. For a moment she could not find her tongue. "My word! I . . . I think it's charming. Laura, I thought you preferred the pale pinks and greens, and this—this is so bright."

"And cheery, Augusta?"

"Well, yes. I find it very cozy and inviting," Augusta declared. It was a room to linger comfortably in all day.

"Well, I was ready for a change, Augusta, so I just got busy."

Augusta laughed. "Well good for you, Laura!" The two sisters had tea and iced cakes in the new sitting room and enjoyed some sisterly conversation.

By the time the two ladies had enjoyed the evening meal together, Augusta had to admit that she'd never known Laura to be better company.

The next two days went by the same way and Augusta was pleasantly surprised when Laura wanted to accompany her to the study as she went over certain papers that had arrived in the two days since Bart had left.

Jason Hamilton had come by the house that afternoon, and Lady Montgomery was startled that Bart had obviously not mentioned to Jason, his best friend, that he was returning to Virginia.

"Well, all I know, Jason, is what he told me. He said he had some unfinished business to attend to there," she'd informed young Hamilton. Jason knew immediately what that "unfinished business" was.

"When did he leave, Lady Montgomery?" Jason had asked her.

"Day before yesterday. I have to confess to you that I would have not been expecting him to make such a long journey so soon after he'd returned home."

"Nor I," Jason remarked. Now he knew what his younger sister was talking about when she'd declared to him that Bart had made her a promise to bring Tawny back. That was exactly what he'd set out to do, Jason was convinced, knowing Bart as he did.

Jason would be going back, too, but he'd be arriving some three or four weeks later than Montgomery. Joy would be elated by the news he would bring back to her.

Jason should have known that he could not outsmart Montgomery. He hadn't expected him to move so swiftly! He should have known Bart's impatient nature would not allow him to linger in England if he was determined to go to Tawny. Nothing stopped Bart Montgomery from getting what he wanted!

Obviously, his best friend wanted Tawny Blair!

Jason knew that he could do nothing to stop Bart from trying to win her. In the end, it would be up to Tawny to decide between the two of them.

Right now, she was still at sea with Captain Crane, but if the *Caprice* had fair sailing, they would be making the Virginia coastline in another week or ten days, he figured.

It was three more weeks before Jason's cargo would be ready for him to sail across the Atlantic toward Virginia. His easygoing nature took hold, for there was nothing he could do to change things. He accepted what fate had handed him.

The next three weeks he spent more and more time at his ship, making her ready for the time he would sail out of the harbor, but often he found his thoughts occupied by Tawny Blair.

He often scolded himself for letting her slip away from him so easily. Damn it, he could have stopped her or at least delayed her and he hadn't! Bart would have done so, he realized.

Maybe he deserved to lose her, since he'd acted so stupidly!

Chapter 21

The *Caprice* had plowed through a very calm sea for the first fourteen days of the voyage, and Captain Crane was puzzled as to why his little passenger was suddenly having all the symptoms of seasickness. That should have hit her much sooner. The girl had no fever or chills, but she was unable to eat any of the cook's nice dinners and she'd stayed in her cabin for the last three days, feeling weak and queasy. The little kitten stayed on her bed to keep her company, and Jeff had kept a constant vigil at her cabin to check on her or bring a bowl of broth in the hope that she could eat a few spoonfuls.

Suddenly, the strange malady was over and Tawny woke up famished. Jeff was elated to bring her breakfast tray. She wasted no time beginning to eat the eggs, thick slice of ham, and flaky biscuits. When Jeff left her cabin he made a point of going to the captain to report that Miss Tawny was as fit as a fiddle again.

Captain Crane was delighted to hear Jeff's news, for he'd been concerned about his young passenger. Too many days had gone by since they'd left the coast of London for her to be suddenly suffering from seasickness, and he couldn't figure out what else it could be. But when she told him that she'd not had any ill effects when she'd crossed the Atlantic on Jason's ship, the old sea captain pondered something else:

Could little Tawny be pregnant? After all, Jason Hamilton was a handsome young fellow and he'd seen the tender embrace he'd given Tawny when he told her good-bye. He knew how two young people could get swept up in passion, so it was possible the pretty Tawny could be carrying Jason's baby.

At least she was feeling better now, and he was happy about that. He could do nothing about what had happened between Jason and Tawny before she boarded his ship. That was their business. All he knew was he was going to look after that little brown-haired miss as best he could, just as he'd want someone to take good care of his own daughter, Kathy.

Tawny felt so perky that she dressed up in one of the muslin gowns Joy had given her and brushed her tangled mass of curly hair. For the first time in days, she felt like playing with Calico. The kitten was delighted to have some attention after lying so quietly for the last few days. Tawny sighed, thinking how she was going to miss her little pet when the ship docked in Virginia.

The captain asked Tawny to his cabin to share the evening meal. Tawny brought back the sweet, cherished memories of his own family, and having her on his ship had made the long days and nights at sea less lonely.

While he'd not mentioned it to Jason Hamilton when he'd booked passage for Tawny, Crane was considering that this might just be his last voyage across the ocean. He wasn't a young man anymore and he found the task more wearing and exhausting than he had even a year ago. There was another consideration: He had a very understanding wife who had put up with his three and four month absences each trip he made. She deserved more of his time.

So, once he made the Virginia coast and got Miss Tawny safely to her destination, he'd head for home and stay there. He knew his dear Kate would be overjoyed at that decision.

It was a wonderful evening for Tawny, too, after the lonely nights alone in her cabin feeling so miserable. Captain Crane was in a talkative mood during the evening, chatting mainly about his wife and children.

"It must be a very lonely life for a married man,"

166

Tawny remarked. "A sea captain is gone so much from his family."

"That is true, Tawny. I happened to be an old bachelor when I married. I was thirty, and that's considered old. My Kate was eighteen."

"Well, it has obviously been a happy marriage, Captain Crane. I can tell from the way you talk about your family that they're very dear to you."

He chuckled. "I've only had two loves in my whole life. The sea was my first love, and then Kate and our family. I've a little secret to tell you tonight. I think this will be my last trip after I return to England. I think I'm ready to stay home, Tawny."

She smiled and patted his hand. "Well, I'm glad that I made this trip with you, Captain Crane."

"Well, so am I, Tawny, and the truth is I didn't even mention this to your friend Jason."

"When you return to England you will probably see him in the harbor. Jason loves the sea and his ship. I don't think he could be happy to be on land too long."

"And I get the feeling that you aren't that excited about the sea, young lady?" Captain Crane inquired.

"No, sir—I love the things of the land. I find the ocean a desolate sight. I can't wait to see the shores of Virginia," she confessed to him.

"Well, young lady—you don't have much longer to wait. We're less than a week away now. In fact, we're only a few days from arriving if I've figured it right. Does that make you happy?"

"Oh, it certainly does, Captain!"

It had been good to see Tawny looking so radiant tonight as they'd shared the evening meal, but once he'd seen her securely locked inside her cabin and he went back to his own cabin, he was convinced that the pretty Tawny Blair might just be having that special glow that comes to a woman's face when she's expecting a child. He recalled his Kate, and her face had never been more radiantly beautiful!

The thoughts Captain Crane was harboring never entered Tawny's pretty head. Not for one minute had she considered that possibility. All she knew was that she'd never felt so sick to her stomach in her young life. Rarely as she'd grown up had she been ill or kept Maybelle from going to the tavern to work. To feel ill was strange for Tawny.

Had she suspected what Captain Crane was pondering she would not have been feeling so happy and light-hearted as she returned to her cabin.

The day the *Caprice* arrived in Chesapeake Harbor, and its captain escorted the elegant-looking young lady from his ship, no one would have recognized her as the same young miss that had left there only a few weeks ago, trussed in jute sack wearing only her nightgown.

She was returning wearing a fancy gown and fine leather slippers on her feet. The gold-colored cape was draped around her shoulders because of the light, misting rains falling over the coast. Jason had stuffed a generous amount of money in her gold velvet reticule before he left her on the ship, so she wasn't penniless.

It was a pleasant surprise to her when Captain Crane had told her that he was going to see that she was safely delivered to her friends, the Camerons. Tawny had to admit to herself that she had been nervous about traveling all alone from the coast to Longcreek. Now she had nothing to fear.

The two of them left the *Caprice* and boarded the buggy he'd hired to take her to Longcreek. As they traveled along the dirt road toward Longcreek, Tawny knew she was not the same young girl she'd been when she was abducted that horrible night after her mother was killed.

Everything about her life had changed since that time. She'd crossed a vast ocean twice now, and she'd changed from a sweet, innocent girl to a young woman who'd been introduced to love by the handsome Lord Bart Montgomery. She'd met and lived with Jason's family on their country estate in England. All this had made a tremendous impact on the little backwoods girl.

The closer they came to Longcreek, the more excited she became. She was glad that it was midday so she could enjoy the sights as the buggy rolled down the road.

When they finally passed by the cottage that had been her home she saw a small boy and girl sitting on the steps. She knew someone else was living there now, but she told Captain Crane that was where she used to live.

He had only glance over at her lovely face to see the sadness etched there.

The old sea captain got the distinct impression that Tawny's home did not hold happy memories for her. Now that he thought about it, as often as they'd talked she had never mentioned her folks. Jason had not told him very much about the girl, either, so he found himself curious about her background.

"I was reared in a small cottage similar to that, Tawny," he told her.

"Really, Captain Crane. Was your father a sea captain like you?" she wanted to know.

"Now how did you guess that, Tawny?" he gave a good-natured chuckle. "He was, so it was born in me, I guess."

"Wish I'd had the chance to know my father. I still don't know who he was. My mother never told me and now she is dead, so I suppose I'll never know him."

"I'm . . . I'm sorry to hear that, Tawny. I think I can understand how you must feel, dear." He reached over to give her hand a fatherly pat. He felt sorry for this young lady, and his kind heart went out to her. He was tempted to insist that she attend to the business she'd come back to Virginia to take care of and get back on the *Caprice* to sail home with him. He was even tempted to invite Tawny to come live with him and Kate in their big old rambling house with its four upstairs bedrooms.

But suddenly the look of sadness was gone from Tawny's face and her brown eyes were sparkling brightly. "Oh, Captain Crane" she exclaimed, "we're here. See over there! That's Cameron Farms! Oh, how good it is going to be to see them again!"

"Looks like a mighty nice farm from here. These Camerons are your good friends then, is that right?"

"Oh, yes, sir—the dearest, sweetest people in the world."

Crane reined his buggy off the main country road to turn into the drive. Hired hands, milling around the grounds of the corral, stopped what they were doing to see who was coming to the farm.

Reba Cameron had also heard the buggy rolling up the long drive, but she didn't recognize the passengers. The husky-looking gray-haired man with a cap set jauntily on the side of his head was not familiar to her. He leaped out of the buggy and rushed around to help the young lady down.

But the minute Reba got a full view of that lovely face, she knew who the young lady was, despite her fine clothes and upswept curls.

Quickly, she leaped out of the chair to rush through the front door. She'd prayed Tawny would return someday, and now she was here.

Unashamed of the tears flowing down her cheeks, she ran down the steps to greet her guests!

Chapter 22

The captain stood by as the two ladies embraced each other with laughter and tears mingling. No one had to tell him how happy the two of them were to be reunited.

Patiently, he waited for them to finally release each other so that Tawny might introduce him. "Oh, Captain Crane — forgive me! I'd like you to meet my very dear friend, Mrs. Reba Cameron."

"My pleasure, Mrs. Cameron." The captain smiled warmly at the attractive lady standing there with her arm around Tawny.

Tawny introduced the captain to Reba and explained to her that it was his ship that had brought her back to Virginia. "He was nice enough to see me safely here."

"Well, Captain Crane," Mrs. Cameron said, "I am truly grateful. Please let me invite you into my house. I think we should all enjoy some refreshments to celebrate Tawny's homecoming."

"Oh, it is so good to be back," Tawny declared as she took hold of the captain's hand to urge him along.

"Dear, I'd like nothing better than having some refreshments, but I've got enough daylight to make it back to Chesapeake so I'm going to have to say good-bye to you right now." He patted her on the shoulder and gave her a kiss on the cheek. He turned to Reba Cameron. "I know Tawny is in good hands, so that takes a heavy burden off my mind. A pleasure to have met you, ma'am."

"You're a good man, Captain Crane, and it was my pleasure, too. I just wish that it would have been possible for you to have stayed longer. We've some awfully pretty country here in Virginia."

"Maybe there will be another time," he told her as he turned to walk away. But he was forced to take one last glance in Tawny's direction. "God be with you, Miss Tawny."

"God be with you, Captain Crane, and a safe voyage back to England." She broke away from Reba's side long enough to give the captain a hug before he leaped back up in the buggy. She stood to watch him travel back down the drive. Only when the buggy went around the bend in the road and he was no longer in sight did Tawny turn to join Reba.

But before the two of them went back to the house, Reba yelled out at one of the men there in the corral to come fetch Tawny's luggage. Then she guided her to the parlor. "Shall we have coffee or tea?" she asked.

"Coffee sounds good to me," Tawny told her, removing the cape from her shoulders. Reba agreed with that, for she'd never been much on tea.

Tawny sat alone in the parlor while Reba went to the kitchen to ask her housekeeper to brew a fresh pot of coffee.

When Reba returned to the parlor it was so good to see Tawny sitting there. "Oh, Tawny—you're home," she exclaimed. "I can't believe it! You can't imagine how worried we were about you. You will never know how wonderful it was to get your letter and know you were all right."

"So you did get my letter? Oh, I hope that Mrs. Thacher got the letter I wrote to her, too," Tawny declared.

"Well, I can't tell you about that, but your letter arrived here about ten days ago, so you can imagine my surprise when I saw you getting out of that buggy."

Tawny smiled. "Well, I had not expected to get back this soon myself, but I had to come back. I've . . . I've scores to settle, and I will!"

Tawny could not delay inquiring about Bill Cameron. "I'm so anxious to see him!"

Reba slowly set her cup down on the table next to her chair and her whole demeanor changed abruptly. "Oh, Tawny, Tawny, my darling, Bill died three weeks ago. I've dreaded having to tell you this ever since you arrived. I wish you could have seen him. He cared for you very much."

Tawny shook her head and did not try to keep the tears from coming to her eyes. The two of them sat there and gave way to their emotions. There was no reason to speak as they silently vented their grief. Reba wished that Bill had known before he died that Tawny was all right. She'd witnessed how he'd seemed to wither away after Tawny had disappeared that horrible night of Maybelle's death.

It took Tawny a long time to gain enough control of herself to ask what had caused Bill Cameron's death.

"It was his heart, Tawny. His heart just gave out. Bill had known about it for quite sometime, I guess, but he'd not said a word to me about it. Knowing Bill, he didn't want me to worry. But now I know why he decided to sell Diablo to Bart Montgomery."

Tawny nodded her head in agreement. It was obvious now why he would have thought of parting with the black Arabian.

"Oh, Tawny, it was such a blessing that you came into our lives when you did. You gave so much to Bill. He had never been happier than he was that last month when you came out here to visit us."

"Oh, I am the one who was blessed. I'd . . . I'd never known how wonderful life could be until I came out here. It changed everything for me."

"I'm glad, dear. That was what Bill and I wanted," Reba told her.

After the two of them had finished their coffee, Reba suggested that she take her to the guest bedroom to get her settled in before the dinner hour. She told Tawny then that she had taken care of all her and her mother's possessions in the cottage. "They're here, Tawny. I saw to that."

The other thing that she told Tawny was that Maybelle was buried on a plot of ground here on Cameron Farms. "That is where I also buried Bill, Tawny. We shall go there tomorrow if you'd like."

"Yes, I'd like that," Tawny replied.

Tawny turned her attention to unpacking her bags. When she opened the doors of the armoire she saw that Reba had already hung up the clothes she had left behind in the cottage. Most of them were the outfits Reba had given her during her visits to the farm back in June.

She hung up all her new gowns beside them and placed the slippers below. She suddenly realized that she now had more clothing than she'd owned in her entire life. Never had she had so many pairs of shoes!

By the time she'd placed all her undergarments in the drawers of the dresser, Tawny decided to stretch out across the bed and rest. Suddenly she felt very tired.

Before she knew it, she was fast asleep. She had intended to change her gown before she went down to meet Reba for dinner, but she ended up taking such a long nap that there was no time to change, so she simply gave the skirt some sharp shakes and brushed out her tousled hair. She'd never worn this nice a gown to sit at the Camerons' table before. It was certainly going to seem strange with Bill Cameron absent from the table, though.

She dabbed a drop of the gardenia toilet water behind her ears and on her wrists before going downstairs to join Reba.

For Reba Cameron it was wonderful to have Tawny sitting at her table to share the evening meal with her. It had been a lonely time for her without Bill there to share her evenings. The days were easier to cope with than the long, long nights. The nights seemed endless to her.

Never had she seen Tawny more beautiful. It seemed to Reba that she'd grown lovelier during the months she'd been away from Longcreek.

Her long brown hair fell around her shoulders and was not put up in the upswept curls as it had been when she'd arrived this afternoon. She looked more like the girl Reba remembered, but there was a regal grace about her that Reba had never been aware of. She decided that there was something she must do before this evening was over. When they had finished their meal and enjoyed an extra cup of coffee, she suggested to Tawny that they retire to Bill's study. "I've something to show you."

Just to step inside the oak doors leading into Bill's study was to feel his presence all around her. Tawny gazed up at the lifesize portrait of Mr. Cameron hanging over the mantel.

Reba noticed her staring up at the painting. Walking over to the liquor chest, she poured herself and Tawny each a glass of sherry. "It's a nice room, isn't it, Tawny? Here, dear—a little sherry will do us both good."

Sinking down into one of the oversize leather chairs, she took a sip of the sherry and Tawny sat down in the other chair across from her.

"Now that you're home, Tawny, I need to talk to you about some things. I'm sure by now you found your things in your room. I had Aurelia hang all your clothing in the armoire."

Tawny told her that she had seen them when she'd unpacked her bags. That was when Reba told her that she'd had Aurelia pack all of Maybelle's things away and put in the storage room in the attic. She told Tawny they'd have it brought down when she wished to look through it.

"There is no rush, for I know there was precious little my mother owned." Tawny smiled sadly.

"As for the furniture in the cottage, Tawny—"

But Tawny interrupted her. "A bonfire would have been the simplest way to dispose of that old worn stuff," she said.

"Well, there were a few pieces that Bill gave to one of his hired hands who had nothing to speak of, Tawny. I hope that was all right. We had no idea when you'd come back and we had to get everything out of the cottage. We did not wish to leave anything there for the landlord to take. He wasn't exactly pleasant to deal with."

"Mother was probably behind in paying him the rent, I'd imagine. She often was. I . . . I am beholden to you and Mr. Cameron for doing what you did for me and my mother."

"Well, dear—it wasn't really all that much," Reba declared. Hesitating to do what she knew she must, she stood and went to the desk and pulled out the drawer. "There was one thing we found in your mother's things, Tawny, that was of value." She took out the small box with the initialed gold ring in it.

"This belongs to you now," she told Tawny, handing it to her.

Tawny opened the box lid and saw the ring with the initial B on it. "I . . . I never saw this," she stammered.

"No, I didn't think you had, Tawny. Your mother had the ring in a concealed spot in her drawer and tied up in a scarf."

"But why would she have done that? I would have figured her to want to wear it."

"Oh, no, dear. She would never have worn that ring for a very good reason."

Tawny looked at her with a quizzical expression on her face. "Why do you say that?"

"Because, Tawny, that ring belonged to your father and Maybelle didn't want you or anyone knowing who he was. Look at the ring, child."

Tawny's long lashes fluttered, and the wildest thoughts went racing through her head. She stared down at the initial B on the gold ring. Reba saw no reason to delay telling Tawny that it was her Bill who was her father.

"I might as well come right out with it. That B stands for Bill—my Bill. He was your father, honey. He didn't know it—never knew it until we found this in Maybelle's things."

Tawny gasped and clutched the ring. "Oh, God—Mr.

Cameron was my father?" Tears and then a smile came to her face. The very thought that that wonderful man was her father filled her with overwhelming joy.

"That's right, honey. I can't tell you the whole story, for I don't know it. Bill didn't even know it. But I can tell you all I know, for I guess Maybelle's side of the story went to the grave with her."

Reba explained that Bill had told her that the ring had been given to him by his father when he was eighteen. He and Maybelle had been very young when they met. Bill was a rowdy, irresponsible young man in his twenties and Maybelle was a local farmer's daughter. They had one brief romantic interlude, and then went their own ways.

"This was long before I came into Bill's life, for he was in his thirties when I married him. You must have been a tot when we married. Maybelle never came to him and told him that she was expecting his child, Tawny. He didn't even know that she still lived around these parts, he told me."

As Reba was talking, Tawny slipped the ring on her finger, for that is where she wished it to be.

"So many years had gone by that Bill never associated the name Blair with a young girl he'd known as Maybelle Blair. But I can tell you that he was thrilled to find out that you were his daughter and that he'd come to know you. We often talked about the strange event that brought you into our lives, Tawny. Bill swore that it was meant to be. I am convinced of that, too."

Before the two ladies left the study to go up the stairs, Tawny was convinced that there was no woman on the face of the earth sweeter or nicer than Reba Cameron.

Reba had told her that after Bill died, she had made a new will, deeding everything to her. "It is your rightful inheritance, Tawny, and this is what Bill would want. We had no children. It should all go to you."

She told Reba good night and kissed her tenderly on the cheek. It had been a very unsettling day for Tawny Blair. So much had happened in the last six months that she found it hard to sort it all out.

But there was one thing she did know, and that was that she was happy to be home! Cameron Farms did seem like her home and now she knew why.

Chapter 23

Aurelia gave Tawny a warm welcome the next morning as she served breakfast. Some of the hired hands recognized the pretty young girl who'd come to Cameron Farms and smiled at her as they moved around the corral.

When they boarded the buggy to go to the plot of ground where Maybelle and Bill had been buried, the men in the corral watched the two striking ladies leaving, but they didn't know that they were gazing upon the future mistress of Cameron Farms.

It was one of those perfect days, with bright sunshine and a calm, gentle breeze rustling through the trees as the buggy rolled up the narrow dirt trail. They traveled toward a high slope of ground in a cluster of trees. It was this slope that Bill had considered one of the most beautiful spots on the farm, for it looked down on the green Virginia countryside and his home.

There was a small clearing where the two graves were, surrounded by tall trees. Tawny knew that it had to be Reba who'd planted all the clusters of wildflowers she spied growing around the plot.

Tawny bent down by the side of her mother's grave and bowed her head in silence. After a few moments, she rose up to stand beside Reba at her husband's grave. She still found it hard to believe that the wonderful Bill Cameron had been her father.

It was Tawny who broke the silence. "It was thoughtful of you to plant the flowers here," she said.

"Bouquets brought from my gardens would have

179

faded fast, so I decided to plant something that could bloom most of the time." Then she turned to Tawny, asking her if she was ready to go back.

As they traveled back to the house, Tawny found it ironic that Maybelle was buried next to the man who'd sired her child, and that Cameron's wife had arranged it that way. Few women would have been as generous toward Maybelle Blair as Reba had been. Tawny could never forget that.

The rest of the day went by quickly for Tawny as she went through the boxes of Maybelle's belongings.

As they were dining later, Tawny inquired about the little brown mare, Coco.

"She is in the stables, ready for you to ride her anytime you'd like, Tawny. Remember she is your horse."

"Then I think I will take her out tomorrow. I'd like to pay a visit to my friend, Mrs. Thacher. She was always so good to me," Tawny declared.

"I remember you speaking about her. Yes, that would delight her, I'm sure. I'm certain she has been very concerned about your whereabouts."

After they had retired to the parlor after dinner Tawny revealed to Reba Cameron her plans after she'd paid a visit to Roberta Thacher. "I've a score to settle now that I am back in Longcreek. I know one of the men who caused my mother's death, Reba."

Reba sat up in her chair with an intense look on her face.

"Yes, I recognized him, and I was shattered to find him a part of the evil plan. I always thought he was a very nice fellow when I saw him around town. The other one was not known to me, but I heard his name when Joe was talking to him that night when they took me away."

"I read and reread that letter of yours when it arrived and imagined what a frightful night that must have been for you, honey. But you didn't mention any names in your letter."

"I know I didn't. I always knew I was going to come back here. I wanted to face Joe Sawyer. I wanted him to know that I recognized him that night. I intend that he pay for what he had a part in," Tawny muttered with the venom of hate churning within her as she recalled that night.

A strange look came to Reba's face. "So that is what has ailed Joe all this time!" she said in disbelief. "Tawny, honey, you could stand before Joe Sawyer for hours and he wouldn't recognize you. You could talk to him until you were blue in the face and he wouldn't understand a word you were saying—you or anyone else. But now I understand what made him go crazy in the head. They say he just sits in a chair and rocks. Neighbors have taken pity on his poor wife and kids, helping her work their farm since Joe got this way. Dear Lord!"

"Well, I guess a higher power took care of him for me," Tawny declared. "I feel no sorrow for him. He showed no pity for my mother or me! There is still the other man to deal with, though."

"And what was the name you heard that night, Tawny?" Reba asked her.

"His name was Pete, and he and Joe were obviously pals."

"Then that could only have been one man—Pete Farrell. He was a neighbor of the Sawyers."

"*Was?* Has he moved away from Longcreek?"

"No, Tawny. He got himself killed right there at the same tavern where Maybelle worked. Got in a fight with some guy and the man stabbed him. So it would seem that this matter has been taken care of for you," Reba told her.

"Well, I guess you are right, Reba," she sighed. "I am glad that I can lay it to rest. I know that my mother was no fine lady like you or Mrs. Thacher, but she didn't deserve what those two did to her."

"Of course she didn't, Tawny. But put all that behind you now, dear. You've got a wonderful life ahead of you. I don't have to tell you that this home is yours to share with me as long as I live and after that, it's all yours."

"Oh, Reba, I don't know what to say to you. In a whole lifetime I'd never be able to repay you for all you've done for me."

What Reba had not yet told her was there was an account in Tawny's name at the bank, established at the same time she'd changed her will after Bill's death.

Few in the town of Longcreek would have envisioned the daughter of Maybelle Blair as a wealthy young lady before she reached her eighteenth birthday. And Tawny did not yet realize this herself.

It was a mild September day when Tawny dressed in one of the riding ensembles Reba had given her months ago and went galloping out of the grounds of Cameron Farms to pay a visit to Roberta Thacher. She had already prepared herself that it was going to be a difficult moment for her to go near the spot where Maybelle's body had lain on the ground. Just the sight of the cottage was going to bring back many unhappy memories. But she could not allow that to stop her from going to Mrs. Thacher's.

As she and Coco approached the two small cottages on the country lane, she was not affected as she had expected to be. Maybe it was her enthusiasm to see Mrs. Thacher, or maybe it was because her revenge had now been satisfied. Maybelle was now at peace with the world where she'd never found happiness.

When Tawny knocked on the door and Roberta opened it to find Tawny standing there, it was like a prayer had been answered for Roberta. The letter had eased the worry, but she had doubted that she'd ever see little Tawny again. But here she stood, looking more beautiful than ever.

Neither of them spoke; they just embraced. When

they finally released each other, wiping the tears of joy from their faces, Roberta led her onto her small, cozy parlor. "Mercy, child," she said, "I never thought I'd get to see that sweet face of yours again. When did you get back to Longcreek?"

"Two days ago. I'm staying with Reba Cameron."

"I know she was as happy to see you as I am. Fine lady, that Mrs. Cameron. Sure was sorry to hear about her husband dying a while back," Roberta told her.

A visit to Roberta's cottage always meant her fresh-baked cookies and hot chocolate, and so it was today. Roberta insisted that she tell her about the young Englishman whose ship she was aboard.

"I met Jason and his friend when they came to Cameron Farms to purchase Mr. Cameron's Arabian. It just happened to be his ship I found myself on when I was abducted that night. Jason took me to his home to stay with his family until he could book passage for me to return to Virginia."

"Sounds like he must be a mighty fine young man!"

"Oh, Jason is wonderful!" Tawny exclaimed.

Roberta immediately assumed that her little Tawny was in love with the young man. She listened to her tell about the palatial estate where his family lived on the outskirts of London. How glowingly she spoke about the young man's family and how nice they had been to her.

"Mercy, Tawny—I'm surprised that you wanted to leave there to return to Longcreek," Roberta laughed.

"I had to, Mrs. Thacher. I had to know what had become of my poor mother, and I could not rest until I knew that justice had been done to the two men who killed her. Now I am satisfied, and I have seen my mother's grave."

"And will you go back to London?"

"I'm not sure what I will do. Reba wants me to stay at Cameron Farms with her," Tawny told her.

"Can't deny that I'd like to see you stay here in

183

Longcreek."

Tawny patted her hand and declared that she'd certainly be here for a while. She realized that she should be getting back to the farm, for time had gone by quickly as the two of them had chatted, enjoying their reunion.

"I'll come by again in a few days, Mrs. Thacher," she promised as she got up to leave.

But there was something else urging Tawny to take her departure from the cottage. She was beginning to feel that miserable, queasy feeling she'd suffered on Captain Crane's ship. She did not prolong her farewell but got up on Coco to quickly gallop away. When she was around the bend of the road and out of sight, she pulled up on the reins. Oh, that queasiness could not be the result of eating Mrs. Thacher's delicious cookies, and she could hardly be seasick, now that she was on land!

After a while, she spurred Coco into motion, but as she rode toward the farm, she was faced with a new possibility. What was happening to her on the ship might have been seasickness, but now she knew better. The many things that had happened to her lately had put her head in a whirl.

Arriving in England with Jason and that marvelous week spent there had been so exciting to her. Being around Jason's sisters and parents had made her forget that she had not had her monthly period. That possibility had not dawned on her during the weeks that she'd been aboard the *Caprice*. She was questioning herself even now. Had it been seven or eight weeks now? She wasn't sure.

But there was one thing for certain: she might be carrying Bart's child. Was she going to follow in her mother's footsteps? Would she have a child who would grow up without a father?

When she arrived at the barn and turned Coco over to one of the hired hands, she slowly walked toward the house, a firm decision made. With her perky head held high, she vowed that she would not be another Maybelle Blair! She'd go back to England and demand that Bart Montgomery marry her. She'd not have his bastard and allow him not to assume responsibility for his act.

As she entered the house, she was glad that she did not encounter Reba, for many things were occupying her thoughts and she needed to be alone for a while.

She had more to consider besides herself, Tawny realized. There were changes to be made in her plans and this was what she must think about in the solitude of her room.

Chapter 24

It was a quiet, subdued Tawny who Reba Cameron encountered at dinner, and she wondered what had caused this change in mood. She could not imagine that her visit with Roberta Thacher had been anything but pleasant. Whatever it was that was troubling Tawny tonight had nothing to do with Mrs. Thacher. But it was obvious that Tawny did not feel free to discuss it with her, so Reba did not press her to do so.

"Was it nice to take a ride on Coco today, Tawny?" Reba asked her.

"Oh, yes. She's such a feisty little thing." She told her how the fiery Arabian had gotten out of hand on the ship and how she'd gone down in the hold to calm him when Bart's expert trainer could not accomplish it.

"Ah, that beautiful Diablo," Reba sighed, recalling the magnificence of the beast.

"Well, you can rest assured that Diablo is living a very fine life." She described the sprawling green estate belonging to the Montgomery family and the Hamiltons' country place that was adjacent to it.

Reba smiled at the young lady who seemed to have suddenly come out of her quiet mood. "You know, Tawny, I was just sitting here thinking that you're not yet eighteen and you've seen more of the world than I have. You have crossed the ocean twice now, and you've seen England."

"I had never thought about it, Reba, but I guess my whole life changed from the moment I came here to Cameron Farms. Remember, I met Jason and Bart here."

"It is strange about life, Tawny. The older I've gotten, the more I realize that but for this or that, our lives would go a different way!"

When the two of them left the parlor to go upstairs to their bedrooms, Reba was pleased to see Tawny acting in a more lighthearted manner. Whatever might have been troubling her seemed to be swept away.

But the perceptive Reba Cameron wondered which one of these two young men attracted the pretty Tawny. Was it the handsome Jason Hamilton with his engaging black eyes, or was it the dashing young fair-haired lord, Bart Montgomery?

She remembered that it was Jason who'd taken Tawny home that afternoon when they were here at the farm. But as a woman, she knew that the imposing figure of Bart Montgomery was enough to turn any woman's head.

When her head rested on the pillow that night, she felt Bill's presence surrounding her. Somehow she felt that she knew that he was looking down on them. He was surely happy that his daughter was back at Cameron Farms where she belonged!

Bart Montgomery was no seaman like Jason, but he had not been out to sea three days before he realized that this ship was nothing like the slick-lined *Sea Princess*.

He wasn't one to roam the decks of any ship, so he spent little time up there with the other passengers. He stayed mainly in his cabin. Time hung heavily on his hands, and there were times when he pondered his sanity about making this impulsive voyage to seek out a pretty girl who'd made him take leave of his senses.

It was a little too late to question his impulsiveness now. He was on his way to Virginia to find Tawny Blair. There was no denying that a part of the urgency to make this voyage was to get even with Jason after the dirty trick he'd played on him.

It seemed he and little Tawny were alike when they felt that they'd been wronged. She'd gone back to Virginia to seek revenge against the men who'd been responsible for her mother's death. He had to admire her spirit and courage. His only hope was that he'd not arrive too late to keep her from getting herself in a mess. Once he got there, he would be more than ready to help her take on the evil pair.

At night, when he lay in his bunk to sleep, his dreams were haunted by Tawny, with her dreamy brown eyes and soft, silken flesh. The intimate moments they had shared were relived as he lay there alone in his bunk and he'd find himself swelling with yearning to encircle her in his arms and make love to her again. He found himself eagerly marking off each day he was at sea.

When the voyage was into the fifteenth day, Bart chanced to meet the captain of the ship out on deck. "Good day to you, sir. Seems as though we're plowing right along. Have we got to the halfway mark yet?" Bart inquired of him.

"Can't say as we've got there yet, Lord Montgomery, but as you said, we're moving along quite smoothly," he answered.

Recalling the number of days it had taken Jason going and returning, Bart was crestfallen to hear that news. But the captain's next remark really put Montgomery into a frenzy. " 'Course, the minute we hit the East Coast don't mean you'll be arriving at your destination, Lord Montgomery. I've two other port of calls before I go southward to the Virginia coast."

Bart's brows arched and a frown creased his face. There was a sharp, snapping quality to his voice when he questioned the captain. "What's this? What are you talking about? My passage was booked for a small port in Virginia."

"And that is where you will go, my friend, but not before we stop in Boston and New York. Then we go on down toward Norfolk. That little dock at Chesapeake is your stop, isn't it?"

Bart was so riled he found it hard to speak. "That's right," he muttered. "No one informed me of this when I booked."

"Well, perhaps you didn't think to ask," the captain declared casually as he left Bart standing to glare at his back as he marched on down the deck of his ship.

But what the captain had said was true: he had not asked if the ship was going directly to Virginia. There was not doubt that all these calls could delay his arrival by a week or so. When he reached his cabin door, he was seething with irritation and beginning to wonder if this was to be an ill-fated venture that he'd live to regret.

But his hands were tied and there was not one thing he could do to change the situation. The captain gave the orders and nothing was going to change that.

Captain Hemphill had an amused grin on his face when he walked away from the young Englishman. He saw the surprise on his arrogant face when he informed him that his ship did not go directly to Virginia from England. He got the very distinct impression that Lord Montgomery was accustomed to having things his own way.

The young man was just going to have to fret and fume, the rugged old captain thought to himself as he went about his duties.

Bart decided to ease his black mood and anger by indulging himself with several sips of the whiskey from his flask. He could not think of anything to make the miserable evening pass faster.

After three or four sips, he began to feel relaxed, so he removed his leather boots and propped his feet up on the small, square table in the center of his cabin. By the time he'd sat there for another hour, he found he had no need for the evening meal. But he suddenly felt the need to lay his head on the pillow, so he stumbled out of the chair to fling himself across the bed.

That night he did not dream of Tawny, but he woke up with a very nasty, throbbing headache and he recalled why he had it. The whiskey had done nothing to change the circumstances.

Now that he accepted what he could not change, it seemed to make the days go by faster. Finally, he was to hear from one of the sailors that the port of Boston was straight ahead. That was the best news that Bart could have heard.

He was even happier that the ship did not linger in Boston.

As the sun was setting over the bay, the ship started to move out through the lapping waters thrusting against its hull.

Bart returned to his cabin with his spirits lifted, and he joined the others for dinner. He met the new passengers who'd boarded the ship in Boston. There was a couple going to Norfolk and a young man traveling to Hampton, Virginia, to his new position as a teacher.

Bart had thought he had seen two ladies and two men getting on the ship, and when he inquired about that to the teacher, Travis Woods, he was told that he had been right. There was another lady, but she'd wished to dine in her room tonight. "That was Miss Norton, and I'm not sure where she's going," Woods had told Bart.

After the meal, Bart bid them all a gracious farewell and went to his room. Tossing aside his coat and unbuttoning his shirt, he sat down to remove his boots. Enjoying one of his favorite cheroots and a nightcap would put him in the mood to retire, he figured.

He took a puff and followed it with a sip of whiskey. That was about the time he heard a soft rapping on his door and a female voice calling out to him. "Lord Montgomery, I'm Darla Norton. May I speak with you a moment, please?"

A puzzled look came to Bart Montgomery as he moved slowly out of the chair and started to button up his shirt—all but the top three buttons.

He opened the door and addressed her. "Miss Norton, is it?" His blue eyes quickly surveyed the young woman he judged to be in her twenties. She wasn't an unattractive lady, but neither was she a pretty one, Bart considered as he looked at her face and golden-blond hair.

"Yes, Darla Norton, Lord Montgomery."

He invited her into his cabin, finding himself a little curious as to how she knew his name."

"Oh, thank you so much. I know I'm being very forward to come to your cabin like this," she cooed in a certain tone that Montgomery immediately recognized.

"Oh, I'm sure you must have a reason." Bart smiled, prepared to play his own little game with her if he must.

"Oh, I did! I understand that you are going to Chesapeake, too, and I thought that was a strange coincidence. I'm going there, too!"

"I guess you could say that, Miss Norton," he replied.

"Oh, please—just call me Darla," she purred sweetly. He was like a handsome blond-haired god, she thought, with those sparking, flashing bright blue eyes of his. But when she found out by chance this afternoon that he was an English lord, she had decided to take advantage of an opportunity that might never come her way again.

Darla was no shy violet and she was certainly no sweet innocent miss. A few gentlemen in Boston could attest to that. This was one of the reasons Darla had decided to move on to another part of the country.

There was a particular reason she'd picked the small area around Chesapeake, Virginia, to cast her lot. The chance meeting of Bart Montgomery was just an extra bonus in her scheme of things.

But Bart instantly saw the boldness in her darting eyes when she looked at him, and he was not about to fall into her little trap.

He'd met enough women like Darla Norton to last him a lifetime!

Chapter 25

A more contemptuous, brazen woman Bart Montgomery had never met. He found that it was impossible to take a stroll on the deck without her suddenly appearing at his side. Darla Norton was becoming a nuisance.

When she knocked on his door in the evening, he ignored it. The next day when she mentioned it to him, he shrugged it off, "I'm a deep sleeper, Darla," he told her. "Nothing wakes me up after I go to sleep."

He was anxious to get to Chesapeake and be rid of her once and for all. But there were still several miles of the eastern coastline to travel before the Virginia shores appeared. It was certainly going to be a welcome sight to him, and, he was glad he'd be traveling on to Longcreek, away from Chesapeake where she said she was stopping.

Captain Hemphill had a remarkable insight about the people traveling on his ship, and there were always passengers who intrigued him. This trip, it was the handsome young Englishman, Bart Montgomery and the foxy little Miss Norton. If ever he'd seen a woman in hot pursuit of a gentleman it was Darla Norton. He'd watched her go through her antics and he found the whole thing amusing. He wagered that Montgomery was going to be hard put to shake her loose. That lady was like a barracuda. He had wondered if she would have been so obsessed with Montgomery if he'd just told her that the man's name was Bart Montgomery when she'd asked him. He'd made the bad mistake of telling her that he was *Lord* Bart Montgomery. Hemphill knew exactly what kind of woman Miss Darla Norton was.

The voyage was nearly over now, and Montgomery would be out of his misery once they arrived in Chesapeake. Perhaps he should let Montgomery know that the ship would be docking in Chesapeake the day after tomorrow.

He got that opportunity the very next afternoon when he happened to meet Bart, who was lucky enough to be enjoying a stroll alone.

"Afternoon, Captain Hemphill," Bart greeted him.

"A good afternoon, Lord Montgomery. A fine, fine afternoon it is, too. You're going to be getting to Chesapeake at a wonderful time of the year. Tomorrow should find you there, barring any bad luck. I am sure that pleases you."

Bart's blue eyes sparked brightly at that news. "Really, Captain?"

"That's right. I know it is a little later than you'd been expecting, but you're almost there now," the captain assured him, as he observed the obvious delight on the Englishman's face.

"Well, I can't deny that I wanted to arrive in Chesapeake sooner, but that doesn't matter now. I couldn't have had any better news."

The captain bid him good-bye and went on his way. Bart turned in the opposite direction to return to his cabin, the best way he knew to avoid Darla Norton. Tonight he decided that the sweet, peaceful solitude of his cabin would be where he'd stay, and he'd have dinner there, too. Tomorrow he planned to make a very hasty departure from the ship.

After a pleasant dinner tray, Bart packed all his belongings in anticipation of the arrival tomorrow in Chesapeake. It was that time of evening for him to enjoy his favorite cheroot and his usual nightcap before he retired for the night.

Because the evening had gone by so quietly, he was feeling smug. Maybe, just maybe, Darla had finally gotten the message that he'd been trying to get through to her for the last few days—that he was not interested in her.

But he was not to be spared. A sudden rap on his door brought him out of his serene mood. Her voice called out to him. "Lord Montgomery—are you all right? You aren't sick, are you?"

At first he made no reply, hoping she would just move on down the passageway to her own cabin. Instead, she kept calling out to him, and he knew that his silence was not going to quiet her.

"No, Darla, I'm fine, but I can't invite you in. I'm working on some papers. Good night!"

"Oh, Lord Montgomery," she drawled. "And here I stand with a nice piece of cake to give you. It would be a delicious snack if you are working so late."

"Thank you, Darla, but I'm not hungry. You take it to your cabin and enjoy it. I have no intention of interrupting my work right now." He muttered impatiently. Damn, she was a bloody pest!

She grimaced and heaved a disgusted sigh. "Well, I'm very sorry I bothered you, Lord Montgomery. I'll say good night to you then," she told him. Her voice was trying to project to him that he had wounded her feelings. The truth was that Darla was very riled that she could not seduce this man, as she had so many others in the past.

Bart suspected that she was only putting on the grand act of being hurt. She was just irked that he hadn't opened his door to her. He just hoped that Captain Hemphill did not alert her to their arrival in Chesapeake tomorrow. He prayed it would come as an abrupt surprise to her.

Right now he was just grateful that she had left his door!

It would have pleased Bart to know that Hemphill

had not mentioned a word to Miss Norton when she had inquired about Montgomery's absence at dinner this evening. He figured to do the young man a favor.

Bart was ready to depart the ship the minute it came to the small dock in Chesapeake. He was dressed and his luggage was placed by the door before he left his cabin to have a hearty breakfast. At least this was a time when he didn't have to worry about Darla coming around. She never stirred from her cabin so early.

By the time he'd finished his ham and eggs, he couldn't believe that he was experiencing the motionless pause of the ship. Had they pulled into the docks, he wondered?

He was pleasantly surprised to see that they had, and he recognized the sights he'd seen when Jason's ship was moored here and they'd taken the brief trip to Longcreek.

Quickly, he turned around to go to his cabin to get his luggage. He slammed into the captain. "I better tell you good-bye now, Captain Hemphill, for I'm leaving quickly and I'll not have another chance to say farewell. My best to you, sir!"

"I understand, son, and my best to you, too," Hemphill replied, watching him make a mad dash across the deck.

Bart managed to get away from the ship without Darla trailing beside him, but as he jauntily marched along the wharf toward the local livery, he glanced back over his shoulder two or three times to see if he could spy her blond head back in the crowd of people on the wharf.

He arranged to hire a horse to ride to Longcreek, and with his one small piece of luggage secured, he mounted up. It was certainly not like sitting astraddle Diablo, but then there was only one black Arabian like Diablo!

196

Having paid the fee to the livery man, he was ready to rein the horse out of the wide doors of the livery. "You oughta' make Longcreek before sunset, mister," the livery man called out to him.

A familiar voice broke through the livery, and Bart saw Darla Norton standing with her reticule in one hand and her luggage in the other. "Well, Lord Montgomery—if you'd hired a buggy I would have asked you for a ride to Longcreek. That's where I'm heading."

"Well, ma'am—I didn't know that." He smiled as he spurred the horse into motion, thankful that he'd decided to get a horse instead of a buggy.

But that sly smile on his face faded when he heard what she'd said. A frown took its place. He thought she'd told him that she was coming to Chesapeake, and now she was saying that she was traveling on to Longcreek. He knew he was not mistaken about that: She had said she was going to Chesapeake.

Bart found that the little roan could not compare to Diablo, but she set a fair pace, and they were approaching Longcreek as the sun was setting. At least he was well ahead of Darla! There was no selection of lodging, for there was only one inn. Greenfield's Inn could provide him with a room and meals and that was enough to satisfy Bart.

By the time darkness was shrouding the small village, Bart had secured a stable at the inn's livery for the horse and been shown to his room at the inn. It was clean and cozy even though it was not luxurious. But luxury wasn't important to him. It was just a place to stay until he could find Tawny. The first place he planned to go the next day was to Cameron Farms.

That evening he dined with the other lodgers at the inn in a homey room with a long table and several chairs lining each side of the table. He was pleasantly surprised by the tasty foods served. The guests could eat as much as they desired from the huge bowls of vegetables and platters of several kinds of meat. The desserts were almost as good as Hattie's, and the selection ranged from pies to three different kinds of cake. Bart was pleasantly sated by the time he got up from the table.

There had been a very nice group of lodgers around the table and Bart had enjoyed the casual conversation he'd shared with those sitting next to him and across the table. The cost of a night's lodging here did not come cheap since it was the only lodging in Longcreek, besides a rundown hotel.

If Darla Norton did not have some family here, then Montgomery figured it would probably be the hotel where she would go. Coming to this conclusion made him feel relaxed, so he didn't glance up constantly while he was dining to see her bouncing through the archway into the dining room.

After the tremendous meal, he felt the need to exercise, so he left the dining room to have a walk before he went upstairs to his room.

Up the street he could see the lights of a local tavern and he could hear boisterous laughter echoing down the street. Bart knew that this must be the place where Tawny's mother Maybelle had worked.

He walked in that direction and puffed on his cheroot as he ambled along. The street where he was walking was quiet except the noise from the tavern. Everyone else was obviously at home for the night.

Some two hundred feet short of reaching the tavern, Bart turned around to walk back to the lodging house. When he was about ready to turn into the walkway of the inn, he spied a buggy coming at a fast pace down the street. There was no mistaking that bright blond head of Darla's guiding the buggy she'd hired at the same livery where he'd last seen her.

Bart quickly ducked behind a huge flowering shrub and prayed that she had not spotted him. God, that woman had been a pain in the neck to him on the ship! He certainly was not going to put up with her

198

now that he was in Longcreek.

Luck was with him this time, for her buggy kept rolling down the street. Bart heaved a relieved sigh and came from behind the shrug to go into the inn.

Tonight there was only one woman on his mind and that was Tawny Blair!

Chapter 26

Tawny's return to Longcreek had filled a lonely void for Reba Cameron. Just to have her in the house and sharing the meals at that long table in the dining room made life more pleasant.

She and Tawny seemed to share many things in common, Reba was now realizing. After Maybelle died, Tawny had no family. Reba's parents had been dead for a long time and she had only one sister, who lived a long way from Virginia. They'd not seen each other for years. Polly had never visited her after she married Bill Cameron and somehow the opportunity for Reba to go to her never came around.

A year ago, Polly had died, but Reba had not even known about it until two or three months later. Finally she'd received a letter from Polly's daughter informing her about her mother's death. Reba had written to the girl and expressed her deep resentment that she was not informed sooner that her only sister had died. She was not feeling too kindly toward her niece for being so irresponsible and thoughtless.

That had been the last contact she had had with her. Reba had figured that her scorching letter was not well received.

Polly had not been one to write often through the years, but Reba had sensed that Polly's life was not too easy after her husband died a few years earlier. Her one and only daughter was no source of joy to Polly.

So Reba considered that she had no family left, either, after Polly died. To have lost her beloved Bill this year caused her to feel completely alone in the world. But now Tawny was here with her, and while she knew that the day would come when the girl would leave, she was going to enjoy the time they would share together.

If Darla Norton's plans went the way she'd plotted them, last night was the only night she'd sleep in the shabby room of that rundown hotel in Longcreek. She'd wondered where that snob of an Englishman, Montgomery, was laying his head. She didn't have enough money left in her reticule to afford even one night's lodging in the Greenfield's Lodging Inn, which was probably where he was staying.

The truth was, after she'd bought her passage to Virginia and hired a buggy to get her to Longcreek, she barely had enough to rent this miserable-looking room and buy herself a meal at a nearby cafe.

Darla couldn't sleep, for she had to ask herself what she'd do in this backwoods place if her aunt would not take her in. This was hardly Boston!

She was going to have to put a heck of an act on for her aunt, for everything depended upon that. At least she'd learned something when she'd struck up a conversation with the young waitress at the cafe. She figured that since it was such a small hamlet, anyone in the town would surely know her aunt, so she'd asked the waitress how she could get to Cameron Farms. "I'm the niece of Bill and Reba Cameron," she'd boasted.

"Really? Well, it was sure too bad about Mr. Bill dying. He was a very loved, respected man around here," the waitress told her.

Darla quickly picked up on that cue. "Oh, I know he was. I know my dear aunt Reba must be terribly lonely," she remarked sadly.

By the time she'd left the small cafe, Darla figured that this might just be the stroke of luck she needed, for she recalled from her mother's reaction how lonely an old widow lady could be after her husband died. So Darla was feeling much better by the time she got back to her small hotel room. She might just find herself a cozy nest with her wealthy aunt.

But she was still nervous about the first meeting they would have tomorrow. She'd laid out her simple blue-flowered frock and a blue satin bow to tie back her blond hair. She wanted to look sweet and girlish tomorrow, so she'd tone down her makeup. A painted face would not do to meet this aunt of hers.

She removed the small flask from her reticule and took a sip of the liquor in hopes that it would hasten her to sleep so she could look her best in the morning. She planned to get an early start out to wherever this Cameron Farms was.

After six hours sleep, Darla was up and ready to get dressed. She figured that an early-morning arrival at the farm would not be considered rude, since farm people always got up early, from what she'd been told by her mother.

While she could have used a couple of cups of black coffee, she decided to hold on to the few coins left in her reticule. Once she arrived at her aunt's there would be plenty of coffee.

She went directly from her room to the livery to get her buggy. In a short time, she was pulling into the drive of Cameron Farms. Darla was already impressed as she went under the archway with the name Cameron printed there. She could see the sprawling big house and stables a short distance away. The property was all fenced in and everything she saw told her that the Camerons were wealthy to own such a place as this.

A few hired hands were milling around the barnyard as her buggy pulled up at the hitching post, but around the house, she saw no one, so she got down from the buggy and secured the reins to the hitching post before going up the path to the front steps.

It was Aurelia who opened the door to admit Darla. Darla announced to the huge black servant that she was Reba's niece.

Aurelia tilted her kerchiefed head slightly. She'd never heard Miss Reba ever mention any niece in all the years she'd worked here. "You say you Miss Reba's niece?"

"That is exactly what I said! Will you please tell her I'm here," Darla said with a snapping tone to her voice.

"Come this way, ma'am," Aurelia urged. She guided Darla to the parlor and told her to please have a seat. "I'll serve you some coffee if you'd like. Miss Reba ain't awake yet, and nobody wakes her until she is ready to get up."

There was an instant dislike between Darla and Reba's black servant and both of them realized it. But Darla told her that yes, she would like some coffee, so Aurelia left the parlor to go to her kitchen. She'd serve her coffee, but she'd not go upstairs to wake Miss Reba. She never did that for no one!

Aurelia returned with the carafe of coffee on a tray. "When does my aunt usually get up in the morning?" Darla asked her.

"Miss Reba gets up whenever the notion strikes her to, miss. Sometimes she gets up early and sometimes she sleeps very late."

The servant set down the carafe and left Darla sitting there alone. Darla glared at her with contempt as Aurelia shuffled out of the room. She didn't like that smart-mouthed servant at all!

She sat there all alone enjoying one cup of steaming hot coffee and then another. It gave her the time to survey the elegant room and the furnishings. A handsome price had been paid for the things she saw in the room. She found herself curious to see this aunt of hers, and wondered if she would bear some resemblance to her own mother.

203

When Tawny had put on the gold-colored riding outfit that Reba had given to her some months ago, it had fit perfectly, but this morning she'd noticed that the waistband of the divided skirt was a little snug. The gold vest would not button with ease, either, so she left it unbuttoned. That Aurelia just fixed too many good meals and she planned to tell her so this morning when she went downstairs.

Giving her hair a few strokes of the brush, she took no time to tie it back with a ribbon nor did she wish to wear the felt hat. Tawny found herself famished for breakfast, so she bounced down the steps and made her way to the kitchen where she knew she'd find Aurelia. As she often did when Reba was still sleeping, she would sit in the kitchen at the little worktable so she could talk to Aurelia.

"Lordy, now aren't you a pretty sight this morning!" Aurelia said with a broad smile on her ebony face.

Tawny returned her smile and giggled. "I tell you, Aurelia, I can't even button my vest 'cause you feed me too good, but I love it! And I'm starved!"

"Well, you sit yourself down and Aurelia will take care of that!"

Aurelia brought her a cup of coffee and a thick slice of the fried ham out of the skillet. When the plate was filled with eggs and biscuits, Aurelia served it to Tawny.

"Lordy, that looks good, Aurelia!" Tawny told her, wasting no time in starting to eat it.

When Tawny was devouring her food, Aurelia sat down at the table with her, having a cup of coffee. "You ever hear Miss Reba talking about any niece, Miss Tawny?" she asked confidentially.

"A niece, Aurelia? No, I can't say that I have."

"Well, there's one claiming to be, right now, out there in the parlor. I never hear her talk about one and I've been here a long time, Miss Tawny."

204

Tawny stopped eating and looked at Aurelia. "What is it, Aurelia? What's bothering you? You know you and I can talk."

"Know we can, Miss Tawny, but there's something about this girl I don't like. You know what I'm trying to say. I know you love Miss Reba like I do and I get the feeling that this lady is up to no good!"

"Well, I'll go in and see if I get the same feelings, too, before I leave for my ride on Coco. Would that make you feel better, Aurelia?"

Aurelia nodded her head. "Oh, that sure would, Miss Tawny!"

"What did you tell her when she arrived and asked about Reba?"

"I told her no one wakes Miss Reba up and I served her some coffee," Aurelia declared. Tawny gave a soft laugh and patted the servant's shoulder.

"I'll go to the parlor and introduce myself," Tawny said.

Aurelia gave her a nod of approval and Tawny left the kitchen and walked down the long hallway toward the parlor.

The vision of Tawny coming through the door of the parlor caught Darla's eyes immediately. This was surely not her aunt. This girl was about her age or younger. But her aunt had no children. Her mother had told her that before she died. So who was she?

Tawny was not aware of the air of sophistication she'd acquired over the last few months. Perhaps it had happened when she was with the aristocratic Hamilton family and in the constant company of Jason and Bart. But it was a very self-assured young lady Darla was facing when Tawny came into the parlor to greet her.

"Good morning. I'm Tawny Blair, and Aurelia tells me that you've come to see your aunt," Tawny said.

"Yes, that's right. My name is Darla Norton and it's nice to meet you, Tawny. I find that a most unusual name. I've never heard it before."

Tawny laughed. "I can believe that. Actually, my name is Tabitha but someone must have started calling me Tawny when I was a tot and it's stuck with me ever since."

The first thought rushing through Tawny's pretty head when she'd entered the parlor and seen the girl sitting on the settee was her mother could have looked like that when she was a young girl. That brilliant gold hair could have been Maybelle's when she was that age.

"Please sit down, Darla, and finish your coffee before it gets cold. As Aurelia told you, your aunt doesn't always get up at the same time every day, but then she doesn't have to."

"I see. And may I ask what you do here? Are you my aunt's secretary?" Darla inquired of Tawny.

Tawny smiled. "No, Darla, I am your aunt's friend— very dear friend. Now if you will excuse me, I was on my way to go riding." She saw something about the girl that she instinctively did not like, an air about her that Tawny did not trust. Aurelia was right!

Tawny went back down the hallway toward the kitchen so she could tell Aurelia that she agreed with her wholeheartedly about this Darla Norton.

Aurelia looked up to see Tawny darting back through the door. "Well, Miss Tawny?" she asked her.

"I think you are absolutely right, Aurelia. But with you and me around Miss Reba, we won't let anyone take advantage of her, will we?" She smiled impishly.

A big, broad grin came on the servant's face. "You right, Miss Tawny!" she declared. "We won't!" She watched the fiesty little Tawny go out the back door of her kitchen and head to the barn. She thought to herself it was a blessed day when that girl came into the Camerons' lives. She'd brought nothing but joy to both of them! She brought joy to this house!

This girl sitting in the parlor now was going to be nothing but trouble, to Aurelia's thinking!

Chapter 27

There was a chill in the air and Lady Sheila Hamilton had had one of her servants light the logs in the small fireplace in her sitting room. She still preferred her garden room, as she called it instead of her sitting room during the day. All the plants in the room were always watered and tended by her, and the servants knew that they were never to bother these plants.

It was in this room she enjoyed sitting by her hearth in the comfortable chintz-covered chair to read a good book. When she tired of reading, she would sit at her lady's desk over by the window and catch up on some letters she needed to write.

This room was her haven for peace and tranquility when things were on her mind, as they were today.

That happy-go-lucky son of hers was not himself lately nor had he been since the day he'd put Tawny Blair aboard the *Caprice*. She figured the young girl had to be back home in Virginia by now, and she knew that it was too soon for her to receive a letter from the girl. Nevertheless, she was anxious for word from her and she knew her Joy was, too. There had not been a day that Joy had not mentioned Tawny.

Her daughters, Angela and Jane had not missed Tawny as Joy had. Angela was so completely occupied with her new beau and it would not surprise Sheila Hamilton if there was not a wedding before the winter was over.

Being the wife of a seafaring family, she was not too happy to know that Jason was preparing to cross the

Atlantic in another week. It was not the crossing she was worried about but the return trip to England. The winter months could make for a treacherous voyage. She was the first to admit that Jason held a special place in her heart since he was her first child and her only son.

As she spent the time in her room during the morning alone doing the things that gave her pleasure, she thought about Tawny. She wondered if the gold cape she'd given her gave her comfort and warmth on the crossing. She was certainly enjoying the warmth of the blazing logs burning in the fireplace. She left the room only long enough to join Addison and Jane for lunch.

When Addison boarded the carriage to go into London to his office and Jane joined her friend to go into the city to shop, she returned to her garden room to spend the afternoon reading. But she had only read a couple of pages when her son came through the door.

"It seems you are the only one home, Mother." he greeted her.

"I am, Son, and I feel quite content and cozy."

Jason ambled over to take the chair on the other side of the hearth. "I envy you, Mother. Of all the people I've ever known in my life, only you seem never to be bored."

"Ah, and I never am. That's the Irish in me, Son. I'm proud of the roots of that heritage. Life's been far more generous to me than I ever expected. The problem with most people, Jason, is that they go through life expecting too much. Life holds no promises!"

A smile broke on his face. When his mother's black Irish eyes sparkled like this, he was reminded of Tawny. There was that same twinkle in her dark-brown ones, he recalled. Tawny had been very much on his mind today, and he did not know why, but he figured that the *Caprice* had landed in Virginia by now and Captain Crane was homeward bound.

What was far more disturbing to him was that Bart

was about to arrive in Virginia, if he'd figured right, or he would soon be there.

Jason had found out today that he was going to be leaving sooner than he'd anticipated. His cargo was being loaded this afternoon and he was going to be shipping out tomorrow. He'd come home early so he could spend more time with his family, as he told his mother.

"And you are happy about this, aren't you, Jason?" she asked.

"What . . . what do you mean, Mother?"

"I mean, dear, that I think that you are anxious to be heading back to Virginia."

"You are talking about Tawny, aren't you?"

"Of course I am talking about Tawny, Jason. I think you are in love with her, dear."

Jason found it impossible to lie to his mother. Her piercing black eyes always seemed to penetrate him.

"If I've ever loved any woman, it is surely Tawny, Mother."

"I thought it was so, Jason."

"She is different from any other woman I've met. Tawny brings out a protective streak in me such as I have for my sisters. I want no harm to come to her."

"I understand what you're telling me, Jason. I am happy that we've had this talk. Now I can see you leave and not be unhappy because I know that this voyage means more to you than just another adventure. You are going to Virginia for answers."

Jason suddenly realized how wise his mother was, for right now he was not too sure of anything. It lay in Tawny's delicate hands as to which man she loved.

His face was serious as he spoke. "Yes, Mother, I go to find the answers. I know that Tawny was grateful to me for everything I did to help her, and as you know she is a very honest, straightforward young girl, but I don't know whether she is in love with me. Love and gratitude are two different things."

"Then it is important that you find out, Jason. For

209

your own sake, you must!" Lady Sheila told him.

He was tempted to confess to her that his best friend Bart Montgomery could already have won the affections of Tawny. There was no doubt in Jason's mind now that Bart's feeling went far deeper for Tawny than he'd realized when they were returning from Virginia. When he'd learned that Bart had left London a few weeks ago, he knew for certain just how obsessed he was with Tawny.

"I will find out, Mother. But whatever happens, I must tell you that Tawny will always be very dear to me."

"And to me, Jason. I liked the young lady."

"I noticed that, Mother." He smiled for the first time.

When he rose to leave the room, his mother called out to him. "Jason, if Tawny is the woman you love, let nothing stand in your way to win her. It will be worth it!"

He gave her an assuring nod as he left the room, for he knew that this would probably be the last private moment they would share before he left. Tonight the family would gather in the dining room for dinner, and he would be leaving in the morning.

He could not have spoke so frankly with his father as he had with his mother. Now he knew, as he'd never known before, who was the spark that inspired his family. That Irish mother of his had always been the one with the sage wisdom to guide the family to seek and find the way to happiness.

In the days to come he'd try to remember all the things he'd listened to her say today.

Across the way from the Hamilton estate, on the bordering country place of the Montgomerys, exciting events were happening that would have pleased Bart had he been here. Harvey Green, Bart's trainer, had taken full charge of the event. If the breeding was a success, Diablo had sired his first colt with a mare brought to the stables to stay for a few days. Green was sure that there would be a prized colt from the union of Diablo and Sir George Howard's fine mare, Morning Star.

Harvey was beginning to realize that this arrogant stallion and his master Bart Montgomery were very much alike. They were both determined to have their own way and he saw this daily in Diablo. Harvey also knew that Bart had left to go back to Virginia to fetch the beautiful Tawny Blair back to England. He'd heard the gossip that had flowed between the two country estates the last couple of weeks. It was amazing how the house servants at the two fine homes overheard the talk going on within those walls.

He did not have to listen to the gossip to know that Bart Montgomery and Jason Hamilton were both vying for the love of the brown-haired beauty. Harvey had to admit if he'd been a younger man, his passion could have been fired by such an enchanting miss. She was a most amazing young lady and he would never forget the afternoon she'd calmed Diablo and paced him back and forth down in the hold of Hamilton's ship.

He could hardly fault Montgomery for seeking out this lady. The likes of Tawny Blair were few and far between. He might never find another like her in his whole lifetime.

Harvey was a middle-aged bachelor himself, and he figured that he had spent about as much time around Bart Montgomery as anyone, with the exception of his pal Jason Hamilton. There were times when they'd got to doing a lot of talking, as men do, when they sat together enjoying a glass of ale or sharing sips of liquor from Bart's flask in the stables during the afternoon. Harvey had the impression that Montgomery was not the marrying kind or at least not ready to settle down with any woman for a long, long time.

However that was before he was smitten by the ravishingly beautiful Tawny Blair. But there was more to that little miss besides her beauty, Green was quick to see that for himself. So had Bart Montgomery!

A woman could be very beautiful but be the dullest creature in the world. This was not the case with Tawny. She could churn excitement in a man just by walking up to him with that smile on her face and her brown eyes dancing with life and spirit. He'd known the feeling himself when he'd been around her.

No, there was no doubt in Harvey Green's mind as to why Montgomery had set sail for Virginia. This time he was not obsessed by a rare Arabian but driven by a wild desire to win Tawny's heart.

Knowing Montgomery, Green knew that he'd not return to England until he did just that!

Chapter 28

Bart Montgomery would have been happy to know just how smoothly things were going back in England. It wasn't only the stables that were being run properly, either. Within the walls of the spacious stone house, things were going just as placidly.

Augusta had gone back to London to spend some time in her own home after the first ten days with her sister. There were no bills piled up on Bart's desk when Augusta left. Laura had worked a few hours every night to see to that.

"Why did you never take this over before, Laura?" Augusta insisted on knowing.

She smiled. "It is really quite simple to explain, Augusta. I was much younger than Edward when we married and he considered me too young to run this big place, so he took charge of everything. I was too young to protest, I guess. Before I realized it, year after year went by. To Edward, I guess I remained that young, helpless girl, even when we both grew older."

Augusta understood her sister as she never had before. "Well, after Bart was born Edward should have known that you were not exactly helpless. As I recall you had a very difficult labor getting that young man here," Augusta pointed out.

"Oh, when I presented him with a son, dear Edward only insisted on pampering me more, Augusta, and I found my baby filled my days so completely that I didn't care that he ran the house completely."

"And so it went on and on, is that right?"

213

"Yes, Augusta, and then Bart stepped into his father's shoes. I guess I allowed it, but that's all changed now. My handsome son is going to be in for a few surprises when he returns."

The two sisters shared a laugh. "I think he certainly will," Augusta agreed. She realized that things were not as they'd always seemed to her. "You've convinced me, dear, that you can easily do without me for a few days. I think I shall go back to London for a while."

"Please do, and when you wish to come back out here to keep me company, I'll love having you, Augusta," Laura told her sister.

Now, Augusta was back for another visit. She was delighted to see that Laura had meant exactly what she'd said. There was no clutter on Bart's desk and the house was running in fine order.

Augusta could tell immediately how well things were going when she chanced to encounter Hattie. She knew everything that went out in the big house. "Scamp don't have to worry about Lady Montgomery," she told Augusta confidentially. "She's just fine without him around. I'm gonna tell him so, too, when he gets himself back here."

Augusta laughed. "You do that, Hattie. I agree with you." She'd always adored this mountain of a black woman who'd worked so dutifully in this house for years and watched young Bart grow into a man. She had the right to take certain liberties, which she certainly did. Augusta knew when she called him Scamp, she did it in a most adoring way.

When the visit was over, Augusta was happy to go back to her own cozy place in London.

It was one of the mornings that Reba Cameron had given way to the urge to sleep late. Slipping into her emerald-green dressing gown, she finally went downstairs to sit in the kitchen to have her coffee and chat with Aurelia.

But when she entered the kitchen and was informed by Aurelia that she had a guest in her parlor, she was not prepared for what the housekeeper told her.

"Says she's your niece, Miss Reba," Aurelia told her.

"My niece, you say, Aurelia?"

"Yes, ma'am, that's what I'm saying."

She took a hasty sip of the hot coffee from the cup Aurelia had just poured for her. "What in the world would have brought her here to Longcreek from Boston?" Her niece she might be, but she was a stranger to Reba. Before her death, she had not even seen her own sister for years.

"I'll have breakfast later, Aurelia," she told her housekeeper as she sashayed out the kitchen door.

When Reba came to the archway of her parlor, she stood for a moment to observe the young lady moving around her parlor, examining various objects. Nothing about the girl reminded her of Polly, so Reba concluded that she must look like her father, but then she'd never seen Polly's husband, either.

Darla obviously sensed her presence. She turned sharply to see the impressive figure of Reba Cameron standing there in her elegant emerald-green dressing gown. She was a most imposing lady!

"Hello, ma'am. I guess you must surely be my aunt Reba," Darla said in the softest, sweetest tone she could manage.

"That's right, and you must be Darla," Reba replied as she moved on into the room. "I understand from Aurelia that you arrived a couple of hours ago, Darla."

"Yes, ma'am I did." Darla walked back over to where she'd been sitting.

"Well, I guess it is long overdue that I meet my only niece. It was always a regret of mine that your mother and I didn't manage to see each other all through the

215

years, and I'm sorry that I never knew she was in such poor health. We shall have a lot of talking to do while you are here on your visit," Reba told her.

Darla managed to force a smile to her face. It was hardly a *visit* she was planning on. She intended to take up permanent residence here, especially now that she'd seen the elegant furnishings and surveyed the grounds surrounding the house, along with the fine stables and barn.

Oh, no, it was hardly a visit she was paying to her aunt!

"Oh, yes, we shall talk a lot, Aunt Reba."

"Well, I've not had my breakfast, so what do you say to the two of us going in to share some. You've not eaten yet, have you?"

"No, just coffee."

"Fine, I'll have your valises taken up to your room."

Darla was not expecting to be taken into the kitchen but rather the fancy dining room they passed through. She didn't like the kitchen, where that servant's eyes seemed to be boring into her all the time she sat there at the small table with Reba Cameron. She was glad when the meal was finished and Reba summoned one of her other servants to show Darla to one of the guest bedrooms.

"I'll give you a chance to get settled in, Darla. I hope you will make yourself at home and come down whenever you wish," Reba told her as they parted and the servant guided her niece up the steps.

She went back to the kitchen and inquired of Aurelia as to Tawny's whereabouts. Aurelia told her that Miss Tawny had gone for a ride on Coco. "She had her breakfast and went in to greet your niece before she left the house, Miss Reba," Aurelia told her mistress. Aurelia concluded that Miss Reba was not exactly overjoyed by the sight of her niece. Maybe she had the same impression of Darla Norton that she and Miss Tawny had

216

upon meeting her.

Tawny had not intended to ride into town when she'd left the farm, but she gave way to the sudden impulse to go to Roberta's, so she turned Coco in that direction as she left the long drive.

Roberta was delighted by Tawny's unexpected visit, but knowing Tawny as she did, she sensed that something was troubling the young girl. At first she did not prod her to talk to her about it.

"Well, dear, I was just hoping that you'd be coming back to see me real soon and you have." Roberta Thacher told her as they sat in the parlor.

"Oh, you must know I would not have stayed away too long, Mrs. Thacher. I've often wondered what I would have done if I'd not had you to run to."

"Well, Tawny dear—I've a confession to make to you. A long time ago I adopted you in my heart and soul. You were my little girl—the one I was never blessed with—and you brought such joy to my life. You can never know!"

Tawny smiled warmly at the matronly lady. "Thank you for saying that, Mrs. Thacher. You were more the mother to me than my own mother was, and I mean no disrespect toward her."

"Oh, child I know you don't. You always had a very generous heart where your mom was concerned. It is not for the likes of me or anyone else to judge poor Maybelle."

"You're right, Mrs. Thacher. Life was cruel to my mother, and I have only found that out since I returned from England." Before she realized it, she was telling Roberta about the incidents that had shaped Maybelle Blair's unhappy life.

"Dear Lord, child—are you telling me that Bill Cameron was your dad? You know that this town has always speculated about who your dad was. Maybelle was a local girl who'd never left Longcreek her whole

217

life so everyone assumed that it had to be someone who lived here."

Roberta was in a state of shock, for never would she have suspected Bill Cameron had been Tawny's father. Like most people in Longcreek, Roberta had always suspected that it was some man who'd gone to the tavern where she worked, probably a man from one of the many ships coming into the shores of Virginia who had wandered in and out of the small hamlet of Longcreek having himself a night of pleasure with the local barmaid.

Dear Lord, how wrong they all were!

Tawny held out her hand and showed Roberta the ring that had belonged to her father and told her that Reba Cameron had found it concealed in her mother's possessions.

"So she knows?"

"Yes, she knows, and she understands, because my father had not met her yet. She is a most wonderful woman, Mrs. Thacher."

"Ah I know she is that, Tawny."

Tawny told her how she had planted wildflowers around Bill and Maybelle's graves on the grassy knoll across the meadows from the house.

"Now, dear—tell me about you," she asked suddenly. "Tell Roberta what is bothering you. You know that I would understand anything you'd tell me."

Roberta Thacher's question took Tawny by surprise. "I know you would, Mrs. Thacher. I . . . I guess that is why I came to you today. I needed to talk to you. There's no way to say it but just to come right out with the truth. I think I might be pregnant."

Tawny might have expected a shocked gasp, but Roberta didn't do that nor did she reproach her. Instead, she asked Tawny, "Which young Englishman won your heart, Tawny dear?"

"Bart Montgomery, Mrs. Thacher."

"Now enlighten me, dear. Was that the one who came here to purchase the Camerons' Arabian or the young sea captain?"

"Bart was the one who bought Diablo."

"Does he know that you could be carrying his child, Tawny?" Roberta asked her.

"No, because I did not know it myself or even suspect it until I got back here."

"Then you must let him know. This will be a test of his love as well as his honor. It is not the end of the world, honey. If you love this young man, and I know you must, then you've nothing to be ashamed about, Tawny. You gave your love and your heart. He is the one to be ashamed if he is not as much man as you are a woman."

Roberta Thacher did not realize how she had eased Tawny's troubled mind. Tawny was tormented by thoughts that she was going to be like her mother, Maybelle, that her child would be born without a father to give it a name.

She was not like Maybelle!

Chapter 29

Riding back to the Cameron Farms, Tawny's spirits were much lighter than they'd been when she left. The feisty little chocolate-brown mare, with Tawny astride, her long curly hair bouncing around her shoulders as they galloped out the lane, was magnificent to behold!

This was the entrancing sight Bart Montgomery was to see turning the bend in the road as he traveled to the Cameron Farms after he left the Greenfield Inn.

There was no doubt in Montgomery's mind who that fetching female was. There was only one Tawny Blair!

He spurred his horse to go faster. The sight of her was enough to spark every fiber in his male body. His excitement mounted as he came nearer and nearer to her.

When Tawny heard the pounding hooves of Bart's mount behind her, she glanced back over her shoulder to see his blond hair flowing over his face, and she gave a sharp yank on the reins. Just the sight of him was enough to make her tremble with a wild exhiliration. Was she dreaming, she wondered, that he was here in Virginia, riding behind her? It did not seem possible that she was seeing Bart. Maybe it was just her wishful thinking that this could be happening.

A few moments later, she knew better as he reined his horse beside Coco. His strong arms reached out to her and they both stretched to reach each other. His blond head bent over so that his lips might reach hers in a kiss.

"Oh, Tawny, love!" he sighed when he finally released

her. "I've found you!" His blue eyes danced lovingly over her face.

"Oh, Bart, pinch me, I must be dreaming!" She gave a soft, lilting laugh.

"Ah, no—you are not dreaming, Tawny, and neither am I. We are together again." He could not resist taking her sweet lips again in a long, lingering kiss.

By the time he released her this time, he saw the impassioned look on her lovely face, and he knew that it was not to the Cameron Farms he wanted to take her so he took charge of Coco's reins to lead them back to the inn.

She was so mesmerized by the sight of him she did not realize that he was now leading Coco as well as his own horse. It mattered not to Tawny in what direction she was going as long as she was there beside Bart Montgomery and his blue eyes were adoring her.

This was what she had yearned for and dreamed about. For a moment there seemed no reason to talk as their two horses slowly paced side by side.

Bart's deep voice broke the brief silence. "I wouldn't have believed that you could have become more beautiful than you were the last time I saw you," he declared to her, "but damned if you haven't."

She said nothing, responding with a smile. She still wasn't completely convinced that this wasn't just a dream. Bart noticed how quiet she was and teased her. "Is this the same chatterbox Tawny I knew? This young lady seems so quiet. Aren't you glad to see me, Tawny? Should I have not come to Virginia?"

Her brown eyes flashed wide. "Oh, you know I'm happy that you are here," she quickly exclaimed, "but I think I'm dreaming all this and you will suddenly disappear."

"I'm not about to disappear, love. It was you who suddenly disappeared without even a good-bye to me."

"I had no idea that I was going to be leaving so

221

soon, Bart. I kept hoping that you would come over to the Hamiltons that last day I was there," Tawny confessed to him.

"And I would have, Tawny, if I'd only known, but I did not figure that Jason would be shipping you out so soon. So I tried to get caught with on the work piled on my desk when I got home." He told her that the same morning she'd left, he'd come to the Hamiltons only to be told by Joy that Jason had taken her to catch the *Caprice* to return to Virginia.

Tawny was pleased at his interest, but she didn't quite understand his next words. "I am not too happy with our friend Jason right now, I must tell you. I don't think he played fair with either one of us."

"What do you mean, Bart? What did Jason do?" Tawny could not imagine Jason Hamilton ever being anything but honest and fair.

Bart told her he'd tell her about that later, for they'd arrived at the inn. Tawny recognized Greenfield's and asked him why they were coming here.

"It's where I'm staying and I wasn't about to share your company with anyone right now. I want to be only with you, Tawny. I didn't cross an ocean to visit with Reba Cameron."

Tawny laughed, for she hardly wished to sit in the Cameron parlor and share him with Reba, either.

Together they dismounted and marched up the walk hand in hand. The look of love was on both their faces for anyone to see. There was an eagerness churning in them as they mounted the steps to the second landing to go to Bart's room.

As they went through the door and Bart closed the rest of the world out, Tawny teased him. "Now, be honest with me, Bart Montgomery—you didn't come to Virginia just to see me. You've heard of another fine horse you wish to purchase, haven't you?"

He whirled her around to face him and his blue eyes

devoured the loveliness of her taunting eyes gleaming up at him. "No, Tawny—you were the only reason I came to Virginia. Do you believe me?"

When he looked at her the way he did, she had to believe that he was speaking the truth. She gave him a nod, for his head was already bending lower so that he might claim another kiss from her honeyed lips.

She felt his heated body pressing against her and that old familiar ecstasy was beginning to flame as he continued to hold her, his lips capturing hers.

His one hand stroked the long hair covering one side of her face and gently he removed it. When he finally released her lips, he was as breathless as she.

Together they sank down on the bed and he removed her clothing as well as his own, for he wanted no barriers between them when he loved her. The sight of her silken flesh was a vision he'd thought about so often since he'd last seen her and made love to her aboard the *Sea Princess*. It seemed like forever to Bart, but it had only been a few weeks.

Like Bart, Tawny was feeling the same fury of the untamed passion he was stirring within her. It was a blazing fire consuming her as she felt his firm-muscled thighs against her legs and his bare, broad chest pressing against her breasts. She felt the flame of fire as his lips trailed down her throat to cover the tip of one of her breasts.

He felt the undulating sway of her body as it surged anxiously against him and he sank deep between her velvety legs.

No longer could he deny himself the paradise she offered to him. He knew of no other woman who possessed the power over him that Tawny did, and his passion swelled and mounted as he heard her soft moans as she swayed and moved in unison with him.

He felt her tiny hands holding his neck tighter and tighter and she gasped as their ecstasy heightened. Ah,

223

he yearned to make endless love to this little goddess as he felt himself give way to the rapture.

They found themselves caught up in a violent tempest, but finally there did come a calm as they lay in each other's arms.

"Oh, Tawny love! Now I know why I was eager to cross that ocean to get to you," Bart huskily murmured in her ear. "You've bewitched me, Tawny Blair. No other woman has interested me since I met you."

Nothing could have made Tawny happier than hearing Bart speak so lovingly, and as she lay there with his arms still holding her, she wondered if she should tell him about the baby she knew she was carrying.

"Please, Bart, don't say such things if you truly don't mean them," she told him. His hand cupped her face as their eyes locked. "You must know that I adore you, Tawny. I think I have since I saw you ambling up to the Camerons' veranda in your bare feet. You were like no other girl I'd ever seen before. You do believe me, don't you?"

"Oh, I want to, Bart! I want to with all my heart!" she admitted.

"Then I must believe that you care for me, too. I am not a man to waste time playing games, Tawny. Either you love me or you don't. Which is it, love?"

A slow, lazy smile came on her face. "Oh, Bart Montgomery, you know the answer to that already! You know I love you."

"And no one else, Tawny?"

"And no one else!" she swore to him.

"And what about Jason, Tawny?"

She was a little startled by this, and her long lashes fluttered as she looked up at him wide-eyed, a puzzled look on her face. "What about Jason, Bart?"

"You mean to tell me that you did not know that Jason was as attracted to you as I was, Tawny?"

"I never felt the same way about Jason as I did

224

about you, Bart, so I guess I didn't think about that," she stammered. "Jason was always so kind to me and I considered him a very dear friend. I . . . I never imagined making love to him as I have with you."

A pleased grin came to Bart's face as he pulled her close to him. "That's what I wanted to hear you say, love. That's all I need to know."

Reluctantly, he rose from the bed as Tawny insisted that she had to leave the inn to return to Cameron Farms. "Reba will be worried that I've met with an accident on Coco, being gone this long, Bart."

"Well, I'll ride out there with you and pay my respects to the Camerons. I'm sure they'll be happy to be brought up to date on Diablo."

"Mr. Cameron died, Bart, just a few weeks before I got back," Tawny told him.

"I'm sorry to hear that. He was a fine fellow," Bart responded. "Your homecoming has not been exactly a happy one then, has it, Tawny?"

"No, but I've had the satisfaction of finding out that the two men who did what they did to my mother received their just punishment."

"Not by your hands, though?"

"No, it had taken place before I got here. One became an idiot, rocking his days away in a rocking chair and speaking not a word to anyone. The other one got himself stabbed."

Bart saw the intensity of emotion on her face and he suddenly realized something about Tawny Blair. She was a lady who could know the fire of passion whether it was love or hate.

"So that can all be put to rest, Tawny."

Together they got dressed so they might ride out to Cameron Farms. The entire morning had passed them by and the midday sun was high in the sky.

As they rode leisurely down the country lane Tawny had the chance to tell Bart how Reba had buried her

225

mother on the grounds of the farm. She was tempted to tell him about learning that Bill Cameron was her father, but there would be another time for that, she decided.

"This is damned beautiful country!" Bart remarked as they approached Cameron Farms.

Tawny thought about what Reba had told her and that also seemed like a dream to her. Someday all this beautiful land would belong to her. But she did not tell this to Bart, either.

"It *is* beautiful country. I was reminded of it when I was in your country. Jason pointed out where you live."

"Never thought about it before, Tawny, but you are right." As she had been tempted to say certain things to him and hadn't, he too, was tempted to tell her that he wanted her to be his wife and return to England with him as soon as possible. He couldn't stay here too long.

Later, before this day was over, Bart would regret that he'd not asked Tawny to leave with him as soon as possible and drawn from her the promise to be his wife.

Chapter 30

Reba Cameron gave a few dabs of the lilac water behind her ears and was ready to join the others for the evening meal. She had to admit it had been an eventful day. First, she was to find her niece at her home for an unexpected visit from Boston. A few hours later, Tawny had come riding in with Lord Bart Montgomery. He and Tawny had met by accident as she was leaving Roberta Thacher's, they'd told her.

She'd invited him to come back out to the farm tonight for dinner when he'd bid them good-bye to return to the Greenfield Inn, and he'd accepted her invitation.

No one had to tell Reba how deliriously happy Tawny was about Montgomery's unexpected arrival back in Longcreek.

Reba had noticed the attraction between Tawny and Bart during his short visit this afternoon. Somehow she'd figured it was the black-haired Englishman, Jason Hamilton, who Tawny was attracted to, instead of Montgomery. Guess that showed how wrong she'd been.

Darla had been upstairs when the young couple returned, and after Bart had left, it gave Reba a chance to speak to Tawny alone. She told her that her niece would be visiting for a few days.

"Aurelia tells me that you met her this morning before you went for your ride," Reba remarked to see how Tawny had responded to her.

"A brief hello and I introduced myself to her."

Tawny dared not say any more than that right now.

There was a perplexed look on Reba's face as she admitted to Tawny, "She's an absolute stranger to me, Tawny. I never saw her before in my life and now she suddenly shows up on my doorstep. I have to ask why."

"As Aurelia is always saying, time will give you the answer, Reba."

"Well, Tawny, if you observe anything you think I should know, I want you to tell me. Just because she's my blood kin and niece means nothing to me—you understand, dear?"

"I understand and I will keep my eyes open for your sake, Reba," Tawny assured her.

"Well, I appreciate that, Tawny. Now, I'm going to leave you to talk to Aurelia and I shall look forward to seeing you at dinner tonight. It will be nice to have Bart Montgomery joining us."

Tawny went to her room to pick out the prettiest dress in her armoire to wear this evening. She went immediately to the armoire, and found the door ajar. Opening both of the doors, she looked over the gowns and immediately made her decision to wear the gold-colored taffeta with the full, lustrous skirt.

With the gown picked out, she went over to her dressing table and pulled out one of the drawers to lay out some fresh undergarments. But the neat, carefully folded pile of lacy garments were not the way she'd placed them. A frown broke on her face and she was immediately irked to think that someone had been rummaging through her drawers, and she knew who that someone was. It could only have been Darla!

She went back to the armoire to examine things more carefully. She knew exactly how she'd placed the slippers on the floor below her gowns and they, too, were askew. Darla had had a busy afternoon. Tawny was furious as she marched out of her room to go to

228

Darla's room and rap sharply on the door.

A lazy voice beckoned her to enter, but Darla was hardly prepared for the look on Tawny's face, her dark eyes blazing. She took no time to greet their new guest as she moved into the room and slammed the door shut.

Pointing her finger in Darla's face, she delivered her warning to the blond-haired girl standing there in front of her. "Don't you dare enter my room ever again without my permission, Darla. Don't you dare . . . don't you dare insult me by lying. I know you were in there going through my things this afternoon. I place things in a certain way! Because this is your first evening with your aunt, I will say nothing, but if anything happens again, I'll go straight to her, and she'll believe me before she would believe you. If you doubt me, then you test it!"

Tawny marched out of the room as angry as she'd entered it, and Darla Norton know she'd met one hell-cat of a woman. She knew she'd have to be more careful in the future, for Tawny Blair was going to have her eyes on her from now on.

Darla knew that she was going to be ill at ease when Tawny was around, so she was nervous about going downstairs to join them for dinner. Tawny seemed very confident about the extent her aunt valued her opinion.

So she dressed with special care and she put just a hint of makeup on her face. Her thick blond hair was tied back neatly with a velvet ribbon.

In her bedroom, Tawny was also dressing with special care for completely different reasons. She wanted to make herself attractive for Bart. She was pleased with the way she looked in the gold-colored taffeta gown, and in her hair she pinned a cluster of gold flowers with green velvet petals.

She took the cherished bottle of gardenia toilet water that Joy Hamilton had given to her and softly dabbed some at her throat and temples.

Satisfied with her appearance, Tawny turned from the mirror. It was time for her to go downstairs to join Reba. Bart could be arriving at any moment.

As the sound of Tawny's slippers echoed along the carpeted hallway, Darla cracked her door to see her moving toward the head of the stairway, so she lingered in her room for a while longer. She wanted to spend no more time around Tawny than she was absolutely forced to.

Reba Cameron was already in her parlor enjoying her favorite sherry when Tawny came into the room. She thought the parlor looked very festive tonight, for Reba had lit several candles and two vases were filled with wildflowers.

Reba had also dressed up tonight in one of her prettier gowns of bright blue, and around her throat she wore her pearls with the matching drops in her ears. They were her most prized jewels, for Bill had bought the teardrop earrings for her when they were first married.

She turned to greet Tawny, who looked like a dream in her golden frock. She stood there thinking that if ever a beautiful young lady should be adorned with jewels it should certainly be Tawny. No princess could have looked more beautiful than she did.

"My, what a picture you make standing there, my dear. Your gown is gorgeous."

"This was one of the gowns Joy, Jason's sister, gave me. It is pretty, isn't it? I never expected to own something so grand." She smiled as she came up to Reba to take the glass of sherry Reba offered her.

"This Joy must have liked you very much."

"Oh, yes, we became friends the minute I arrived at Jason's home. Jason's mother and his other sisters were very nice, too."

"And his father?"

"At first I found him a little reserved, but he was just as nice as the rest of them."

They had just taken their seats when Aurelia escorted Bart into the parlor. He looked very dashing as he strolled in, dressed in his fine-tailored deep-blue pants, snowy white shirt, and blue-striped coat. Reba Cameron thought he was a magnificent figure of a man and she could see why Tawny had lost her heart to him.

"Good evening, Lord Montgomery," Reba greeted him.

"Good evening, Mrs. Cameron. Good evening to you, Tawny," he said as his blue eyes appraised the beautiful curves of Tawny's figure in the taffeta gown.

When he accepted a glass of sherry, he suggested that she just call him Bart. "I would feel more comfortable if you would," he told her with a charming smile on his face.

"So I shall then." The next thing she was eager to ask him about was Diablo. He assured her that Diablo was happy in his new home and that he expected by the time he returned to England to hear from his trainer, Harvey Green, that Diablo had sired his first colt with Sir George Howard's fine mare.

"Oh, how wonderful! I'd love to see that first foal!" Reba exclaimed excitedly. She also thought about Bill and what a joy that would have been to him.

"Well, I invite you to come visit me in the springtime, Mrs. Cameron, and I will be delighted to take you to see that colt."

"You are very nice, Bart, and I must confess you are tempting me, but we'll just have to wait and see what spring brings," she replied.

Bart might have been talking to Reba but his eyes kept going back to Tawny. God, she was gorgeous tonight!

Reba heard the chiming of the clock on the mantel and it occurred to her that Darla had not come downstairs yet. The girl had had the whole afternoon to nap and she was surely up and dressed by now. She knew that Aurelia would be coming to the door shortly to announce that dinner was ready.

It was at this moment that Darla came sauntering through the door. She stopped short as she spotted the familiar figure of Bart Montgomery standing by the end of the settee looking down at Tawny Blair and her aunt.

She felt very awkward and nervous as she approached them. But Darla was no more startled than Bart when he glanced over to see the blond-haired woman coming into the parlor. What under God's green earth was she doing here at the Camerons'?

"Well, Darla, I was wondering what had happened to you. I know you've met Tawny, but I'd like you to meet my other guest, Bart Montgomery."

A smug smile slowly came to Darla's face as she addressed Montgomery. "Well, hello, Bart — it's a small world, isn't it?"

Reba cast a glance in Bart's direction and then back to her niece. "You two know each other?"

"You might say that, Aunt Reba. I met Bart when I caught the ship in Boston to come here."

No one had to tell him the hell this woman could create and he had to admit to himself that he already suspected that this was exactly what she'd try to do.

"Hello, Darla. I . . . I don't think you mentioned in our brief encounter that Cameron Farms was your destination," he said, trying to sound more casual than he was feeling.

It was obvious to Reba Cameron that her niece Darla was not exactly the most pleasant sight Bart could have seen. She also darted a glance down at Tawny, who had a perplexed look on her face.

The gay air that had been in the parlor before Darla had appeared had now vanished. Reba was happy that Aurelia announced dinner.

Reba made a point of directing Darla to sit on her left and Tawny on her right with Bart seated by Tawny's side. What was interesting to Reba was Aurelia's manner when she served her niece.

Aurelia did not like Darla, Reba sensed. She'd have to keep this in mind, for Aurelia was rarely wrong about people. She had an inborn instinct.

Reba was very aware that during dinner Tawny became unusually quiet and her lovely face wore no smile. Bart was aware of it as he sat beside her. She had not glanced his way since they'd left the parlor. He was determined to make her do so as he made a point of telling her how beautiful she looked tonight.

"Why thank you, Bart," she responded with her eyes looking directly at him, but he sensed a chill in those beautiful brown pools.

Darla was wishing that she had dressed more daringly. Had she known that she was going to be seeing Bart Montgomery tonight, she would not have dressed so plainly.

But that was about the only word Bart got to say before Darla started chatterboxing again. She seemed determined to let Tawny and her aunt know about the number of days and nights the journey took from Boston to the coast of Virginia.

Bart saw the devilment in her blue eyes when she spoke. "Well, Bart — it was a little more than a brief encounter that we had. My goodness, I think we saw each other every day and most nights."

Montgomery wanted to wring her neck. He knew exactly what she was trying to do. He noticed how Tawny quickly turned around in her chair to glare at him. He yearned to tell this brazen young woman what he had truly felt about her back on the ship as

233

well as now, but he did not wish to insult Reba Cameron.

Bart was glad when the dessert was served and the meal was finally coming to an end. But Bart was not any more relieved than Reba. She was very upset that such an enjoyable evening had suddenly changed from the moment her niece appeared. She knew one thing and that was she'd not tolerate this under her roof. Darla would not come into her home and disrupt it.

Bart Montgomery was determined to get Tawny alone and clear up any misconceptions she might have construed from Darla's devious innuendos.

The minute they rose from their chairs to leave the dining room, he wasted no time reaching out to take Tawny's hand. "If you'll excuse us, Mrs. Cameron," he said to Reba, "I'll take Tawny for a stroll so I can enjoy my after-dinner cheroot."

He did not care that Tawny seemed reluctant to follow him. He was determined that she would! He had no intention of returning to the parlor and have Darla do more of her devilment.

"Why, of course, Bart. It's a lovely evening for a stroll. Besides, my niece and I have a lot of talking to do since we've never met before. Isn't that right, Darla?"

"Oh . . . oh, that's true, Aunt Reba," Darla stammered as she watched the handsome Montgomery guiding Tawny down the hallway toward the front door.

The minute the door was closed and it was only Bart and Tawny in the darkness alone, the air seemed so refreshing and clean.

Tawny seemed to relax, too. Bart's hand released her, only to slip around the back of her waist. "We will walk for a while, for I have some talking to do to you, Tawny."

"I think you do, too, Bart," she declared as she fol-

234

lowed him.

But he never lit up his cheroot, for the minute he had led Tawny far enough away from the house, he whirled her around to press against him. "This is the only reason I came here tonight, Tawny. I only want to be with you!" His lips captured hers for a long, lingering kiss.

When he released her, he looked down into her face with a serious look on his face. "Tawny, I've got only one thing to say about what happened tonight," he said. "You can believe me or you can believe Darla Norton. The choice will be yours, but I vow to you that I had nothing to do with her on that trip down the coastline. I will say this for your sake and Reba Cameron's sake: that girl is not to be trusted."

But before Tawny could reply, he had taken her half-parted lips in another sensuous kiss. When he released her again, he urged her to tell him that she believed him.

"Oh, I want to, Bart."

"Well, love, that must come from you and I can't force it. I will tell you this before I take you back to the house. You know where I am and you just ride Coco there whenever you want to see me. I don't want to hurt Reba Cameron's feelings, and I fear I won't be able to bridle my tongue if I'm around her niece again."

"What is it you're not telling me, Bart?"

"There is no time to tell you tonight, but I will soon. I'm leaving, Tawny, when I see you to the door. I hope Mrs. Cameron will not be angry with me for that, but I have no intentions of being near Darla Norton."

"You are very serious about this, aren't you, Bart?" Tawny asked him.

"Very serious, love. Come to me tomorrow at Greenfield's and we'll enjoy the day together."

By now he had walked her back to the front door and he took one last kiss before he left her to go to the hitching post to mount his horse. Tawny watched him until he rode out of sight in the night's darkness.

She found herself curious about what Bart was going to tell her about Darla Norton!

Chapter 31

When Tawny entered the parlor where Reba was sitting with her niece, they both looked up to see only Tawny approaching them. Darla glared beyond her, expecting to see the handsome Montgomery following. A puzzled look came to her face as Tawny took a chair across from Reba. "Bart just decided to go on to his horse and ride back to Greenfield's," she informed her aunt. "He told me to tell you how wonderful the dinner was."

"My goodness, you'd think he would have come in to say good night," Darla said, and it was obvious she was piqued.

Tawny was out of patience with Darla as it was, so her tongue was a bit sharp as she replied, "I've done that for him, Darla."

"Well, the hour is late and I can see why he would be wanting to get back to town," Reba declared understandingly to Tawny, but she rather suspected Bart Montgomery's urge to depart was the annoying presence of Darla. She sensed that he had found her a nuisance during the evening. Reba was already wishing that her niece had never come here.

It didn't surprise Reba at all that Tawny did not linger in the parlor long after she'd returned from saying good night to Bart.

After Tawny had left, Darla turned to Reba. "Well, I guess we've been deserted, Aunt Reba," she said. "For me the night is too early to go to bed."

"Well, perhaps the nap you took during the afternoon

has made you wide-eyed tonight, Darla. As long as you are a guest here, I guess I'd best tell you our routine so you'll know. Aurelia fixes only one breakfast, and that's at eight. I sometimes don't have breakfast if I sleep late as I did this morning."

She went on to tell her that lunch was at twelve, and dinner was always at seven. "We all keep our own bedrooms in order. Aurelia is getting too old to do the cooking and all the housework in this big place. I'm sure you understand that."

"Oh, yes, ma'am. I rarely eat breakfast anyway." Darla replied sweetly.

"I was sure you would, dear. Now I think I'll retire, too. Shall we go upstairs together?" She made the rounds to blow out the candles still burning. Darla could hardly protest when Reba was already dimming the huge lamp in the center of the round table.

They left the parlor together and mounted the stairs. Reba told her niece good night as she came to her bedroom door, but before she went inside she happened to glance down the long hallway and noticed a light gleaming under the threshold of Tawny's door. So it was not a matter of Tawny being ready to go to bed that had prompted her to come upstairs, which was exactly what Reba had thought.

Reba wasn't sleepy, either, but she had some thinking to do and she needed to be alone. Once she had undressed and got on her gown and robe, she went to her dressing table to open the drawer where she kept special items. The small packet was not very large, for her sister had not written her often. She took the letters tied in a pale-blue ribbon in her hand.

Sitting down in the chair next to the nightstand, she heightened the wick of the lamp to give out more light. She spent the next hour reading over the old letters from Polly. Halfway through them, she realized that some were a year apart, and in most of the later letters she had complaints about her daughter. She mentioned that she was finding Darla hard to manage since her husband was no longer around to lay down the law to her. It was Polly's last letter that Reba read not once but twice. She complained that her days working in the mercantile store were long and hard and her lazy daughter did not turn her hand to do a thing around the house to help her out. Polly had found Darla an afternoon job in a bakery next to the store where she worked, but Darla had been fired after a couple of weeks.

Reba sat there for a long time after she'd finished reading the letters. Had Darla come here thinking that she was going to live off her generosity and do nothing? That young lady was going to be in for a few surprises if that was the case!

Tomorrow she was going to ask her a lot of questions.

Putting the letters back into the drawer, she decided to go to bed, for there was nothing she could do tonight.

Down the darkened hallway, Darla had kicked off her slippers and removed her frock, flinging it over the chair. Sitting on her bed with her back propped up against the pillows, she dwelled in her own musings. A wicked grin came to her face. Oh, how she'd made that Bart Montgomery squirm this evening, especially in front of her aunt and Tawny Blair! It was good enough for him. On the ship she had sensed that he considered himself too grand for the likes of her.

She had definitely noticed that Tawny did not seem pleased about hearing that they knew each other. Now, Darla considered she had herself a very powerful weapon to use against Tawny. Now she knew that Tawny loved Montgomery. Darla was determined to get even with her for that arrogant way she'd marched into her room this afternoon and dared to give out her

239

warning.

She knew where Bart was staying, because Tawny had mentioned the Greenfield Inn. She should have known that it would not be that shabby hotel where *she'd* stayed that first night.

Tomorrow she was going to get started on her own plans, and with that in mind, she wanted to get up bright and early, so she dimmed the lamp and slipped under the soft pink coverlet. Sleep came quickly for Darla, for it had been a long, interesting day. More than ever she was determined to share some of the luxury she'd found at Cameron Farms. Why shouldn't she? Why should she have to work so hard when Tawny Blair enjoyed her aunt's generosity.

When Bart arrived back at the inn, he stopped at the desk. "I am expecting a young lady in the morning bringing me some papers to sign," he told the clerk. "She will have my permission to have the extra key in your rack, Mr. Kramer."

The elderly clerk assured him that he would leave word when he left the desk late tonight and Bart thanked him, turning to go to his room. He did not doubt for a minute that Tawny would ride to the inn, for he'd seen the curious look in her brown eyes when he'd promised to tell her some things about Darla Norton.

Anticipating Tawny coming to him tomorrow, he began to get undressed for bed.

No one could have been more surprised than Aurelia when the fair-haired Darla came bouncing into her kitchen. "Good morning, Aurelia. My aunt told me if I wanted breakfast I had to get downstairs by eight, so here I am," she giggled.

240

"Yes, that's right. So if you'll just have a seat over there, I'll get your plate ready. You want ham or bacon?"

"You mean I sit here in the kitchen?" Darla asked, raising an eyebrow.

"This is where Miss Reba and Miss Tawny sits, so I'd say so," Aurelia informed her.

Shrugging her shoulders, Darla went over to the oak table to take a seat. She told the servant she'd have a slice of ham and a few pieces of bacon. Aurelia brought the plate to the table and poured a cup of coffee and then returned to her stove.

There was no chatter between the two of them as Darla ate her breakfast in silence, then got up to go toward the back door.

Aurelia inquired where she was going. She saw the indignant look on the young girl's face as she turned sharply around. "Your aunt might inquire, Miss Darla!"

Darla could not argue with her about that. "Oh, I am going for a ride. Aunt Reba told me I could." She turned around haughtily to leave.

When she got to the barn, the young hired man was told by Darla that she wished him to saddle her up a horse.

"Which one would you like, miss?" he asked her. "This roan is a fine mount, ma'am."

"No, I think I'd like to ride that brown one in the next stall," Darla told him.

The young man scratched his head and shook his head. "Can't rightly do that. That's private property — she belongs to Miss Tawny."

Darla laughed. "Young man, I'm Reba Cameron's niece, and my aunt has given me permission to ride any horse on this farm and that includes Tawny Blair's horse. I don't want to go back in the house and tell my aunt you've refused me."

He knew nothing to do but obey her command.

There was no way he wanted to rile the boss lady, Miss Reba. So he saddled Coco and Darla immediately mounted. Long before Reba or Tawny went downstairs, Darla was riding toward Longcreek.

Tawny was up and dressed in her divided skirt and matching vest of deep-green twill. She wanted to be sure she looked her best when she went to see Bart at the inn. Straightening the collar of her ecru blouse, she was satisfied as she looked in the mirror. She was tempted to tie her hair back with a ribbon but changed her mind and let it remain free and loose.

Before she went to get Coco to ride to Greenfield's and Bart she wanted a hot cup of Aurelia's black coffee. Jauntily, she left her room and dashed down the steps toward the kitchen.

"Well, good morning, Miss Tawny," Aurelia greeted her, already reaching for the coffeepot, for she knew what Tawny wanted. She rarely ate breakfast.

"Thought Miss Darla was you when she came in a while ago," the servant commented.

"Darla's already up?" Tawny was surprised to hear that.

"About an hour ago. Left to go for a ride. She told me to tell Miss Reba if she asked."

By now Tawny had finished the cup of coffee and she headed for the back door to go to the stables. She told Aurelia good-bye and rushed out the door. The servant had barely turned around before Reba was coming slowly through the door with her robe and gown still on.

Once again, Aurelia reached for the coffeepot and carried the cup over to the little oak table where Reba had taken a seat. "Miss Tawny just dashed out the door," she told Reba.

"Going for a ride, I'd bet," Reba remarked as she took the first sip of coffee.

"Yes, ma'am. Sure she was. Had that riding skirt on

you gave her." Aurelia went back to her stove and Reba sat there sipping her coffee and looking out the kitchen window. Suddenly she set the cup down on the table as she observed a streak of green marching from the stable toward the house. Something about the way Tawny was walking and the stormy look on her face told Reba that she was in a raging fury.

The back door was slamming with a mighty roar as Tawny stomped through the door, her brown eyes sparking with furious fire. She didn't see Reba Cameron sitting in the corner as she approached Aurelia. "Damn her! Damn her, Aurelia! She took Coco!"

Never had Reba ever seen Tawny so angry. She rose from the table and addressed Tawny. "Are you saying that *Darla* took Coco?"

"I'm saying exactly that, Reba! Ben told me he tried to refuse her but she told him that you'd said she could ride any horse she wanted," Tawny told her.

"I did not tell her that, Tawny. Besides, Coco is your horse. When she returns I shall set this straight once and for all," Reba declared in a firm tone. Now Tawny was not the only one angry. Reba Cameron was seething and she was not going to tolerate this place being turned upside down by anybody!

Aurelia went back to her stove, shaking her head as she thought to herself that she just knew that girl was going to make trouble when she arrived here yesterday morning.

Reba urged Tawny to join her for another cup of coffee and Tawny agreed, hoping that Darla would return with Coco so she could leave to go to Greenfield's.

"It won't happen again, Tawny, I promise you," Reba assured her, patting Tawny's hand.

Tawny didn't say anything, but she knew it wouldn't. When she next saw Darla she was going to let her know it better not!

Chapter 32

Reba left Tawny in the kitchen with Aurelia after she'd had her second cup of coffee. Tense and angry, she'd mounted the stairs to her room. She didn't need all this trouble right now. Having Bill die had been a devastating blow to her. When Tawny had returned a few weeks later, life had taken on a renewed hope for happier times again for Reba. But now Darla had arrived and everything seemed to be falling apart again. She was damned well not going to see that happen if it meant she would be forced to send her niece away. Tawny meant much more to her than Darla ever would.

Back in the kitchen, Tawny sat at the table in silence as she continued to look out the window for some sight of Darla returning with Coco. Finally her patience was worn thin and she got up from the table. Darla was not going to cheat her out of this day with Bart. Aurelia watched her go hastily toward the door. "You leaving, Miss Tawny?"

"Yes, Aurelia. You can tell Miss Reba that I'm keeping my appointment with Bart. I'll ride another horse."

She went to the barn and had the young man saddle up the roan. But she made a point of telling him that he was never to allow Coco out of this barn again. "Miss Norton does not have any right to Coco. That is my horse and you can confirm that with Miss Reba!"

Putting the roan into a fast gallop, she rode out of the stables and down the drive toward Longcreek.

* * *

Tying the reins to the hitching post, Darla pranced up the walkway leading to the front entrance of Green-field's Inn. Without hesitation, she boldly marched up to the desk clerk and asked for Bart Montgomery's room. Darla was well seasoned in this back in Boston, but she expected to find the inn here in Longcreek more restrictive. She was delightfully surprised when the clerk handed her the extra key in the rack and smiled. "Yes, ma'am—Mr. Montgomery told us last night that you would be arriving this morning."

Darla didn't have to use the clever lie she'd conjured up to use on the clerk and she also knew that Bart and Tawny had planned the rendevous when they had been saying their private goodnight. A sly smile was on her face as she mounted the stairs to the second landing.

When he heard the noise at his door, Bart had just gotten up and slipped into his pants. He'd just finished shaving and was ambling around the room barechested as he prepared to put on his shirt. But thinking that it was Tawny at his door, he made no effort to put his shirt on. In fact, he was overwhelmed with delight that she was so eager to come to him, for he had not expected her to get to the inn for another hour or so.

But when that brazen, blond hussy came sauntering through his door, he was utterly flabbergasted. "Wha-what the hell are you doing here, Darla?"

"Why, Bart—you could hurt a girl's feelings talking like that!" she smirked.

Hastily, he grabbed his shirt, for he realized exactly what had happened downstairs and how she'd managed to obtain the key. He could hardly fault the desk clerk after the orders he'd left last night.

He buttoned his shirt as she watched him, purposely moving so that he might block the doorway. "A woman has a right to have her feelings hurt when she has been too presumptuous. Now, I'll take the key there in your

245

hand."

Darla gave out a girlish giggle. "No, I think I'll make you work for it, Bart."

Bart's blue eyes blazed with fury. "I've no time for your stupid games, Darla. Don't you get the message? I tried to tell you on the ship, but it obviously didn't register. I dare you to drop that key in your bodice, for my touch won't be a gentle one. I will get that key before you leave this room."

Something about the look in his fierce blue eyes urged her to not trifle with him, so she stretched out her hand to him and he took the key. "Now, Darla—get out of here just as fast as you can. I'm expecting a lady to visit me."

"I'll be glad to leave, Bart Montgomery. You are not much fun anyway!" Darla shrieked at him as she turned to go. As soon as she was outside the door and slowly started walking down the hall, she was shaken by what had happened.

Obviously, Bart Montgomery considered Tawny Blair a lady and he labeled her a tramp—or worse. Well, maybe she was, but she didn't care. Being a lady had certainly not rewarded her own mother with a glorious life. She certainly didn't want that kind of life of hard work.

She knew she had some thinking to do before she returned to the farm, so when she got back downstairs she noticed the busy dining room of the inn. It had a warm, cozy air about it, so she decided to go in and have a cup of tea before she rode back to the farm. She would also have a perfect view of the entrance when Miss Tawny Blair appeared.

She kept her eyes focused in that direction for the next half hour.

But Darla was not about to see Tawny enter the inn. All Tawny had to see was Coco tied at the hitching post. There was no shadow of doubt in Tawny's mind as to who Darla Norton was visiting. Well, she might be naive, but she was not a fool! The two of them would not play her for one, she vowed.

But she did leap off the roan and take Coco. Right now, that was the only thing that mattered to her. That bitch could ride the roan back home. Tears spilled down her lovely face as she rode home. But the closer she got to Cameron Farms, she more she knew that she could not live under the same roof with Darla Norton. But what was she to do? She didn't know!

Cameron Farms might be hers someday, but now it wasn't. It belonged to Reba Cameron, and Darla was her niece so she couldn't order her to leave. Reba would have to do that.

Suddenly Tawny knew what she would do for at least a few days. She'd go to Mrs. Thacher's. It would be best for everyone, for she wasn't sure about what she might do when she encountered Darla. She knew that Roberta Thacher would welcome her to her cottage.

When she arrived back at the farm and was going through the kitchen, she did not see Aurelia sitting at the table until the servant called out to her. "See you done got your Coco back, Miss Tawny."

"That I did, Aurelia," she declared, making no effort to tell her how as she dashed on out the kitchen door to go up to her room to pack. She had every intention of taking Coco with her when she left here. Mrs. Thacher had an old shed at the back of her house that would do to quarter Coco for as long as she stayed there.

Once in her room, Tawny started gathering up some of her things to take to Roberta's when there was a rap on her door. Reba stood there, and as she walked into the room, she looked at Tawny with concern and asked what she was doing.

"I was going to find you before I left, Reba. I'm . . . I'm going over to Mrs. Thacher's for a few days. She's

247

been feeling poorly so I thought I'd help her out. She always helped me when I needed her." It did not exactly sit well with Tawny to lie to Reba, but she wanted to spare her feelings.

Reba looked at Tawny's face and she knew she was not telling her the truth. This pained Reba deeply. She walked over to the young girl she loved so dearly and put her hands on Tawny's shoulders. "There have never been any lies between us, dear, so let's not start now. Aurelia told me you rode Coco back in. Where did you find her? Tell me, Tawny!"

A mist of tears was in Tawny's brown eyes even though she was desperately fighting not to cry. "I found her tied at the hitching post at Greenfield's Inn. Need I say more, Reba? Right now, I want no part of Bart Montgomery or your niece, so it's best I'm not here when she returns. She'll have the roan to ride back here on. I switched horses." She should have brought the roan back, too!

Reba's eyes went to the floor and she shook her head. "I wish she'd never come here, I swear it! Perhaps you are right to go to Roberta's, and while you are there I will do what I've got to do. This is your home—not Darla's."

"I'm glad you understand, Reba, for I'd not hurt your feelings for anything in the world," Tawny declared, wiping a tear from her eyes.

"It will be taken care of, and quite quickly! But what shall I do if Bart Montgomery comes here seeking you out, Tawny?"

"Tell him I went to some friends but I didn't tell you which ones. He won't know who they might be."

"Are you sure this is what you want, Tawny?" Reba asked her.

"Very sure, Reba! I don't wish to see him—not now!"

"All right, dear. I'll do as you say."

By now, Tawny had all the things she wished to pack

in the small valise and she was ready to leave. "Everything will work out, Reba. Nothing can ever destroy what we have, not even Darla! I'll keep in touch with you."

"Do, Tawny," Reba urged her as Tawny prepared to go, but Tawny had to tell Reba one more thing before she left. "Watch out for her as long as she's here, Reba. I said nothing about this to you, but the first afternoon she was here, she invaded my room and went through all my drawers."

"My God, why didn't you tell me?"

"I gave her a harsh warning and I hoped that would be enough to stop her mischief. Obviously, it wasn't!"

There was a sad look on Reba's face as she watched Tawny start for the door. "Thank you, honey. I'll keep what you've told me in mind."

Reba stayed in Tawny's room for a few moments before she emerged to the hallway. Anyone who knew Reba Cameron knew she was a woman of action. She did not intend to waste an entire afternoon, so she immediately summoned her foreman to her study. She had already taken from the safe the funds necessary to cover the expenses involved of ridding herself once and for all of her niece. She would send her back where she had come from.

When the foreman entered the study, she wasted no time in telling him that she wanted him to travel to Chesapeake to secure passage on the first ship going up the coast to Boston. "My niece is returning to Boston as soon as possible, Mart. I've included enough there for your night's lodging and meals in Chesapeake. I want you to get started at once. I'll have Walt take over your chores until you return."

"Yes, ma'am, Miss Reba," he replied. She might be a woman, but few were like Miss Reba. There was no question ever as to who was the boss around here now that Bill Cameron was dead.

Now that that was done and Tawny had departed, Reba found there was no contentment she could find in this house as she roamed around waiting for Darla to return.

She was filled with mixed emotions, for she did not relish her return but she was also anxious to confront her with her devilment.

She did not have long to wait, for Tawny had not been gone an hour and Mart was already on his way to Chesapeake when Darla came riding in on the roan.

All her watching for Tawny to appear had been in vain, and when she'd finally left the inn to find the roan in the place of Coco, she was feeling rather satisfied. Obviously, Tawny had arrived and found her horse tethered there and switched it for the roan. But Tawny was obviously piqued so she'd made no effort to come into the inn. That was enough to give Darla some satisfaction.

But Darla was soon to learn that she was not dealing with a woman like her mother Polly when she encountered her aunt Reba. Polly had been a simple, easygoing woman who'd allowed her daughter to intimidate her. This was not the case with Reba Cameron!

As Darla started to rush up the stairs, a voice below called out to her. "Darla, come down here! We've got some things to talk about!"

She had only to look at her aunt's face to know that she'd pushed her luck too far. Her blond head was whirling crazily trying to construe a story that would soothe her aunt's ruffled feathers — and there was no doubt that they were ruffled!

"All right, Aunt Reba," she replied in the sweetest tone she could muster.

But this didn't impress Reba at all. She turned her back on Darla as she went back to the parlor.

There was a smirk on Darla's face as she followed her aunt. She hated the arrogant bitch with a passion for thinking she could dare to lay down rules to her. Who did she think she was anyway?

But Darla was hardly prepared for the news she was about to hear from her aunt Reba!

Chapter 33

When Darla was finally dismissed by Reba Cameron to her bedroom, she knew she had encountered a domineering, unrelenting lady she could never outsmart. How she and her mother could have been sisters Darla would never figure out! They were completely different.

It was a very subdued, scared Darla Norton who went into her bedroom after the stern lecture she'd just received from Reba Cameron, who'd told her in no uncertain terms that she had no right to lie as she had to the stableboy and that she had absolutely no right to take Tawny's horse, Coco.

Darla now realized she should have played it smarter and courted Tawny's friendship instead of making her an enemy, as she'd obviously done. Tawny Blair held a high place of esteem with her aunt. It was too bad that she'd found that out too late for it to do her any good.

Darla accepted that today she had destroyed any hopes she might have had to enjoy a life of ease. What had it profited her to go to Greenfield's to see Bart Montgomery? He had looked down his aristocratic nose at her, so she was asking herself why she'd wasted her time for nothing.

Was it her destiny to be as doomed as her own mother? Perhaps that was the answer. Obviously it was, for her aunt had informed her that she was booking passage for her to return to Boston as soon as possible, and she'd said it without blinking an eyelash. Darla knew that she meant every word.

Heartlessly, Reba had told her that she would give

her the funds to keep her for two months after she arrived. "The rest is up to you, Darla, to find yourself a job. I feel no obligation to support you beyond that."

The evening meal was a strained affair. Tawny was absent from the table and Reba had sought not to explain that to Darla. Darla dared not to be so bold as to ask.

All day long, back at the inn, Bart Montgomery had waited and wondered why Tawny did not show up. He did not give up hope until the afternoon grew late.

He knew one thing, and that was tomorrow he was riding out to Cameron Farms to see her. He had no way of knowing that Tawny had come to the inn, found the evidence that Darla was there, and left sadly disillusioned.

Last night she was sure Bart loved her, as he'd told her he did, and that he'd come all the way from England just to see her again. That had meant everything to Tawny. But how could he love her when he had Darla in his room? Now she realized why the sight of Darla at Reba's had stunned him when he'd come to dinner.

Tawny had plenty of time to think after she arrived at Roberta's. She had been a fool to not see it last evening. Darla had thrown out little hints all evening that they had become well acquainted traveling those days and nights on the same ship.

Tawny was grateful that Mrs. Thacher did not prod at her as to why she'd come to spend a few days with her. She just accepted Tawny with delight. But Mrs. Thacher was a wise, sensitive lady and from just the way Tawny spoke her name, she figured it had to be something to do with that young niece of Reba's.

Longcreek being such a small place, the whole town knew about any newcomer arriving there, so Roberta had heard about Darla's arrival.

She and Tawny had enjoyed a pleasant evening and a tasty meal. Afterward they sat in Roberta's parlor, talking, until Roberta confessed to her that she was going to have to call it a night. "Now, honey, I know that you probably aren't sleepy, so you just make yourself at home. You stay up just as long as you like 'cause it won't bother me," Mrs. Thacher assured her as she prepared to leave the parlor.

"If you're sure it won't bother you, I think I will. I might just go out and sit on the step for a while. I used to enjoy doing that when Mother was working at night."

"I remember, Tawny. I used to see you out there some nights when we had a bright moon out," Roberta told her. She gave the girl a warm smile and turned to leave the room.

After she was gone, Tawny dimmed the parlor lamp lower before she went to sit on the step. Sitting there all alone in the night's quietness she could not resist glancing across the way at the cottage that had been her home all her life. Somehow it did not look the same now as she saw the lamplight glowing through the windows. The family living there now was still up.

Whoever they were, they'd certainly made a lot of changes around the place. A painted wooden bench sat under the spreading oak tree, and window boxes filled with flowers were placed at the front windows. She could make out the ruffled curtains hanging at all the windows and she could imagine how much nicer it was inside now. There were no weeds growing knee-high around certain areas of the yard as there had been when she and Maybelle lived there.

The man living in the cottage had already gone to the woods to cut and haul their supply of wood for the coming winter.

What had happened in her life since just last spring! It was only a short period of time, but it seemed like more than just a few months to Tawny as she sat there thinking about the past. But it was rather foolish to dwell on the past, for it was the present she should be concerned about, she realized.

By now, Tawny had to come to terms with the truth that she surely must be pregnant with Bart's child, but he obviously wasn't ready to marry her.

As she sat there a voice reminded her of something: *She was not going to be like Maybelle even if the child didn't have a father.* Tawny would not be penniless and forced to find employment in a tavern. Someday she'd own Cameron Farms and she had been amazed at the sum Reba had put in the bank for her just recently.

She would not be forced to exist as Maybelle had all her life. Somehow, those thoughts had a soothing effect on her and she felt ready to go inside to bed.

Amazingly, she slept soundly and Bart Montgomery did not haunt her dreams.

Bart was admitted to the house by Aurelia when he arrived at Cameron Farms. When he told her he wished to see Tawny, the servant told him that she wasn't here.

"Where is she then, Aurelia?" His blue eyes prodded her.

"I can't rightly tell you that, sir. You gonna have to talk to Miss Reba about that, so I best get you to the parlor until she gets downstairs." She guided the tall Englishman toward the parlor, thinking to herself that he was a handsome devil. She could see why Miss Tawny had lost her heart to him. He had the brightest, bluest eyes she'd ever seen.

"You just have a seat and I'll go tell Miss Reba you are here. You like any coffee, Mr. Bart, while you're waiting?"

Bart told her that he didn't care for anything and thanked her.

Aurelia left him to go tell Reba Cameron that he was in the parlor. This was one of those times when Aurelia felt she should go to Miss Reba's bedroom.

Reba was already up when Aurelia knocked on her

door, and her servant wasted no time in telling her why she'd come upstairs.

"I'll be right down, Aurelia. You tell him that." Reba informed her as she started to put some order to her hair.

Aurelia went back to her kitchen and Bart waited impatiently, hoping that he'd not be subjected to Darla's presence in the parlor.

But Darla was still sleeping soundly, for it had been dawn before she finally drifted off to sleep. Before that, she had tossed and turned with all the things on her mind. Sheer exhaustion had finally taken over.

"Good morning, Bart," Reba greeted him.

Eagerly, he rose. "Aurelia told me that Tawny isn't here and that I should speak to you. I hope that I've not disturbed you."

"Not at all. Please have a seat. If you don't mind I'll be having my morning coffee while we talk and perhaps you'll join me." She smiled, knowing that Aurelia would be bringing in a tray even though she had not requested it.

As she finished speaking, Aurelia indeed came trotting into the parlor with a carafe of coffee and two cups on a tray. As soon as she left, Reba turned to Bart. "All I can tell you is that Tawny left yesterday to go visit a friend," she told him. "Was she expecting you to come out here this morning, Bart?"

"Tawny was supposed to have come to Greenfield's yesterday. We were to have lunch together, but she never showed up and I waited all day for her," he declared.

"And you were there all day so you would not have missed her by chance?" she said, playing her own little game with him. By now, Reba had figured out exactly what had Tawny so disturbed, besides the fact that Darla had taken Coco. She'd ridden to the inn to keep her engagement with Bart, but when she spied Coco at the hitching post she'd switched horses and left without going into the inn.

256

"I was there all day long. By late afternoon, I knew that she wasn't coming," Bart told her.

Reba was pulled in two directions, for she felt that Bart was being completely honest with her, and she feared that Tawny had jumped to the conclusion that Bart was having a rendevous with Darla.

"Do you know the friend she is visiting, Mrs. Cameron? I've not traveled to Longcreek to waste my time. I came because of Tawny and my concern for her. You've probably guessed that I care very much for Tawny."

"I appreciate you being so honest with me, Bart. I have to confess that I had sort of figured that out, but then Tawny is a most beautiful young lady," Reba remarked with a gleam in her eye. She was tempted to tell him where he might find Tawny, but she did not want to do anything that would displease Tawny. Perhaps it was better that Tawny have a day or two to cool her temper, for never had she seen the girl so furious as she'd been yesterday.

"I'll tell Tawny that you're anxious to see her as soon as you can if she comes back to the farm in the next day or two. She won't be gone long, I'm sure."

"And you don't know which friend of hers she went to visit?" he quizzed. It was awfully hard for Reba Cameron to lie to him with those blue eyes locking with hers as they were.

"I just can't recall that she told me when she left on Coco, Bart. I'm terribly sorry about that."

Bart Montgomery left Cameron Farms feeling perplexed and puzzled. He didn't understand what was going on, but he knew damned well something was.

After Montgomery left, Reba was flooded with guilt about lying to him. She felt she should have told him the truth. There was no point in these two young lovers being miserable when they could work out their differences if only they'd get together.

But the thing that riled Reba the most was she knew

their misunderstanding would never have happened if Darla had not been here.

Tomorrow she was going to Mrs. Thacher's to have a talk with Tawny. She must, for both those young people's sake. Love was a fragile thing and she didn't want Tawny to let it slip through her fingers.

She knew that if Bill Cameron were here, he would urge her to go talk to Tawny as one woman to another!

Part Three

Treacherous Trickery

Chapter 34

Reba had never considered Tawny stubborn during the time she'd known her, but she faced that kind of young lady when she went to Roberta Thacher's cottage to talk to her the next day.

"Well, honey—I just don't want you to be sorry later that you didn't give him a chance. He seems to want to talk to you, Tawny."

"Oh, Reba, I appreciate you being so kind, but I just don't want to see Bart right now." She couldn't explain it to Reba when she didn't understand it herself. The pain that had stabbed at her when she rode to the inn and found Coco at the hitching post was overwhelming. Jealousy had swelled in her to think that Darla was there with him. It was only the day before that she'd been in that room and she'd given herself to him so completely in the ecstasy of passion they'd shared. Never had she loved him so much and she was certain he loved her just as much.

She didn't fault Bart that the bold Darla Norton had taken it upon herself to ride Coco and come to the inn, but she could not excuse him for inviting her into his room and allowing her to stay there for almost an hour. This was the torment she was enduring. She had no way of knowing that Darla had only been in the room for five minutes, or that she had been in the dining room for almost an hour.

She could not bring herself to tell Reba about this right now, so she just told Reba to tell Bart that she didn't wish to see him.

"Tawny, are you sure this is what you want me to say to him?"

"Yes, Reba, I'm very sure!" she declared in a very firm voice.

Seeing the futility of trying to change her mind, Reba prepared to leave the Thacher cottage. "Guess I had things figured all wrong, Tawny. I would have sworn you were in love with Bart Montgomery."

Her remark brought a quick response from Tawny. "Maybe I am but maybe—maybe right now I'm . . . I'm a little disappointed about some things, Reba," she stammered.

Reba smiled. "Well, honey, let an old married woman tell you something about loving a man. We all have our times of being hurt and disappointed, but you never solve anything if you don't talk it out. Bill and I had our fair share of fusses over the years. Bill was a quiet one when he was out of sorts with me, but I made him talk to me."

She said no more as she walked out the door. It was only later that Tawny thought about what she'd said. As she lay in bed that night, she wondered if she had played the role of a coward by not marching right up to Bart's room and confronting him with Darla.

That evening over at Cameron Farms, Reba did not hesitate to confront her niece. She waited until after they'd dined, for the situation had been strained for both of them the last twenty-four hours. Reba wasn't heartless; there was a very gentle side to her. It was only when someone crossed or tried to use her that she could be hard and unbending. Now that Mart had returned with Darla's passage booked for three days from now, she intended to inform the girl tonight that she must leave Longcreek.

After they'd finished the cherry pie Aurelia had baked, Reba asked her to bring coffee to the parlor. "I've some things I'd like to talk to you about, Darla," Reba told her niece.

After Aurelia had served the coffee and left, Reba began to speak to the solemn-faced girl sitting across from her. "I've secured passage for you to Boston in three days, Darla. No one regrets more than I do that your visit has to end this way. If coming here cost you your job, then you'll return to Boston with enough money to carry you while you find another."

Darla sat there silently as she sipped the coffee. But Reba had much more to say, and she wasted no time saying it.

"I don't know where you got your ways, but I know one thing for sure, and that is that my sister Polly was a good soul. I find it disgusting to think the very first afternoon of your visit you're discovered nosing through Tawny's bedroom."

This made Darla bristle, but she still did not say anything. Reba continued to let the girl know exactly why she was being sent back to Boston. "Your boldness was embarrassing to Lord Montgomery the night he came to dinner. You must have known that he is very attracted to Tawny, but yet you tried to hint that you and he were more intimate than you were. Don't try to tell me otherwise. Then as if that wasn't enough for you to stir up trouble, the next morning you take Tawny's mare when my stable-boy tried to refuse you."

"So Tawny is the one who's tattled to you and caused all this misunderstanding," Darla snapped, finally giving way to all the restrained resentment that she was being asked to leave.

"Not Tawny at all. This is Tawny's home, Darla, and she is the one who took her leave because she'd have no part of you after she found out you'd brazenly gone to the inn uninvited by Bart Montgomery. No lady would have done that, Darla!"

"Well, I guess I'm not any fancy uppity lady like Miss Tawny Blair with all her grand airs," Darla smirked.

It took all her willpower to keep from going over and slapping her smug face, but Reba managed to do it. "Let me tell you something about Tawny Blair, Darla. I doubt that you ever went around in your bare feet most of the year or ragged clothes. Maybe Polly was poor, but I know your clothes were always mended, and that Polly worked her fingers to the bone to keep you in shoes. No, Darla, Tawny was hardly born to a life of luxury. But when your actions yesterday urged Tawny to leave, you signed your fate here. So you must leave. I won't allow you to continue to do what you managed to do in only a few days' time to my home and Tawny's."

Darla didn't figure that she had anything else to lose by asking, "May I dare be so bold to ask why you have constantly talked tonight about this being Tawny's home? I know you and your husband didn't have any children."

"It's quite simple, Darla. Bill and I adopted Tawny in our hearts after we met her. You're right, we didn't have a daughter, but we thought of Tawny as our daughter and so she shall always be."

Now Darla knew why Tawny was so self-assured when she'd threatened to go to Reba if she caught her in her room again. She wished that she could be as lucky as Tawny, but she rather doubted that she ever would. She didn't possess that quality to draw people to her as Tawny Blair did, so she might as well accept it.

"Well, Aunt Reba—I'll try to be on my best behavior so I will cause no more embarrassment to you while I'm here. In three days, you and Tawny can have your happy home back again." She got up from the chair and moved to leave the room.

Reba sat thinking to herself about Polly and how sad she must have felt to have raised such a despicable daughter. "It could have been nice for you and me both, Darla. I fear you have a set of wrong values about life." Reba sighed dejectedly as she watched the young girl go toward the door.

A smirk was on Darla's face as she whirled around to look at her aunt. "Ah, Aunt Reba—it would never have worked for me here at Cameron Farms," she retorted. "I knew that the first afternoon I was here. I find it a very dull and boring place. Why did you think I was seeking a little excitement with that handsome Englishman? Well, there are plenty of eager, lively gents back in Boston!" Darla turned and walked out of the parlor.

Reba Cameron realized that for the first time she'd probably heard the truth spoken by her niece. More than ever, she knew she'd made the right decision to demand that she leave. Walking over to the liquor chest, she poured herself a glass of sherry to take with her to her bedroom. She thought about how nice it would be to have Tawny back and to share the evenings with her again.

As she mounted the stairs and walked down the darkened hallway of the second landing, she realized how lonely the darkness under Tawny's bedroom door seemed.

Reba Cameron would not have rested so peacefully that night if she had known that Darla was still plotting with devilment brewing in her blond head. Now that she knew exactly how things stood between her and her aunt, she planned to take as much as her valises could carry back to Boston with her. Darla's blue eyes had carefully scrutinized the spacious house the last few days and there were things sitting around everywhere that she could easily sell once she was back in Boston.

She wasted no time tonight by going to bed too early. Instead, she immediately started packing one of her valises so she would have some idea about just what she could stuff in the other one. In this one guest bedroom alone there were dainty little porcelain figurines and cut-crystal trays, so she helped herself to a pair of the figurines and one of the trays and wrapped them protectively in her chemises. In three days' time she figured she could acquire quite a bit of loot. Tomorrow she would slip back into Tawny's room and help herself to some of those fancy lacy undergarments she'd seen in the drawer of her dressing table. Who would ever know they were missing, since Tawny intended to be gone as long as she was there at the farm. By the time Tawny returned, she would be well on her way to Boston.

Darla had never seen Tawny wear any jewelry, but her

aunt had many exquisite pieces of jewelry and that was something else that whetted her greedy appetite. But she knew that she would have to be very careful about that. That would have to take place at the very last moment of her stay here.

The scheming Darla Norton intended to use the next three days to feather her nest. Her voracious nature was not going to show any mercy for this wealthy aunt of hers.

Having decided how busy her day was going to be tomorrow, Darla finally dimmed her lamp and crawled under the coverlet to go to sleep.

Tawny was desperately tempted when she woke up the next morning to pack her few belongings into her valise and saddle up Coco to ride back to Cameron Farms. Why should she allow the likes of Darla Norton to push her out of her home? Had Reba not told her that Cameron Farms was her home?

But pride churning deep within her demanded that she not be at Cameron Farms in case Bart should come there to see her. She knew what his silken tongue and smooth ways could do to her. He could convince her that absolutely nothing had happened between him and Darla. She would be helpless to resist him if he so much as took her in his arms. No, it was time she tried to tame this wild passion she felt for Bart Montgomery until she was sure beyond a shadow of a doubt that he loved her as devotedly as she loved him. Only then would she surrender to him again.

When she had dressed and shared a breakfast with Mrs. Thacher, she told Roberta she was going into town to make a few purchases. At first she had planned to go to the bank to see if she could draw some of her money out, but as she was dressing and preparing to leave, she'd picked up her reticule. For the first time since she'd arrived back in Longcreek, she recalled that Jason had told her he'd put funds there in case she needed them. What she had not realized was just how much he had given her!

She had no reason to go to the bank today, she realized as she told Roberta good-bye and left the house. It was a good tonic for Tawny to go to the mercantile store and walk up and down the one main street of the small town with her pretty head held high and proud.

She bought enough yards of pretty muslin and lace for Roberta Thacher to sew herself a lovely frock and she bought her a soft woolen rose-colored shawl. She picked various yarns that she knew Mrs. Thacher would enjoy using for her knitting and also bought skeins of embroidery thread. Tawny's last stop was at the bakery to buy some delicate fruit tarts.

She was feeling very lighthearted and happy when she mounted Coco to go back to the Thacher cottage.

Now she realized just how much labor Mrs. Thacher had put into that dress of hers to make it attractive for Tawny to wear on that first visit to Cameron Farms to have lunch with Reba and Bill Cameron!

Maybe the gift of the shawl and the lovely material she'd bought today would tell Mrs. Thacher how much she appreciated all the thoughtful things she'd done for her for so many years. She owed her so much!

Tawny also realized something else she had not thought about until today. There was another person she owed a lot to, and that was Jason Hamilton!

Chapter 35

Darla's day went very well, just as she'd plotted it. She made sure that her aunt was downstairs before she dared to venture into Tawny's room. She helped herself to half the pile of neatly folded sheer undergarments. She didn't try to take any of the gowns, for they were far too bulky, but she did take one pair of slippers.

She already knew that Tawny had nothing of value in the dressing-table drawers, but she did take advantage of being upstairs alone to go through the other guest bedrooms to see what she might take that would be small enough to conceal in her valise and not be noticed until after she was long gone. She'd been here long enough now to know that old Aurelia did not clean the two extra bedrooms every week, so she was sure she'd be gone before those rooms were dusted and aired.

The booty she found there was nothing much, but the small silver box and miniature silver vase were worth taking, so she slipped them into her pocket. There was a beautiful small framed mirror sitting on one of the dressing tables, but she passed that by.

Slipping back to her own room, she placed the purloined items into the valise she'd started to pack last night. She closed and secured it before lifting it off the bench at the end of her bed to set it on the floor.

She felt the need for some lunch, so she left her room to go downstairs to the kitchen. Other than to request her lunch, Darla had nothing to say to the servant and Aurelia sought not to engage her in conversation. As she got up to leave, she did inquire about her aunt and her whereabouts.

"Can't rightly say, Miss Darla. She may have gone out to the barn to talk to her foreman," Aurelia told her.

Darla went to the parlor, but Reba Cameron wasn't there. From there she went down the long hallway to the study, but she wasn't there, either. Many interesting items were on the desk and end tables and the long mantel was lined with pieces of pewter, but Darla dared not touch those, for she knew her aunt considered this room to be sacred.

Darla saw many things in that elegant parlor, but Reba spent too much time in there for her to be foolish enough to take something that her aunt would immediately miss. She restrained her avaricious ways and left the parlor empty-handed.

It was only a few moments later that her aunt and Bart Montgomery entered the parlor. Reba had been coming from her barn when he rode up the drive.

Reba was beginning to feel sorry for the confused young man accompanying her into her parlor. She did not like the position Tawny was putting her in.

"I don't understand this, Mrs. Cameron. This is not like Tawny at all. Is . . . is she ill? Is something being kept from me?" He looked at her with his intense blue eyes demanding an honest answer, and urging Reba to tell him the truth.

She decided to answer him with some truth. "I don't think I exactly understand, either, Bart, but to answer your question about Tawny's health, I can tell you I am sure she isn't ill."

Bart wasted no time sitting down as Reba had invited him to do. There was one other person he recalled Tawny constantly talking about when they were together. He was going to seek out a Roberta Thacher.

"Well, Mrs. Cameron—I won't take up any more of your time. I'm going to start making a pest out of my-

269

self. But could you direct me to the home of Mrs. Thacher's? I'm going to pay a call on her this afternoon," he told her.

Reba had trouble keeping a calm look on her face. In a way she was pleased, for it was there he would find Tawny and she had not had to tell him. She was happy to direct him to Roberta's cottage.

She watched him leave and she prayed a silent little prayer that when he got to Roberta's that Tawny would not allow that stubborn pride of hers to turn her back on this man who loved her dearly.

Bart went in the direction Reba Cameron had told him, but no one answered the door when he knocked, so he dejectedly walked back down the path toward the hitching post and mounted his horse to go back to the inn.

He was feeling quite irritated by the time he arrived. The idea struck him that he was also giving way to very foolish folly for a man his age. Five years ago, he might have gotten so lovestruck as to have done what he was now doing, but no woman had ever had him going such circles as Tawny Blair!

By the time he got back to the inn, Bart had made a decision that he could only stay here in Longcreek so many days, and if Tawny did not wish to be with him, then he might as well accept that so he could return to England. But it galled him to think that for once he might fail to accomplish what he'd set out to do. It had been his intention that Tawny was going back to England with him!

Roberta Thacher was walking down the road from the neighbor's house she'd been visiting when she saw the handsome young man mounting his horse tethered at her hitching post and gallop away. She knew that no young man like him was coming to her house to call on her so it must be Tawny he was coming to see. Mercy, he was some fine figure of a man, she thought to herself.

When Tawny returned to the house a short time later, Roberta told her about their visitor.

"That was Bart Montgomery, Mrs. Thacher," Tawny told her as she laid down her packages.

"My goodness, he's some good-looking fellow!" Roberta exclaimed.

"Oh, Bart is that!" Tawny agreed with her.

"Is that the young English lord you told me about, Tawny, honey?"

"Yes, Mrs. Thacher—he is the one." Tawny found it hard to sound casual when she spoke about Bart Montgomery.

But she didn't fool Roberta Thacher for a minute, for she'd known Tawny all her life. The girl couldn't mask her feelings around her.

"He's the man you love, isn't he, dear?"

Tawny's brown eyes glanced up to meet hers and she couldn't lie. "Yes, I love him. But I'm not too sure he loves me."

"Why, honey, now why would you say that? My goodness, the man came by here today, didn't he? He sure wasn't coming to see me! It would seem to me that a man must care very much for a woman to come all the way from England to see her."

"I would like to think that, too, Mrs. Thacher, but I've got my reasons for having doubts," Tawny replied.

"Well, Tawny dear, I won't pry into your business," Roberta told her as she changed the subject and asked her if she'd had a nice afternoon shopping.

"Oh, I had a wonderful time, and I hope you'll like what I got here for you. Here, Mrs. Thacher—these are for you." Tawny handed her the packages.

"Oh my goodness, Tawny—all of this is for me?" Roberta took the mountain of packages and opened each and every one of them to find the beautiful things Tawny had purchased for her.

271

"Oh, Tawny, how thoughtful and sweet you are!" Roberta declared as she examined all her gifts.

"It's very little for all the things you gave to me over so many years, Mrs. Thacher, and they meant so very much to me. You'll probably never know how much!"

"Come here, child, and let an old lady give you a hug." Roberta took her in her arms to give her a warm, loving embrace.

Tawny felt so happy that she'd brought Mrs. Thacher the gifts, for she had only to look at her face to know how thrilled she was to have the yarns and embroidery thread. She'd watched her fingers caress the shawl and knew how she prized it.

Tawny insisted that Roberta just sit in her parlor and she prepared their supper that evening. Roberta allowed her to have her way.

Mrs. Thacher had complimented Tawny after supper that she was a much better cook than she'd realized. "I guess I'd forgotten that it was you who did all the cooking when your mother worked," Roberta told her.

"Yes, I did. It seems like a lifetime ago. So much has happened to me since those days I lived at that little cottage."

"I guess so. You've changed a lot, Tawny. I can see that, but it's all been for the better. I've seen you go from a wee tot to a young miss roaming around this countryside. Now I see before me a lovely young lady and I'm proud to say that I shared a part of your life, Tawny."

"Without you I don't know what I would have done at times, Mrs. Thacher, I swear it!" Tawny admitted.

"I'm happy I could do what I could. Looking back now, I wish I'd been a little kinder to poor Maybelle."

"Well, I won't be faced with the same dilemma as my mother was when she found herself pregnant. There is no doubt now that I am carrying Bart's child." She saw no reason not to tell Mrs. Thacher that Reba Cameron had made a new will when her husband Bill died.

"Cameron Farms will be yours someday, child?"

"That's right! I could not believe it myself when she told me," Tawny declared.

"Well, Reba Cameron is some kind of lady, I must say!"

"My father was a very lucky man," Tawny said. Only later had she realized how easily she'd spoken of Bill Cameron as her father.

"Oh, Tawny dear—this makes me most happy. You are a lady of substance. You will never have to face the same perils as your poor mother."

"No, I won't. I've thought about this so much, Mrs. Thacher, and I know how this town looked down on her. She didn't deserve it. It makes me love her much more. I'm only sorry that I can't tell her."

Roberta Thacher reached over to pat Tawny's hand and assure her. "She knows dear. I am sure she knows."

Coming from this dear lady, Tawny believed her.

When she laid her head on her pillow that night, Tawny was at peace with herself. It really did not trouble her that she might be faced with having Bart's child without him as her husband, for she'd manage to do it without him.

As she lay in bed she came to another conclusion: that she was playing the role of a coward to allow the likes of Darla Norton to run her away from her home.

Tomorrow she was going back to Cameron Farms. It was not Darla's home, it was hers!

The next morning she woke up early and immediately started gathering her belongings together. She hastily dressed and told Roberta that she was going back to the farm. Roberta did not try to stop her, for she knew that this was right for Tawny.

Cameron Farms was where Tawny was going to find the answers to what was troubling her, Roberta Thacher knew. Happiness swelled in her to know that Tawny

273

truly had a home.

She knew that life was going to be kinder and gentler to Tawny than it had been to her mother.

Chapter 36

The lovely Tawny Blair coming through the kitchen door was a glorious sight for Aurelia. "Well, bless my soul—it's about time you got yourself back home, Miss Tawny."

Tawny gave a soft little laugh and warmly embraced the black servant. "You suppose I could have a cup of coffee, eh?"

Aurelia chuckled. "Now, you know you can. Better than that, do you want some ham and eggs maybe?"

"No, just coffee is all I need," Tawny told her as she sat down at the table. "Is Miss Reba doing all right?"

"Seems to be, Miss Tawny. Miss Darla's being sent back to Boston in the morning." Aurelia told her, knowing that this news would please Tawny.

"I'm happy to hear that for Miss Reba's sake," Tawny commented as she took the first sip of her coffee.

"Did Miss Reba know that you were planning to come back this morning?"

Tawny told her that Reba did not know, but she had no doubt that she'd be as happy to see her as Aurelia had been. Tawny enjoyed a second cup of coffee and some more chatter with Aurelia before she left the kitchen to go upstairs.

She had not been inside her bedroom very long before she discovered that her drawers had once again been plundered and many of her undergarments and lacy chemises were missing. She rushed over to the armoire to see that all her gowns were on the rack. She heaved a deep sigh of relief for that and was about to close the

275

double wooden doors when she chanced to glance down at the floor to see the vacant space where her cream-colored slippers had been placed when she left to go to Roberta's.

She did not have to wonder where they were. Darla had taken them! Tawny wondered to herself just how many other things in this spacious house she'd managed to pick up.

She left her bag on the floor and went to Darla's door, unceremoniously marching in. She said not a word as her brown eyes scanned the room until she saw the secured valise on the floor and an open one on the bench at the foot of Darla's bed.

She ignored the open one and immediately opened the latched one, flinging articles all over the room.

By now Darla had roused up in sheer shock to see Tawny in her room. "Wha-what in hell do you think you are doing, Tawny Blair?"

Tawny was already holding one of her cream-colored slippers so she knew she would soon come across the other one. "I'm taking back what you hoped to steal from me, Darla Norton."

When she had completely emptied the valise and found her slippers and undergarments, she turned her eyes in Darla's direction.

"My, my—seems some of Miss Reba's things found their way into your little valise, too. I suggest you put them back before this day is over, Darla." Tawny didn't care that she stepped on various articles of clothing belonging to Darla as she went out the door.

For the longest time Darla just sat there on the bed staring at her things lying on the floor. Oh, how she hated that little bitch! Why had she come back here today of all days? If only it had been tomorrow she would have been gone!

What had prompted her to come back so soon? Darla wondered. Well, it really did not matter now, for all her carefully laid plans would never work out, Darla dejectedly realized. For the next half hour she fumed and cussed Tawny Blair as she gathered up her things.

When Tawny returned to her room and placed her things back where they belonged, she changed her clothes from the riding skirt she'd had on to the deep-green muslin frock she'd not worn since she'd arrived back here from England—the one young Rudy had given Jason to give to her when she was aboard the *Sea Princess*. Now she had the right slippers to wear with it! She slipped her dainty feet into the cream-colored shoes.

Perhaps it was the slippers that reminded her of Joy Hamilton or maybe it was the dress that reminded her of Jason, but her thoughts were very much on the Hamilton family today.

Forever she would remember their kindness to her.

Something else was on Tawny's mind this morning now that she was back at the farm. She intended to pay a visit to her mother and father's grave. As soon as she had a chance to see Reba and let her know that she was back to stay, she planned to take the buggy up to the little plot on the knoll about a mile from the house.

She rather suspected that Darla would not be coming downstairs too soon now that she knew Tawny was back at the house. Perhaps that was the best place for Darla to keep her out of mischief, Tawny thought to herself.

When Tawny had finished brushing her hair, she left her room to see if Reba was in the kitchen having her morning coffee.

But as she was almost at the base of the steps, she saw Reba coming from the front door. The foreman had obviously just handed her the mail and she was absorbed with that.

"Good morning, Reba!" Tawny greeted her with a smile on her face. Reba looked up to see her, so thrilled at the sight of her standing there that she let some of the mail fall from her hands.

"Ah, Tawny, you're home! Lord, it's good to have you back here!" Reba declared, rushing to fling her arms around her.

"It's good to be back, Reba. Had your coffee yet?"

"No, was just going to the kitchen when Mart brought me some mail. Join me?" Reba urged her as the two of them moved down the hallway.

Together they went into the kitchen. It was only when they sat down at the table and Aurelia had brought them each a cup of coffee that Reba Cameron noticed that one of the pieces of mail was addressed to Tawny.

"Seems you have a letter from England, Tawny," Reba declared as she handed it to her.

"For me?" She figured that it must be from Jason, but after she opened it she realized it was from Joy Hamilton. Noticing the date, Tawny saw that she'd written it only a day after she'd left England. Joy wrote how much Tawny was already missed by all the Hamilton family. But the part of the letter that made Tawny's heart beat faster was that Joy had told her that Bart had come to see her the same day Jason had put her aboard the *Caprice*. He was very disappointed to find out that she was already gone, Joy had stated. Tears almost came to her eyes as she read that Bart had vowed to Joy that he was going to bring her back to England with him. By the time Tawny received her letter, he would probably be there, Joy wrote. Surely he did love her after all, Tawny thought to herself.

It was the last paragraph of Joy's letter that made Tawny feel torn by mixed emotions:

Tawny, I think you have two Englishmen in love with you. I could swear to you that my brother Jason is in love with you, too. He hasn't been the same since you left, and now he's planning to return to Virginia. He tells the family that he has an assignment of cargo going to Chesapeake, but Mother and I both know that it is you he's going there to see. By the time you get this letter, Jason will be leaving England.

Tawny read the last paragraph twice. She thought about Jason and how wonderful he'd been to her. How could she possibly tell him that she didn't love him, that it was Bart she loved, Bart's child she was carrying?

Reba had detected the varied emotions reflected on Tawny's expressive face. Her smile had changed to a more serious, thoughtful look as she'd read her letter.

Suddenly, Tawny glanced up to see Reba looking at her. "It was a letter from Joy Hamilton, Jason's sister. We became very good friends in the short time I was there," Tawny told her.

"Well, it was nice of her to write you. I trust everything is well with the Hamiltons?"

"Oh, yes—everything is just fine. Joy was missing me," Tawny told her. She saw no need to mention the fact that Jason Hamilton was also going to be arriving in a couple of weeks. Bart Montgomery probably would not know this, Tawny realized.

When the two of them left the kitchen, Tawny told Reba that she planned to go to the cemetery plot and take some flowers to the graves.

"I think it best that I stay around the house, Tawny. I'll see you later, dear," Reba told her as she prepared to mount the stairway and Tawny went in the other direction to ask Mart to prepare the buggy for her.

She went to the garden to pick a basket of flowers to take to the grave. There were not as many blooming now as there had been when she and Reba had made that first trip up to the grassy knoll.

Autumn was here now, and the summer was gone. Tawny had not thought about it until now, but in the second week of October she would be eighteen. Before her next birthday came around she was going to be a mother. This frightened her, she realized as she strolled through the grounds surrounding the house.

With her basket filled with a mixture of wildflowers and the white-and-yellow asters, she went toward the

279

barn to see if the buggy was ready.

Mart gave her a warm greeting. "Nice to see you home, Miss Tawny. Got yourself a lot of pretty flowers there."

"Good morning, Mart. The flowers *are* pretty, aren't they? There just aren't too many of them. How's your family?" she asked as he assisted her up into the buggy and handed her the basket to place on the seat beside her.

"Oh, they're just fine, Miss Tawny. Young Billy lost a tooth last night," he laughed. Tawny laughed, too, for she remembered Mart's young son and knew that Mart had named his son Billy because of his great esteem for Bill Cameron.

He watched the young lady guide the buggy out of the barn gates and he thought to himself how she reminded him of his boss when she laughed. She had that same twinkle in her dark eyes. Maybe that was why he had taken to her the first time she'd come to the farm back in the early spring to visit the Camerons. He'd been there in the barnyard when Bill Cameron had brought her around to see his horses, and it was obvious to Mart that Bill Cameron had been very fond of Tawny to have bought her the feisty little mare, Coco. He was a generous man, but he would not have done something like that if he had not thought a lot of that young miss.

Suddenly Mart knew what Miss Tawny reminded him of, and it was that magnificent black Arabian Mr. Bill Cameron had owned. Like Diablo, there was a regal air about Miss Tawny, with that pretty head of hers held high and proud. The very sight of her was enough to make a man stare with wonder and admiration.

She was that rare breed of a woman a man didn't see too often!

Chapter 37

As Tawny pulled the buggy into the grove of trees, she noticed that the flowers planted there were blooming profusely as if it were midsummer or spring.

She got down from the buggy and tied the reins to the trunk of a small tree. Getting her basket from the buggy, she walked over to the graves to place layers of flowers between the two graves.

They lay side by side now as they had when they were lovers for that one brief interlude of their young lives. Maybelle would never have imagined this would come to be, Tawny thought to herself.

Once all the flowers were taken from her basket, Tawny sank down on the ground and spoke as though her mother could hear the words. She told her of the baby she was carrying and about the man she'd given her heart to as willingly as Maybelle had given her love to Bill Cameron.

"Now I find myself exactly as you did, Mother — afraid, just as you probably were afraid. I wish you were here for me to talk with."

A gentle breeze rustled through the tall tree branches in the grove. It was almost as if the swaying branches were humming their soulful tune to her. The answer came to Tawny as she sat there listening, and she would have sworn that it was Maybelle's voice she heard.

After she gathered up her empty basket from the ground, she moved to her buggy to go back to the house. She knew she'd made the right decision to return. She should never have indulged her fit of temper and left in the first place. She was only being absorbed with her own selfishness and not thinking about Reba Cameron at all. She urged the bay into action so she could get back to the house as soon as possible.

In fact, she was going to stay close to Reba Cameron's side for the rest of the time that Darla Norton was in that house. She would not trust that girl any farther than she could throw her!

As soon as she'd turned the buggy back over to Mart, she made straight for the house, but she didn't find Reba in her parlor or working at her desk, so she went to the kitchen to ask Aurelia where she might find her.

"She went into Longcreek on some errands, Miss Tawny, but she will probably be getting back before too long. Nothing ain't wrong, is it?" Aurelia thought she noted an anxious look on the girl's face.

"No, Aurelia, nothing is wrong. Did . . . did Darla go with her?"

"No ma'am! She's still upstairs as far as I know. She ordered a tray this morning and that's the last I heard of her all morning. That's just all right with me. Vera brought the tray back down a while ago. She'd done a fine job of cleaning up the plate, so I don't expect she'll be eating any lunch. Don't know where she managed to put it."

Tawny figured that she knew why Darla wanted to keep to herself today. The thought of facing Tawny after the episode this morning would not exactly be pleasant for Darla.

In fact, it wouldn't surprise Tawny if Darla remained upstairs in her room the whole afternoon!

When she left the kitchen, Tawny went directly upstairs. But before she went to her own room, she checked the two guest bedrooms to see if Darla had put the articles back where they belonged.

She was pleased to see that Darla had done as she'd demanded. When she got to her own room, she took a fast glance to see if her things had been bothered while

282

she was away.

Darla was aware that Tawny had come upstairs, and she heard the slight squeaking of the doors opening to the other bedrooms. She smiled to herself, for there was nothing Tawny could fault her about now since everything was back in its place.

The whole day seemed to drag on endlessly, and Darla was welcoming the dawning of the next day when she would be leaving this place. She didn't enjoy thinking about this last evening, and she knew that her sleep would be a restless one tonight.

Darla tried to soothe herself by thinking about the trip back up the coastline to Boston. Perhaps she would meet some interesting gent along the way and she'd be able to put this miserable situation behind her. If not, there was Boston to look forward to. She knew a few people there and there were far more exciting nighttime activities than in Longcreek.

She realized that coming here had been a big waste of time. Life on this farm was dull and boring! She did not find an evening stroll around her aunt's gardens stimulating and hearing the song of a whippoorwill in the pasture was not sweet music to her ears. She thrilled more to the toe-tapping music she could sit and listen to at the corner tavern near her boardinghouse in the city.

The fresh country air did not invigorate her. Parading through the milling crowd of the city's streets was far more exciting to her.

No, she was not cut out to be a starry-eyed country girl like Tawny Blair, and as far as the wealth she'd not been able to share, as she dreamed about when she'd come here, Darla figured that she'd fill her coffer when she got back to Boston by being much smarter than she'd been in the past. Tawny Blair had taught her that a wide-eyed sweet innocent could attract a certain kind of man much more easily than her own bold, brazen ways. Oh, she'd play the same games she'd played before she came here, only this time she'd play the cute, coy blonde. She suspected that the effect might urge the fellows to coddle her and be as protective of her as Bart Montgomery was with Tawny. It was worth a try, she was convinced.

Reba had drawn a tidy sum out of the bank, but only a small portion of it was to be given to Darla. She felt the amount she'd decided to hand to her niece when she left would be generous enough that Reba's conscience would be eased.

With the fat roll of bills in her reticule, she went on down the street from the bank to the one and only jewelry shop in Longcreek. There was a birthday present to buy for Tawny. Someone as lovely as Tawny should have a few pieces of jewelry, Reba had decided, and there was something very special about one's eighteenth birthday.

She'd known Mr. Simpson, the jeweler, for years and she'd decided to ask his opinion. He also knew Tawny, so she knew that he would help her pick out the right piece.

When she entered the small shop, she received a friendly, warm greeting from Seth Simpson. Bill Cameron had purchased several pieces of jewelry from him over the many years he'd been in business here in Longcreek.

"Well, Miss Reba, it's been a while since I've seen you," Seth greeted her.

"Seth, I've come to you in search of a birthday gift for a very special young lady. You know Tawny — Tawny Blair."

"Oh sure, I think we can find something for her. What birthday is this?"

"Her eighteenth."

Seth shook his head and declared, "That little miss is eighteen? Lord, I find it hard to believe how fast the years fly by. That's a sign we're getting old, you suppose?" he chuckled.

"Don't know about you, Seth, but I'm not going to admit to it just yet." She told Seth what she had in mind for a gift.

She saw a smile come to his face as he started to speak. "Just a minute, Miss Reba, while I go to the back of the shop. I've got something back there I want to show you. I think you might find it just what you're looking for."

He disappeared behind the draped doorway leading to the back of his shop. He quickly returned with a small velvet case and handed it to Reba. "You see for yourself if this would not be the perfect gift for Tawny."

The ring was a sparkling smoky topaz encircled with small diamonds, and in the case with it were matching earrings.

"Oh, Seth! Seth!" she sighed with delight. "I could not have asked for something more perfect. The topaz sparkles like Tawny's brown eyes."

"Exactly what I thought when you told me it was for Tawny's eighteenth birthday. I thought about those brown eyes and hair of hers. Always thought she was the prettiest little youngster when she'd trot up this street by my shop."

"Well, Seth, I think you've made a sale. How much is it?" Reba asked, loosening the ties of her reticule.

Seth quoted her a price that Reba Cameron considered very fair and less than she'd planned to spend on the gift, so she didn't hesitate a minute counting out the money. Seth declared that he'd like to see Tawny's eyes when she opened her gift. "She's sure going to be one thrilled young lady, I think."

"I think she will be, too, Seth, and I am so pleased with it. I wanted something special for her, and I feel I found it," Reba told him as she put the case in her reticule.

After they sat for a while longer to talk, as longtime friends do when they've not seen each other for a while, Reba left the shop. She accomplished what she'd intended.

She traveled back to the farm in the grandest of spirits.

Darla Norton figured that she had seen a fair share of handsome men in her life, but not one of them came up to the dashing figure of Bart Montgomery as he sat so arrogantly in the saddle riding his horse up the long, winding drive.

She had been sitting by the window in the bedroom when she noticed him coming up the drive. His blond hair fell over his forehead as he came galloping up to the front of the house. His firm male body was very exciting to Darla. The pants looked like they were molded to him, and the white shirt was open at the neck. She watched him and felt titillated by the sight.

This time he was going to find Tawny home, and she knew that was why he was coming out here. Suddenly, she jumped up out of the chair to dash to the door. Maybe, just maybe she still might be able to torment the snobby Tawny a little before she left this farm once and for all! She still had a score to settle with Miss Tawny Blair!

With this in mind, she rushed to the landing hoping she might be the one to greet Bart Montgomery at the front door.

Luck seemed to be with her this time, for she opened the door before Bart had a chance to knock. He was hoping that it might be Tawny eagerly opening the door to greet him.

But it was Darla Norton standing there, inviting him to come in.

Chapter 38

Tawny had heard the pacing hooves of Bart's horse and assumed Reba might be returning from town, for she had not seen the rider. She was standing at the top of the stairway when she saw that it was Bart in the entrance and Darla was beside him, looking at him with a smile on her face.

She was tempted to turn quickly around and return to her room when Bart's blue eyes gazed up to see her standing there. They both stood there, staring at each other without saying a word. Tawny felt the magnetic force of him as she stood there looking down at him and Darla.

Well, she wasn't going to tuck her tail and run this time, Tawny decided, so she slowly started to move down the steps. Bart watched the sensuous sway of her curvy body as she descended the stairs. He was immediately fired with desire for the love only she could give to him.

Darla watched Bart as Tawny came up to them, and it was as if she was a ghost, for neither of them seemed to know that she was standing there. But she wasn't ready to oblige them by making a departure just yet.

"Good afternoon, Bart," Tawny greeted him with a forced smile on her face. She would not have dared to address him as she might have if Darla had not been standing there.

"Afternoon, Tawny. I'm . . . I'm glad I finally managed to find you home," he responded, hardly knowing how to act with all the strange things going on between them the last few days. Then there was Darla standing there, ogling them both.

"Well, don't you suppose we could move out of the hall and go to my aunt's parlor?" Darla broke her silence to remind them that she was there.

Tawny's dark eyes turned to Darla. "I'm sure you'll excuse us, Darla," she told her. "Bart and I have to talk."

Bart was as much taken by surprise by this commanding air of Tawny's as Darla was. "Well, I guess I know when I'm not wanted!" Darla could only stammer, and she flounced around to leave the two of them.

"That's exactly right, Darla. You aren't wanted," Tawny told her as she turned her back on them.

An amused grin came to Bart's face as he watched Darla leave. He was glad Tawny had gotten rid of her so they could be alone.

He'd never seen this side of Tawny Blair, but he rather liked it, he had to admit. He also swore as he'd watched her come down those steps and approach him that she never looked more radiantly lovely. He was beginning to think that each time he saw her she seemed to be more beautiful than the time before.

"Shall we go into the parlor, Bart?" She invited him to follow her and he was eager to oblige her. When she took a seat on the settee, he sought to sit beside her instead of on the opposite chair.

His hand reached to take hers. "Why have you been avoiding me, Tawny?" he asked her. "You know bloody well I came here only to see you and you gave me every reason to think that first night you were happy I had come. Then suddenly you seemed to want no part of me."

"Things happened, Bart," she said, finding it hard to be casual and aloof with him.

"What kind of things? Tell me, so maybe I can understand some of this confusion. I waited all day for you to come to the inn and you never showed up."

Tawny tilted her pretty head. "Oh, did you wait alone,

Bart?" she asked him. "I came to the inn as I said I would. I was slightly delayed, though. You see, Darla Norton took Coco, so I kept waiting for her to return so I could have my horse back. Then I wanted to inform her once and for all never to take my horse out again without my permission."

"She took Coco without asking?"

"She did. After I waited for almost an hour, I finally rode to the inn to meet you, but the first thing I saw was Coco tied to the hitching post. Now, it wasn't too hard for me to know who'd she'd come to the inn to see and who she was with, so I turned around and came back to the farm."

So that was what all this was all about! He was rather pleased that Tawny was jealous. Impulsively, he reached out to bring her into his arms, for he intended to kiss her and wash away all her doubts that he had an interest in Darla Norton. "Oh, honey, you don't think I care about Darla?" But Tawny didn't give way to the sweet surrender he'd expected from her.

"Darla was not in your room that day?" Her brown eyes were fired brightly as they locked with his and she moved away from him.

"She was not in my room any damn hour if that's what you mean, Tawny. Now, if you'll just listen, I will tell you what did happen, which I could hardly help."

"I'm listening, Bart."

He told her how he'd instructed the desk clerk to allow her to come up to his room. "When Darla Norton came to the inn and asked for my room, the clerk assumed she was the young lady I'd been speaking about the night before so he gave her the key."

"So you did not know she was coming? My, what a surprise you had!"

"Tawny Blair, don't be flippant about this! We've already wasted a lot of pleasant time." He urged her closer to him, and she found it impossible to resist the sweet persuasion of his powerful arms. When she was almost ready to let him kiss her, as she knew he was about to do, she recalled just how long Aurelia had mentioned that Darla had been gone from the house.

So once again she pulled away from him, and Bart frowned as he raised a questioning brow. "What is it now, Tawny? Why are you so damned determined to make both of us miserable? Will you please explain this to me?"

"Then where in the devil was she if she wasn't with you? I know she'd been there for over an hour when I found Coco. You tell me that, Bart Montgomery!"

"I can't tell you what I don't know, Tawny. I know she wasn't in my room five minutes, and you can believe that or not!" Bart was becoming impatient with all the accusations she was tossing at him. No woman had ever dared question him as Tawny had been doing. He had found her to be so different this afternoon from the young girl he'd known. What was this sudden change all about, he wondered? *Something* had changed her since that first night he'd arrived in Virginia.

It was more than just her jealousy of Darla. She had to know that he'd never care for the likes of Darla. There was something else troubling Tawny, and damned if he knew what it was.

Bart knew that he had been honest with her, and that was all he could do. She either believed him or she didn't. He sat there waiting for her to say something, but she made no comment one way or the other.

"Well, do you believe me or not, Tawny?"

"I want to believe you, Bart."

His blue eyes flashed as he gave her the hint of a grin. "Well, I'm at least glad to hear that!"

Tawny would never know what she would have done next with Bart sitting there looking so devilishly handsome with that crooked grin on his face if Reba Cameron had not happened to walk through the parlor door when she did.

It was a wonderful sight to Reba to see the two young

people sitting together. They made such a fine-looking couple! She was feeling in high spirits anyway, and this just heightened them.

She greeted both of them but quickly excused herself to go upstairs so that they might enjoy their privacy. But Bart was already getting up from the settee to announce that he was preparing to leave anyway.

"Well, why don't you join us for dinner tomorrow night, Bart?" Reba requested. Tomorrow night Darla would be gone, and that was enough to make it a festive occasion.

"Thank you, Mrs. Cameron. I shall be happy to accept your invitation," he told her. When Reba had given the two of them a farewell wave of her hand and exited the room, Bart turned back to Tawny. "Do you want me to come tomorrow night, Tawny?" he asked her.

There was a look of pleading in his blue eyes that she would never have expected to see in the arrogant Bart Montgomery's eyes.

"Why would you have doubts, Bart? Of course I want you to come." She gave him a loving, warm smile.

"I've been puzzled about you, love. I guess I still am, but I've never lied to you, Tawny, and I won't start now. Remember that I told you that I didn't have time to play games, and I still feel the same way. I want you, Tawny. I always have!"

Before she could pull away or protest, she found herself firmly encased in his arms and his lips demanding that she return his kiss. She was powerless to refuse him even if she'd wanted to. She really did not want to, for it had been so long that she'd denied herself the ecstatic joy of his sensuous lips caressing hers.

When he finally released her, she felt limp and breathless. His blue eyes searched her face. He didn't know what kind of little games she'd been playing on him the last few days, but he was convinced now that Tawny loved him just as much as he loved her. The passion surging in her body was just as untamed as his when they were pressed close to each other and their lips touched. The flames of desire sparked a fire that would never be put out as long as either one of them lived.

He knew it, and he was determined to prove to her that she felt the same way. Whatever it was that was making her doubt it, he would see that she was convinced she could not love any other man as she loved him.

Before he sought to release her from his arms, he murmured softly in her ear, "Tawny, love! Oh, Tawny love! You still don't realize what you do to me, do you?"

She wanted to believe him, and he was so convincing.

He suddenly released her and turned to leave. Tawny watched his towering figure leave the parlor, and she knew it was hopeless to try to stay angry with him. Besides, he'd given her much to think about. She had to trust the man she loved—the man who was to be the father of her child.

As she climbed the steps to her bedroom, she felt alive again with happiness. The torment and pain she'd been feeling for the last few days was washed away. Bart possessed the magic to make her forget.

Perhaps she had been too hard on Bart. If he had told her the truth about Darla, then she had been wrong. If only Darla Norton had not come to Cameron Farms, none of this would have happened! It was enough to make her rejoice that in the morning she would be gone from here and tomorrow night would be a night to celebrate.

Maybe that was why Reba seemed in such high spirits! Maybe she was feeling the same way, Tawny thought to herself.

But there was tonight to go through yet, and Tawny wondered how that would go. She could only pray that it would be as peaceful as possible with Darla around. For Reba's sake, she was going to try to make it go that way.

But what Tawny could not know was that Darla had not gone directly upstairs after she'd left them. She'd positioned herself behind the archway to listen to them talk. It was only when she'd seen her aunt arriving that she scurried up the stairway.

So Tawny *had* been jealous when she'd found Coco at the inn and suspected she'd been with Bart all that time. A smug smirk came to Darla's face as she listened to the smooth-tongued Montgomery trying to convince Tawny that he'd had nothing to do with her. True, he hadn't, but neither could he ever prove that she was only in that room five minutes, and Darla knew that.

She still planned on giving Tawny one more sleepless night before she left! There were seeds of doubt that she could plant in Tawny's mind about that arrogant Bart Montgomery before she left, and she was going to delight in doing just that.

Oh, yes, she wanted to make both of them hurt as they'd made her hurt!

Chapter 39

Tawny felt she should excuse herself as quickly as possible so Reba and her niece could have a private evening together, since this was the last one Darla would be spending here. She bid Darla a polite good night and turned to Reba. "I'll leave you and Darla together to share the rest of the evening." she said. "I'll see you tomorrow."

Reba gave her a nod, letting Tawny know that she understood. After Tawny had left the dining room, she remarked to Darla, "Tawny is always a very thoughtful young lady. It was kind of her to allow us this time alone, for there are some things the two of us must talk about tonight. We won't have the chance to talk in the morning when Mart is taking us to Chesapeake."

Reba wasn't looking forward to making the trip in one day, but she certainly did not wish to stay overnight in Chesapeake. She'd even thought about just sending Darla to Chesapeake with Mart in the buggy, but Reba wanted to be sure Darla got on that ship. Knowing the girl could not be trusted, this was the only way she could be sure.

Reba took Darla to the study after supper and invited her to share a glass of sherry with her while they talked. Darla was more than happy to accept her offer.

"Tell me, Darla, do you have a lot of friends back in Boston?" Reba asked her.

There was a stately air about Reba Cameron that Darla had to confess that she admired. It was too bad her mother Polly could not have been more like Reba. The two looked or acted nothing alike.

"Yes, I've got a lot of friends there. Lived there all my life, remember?"

"That's right. I always found it funny that Polly ended up in Boston instead of Virginia, for she loved it here so much."

"My father liked it in Boston. He liked the city living, so I guess you might say I'm like him."

"Yes, I suppose you could say that. You must also look like him, too. You see, I never met Polly's husband—your father."

"Well, you and mama didn't really have a lot in common, shall we say," Darla retorted as she sipped the last of the sherry.

She had not expected to be offered a second glass, but Reba did offer so she accepted it.

"I'm accompanying you tomorrow to Chesapeake, Darla, to see you safely aboard the *East Wind,* which is the ship taking you to Boston."

"You don't have to bother—really."

But Reba assured her she was going to do it. "But while we are together, I've thought there are some other things to be said while I'm alive, Darla. Since you are Polly's daughter—my niece, I'm going to give you your inheritance tomorrow when you leave. It should be enough to keep you comfortable for two or three months. Now, mind you, it won't provide any luxurious living, but then it beats the way your poor mom had to live. When I die, all I own—Cameron Farms and everything else—has been willed to Tawny. I have no reason to tell you this other than to save you coming back to Virginia thinking you might gain something from the trip."

"I don't think you have to worry about that, Aunt Reba. I wouldn't have done so even if you'd not told me all this."

"It is only that I intend to put my cards on the table with you, Darla. So now you know, and I guess as I sit here and think about it, I might as well give you this tonight." As she spoke, Reba pulled out the drawer of the desk and got the roll of bills she'd placed there when she returned from town.

"Here you are, Darla, and I hope you make good use of it," Reba told her as she handed the money to Darla.

Darla's curiosity was whetted and she took the roll of bills greedily. Wanting to know how much her aunt was giving her urged her to gulp the sherry hastily so she could bid her aunt good-night and go to her room.

Reba sensed how she was feeling so she obliged her. "Well, Darla" she announced, "we've got to get up early in the morning, so I guess we'd best get ourselves to bed, don't you think?"

"Yes, I guess we should," she agreed, gulping the last of the sherry. She got up from the chair to follow her aunt out of the study.

When they reached the second landing, they said their good nights as they went to their bedrooms. Anxiously, Darla rushed over to the bed and brightened the lamp on the nightstand. She counted the money in the roll. It wasn't much of an inheritance when she considered how much Tawny Blair was going to get someday, but it was more money than she'd ever held in her hand at one time. With five hundred dollars in her reticule, she could manage very nicely in Boston for a few months.

She undressed and slipped into her gown and robe. She had one more thing to do before she retired. She had a last-night call to pay to Tawny Blair. It would be her final good-bye to the brown-haired miss who'd caused a lot of things not to work out for her the way she'd planned.

She was pleased to see that Tawny's light was still gleaming under the threshold when she emerged from her bedroom door. She gave a soft rap on the door, for she did not want her aunt to know she was paying a call on Tawny.

Tawny opened the door to see Darla standing there and a frown immediately creased her face. "It's a little late, Darla, and I was getting ready to go to bed. What do you want?" Instinctively, Tawny knew that she was up to something. Darla Norton was like a poison and everything she came in contact with suffered from her touch, Tawny had decided.

"I want nothing, Tawny—really! I just thought since you and I have been at odds ever since I arrived, I'd like to mend the fences, shall we say."

Reluctantly and against her better judgment, Tawny invited her into her room. "I can't imagine anything we have to discuss, Darla."

"Well, I'll grant you we don't have a lot in common, Tawny. But there is something I intend to set straight with you before we part company. The thing that made you take an instant dislike to me was Bart Montgomery, and I'll not deny to you that I carried on a full-fledged flirtation with him aboard the ship. Why shouldn't I have? He is a damned handsome man. When he happened to show up here, I continued to do what I'd done on the ship. Hell, I'm a born flirt."

"What is your point in telling me all this tonight, Darla? I realized exactly what you were doing that night. It was all very obvious that you were throwing yourself at him."

Darla gave her a smile. "Back in Boston, it would not have been so ridiculed, Tawny." She turned around, swaying her hips as she sauntered toward the door. "I'm a city girl, Tawny—not a simple backwoods country girl like you. So I have some advice to give you. If you plan to love a man like Bart Montgomery, you better expect to be challenged constantly. You'll never be able to hold him with your simple, naive ways."

She made a hasty exit out the door, hoping that she'd given Tawny some things to think about that would give her a restless, sleepless night. Darla smiled as she went back into her room, for she'd seen the look on Tawny's face as she'd spoken and watched the nervous fluttering of Tawny's dark lashes.

Tawny tried desperately to ignore the things Darla had said as she prepared to go to bed. Maybe she *was* just a simple country girl, very naive and innocent compared to the wealthy Englishman, Bart Montgomery. What would it be like to be his wife? It would certainly be different than being the wife of someone like Bill Cameron here in Virginia. She'd never really given this any thought before tonight.

Would women always be fawning over him? If that was true, she would surely be miserable, even though she loved him dearly. All she had to do was recall how jealous she'd been when she'd suspected that Darla was in the inn with Bart.

Could she ever possibly hope to hold him if they were married?

If Darla had hoped to give her a restless night, she had certainly managed to do just that, for Tawny found herself thinking about a number of things as she lay there in the darkness. Another thing gnawed at her, and that was the fact that Bart Montgomery had never in all his amorous moments with her proposed marriage. Oh, he'd told her that he adored her and that he loved her. But Tawny had to remind herself that he'd never asked her to be his wife and share his life.

Perhaps, as Darla had said to her tonight, perhaps she'd presumed too much from this Englishman, who vowed he loved her.

Maybe she should find out just what his intentions were before she went any farther with him. But how could she fight the forceful power he seemed to have over her that made her surrender so easily? She had no answer for that, for she felt herself yielding to him this afternoon as he sat there on the settee beside her.

Tomorrow night he would be coming to dinner, and she knew that she'd find it hard to resist his winning charms when she was around him.

The dawn was breaking when Tawny finally found herself falling to sleep. She had Darla Norton to thank for that!

She was finally sleeping soundly when Reba and Darla dressed to leave for Chesapeake. But when she did finally get out of bed, she was thinking to herself that it was going to be good not to be seeing Darla Norton around here anymore.

When she heard the clock chiming twelve, she couldn't believe how she had slept half the day away. By the time she went downstairs and into the kitchen for a cup of coffee to help her come alive, the Cameron buggy was approaching the outskirts of the little port city of Chesapeake.

Reba was finally feeling confident that nothing had gone wrong to delay them, but she'd also sensed that Darla seemed jubilant about getting to Chesapeake to catch the ship that would be taking her back to Boston. Darla was indeed feeling a great sense of joy, for she had been able to outfox both Tawny and her aunt Reba.

It had happened quite by chance early this morning, and this time she'd had no plans. But she'd heard her aunt's door open and she'd opened her own door slightly to see that Reba was dressed when she went down the stairs.

Reba had her reticule in her hand and a shawl over her arm. Her bonnet was already on so Darla knew she would not be coming back to her room before they left. The time was too near that they would be departing. Darla hastily gathered up her valises and her reticule to leave the room, but she darted into Reba's room just long enough to see if there was something she might slip into her reticule.

There would be no time for anyone to discover what she'd done until she was long gone. Darla's blue eyes sparkled with excitement when she spied the two exquisite strands of pearls with the diamond clasp lying on the dressing table. Beside it were the matching earrings that her aunt had worn the night before. Darla quickly snatched them up and put them in her reticule. Slipping out the door, she made for the stairs.

As she went down the steps, she smiled as she thought how she was going to have the last laugh on her aunt and Tawny Blair. Never had she been happier or more satisfied than when she was aboard the buggy riding away from Cameron Farms.

By the time Reba Cameron returned home to discover her pearls were missing, Darla would be long out to sea, traveling up the coastline toward Boston.

For once, Darla told herself, luck had been on her side. Maybe life would change for her, she wanted to believe!

Chapter 40

When Reba got back into the buggy beside her foreman and he was urging the bay back toward Longcreek, she sighed. "I'm not as young as I used to be, Mart. I'm going to be weary by the time we get back home."

He smiled. "Oh, Miss Reba, all us old-timers around the farm will forever see you as being young. You know, there are a few of us left around here that recall the day Mr. Bill brought his young bride home."

"That seems like a long, long time ago," she said laughing. "I don't know how I'd have managed after Bill died without you and Fred, Mart."

"Well, ma'am—I guess I would have to say I don't know how some of us would have made it without the Camerons. Cameron Farms gave me and mine a good life. Always had a roof over our heads and food in our bellies. I worked for a good man and a fine lady."

"Thanks, Mart. It is nice of you to say that."

The two of them talked of many things as they rolled along the country road leading them back to Longcreek and the farm. It made the time go by faster, for both of them were feeling the weariness of the trip back. While Reba Cameron said not a word to him about this young niece they'd seen off on the *East Wind,* Mart got the feeling that it was good riddance that she'd gone back where she'd come from. He had heard the gossip around the barn and corral that Miss Tawny had gotten real riled when Darla had taken her horse Coco out without her permission. Knowing Miss Tawny, he could imagine how that set with her.

As beautiful as the sunset was, Mart and Reba Cameron saw the wonderful sight of the farm coming into view. Both of them were more than ready for the comforts of home after the long day they'd put in today.

They sank into a serene silence for the rest of the ride as each of them gave way to their own private musings. It was as though the two of them were also weary of talking.

They wasted no time once they arrived at the barn in hastily saying good-night to go their separate ways. Mart went toward his own small cottage to join his family for a good meal and preparing to get to bed early to meet the next day's chores around the farm.

Reba stepped through her front door to smell the good aroma coming from Aurelia's kitchen, but she did not make any effort to go there. She slowly climbed the stairs to go to her room. A warm, relaxing bath was what she desired to wash away the dust of the long ride and she intended to lie across her bed for a while before she dressed for dinner.

Right now, she was too tired even to go in to see Tawny. But there was one comforting feeling, and that was Darla was no longer under her roof.

By the time the sun had set and darkness was covering the gardens below her bedroom windows, Reba had enjoyed the relaxing bath she'd anticipated and was lying on her bed. But she no longer felt so tired and she certainly was not sleepy.

She suddenly remembered that she'd invited Bart Montgomery to come to dinner tonight, so she jumped up from the bed to get dressed. Now she knew why she had smelled such delicious aromas coming from Aurelia's kitchen. She had told her cook that they would be having a guest for dinner.

She took her favorite black gown from her armoire, it was the perfect gown to wear with her cherished pearls.

After she had slipped into the black gown, she sat down

at her dressing table and opened her jewelry chest. It was a shame she never wore the beautiful pearl ring Bill had given her. Most of the time it lay there in the velvet-lined chest so she decided to wear it tonight along with the matching necklace and earrings.

It was only after she'd slipped the ring on her finger and sought her necklace and earrings that a panic broke within her. There was no sight of her necklace in her jewelry box or atop her dressing table, nor were the earrings anywhere to be found. She urged herself to calm down. As someone would backtrack through a forest, so did Reba. She'd worn the necklace last night, she knew, and now she remembered that she had not placed the earrings or the necklace back in the case. They lay there on her dressing table last night and so they had lain there this morning.

For a moment she sat in silence, thinking. She had left her room and gone downstairs. Darla had joined her a few minutes later. Reba had her answer as to where her lovely pearls were. They were with Darla, and she knew that never again would she wear them around her neck.

That despicable little bitch had stolen her necklace and earrings just before she'd left! Reba accepted that she could do nothing about it now, but she prayed she never showed her face around here again, and she rather doubted that she would.

She settled for the one strand of pearls and the pearl stud earrings she'd favored before Bill presented her with the exquisite jewelry Darla had helped herself to. It looked very nice with her gown, but she was still devastated by the loss of something she'd cherished so dearly.

With a dab of the lilac toilet water at her temples, she turned away from the dressing table to go down to her parlor to wait for Tawny and Bart Montgomery to join her.

When she went to the parlor she was glad that Tawny had not arrived. She wanted a moment or two to pour herself a glass of sherry and calm her frayed nerves, for she was now wondering what else she might find missing in her home.

Tawny had seen Reba return late in the afternoon and watched her walk up to the house. She looked tired and Tawny made no effort to bother her. Reba had put in a very long day on the road seeing Darla off on the ship, but there was the consolation that Darla was at last gone.

Shortly after she'd seen Reba return, Tawny had begun to dress for dinner. She chose the rich brown silk gown Joy Hamilton had given to her, one she'd never worn before. She was pleased with the way it flattered her figure, with the low, scooped neckline and long, fitted sleeves.

She attempted to pull her hair up into the sophisticated upswept hairdo the Hamilton's maid had fashioned one night when she was in England. She found that she had done a very good job as she surveyed herself in the mirror. The reflection she saw there was of no simple-looking country girl, as Darla had called her last night. All day Darla's remarks had paraded through her mind over and over again.

Tawny had never thought about Bart Montgomery as a sophisticated man of the world, rich and experienced. She had only considered him the handsome young man who'd stolen her heart from the minute she spied him on Reba's veranda. It had never meant anything to her that he had the title of a lord. So, as Darla had delighted in telling her, she probably *was* very naive when she compared herself to Darla.

Tonight he was going to see her in a different way, Tawny decided. Her mirror told her that she looked very attractive in Joy's silk gown.

There was only one thing that Tawny noticed tonight as she dressed and there was no denying the fact that all her gowns were tighter around the waist than they had been a month ago.

There was no doubt in her mind that she was pregnant,

and her figure was reflecting it. She pondered if she should honestly confront him with this and see if he truly cared enough for her to offer marriage.

But Tawny wanted him to ask her to marry him of his own free will and not just because she was going to have his baby. Maybe tonight she would have the answer to just how much Bart cared for her.

But for now, she forgot about all this to go downstairs to join Reba and share a glass of her favorite sherry as they waited for Bart to arrive.

When she walked through the parlor door, Reba sat there looking very elegant in her black gown. As she usually did in the evenings, she had lit all the candles in her parlor. Someday, Tawny thought, when she owned a home, she was going to have her parlor glowing with the twinkling light of candles and vases of fresh colorful flowers just like Reba did.

The two women greeted each other and Tawny sat down as Reba served her a glass of sherry. Tawny looked very lovely tonight and Reba was quick to tell her so.

"And so do you! I trust you got Darla on the ship and everything went well," Tawny said as she took the glass from Reba's hands.

"Oh, yes—she's on her way back to Boston. With her are my pearls, I'm sad to say," Reba informed her.

"Oh, no! How . . . when did she manage to do that, Reba?" Tawny asked with a displeased look on her face.

"Obviously this morning after I left my room to go downstairs. I never came back up so I didn't find them missing until I returned home from Chesapeake. I'd taken them off last night and laid them on my dressing table."

"That wicked little witch! How could she have been that mean?"

"Oh, it's easy for someone like Darla, Tawny. She cares about no one but herself. Bill had given those jewels to me and I shall miss wearing them, but I can do nothing about it now."

"I know how much you loved them, Reba, and I'm just

so sorry that she managed to leave with them." Tawny was sorry that she had not been able to stop her as she had earlier from taking what did not belong to her. She saw no reason not to tell Reba now what had occurred the morning she'd returned to the farm.

"I marched into her room and dumped everything out of her valise and there were my undergarments and some little trinkets placed around the two other bedrooms. Oh, I gave her a tonguelashing and hoped that I'd put the fear of God in her to not try that again, but obviously I hadn't," Tawny told her.

"As you said, Tawny, Darla is a wicked person, I'm sad to say, and my poor dead sister was probably very aware of it, too. Well, we shall rejoice that she's gone and won't trouble either of us again."

Reba had not planned on giving Tawny her birthday gift tonight, but perhaps it would make the evening more festive and gay. Reba thought how divine the ring and earrings would go with the brown silk gown.

She asked Tawny to excuse her for a moment while she went to the study to get the velvet case she'd placed in Bill's safe. Excitedly she dashed back to the parlor and handed the case to Tawny. "It's my birthday gift to you, honey. I know it's a week or two away, but when I saw you in that pretty gown, I just couldn't resist going ahead and giving it to you now."

Tawny opened the case to see the flashing diamonds circling the topaz of the ring and earrings. Never had she seen anything so magnificent! "Oh, mercy! Mercy, Reba — I think I'm going to faint," she gasped as she slowly sank down on the settee. Her hand trembled as she placed the ring on her finger. It fit perfectly.

Reba came to help her put the earrings on her dainty ears. "Bart Montgomery's eyes are going to pop out of his head when he sees you tonight, Tawny!" Reba gave out a girlish giggle. "Let me look at you."

Tawny turned so Reba had the full view of her lovely face with the exquisite jewels dangling from her ears.

"Come over here and have a look at yourself in the mirror," Reba suggested. Tawny walked to the console table where the gilt mirror hung. She'd never worn a pair of earrings before, but she smiled with delight at the image she saw in the mirror. "Oh, Reba—I . . . I just don't know what to say to you. I love them!"

Reba stood with admiration gleaming in her eyes as she recalled this young girl she'd first met, with her ragged skirt and her bare feet. Now she could have been a princess in her fine silk gown and jewels. Reba felt a degree of pride as she looked at this young lady.

Bill would have approved wholeheartedly of her gift to his daughter. How happy and proud he would have been tonight if he had been sitting in the parlor with them! But then Reba always felt his nearness when Tawny was around her. She had only to look at Tawny's warm brown eyes and see Bill reflected there.

She could not help thinking what a shame it was that her niece could not have been as nice as Tawny.

Chapter 41

Bart Montgomery had always thought Tawny Blair was the most beautiful, enchanting young girl he'd ever seen in his life, but when he stepped into the Camerons' parlor tonight the sight of her actually took his breath away. She was gorgeous!

He could have escorted her to any grand affair in London and she would have made any man's head turn to admire her breathtaking loveliness. He came up to her and declared, "You look beautiful—absolutely beautiful tonight!" It did not matter to him that Reba Cameron was standing there observing him.

"She does look lovely tonight. I agree with you, Bart," Reba remarked as she urged him to sit down.

As Reba served him a glass of sherry, Bart's eyes danced over Tawny's face and the shimmering silk of her gown. He'd never seen earrings dangling from her ears before, but she surely should wear them more often, and he would have to remember to buy something she could put on those pretty ears of hers, for Tawny was meant to wear jewels.

His blue eyes darted downward to see the exquisite ring on her slender finger. His hand lifted hers up to look at it. "I've never seen you wear this before, Tawny."

Softly, she laughed. "Because, Bart—I just got it tonight. Reba gave me the ring and earrings for my birthday."

"Damn, I didn't know it was your birthday!" he declared.

"It isn't, Bart. I just decided to go ahead and give

Tawny her gift early, for I thought it would look so nice with the gown she was wearing," Reba told him, easing his embarrassment that he had no gift for her on her birthday.

"And when is this young lady's birthday, Mrs. Cameron?" he asked Reba, in lighthearted jest.

"The fourteenth of October, Bart."

"I'll have to remember that," he grinned.

Tonight there was laughter around the dining table as they enjoyed Aurelia's delicious meal and a bottle of wine from the Camerons' cellar.

Later, when they retired to the parlor, Bart was pleased that Reba insisted that he enjoy a cheroot if he wished. "Bill always smoked his cheroots right after dinner, and I have got to confess to you I've missed the smell of them," she graciously suggested.

He did not hesitate taking out the silver case from the pocket of his coat and lighting up one of his long cheroots. Tawny watched him and recalled those nights aboard the *Sea Princess* when they would stroll the deck and he would smoke one.

She smiled at him and he returned her smile. When she told him that she'd heard from Joy Hamilton, she could have had no idea that the comment would bring such a change of mood.

"And how are the Hamiltons?" he'd asked her bluntly.

"Oh, they seem fine. Angela is getting married soon, so you can imagine how busy Lady Sheila is, preparing for her daughter's wedding."

"And what's Jason up to? Did Joy tell you? What faraway place is he getting ready to sail to?"

"Here. Jason is probably at sea now to come to Virginia," Tawny told him. The expression on Bart's face did not change at all, but she saw how brightly his blue eyes flashed.

He tried to keep his deep voice cool and casual as he inquired about his old friend's departure from England. Tawny told him that Joy's letter had been written the same week that she'd departed from England to come back here. That was all Bart had to know to figure Jason Hamilton could be arriving anytime.

Bart knew that he'd wasted too much valuable time since he'd arrived back here. He should have convinced Tawny days ago to leave here with him, and they should have been sailing back to England by now. It was not that he did not feel that Tawny loved him and not Jason Hamilton, but he knew that Jason had a special place in Tawny's heart. He was not going to stand by and see her confuse that feeling with the rapture of love they shared.

It was a forced laugh he gave. "Well, I'll be darned! So old Jason is coming back this way."

Those all-knowing, experienced eyes of Reba Cameron had noticed something that Tawny had not sensed while she was talking about Jason Hamilton. The news Tawny just told him had not pleased Bart Montgomery at all. Oh, he was a very sharp, clever young man, she knew, and he'd disguised it very well.

She figured that this was the proper time for her to leave the young couple alone for the rest of the evening. She gracefully rose to announce, "Well, I'm sure you young people will excuse me. I've had a very long day, but don't let that stop the two of you from enjoying the rest of the evening."

Tawny got up from the settee to embrace her and thank her for her gift. "It has been the nicest birthday I have ever had, Reba."

"Well, honey, I'm glad." She turned to bid Bart good night. He rose to take her hand in his and thank her for the delightful evening.

When it was only the two of them alone, Bart felt the Cameron parlor was not exactly where he wanted to be to convince Tawny that she must return to England with him. But Tawny felt that this was the perfect setting and perfect night for Bart to propose to her. All night long his eyes had adored her, and she was feeling very romantic and sentimental. She was sure he might just be preparing to do that when he rose from the settee to blow out the many candles all around the room. When he came back to the settee, his arm went around her as he pulled her close to him. "I adore you, Tawny Blair, and I never saw you look more beautiful than you do tonight."

"Do I really, Bart?"

"You know you do. You must know you've driven me crazy all night long. It's sheer hell for a man when he wants to make love to a beautiful woman and he can't."

She laughed. "Oh, Bart Montgomery, you are a devious man. I think I am becoming convinced of that. We all had a wonderful evening and you were certainly enjoying yourself, too, I think."

"I didn't say that I wasn't, but I can't exactly love you like I want to here in this parlor, Tawny love. My time is growing short and I'm going to have to be going back to England. I want you to come with me. I told you that it was my only reason for coming back here in the first place."

"And if I agree to come with you, Bart?"

"Then I'll be the happiest man alive. Come to the inn tomorrow so we can be alone."

"I'll be there, Bart," she promised him. While he'd said that he wanted her to go back to England, she wondered if he meant that he wanted her to be his wife. Before she ever boarded any ship to leave Virginia, she had to know exactly what his intentions were.

Bart left shortly and she went up the steps warmed by his farewell kiss still searing her lips. There was no question that she wanted to be with the man she loved, especially now that she was certain she was carrying his child, so that meant going to England. But there was another part that yearned to stay here at Cameron Farms with Reba Cameron.

What was the answer? Did she follow her heart's desire and tell Bart Montgomery that she was willing to leave with him anytime he said? Did she ask him when he spoke of her going back to England with him if he was talking about the future they would share together as a man and wife?

Maybe it was time she talked to Reba Cameron for there was no one she had more faith and trust in. She decided that she'd do it tomorrow before she rode into Longcreek. Maybe she would be better prepared to face Bart when she saw him.

She was reluctant to remove the earrings, but she did. The ring she left on her finger as she prepared to undress. Now she wore a ring on each of her hands, and she couldn't say which of them she prized more highly. The simple gold ring with the letter B on it was treasured very much knowing all the years her father had worn it.

Life had been very generous and kind to her lately, Tawny had to admit as she crawled under the coverlet of her bed.

By the time Bart Montgomery had ridden through the late night, many thoughts occupied him. The news that Jason could be arriving anytime could certainly complicate his plans for him and Tawny. He could not forget the influence Jason seemed to have with Tawny. Maybe her feelings for him were those she would have for an older brother, as she'd once told him, but he knew that Jason certainly didn't feel about Tawny as he did his three sisters.

Now, there was another thing gnawing at him especially after this evening. Somehow, he had the feeling that she was not going to be willing to leave this place and Cameron Farms.

What he was asking himself now, was if he was ready to offer her marriage to get her to come to England with him. That had not exactly been his intention when he left home. Marriage was a lifetime commitment, and Bart had not given any thought to that.

He knew he adored Tawny, and cared for her as he'd never cared for any other woman in his whole life. No woman had driven him as wild with desire and passion as Tawny Blair did, but did all this mean he wanted to marry her? That was something he'd always shied away from. From the time he was twenty, he'd played the elusive bachelor around London and so had his best friend, Jason.

But what if this was the only way he could get her to go back to London with him? A little voice kept haunting his sleep that night, telling him that he'd better decide just how much he cared for her.

Tawny dressed in her brown twill divided skirt and the gold checked blouse. She found herself struggling with the waistband of the skirt to get it fastened. She could no longer ignore how her waistline was expanding the last three weeks.

Pulling on her brown leather boots, she wondered if it was obvious to anyone else around here. Aurelia's eyes seemed to see everything, and Reba was most perceptive.

She took the long-sleeved twill jacket with her as she left the room. There seemed to be a chill in the air this morning.

She was surprised to find that Reba was already in the kitchen when she arrived. She seemed in a cheerful mood, as she had been last night.

"Think I had the best night's sleep I've had in a long time," she said. Tawny understood what she was talking about. Darla was not under her roof anymore.

"You look awfully pert and pretty this morning. Am I right that you and Bart have some plans for today?" she asked Tawny.

"Yes, I'm going to see him shortly. But I wanted to talk to you before I left for Greenfield's if you've got the time," Tawny told her.

"I've got all the time in the world, honey. This afternoon I am going to see a couple of old friends I've not seen in a long time, but that's a long time away."

When Reba asked her if they should have their talk here

or in the study, Tawny suggested the study. She knew that something was troubling Tawny and what she wished to speak to her about was not for Aurelia's ears.

As the two of them walked to the study, Tawny was almost wishing she had not said anything to Reba. But it was too late now!

Chapter 42

Tawny was reluctant to start talking once they reached the study and Reba had to encourage her to tell her what was on her mind. "After all, we're friends, and friends can talk about anything."

"Oh, of course we are friends, Reba. I've no better friend than you." Tawny smiled weakly. "The simple truth is, I don't know how to begin, I guess."

"Well — just spit it out. That's the simplest way."

"I guess you are right. It has to do with Bart Montgomery."

Reba smiled. "I rather suspected that."

"He wants me to go back to England with him and he's going to be leaving very soon, he told me last night."

Reba chuckled. "Told you you'd knock his eyes out last night, didn't I? He asked you to marry him?"

"No, Reba, he didn't propose, if that's what you mean."

Reba bristled. "If you accompany him to England of your own will, Tawny, then it would only be as his bride or his mistress. I'm sure you must realize this."

"He tells me he adores and loves me."

"Then, Tawny, it's time the young man asked you to marry him if he wants you to leave your home to go to England with him. That's the best advice I can give you, dear."

"But he could refuse to marry me, Reba."

"Then you better find out if you're wasting your time with him. There are other men in this world and you're a beautiful girl. You've a home and people that love you, so you don't have to be at any man's mercy, Tawny."

315

"I realize this, but there is something else I've been wanting to tell you, and I just didn't know how."

"Well, it's time you did. Come out with it. I've lived a long time, honey, so not too much would shock me."

Tawny sighed. "I . . . I think—no, I know I'm pregnant with Bart's child. I was sure when I got back here from England."

"So it happened when you were aboard the *Sea Princess* as a stowaway?"

Tawny nodded her head.

Right then, Reba Cameron was not feeling too kindly toward that older Englishman who had taken advantage of a sweet, innocent girl like Tawny. "It would not be the end of the world if you had your baby without a father," she said. "I mean no disrespect, honey, and you know that, but you're not in the position your mother was in when she found herself expecting you. But I must ask you, even though I think I already know the answer to my question. Do you love Bart Montgomery?"

Once again, Tawny nodded her head.

For a moment, Reba said nothing. There was only one thing she could advise Tawny about, and she knew it would be sage advice. There was nothing she could do about Tawny's heart and the way she felt. Tawny knew she spoke from the depth of her heart when Reba urged her not to leave with him, if it would not be as his wife. "Whether you carry his baby or not," she added.

"I won't, Reba. I promise you that," she assured her. But Tawny also knew how vulnerable she was when she was with Bart Montgomery.

"You're a young lady with your whole life ahead of you, Tawny."

Meekly, Tawny told Reba she appreciated her advice very much. She was glad she'd had the talk with her before she left to go to Greenfield's Inn.

Anyone seeing the brown-haired Tawny astride her

chocolate-brown mare galloping down the country lane would have admired them. Her long-sleeved twill jacket felt good, for there was a nip to the air as she swiftly rode down the lane. Her long, loose hair flowed back from her face. She was suddenly struck by the thought as she rode to the inn that as she grew larger with the child she was carrying she would not be able to ride Coco. A wave of sadness washed over her at this prospect.

The ride into town also gave her time to dwell on the things Reba Cameron had said to her. She never questioned for a minute that Reba had her best interests at heart.

Bart was standing on the front porch of the inn when she arrived, and by the time she had leaped off Coco and was tying the reins to the hitching post, he was by her side. "I've been looking for you to ride up. I thought you would never get here." There was a boyish exuberance about him as he clasped his hands on her waist and took a kiss from her sweet-honeyed lips.

As he broke away from her to look down at her face, there was a glint of mischief in his blue eyes. "Sweeter than any wine I ever tasted," he told her.

It was hard to resist such power as Bart possessed, she thought as she returned his smile. But in the back of her mind was the warning of Reba Cameron.

As the two of them walked up the pathway to the inn's entrance, Bart's arm went to the back of her waist, but his eyes were directed at her all the time.

His eyes were not the only ones ogling the lady walking beside Bart. Many of the guests at the inn were staring at the striking young couple as they mounted the two steps and walked across the porch to the front door.

From the foyer, the delicious aromas of the dining room permeated to the lobby. "Would you like some lunch, Tawny?" He added that the food here at the inn was quite tasty.

"Yes, that would be nice."

They took a seat in a secluded corner of the dining

317

room. The older couples sitting there exchanged smiles as they observed the romantic young couple holding hands.

Tawny and Bart didn't notice that they were being stared at for they had eyes only for each other. Tawny decided that it was time she did as Reba Cameron had suggested. "When do you leave, Bart, for England? You haven't told me."

A grin came to his face. "Well, that has sort of depended on you all along—ever since I've been here. There's a ship leaving in five days if you can be ready to go then, love. What do you say to that?"

She tilted her head to the side with a quizzical look on her face. She hesitated a moment before she remarked, "Five days doesn't give a lady much time to prepare for a wedding, you know?" Tawny watched Bart's face intensely.

His reaction was enough to dishearten her. She watched as his blue eyes flashed with surprise and he seemed unable to speak for a minute. "A wedding? I . . . I haven't thought about that, Tawny."

"Oh, I see."

His hand squeezed hers tightly as he tried to soothe her concern. "I guess I figured that our love was the most important thing. A wedding is merely a ceremony anyway, and it surely doesn't bind two people any closer than we are right now."

"Then I would be traveling back to England with you as your mistress, Bart?"

A frown came to Bart's face. He lowered his deep voice. "You'd be going back to England as the woman I love, Tawny. What is the matter with you? I can't seem to figure you out since I've come back to Virginia. You're not the same girl I knew when we sailed to England." He knew now that he was right; Tawny had changed.

"I'll agree with you about that, Bart. That girl had never loved or been loved by any man."

"So at least you will agree with me that you love me and I love you?" Bart's eyes were searching her lovely face for an answer.

"Yes, Bart, I love you," she confessed quite candidly.

"Look, this damned dining room isn't the place for us to talk. Are you through with your lunch?"

She nodded her head, so he summoned the waiter for their bill. Tawny knew she had to make a hasty decision, for if she accompanied him to the privacy of his room, she would surrender to his forceful arms that would be holding her as soon as they were behind closed doors.

When the bill was paid, Bart assisted her from the chair and guided her back into the lobby, intending to take her toward the stairs leading up to the second landing. But Tawny suddenly stopped and he looked down at her, asking her what was the matter.

"Nothing's the matter, Bart, but I just thought it might be nice to stroll the gardens. It's a beautiful day and we could talk all we want to."

"Fine, love—if that's what you'd like. It really doesn't matter to me as long as I'm with you. You surely must know that by now. I can't think of anything else I can do to prove it to you," he told her as he turned around to go out the front entrance instead of down the hallway.

When he said such sweet words to her, she felt herself mellowing, and she was almost tempted to tell him that she'd changed her mind. She would prefer to go to his room. But she didn't, for something told her to remember the one thing he could do to prove his love and devotion to her was to ask her to be his wife. This had suddenly become very important to her.

As they started their leisurely stroll around the garden and Tawny mused about all the things puzzling her mind, Bart was trying to untangle so many things troubling him about her.

When he asked a woman to marry him, it would be his decision as to the time and the place, and he found Tawny's earlier remarks had not exactly set well with him. Her question had stunned him. As much as he adored this breathtaking beauty, he'd not permit her to push him into a hasty marriage.

The elusive bachelor in him bucked up against such tactics, and he wondered why she'd done it. And why had she proposed that they stroll the gardens instead of going to his room? Had her ardor cooled? One could assume that. Her mercurial moods had him puzzled, and he could not say he liked this new side of her.

Bart Montgomery had never been a patient man, and he saw no reason to start being so now. He took hold of her shoulders and turned her around to face him. His eyes had a fierce gleam in them when he spoke. "Tawny, love, I told you a long time ago that I had no time for playing games and I was of the opinion that you felt the same way. If you don't feel the same way you did about me, then tell me right now and I'll waste no more of your time or mine."

"What is the matter with you, Bart? Why would you say something like that? I feel exactly the same as I've always felt about you. Is it because I asked you if we were going to be married before we departed for England?"

"I have to admit you took me by surprise, Tawny," he muttered.

"Why would it seem so unreasonable to you, Bart? Is it too much for a lady to expect from the man who says he loves her?" Her eyes still searched his face for the truth. She started once to add if it was too unreasonable when the lady was expecting a child, but she still clung to the hope that she'd not be pushed to do that.

"If someone is in love, they trust that person, Tawny. They have faith in them," he solemnly declared.

"And if I agree to go back to England with you because I love you so very much and we are not married before we leave, then I must have faith that you will do the honorable thing once we are in England?"

She was doing it to him again, damn it! "Why are you so damned obsessed about marriage suddenly, Tawny?"

"Because, Bart I don't intend to end up like my mother. I'll not be another Maybelle Blair. I am Tawny Blair and I'm a lady who demands your respect!"

Before he realized what she was about, she was dashing away from him like one of the frightened little does in the woods where she liked to roam. As he started around the corner to pursue her so he could talk some sense into that pretty head of hers, he slammed into an elderly couple taking their afternoon stroll. The impact of his rushing body caused the two of them to fall to the ground. By the time he'd helped them up and apologized as he lingered to see that he'd not injured them, there was no sight of Tawny or her horse at the hitching post. She was already gone.

At first he was urged to go get his horse and ride after her, but maybe it was better that he let her simmer down. Tomorrow he would ride out to Cameron Farms and convince her that he loved her enough to marry her if that was what she wished.

He had not exactly planned it that way, but if that was what it took to win Tawny, then he'd do it!

Chapter 43

She stumbled several times as she ran blindly toward the hitching post and frantically jerked the reins loose. She hastily mounted Coco, and tears flowed down her cheeks as she spurred the little mare into action. They moved swiftly down the street from the inn and around the corner when the sight of a familiar figure sauntering down the dirt road made her pull up on the reins to bring Coco to a halt. Her hand went up to her face to wipe the tears away.

"Dear God, Jason! It is you," she excitedly shrieked.

The sight of Jason walking down the road with his black eyes sparkling and that warm friendly smile on his face as he recognized her was the tonic she needed right then.

"In the flesh, Tawny!" he laughed as he rushed up to help her off Coco. They enclosed each other in a warm, loving embrace right there in the middle of the road.

"Oh, Tawny, it's good to see you again," he declared as his arms slightly released her to look down at that lovely face he remembered so vividly.

"It's good to see you, too, Jason. I got Joy's letter and she told me that you were shipping out to come here. But I didn't expect to see you this soon," she exclaimed, as they still held each other.

"Just couldn't stand to be away from you any longer, Tawny, my girl," Jason told her, in that lighthearted Irish way of his.

"Oh, Jason," she giggled. But Jason Hamilton had now had time to look long enough at her face to tell that she had been crying.

"Suppose that little mare of yours could carry the two of us? I was going to suggest that we go back to the inn so we could have a nice little visit."

"Of course she can. Come on—let's go," The idea appealed to Tawny, for she was not ready to go back to the farm or talk to Reba just yet. Besides, Jason always seemed to have a way about him that consoled and comforted her. Right now, she had the need for this!

Jason mounted up behind Tawny on the feisty little mare, and Tawny reined her around to go back to Greenfield's praying that they wouldn't encounter Bart when they arrived. As they rode the short distance, Jason confessed that he had been on his way to the livery to get a horse so he could ride out to Cameron Farms to see her.

Luck was with her, and Tawny did not run into Bart as she accompanied Jason up the stairway to his room. He told her as they made their way to his room about his good luck in finding a ride from Chesapeake to Longcreek with a local farmer. "Luck was with me, so I got here sooner than I expected, Tawny," he told her.

"So you landed this morning?"

"That's right, and here I am with you before the sun is setting."

Tawny thought to herself that there was no one like the happy-go-lucky Jason Hamilton. No one could bring a smile to her face or lighten her mood like him!

When they were inside Jason's room, he went over to where his luggage was lying on the foot of the bed. "I've some letters to deliver to you, Tawny. One is from my mother and the other is from Joy." He walked over to hand them to her and told her that he was going to see about having coffee sent up from the dining room.

"I feel the need for some coffee, and that will give you time to read your letters by the time I get back upstairs."

"Yes, Jason—that would be nice," she replied.

He gave her a big grin as he rushed through the door, and she turned her attention to the two letters in her hand.

It was Joy's letter she opened first. The letter was like Joy herself, breezy and cheerful. She told Tawny about all the commotion going on, what with the preparations for Angela's wedding in a few months. Lady Sheila Hamilton wrote about the same things and expressed how much she was missed. She wrote that she hoped that Tawny once again would be returning on her son's ship with him when he left Virginia.

Tawny was just folding up Lady Hamilton's letter when Jason returned carrying the tray himself. "Well, it was faster this way and I didn't want our coffee getting cold," he told Tawny.

Tawny laughed as she went over to assist him with the tray. She closed the door he'd had to leave open. Bart was still very much on her mind and his room was only a short distance away. He could come sauntering down the hall at anytime.

When they had their coffee and settled on the matching chairs by the double windows, Jason lifted his cup in lighthearted jest to propose a toast. "Here's to our reunion, Tawny!" She took a sip of her coffee as Jason was doing.

"How have things gone for you, Tawny? The Camerons are elated to have you back, I know."

Tawny informed him about Bill Cameron's death and that Reba was managing the farm now alone. She also told him about her mother being buried at Cameron Farms and that the two men responsible for Maybelle's death had suffered their own punishment.

"Well, honey, sounds like all the loose ends you wanted to come back to see about are now taken care of. That's good! You can come back to England with me and I won't have to worry about you." He smiled.

"Oh, Jason, you are such a dear, but then you always have been since the day I met you at Cameron Farms," Tawny told him.

"Ah, Cameron Farms—guess that place will always

have a special place in my heart, Tawny." Jason was wondering how he was going to bring up the subject of Bart Montgomery, for he knew that he'd surely arrived by now. He also wondered if Bart was the reason for Tawny's tear-stained face when they'd happened to meet. He'd wager that Montgomery was staying right here in this inn.

"Bart is still here, isn't he? I heard that he was coming back a few weeks ago before I left England."

"He is. And right here is where he is staying."

"Figured he was." Jason had only to look at Tawny's face to see that the subject of Bart had an unpleasant effect on her. So he tried to keep up that happy-go-lucky air of his. "I'm jealous! He's had you exclusively for three weeks, so I've some time to make up for."

Once again he had brought a smile to Tawny's face and for that he was glad. "Oh, Jason, you couldn't have arrived at a better time!"

"Well, honey, you must know how I feel about you. I'm here and I won't lie to you, Tawny, that this was part of the reason I took on this cargo. I wanted to see if you got here safely and if you were all right back in Virginia. My family and I took you into our hearts." Now Jason's black eyes were warm with the depth of emotions he felt and his manner was more serious than he'd intended.

"I know that, Jason, and it means the world to me." But this more serious mood was also a little disconcerting; what if Jason confessed that he loved her. The look in his black eyes right now said that he did.

"Well, you just always remember that, Tawny. I'm afraid I'm not going to be here for as long as Bart. I won't wait to get back across the ocean before the winter winds set in. I prize the *Sea Princess* too much for that."

"And do you wait out the winter in England, Jason?" she asked him.

"Oh, I spend more time there in winter, but then there are always the warmer waters I can sail to."

She sought to tease him. "I think the *Sea Princess* and the sea are the loves of your life."

His black eyes flashed brightly as he spoke to her with such sincerity she had to believe him. "Up to now they were, Tawny. Nothing meant so much to me in my whole life. But then I met you. I guess what I'm trying to tell you, Tawny, is that when I said a while ago that I wanted to take you back to England with me, I meant that I wanted you to return to England to be my wife."

"Oh, Jason!" She could not hold back the tears flowing down her cheeks. So desperately she'd wanted to hear Bart Montgomery say what Jason just now had said.

Seeing her cry was enough to urge Jason to move over to her and put his arms around her. "Didn't intend to make you cry, honey."

"I know you didn't, Jason," she sobbed. "It's just that . . . just that you are so good to me—so sweet!"

He kissed her damp cheek tenderly as he laughed. "I'm not sweet at all. Just ask my mother and she'll quickly tell you that I'm a devil."

"I don't know what to say to you, Jason. You've paid me a great honor, but right now I'm so mixed up I can't think straight."

"Don't worry about it right now, Tawny. I'll be here another few days. We both know how a day or night can change everything. Now has some other bloke already made you promise to marry him?" he asked her in that special way of his.

"No, Jason, I've not promised to marry anyone else. I can assure you of that," she replied.

"Well, that's enough to satisfy me then."

The afternoon had gone by so swiftly in Jason's company, but looking out the window, Tawny could see that the sun was sinking low in the western sky. She knew that she must be leaving the inn to get back to the farm before dark.

Jason escorted her back to the hitching post and they said their farewells. But he promised that he would be riding out to the farm tomorrow to see her and pay his respects to Mrs. Cameron.

326

As they left the lobby of the inn, Tawny became nervous until she had mounted up on Coco and was riding away. Only then did she begin to feel confident that she would not be encountering Bart Montgomery.

But she was in a quandary now more than ever since Jason had asked her to marry him and return to England with him.

She could marry Jason, and there would be a father for the child she carried. Never would she have to worry about him not being a devoted, caring husband. But she did not love Jason as she did Bart Montgomery.

She was convinced that Bart had given her the impression this afternoon that he was not at all interested in marrying her even though he wanted to take her back to England when he left. But what did she have to look forward to when he tired of her? What would he do when he found out that she was having a baby?

When her soft curves were no longer there and her body grew heavy with the baby, he might not be lured to her with the flaming passion he felt now. She could find herself in a strange country discarded by Bart Montgomery and she would be in the same dilemma as her mother had been.

By the time she approached Cameron Farms, she vowed that she'd never put herself in that position. Better she marry a man who loved her and would marry her even though he was not the father of her child, she told herself.

However, she would never lie to Jason, nor would she marry him without telling him that she was carrying Bart's child. He had the right to know the truth.

Just knowing Jason was here in Longcreek and cared as dearly as he obviously did for her was enough to ease the pain Bart had inflicted earlier today. She had instantly sensed his reticence when she had mentioned marriage. That was enough to shatter her hopes and destroy all the romantic dreams of a future shared with Bart Montgomery.

Maybe Lord Bart Montgomery did not consider that

she was good enough to be his wife but good enough to be his mistress.

Well, his mistress she would not be!

Chapter 44

Tawny did not fool Reba Cameron for a minute. Reba knew that Tawny was not telling her the truth about all of her afternoon. Oh, she could believe that the surprise of meeting up with Jason Hamilton delighted Tawny, but when she spoke of Bart, there was a look in Tawny's eyes that gave her away.

But Reba had lived long enough to know that affairs of the heart were a very private matter that no one could intrude on, so she didn't even try. They were something Tawny would have to decide on herself.

Tawny had no inkling that Reba was not convinced that she was feeling as happy as she was trying to appear to be as they shared the evening meal. She did not inquire about Reba's afternoon spent visiting her friends, and Reba did not mention to her that she'd paid a visit to Roberta Thacher this afternoon and found her ailing.

Reba retired early to allow Tawny some time alone. Besides, she planned to pay a visit again tomorrow to Mrs. Thacher, since the elderly lady had no one to look after her.

Reba was right, for Tawny did welcome the chance to go to her bedroom to think about the events of this strange day. As she slowly undressed and hung up her gown in the armoire, she thought about the two men who held such special places in her heart. Before she slipped her nightgown over her head, she looked at herself in the full-length cheval mirror. There was no denying it; her waistline was not so tiny anymore. The time that she could hide her dilemma was growing short.

Loving a man with all her heart and soul had caused all this, she chided herself. Foolish, romantic dreams had to be forgotten now. She'd had her fling at folly, and now she had to think in more practical terms. This child had to have a father if she didn't want to become another Maybelle Blair. Jason Hamilton was the answer to all her problems.

Tomorrow she was going to try her best to forget that Bart Montgomery ever existed and return the unselfish love that Jason Hamilton was willing to give to her. She would be a good wife to him, for he certainly deserved that.

This was her decision when she crawled under the coverlet on her bed.

It was inevitable that the two Englishman would encounter each other at Greenfield's Inn. Jason had already gone down to the dining room and was seated at the table when he looked up to see the tall, arrogant-looking Montgomery coming through the archway from the lobby. He made no effort to get up from his table to greet Bart. The truth was, Jason wasn't too sure how Bart would react when he did meet him, as he had known they surely would.

So Jason decided that he'd just sit at his table and wait until Bart spotted him in the room. He'd already ordered his dinner, so while he waited, he let his eyes roam around the room in the opposite direction from where Bart had taken a seat.

It didn't take Bart too long to recognize his black-haired friend across the room. He immediately rose up from the table to march across the room to Jason's table. Out of the corner of his eye, Jason saw his towering figure weaving around the other tables to come to his.

"Well, Jason—here we both are again in Virginia," he greeted Hamilton. "When did you arrive here in Longcreek?"

"Yes, we're back again, it seems. I hear you've been here a while. I just got here this afternoon," Jason informed him.

"Are . . . are you dining alone. If so, perhaps I might join you?"

"Be my guest, Bart. I have no one joining me," Jason replied.

"So you haven't seen Tawny yet, eh?" Bart asked him as he motioned to his waiter.

"Well, no—that's not correct. I did see Tawny this afternoon. She's looking wonderful, isn't she? I was glad to see that everything had gone so well for her since she'd been back."

His remark was rather startling to Bart Montgomery. She was hardly looking happy when he'd last seen her. When she'd rushed away from him in the garden, she was in a very sad mood, but he had no intention of letting Jason know this.

"Yes, I agree with you. She looks magnificent. I guess then I don't have to fill you in on what's happened to her since she's been back."

Jason quickly replied that he thought she'd brought him up to date on everything. "I was happy to hear her news, with the exception of Bill Cameron's death. I was very sad to hear that."

"Well, Mrs. Cameron seems to be carrying on bravely," Bart said.

"Oh, I'm sure she will. She is a fine lady." It was as if they were parrying with each other and both were very aware of it.

Jason's dinner arrived. He'd ordered before Bart had entered the dining room and Bart now took the opportunity to order his. Jason's beefsteak looked so appetizing that he ordered the same. He insisted that Jason go ahead and begin.

Jason gave him one of those familiar grins, declaring that he had no intention of letting it grow cold. It was a strange situation the two Englishmen found themselves in, for uppermost in both their minds were thoughts about Tawny Blair.

She would have been shocked to know that the two Englishmen were taking their evening meal at the same table while she dined with Reba Cameron.

Jason's full attention was devoted to devouring the thick juicy steak, and he carried on no conversation with his old friend. By the time he was enjoying the last few bites of his meat, Bart was being served his dinner.

Jason had another glass of wine as Bart ate his steak. "Good food here at the inn," Jason remarked, and Bart merely gave him a nod of his head.

When Bart finished his steak, he, too, had another glass of wine. It was finally Bart who brought up the subject that was on both of their minds. "Guess there's no point in not putting our cards on the table, Jason. You know that it was Tawny who urged me to come back here, and I guess it was Tawny rather than any cargo that brought you back here."

"I won't deny that, Bart," Jason readily admitted to his old friend.

"One of us is going to be the winner and one of us the loser, old friend. I don't intend that the loser be me," Bart declared with a grin on his face.

"I've known that for a long time. But I'm willing to gamble even if I do end up being the loser, Bart."

"That's where we're different, Jason. Guess we always have been 'cause I refuse to be a loser. I always get what I set out to get and you ought to know that."

Jason laughed. "Oh, I know that, Bart, but this might be the one time in your life that you lose."

Bart's dark brow raised and Jason knew that was a sign he was getting riled. "Don't you believe that, Jase!"

"Well, we'll both know the answer before too long, and if Tawny decides that it's you, then I'll wish both of you all the happiness in the world."

"Well, that's not my way, Jason, 'cause I'll fight you to the bitter end," Bart informed Jason.

"Well, I'll keep hoping until she tells me no, and as yet she hasn't," Jason taunted him.

"What do you mean, she hasn't told you no?" Bart asked, leaning across the table.

"I mean she has not agreed to marry me, but then she has not said no," Jason candidly told him.

"You asked her to marry you?" Bart muttered. He had not expected his friend to have been so bold or daring. No woman had ever held Jason's interest like the sea and his ship. While he might have been attracted to Tawny, Bart had not thought him to be this serious as to propose marriage.

"As a matter of fact, I have. I see no reason that you should not know, Bart."

Bart leaped out of the chair and the fierce anger surging within him exploded, "You double-crossing ba—"

"Don't say it, Bart!" Jason interrupted him as his own black eyes blazed like coals. "I won't take that even from you, Bart Montgomery! But then, I don't want to make myself look like a fool here in this dining room."

Bart shook with such rage that he knew he must get out of the room and away from Jason Hamilton. So he turned from the table and marched out. He didn't stop until he was outside the front door in the cool night air. The chilly air had a calming effect on him.

He was tempted to pull his horse out of the livery and ride to Cameron Farms right then. Once and for all, he would prove to Tawny that she was his woman. Jason Hamilton or no other man could ever make her feel like he had. She had to know this. If she married Jason, she'd always be haunted by those moments of ecstasy they'd found in each other's arms. Bart was convinced of this.

By the time he had cooled his temper enough to go back inside the inn, he'd decided if marriage was what the little minx wanted, then he'd marry her. The first thing he'd do in the morning was go to the jeweler in Longcreek to purchase her the most beautiful ring he could find to assure her of his intentions to marry her.

If a wedding was what she wanted, then they would have one before they boarded the ship to sail for England. He'd show that Jason Hamilton who was the winner!

Having made her decision the night before, Tawny eagerly welcomed Jason Hamilton when he appeared at the farm bright and early the next morning. Reba Cameron gave him as friendly a welcome, for she had always been even more impressed with the young sea captain than she had been with Bart Montgomery.

She liked his gentle, easygoing nature more than the more arrogant air of Montgomery. Tawny seemed so happy and at peace around Jason, Reba observed.

The young couple left the house because Tawny had suggested to Jason that he accompany her to visit her mother's grave. While they were on the grassy knoll and Tawny had placed the bouquet of flowers, she turned to Jason. "I'm ready to leave, Jason," she told him. "I'm ready to go with you any time you say. That is why I wanted you to come here with me this morning. I wanted to tell you that I will go back to England with you and I'll be most honored to be your wife if you want me."

"Tawny, I'm the one who is honored," he responded, taking her small hands up to his lips.

"Jason, I've something else to tell you before this goes any farther. I could never marry you without telling you that. I'm . . . I'm sure I am carrying Bart's child. But he's not asked me to marry him as you did. Oh, he wants me to go back to England, but when I asked him yesterday if he meant that we should be married, he hedged."

"Tawny . . . Tawny, you don't need to tell me any more and put yourself through all this torment. None of it matters to me or how I feel about you."

That scoundrel Montgomery was not going to get a chance to use his winning charms on Tawny again if he could prevent it. He was going to get her to leave here with him as soon as possible.

334

He urged Tawny to sit down on the thick carpet of grass. His hand held hers as he asked her if she was sure she wanted to go to England with him.

"I'm sure, Jason. I thought about it all night."

"How long will it take you to be ready to leave here?"

"I have only a couple of valises to pack, if that is what you mean."

"That is exactly what I mean."

"Jason—could we take Coco?" she asked him in a hesitating, almost childlike way. "I would hate to leave her behind."

He laughed and gave her an assuring hug. "Don't see why Coco would cause any problem after we managed to handle that fiery Arabian, Diablo. Never thought about that, but we'd have no need of a buggy."

But Tawny quickly pointed out her two valises, and Jason quickly agreed with her. "I should know better than that having all those sisters. Ladies just don't travel as light as men do."

When the two young people returned to Cameron Farms and told Reba of their plans, they looked so happy she could not feel too sad. Knowing Tawny as she did, Reba had no doubt that she'd told him quite honestly that she carried another man's child and Jason had still wanted to marry her. That was enough to win Reba Cameron's approval.

One hour later Tawny's luggage was packed and she had changed into the riding ensemble for the trip to Chesapeake. She had gone to the kitchen to say a fond farewell to Aurelia and a very emotional good-bye to Reba. Reba promised that in the springtime she would come to England to see Tawny and Jason. It was a promise that Reba planned to keep, for she knew there would be a baby by that time and that baby would be her Bill's grandchild. Nothing would keep her away from England.

She watched the two young people leave and she was filled with bittersweet thoughts as tears of sadness and joy rolled down her cheeks. Tawny had made the choice she felt she had to make, and Reba understood. Jason Hamilton would make her a fine, devoted husband and Reba also understood that Tawny was haunted by the fear that she could end up like Maybelle if she had her baby without a husband.

What a tremendous burden and torment must have been lifted off of Tawny's shoulders when Jason had returned to offer her the haven of his love and protection!

But Reba knew she was not marrying the man she truly loved!

Chapter 45

Jason lingered at Greenfield's Inn long enough to pay his bill and gather up the few belongings he'd brought from his ship when he'd left Chesapeake yesterday. He and Tawny had covered several miles by midday. By the middle of the afternoon, they arrived at the small dock in Chesapeake.

As soon as he had Tawny situated in his cabin, he went out on the deck to find Rob Gavin, his first mate, to instruct him that they were to prepare to sail away from the port.

An hour later, Rob and some of his crew had lowered the little chocolate-brown filly into the hold without any problems. She'd been docile compared to the rambunctious Arabian.

When Jason returned to the cabin to assure her that the little mare was safely in the hold and seemed very content, Tawny was relieved.

Jason could not linger in the cabin, for he had to get to the deck of his ship to see that all was in order for them to leave.

When she felt the sudden jerk of motion that told her that she was once again leaving the shores of Virginia, she went over to the portal to look out. She saw one of the most beautiful sunsets she'd ever seen in her whole life. The deep hues of purples, roses, and golds were magnificent. She stood there mesmerized by it. She told herself that she was going toward a wonderful, beautiful life like the sunset outside her window. She had to believe this or she would never have left Cameron Farms.

When Jason returned to the cabin later, she had washed

the dust from the long buggy ride away from her face and brushed her hair. The divided skirt and blouse had been discarded for one of the pretty muslin frocks.

"Well, you don't look like the girl I left in this cabin a few hours ago. My, how pretty you look—all refreshed and beautiful!" he told her.

"I feel very at home here, Jason. I remember many days and nights in this cabin." She smiled and walked over to him and placed her hand on his shoulder. "It's different this time, Jason. I'm certainly no innocent young thing and I don't want you to deny yourself the rights of your captain's cabin. I want you here."

He saw she was quite serious and he appreciated what she was saying. "All right, Tawny, I'll stay here with you, but I'll hang a hammock. I won't sleep with you until we are married. That's the way I want it."

She nodded her head, and a slow grin came to both of their faces. Once again she was thinking to herself that there was no other man in the world like Jason Hamilton. She reached up to tiptoe to plant a kiss on his cheek as she told him, "And so it shall be, Jason."

Later, they shared a tasty dinner, then Jason left her to check out his ship. When he returned to the cabin, he brought a bottle of wine. "By the way, Rudy said to tell you welcome aboard and he looked forward to serving you again."

"Ah, dear little Rudy! I shall look forward to seeing him, too," she told Jason as he got two glasses from the low chest.

They sat at the square table and lifted their glasses to toast their future. Jason grinned. "I guess you know that no one will be happier than Joy when she learns that you're going to marry me."

"I know. Joy and I became very close the first minute we met."

"Well, Joy was not the only one. There were many discussions around our table after you left, Tawny. I guess one of the most fascinating things about you is the power you have to charm people. It is a gift, you know?"

She gazed at him and smiled.

Jason was convinced that she did not realize how bewitching those big brown eyes of hers could be.

He figured that it was time he allowed her to get to bed while he took a final tour around the deck of his ship. "It's been a very long day and I'm sure you want to get some rest. I'm going to let you get ready for bed." He got up and went toward the door.

Dear Jason—how different he was from his friend, Bart Montgomery!

She wasted no time after he'd gone out the door in getting into her nightgown. She dimmed all the lamps except one. She lowered the glow of that one so that he could still see how to hang the hammock when he returned to the cabin.

When Jason returned he moved through the dimly lit cabin as quietly as he could so he would not disturb Tawny if she was asleep. Once the hammock was hung, he undressed. It had been a long time since he'd struggled into one of these hammocks. They were very comfortable but a bother to get into.

It took him a couple of times before he finally got his body just right. Tawny was observing him and she held her hand over her mouth to suppress a giggle.

She knew he was cussing the fact that he'd failed to dim the one remaining lamp so she softly ordered him to stay where he was now that he'd gotten himself so comfortable. "I can do it much easier than you, Jason," she laughed as she quickly scampered over to the table.

"Good night, Jason."

"Good night, Princess," Jason replied with a grin on his face.

Bart Montgomery was rarely ill at ease or nervous about

anything, but when he went to the jeweler to pick out a ring for Tawny, he was flustered. Seth Simpson noticed it the minute the tall, blond-haired young man walked inside the door.

"Morning, young man," the jeweler greeted Bart. "What can I do for you?"

"I'd . . . I'd like to see a ring," Bart mumbled.

"A ring, is it? A ring for a lady—maybe a special lady." Being a very talkative fellow, Seth told him that there were rings bought for a sister or a mother. Then there were rings a man bought for a special young lady.

"This is for a special young lady, as you said."

"Next question, young man, is what gem are you interested in? A diamond, I would suspect."

"Yes—a diamond."

Seth bid him to have a seat while he went to the back of his shop. All the time he searched some of the trays in his safe, he was wondering who this young man was. Simpson knew all the local young gents. Seth could tell from the way he spoke that he was not from Virginia. He also suspected that this gent wanted something very impressive. No ordinary diamond ring would suit him.

Seth searched for the one he felt would catch this fellow's eyes. Would he accept the very spectacular diamond encircled with blue sapphires that were so exquisitely cut? It was the most expensive ring in his entire collection and Seth knew that was why he'd never sold it here in Longcreek. Few ladies dressed so fine here to wear such a magnificent ring.

He took it out of the tray and placed it on the velvet cloth to display it to Bart Montgomery. To Seth's great delight, Bart immediately fancied it and asked the price.

Not a muscle flinched when Seth told him the price and he informed the jeweler he wanted the ring. Seth had no idea that it was Tawny Blair the ring was being purchased for when he sighed and smiled. "That lady is certainly going to be happy when you present her with this, young man."

"I hope so," Bart said as he handed Seth the money for the ring. Seth pocketed the money, thinking to himself that he was going to lock up the store and spend the entire afternoon fishing. He could well afford to do it. In fact, if he wanted to take off the whole week he could do it, and he damned well might, he thought as he told Bart good-bye and watched him walk out the door.

With the ring secured in the pocket of his coat, Bart was ready to ride out to Cameron Farms. He felt very confident as he rode down the dirt road that if he asked Tawny to marry him and gave her the ring, she would surely agree to go back to England with him. If she did, then he was going to secure their passage before this day was over on the first ship he could find sailing for England.

It was almost noon when he galloped up the long drive of Cameron Farms. The barnyard was alive with the activities of the hired hands.

Reba was up and dressed, for she was preparing to go into town to check on Roberta Thacher. She was just a little concerned about the older lady and she had never got around to telling Tawny about her ailing, with the way things happened so swiftly yesterday.

She was in her parlor when a deep voice called to her and she turned away from her mirror. "Bart! Bart Montgomery!"

He gave a spirited laugh. "Why, Mrs. Cameron—is the sight of me such a shock?"

"Guess it shouldn't be," she said, trying to gain her composure. It was just dawning on her that she was going to be the one to face Bart and tell him that Tawny was gone.

She invited him to sit down as she placed her bonnet on the table.

"Please, Mrs. Cameron, don't let me hold you up," Bart said. "It's obvious you were preparing to leave the house. I was coming to call on Tawny."

It was going to be difficult to tell him what she must but she knew of no way to make it easy. "Tawny isn't here, Bart."

"Well, could I wait until she returns then?"

"Bart, that could be a very long wait, I'm afraid. She left here with your friend, Jason Hamilton. By now I would say that they are far out to sea going toward England."

"What are you saying, Mrs. Cameron?" his eyes flashed with disbelief and despair.

Reba realized what a stunning blow she'd delivered. "I don't enjoy being the one to tell you this, but I suppose I must. Jason Hamilton asked Tawny to marry him and she accepted. So they left to go to his ship and sail for England."

Bart felt as if he'd been hit in the gut with a mighty blow of a club. He could not speak in his state of shock. It pained Reba Cameron as she looked at him to see the misery in his eyes.

"I'm sorry, Bart. I truly am, but Tawny must have felt very strongly about this or she wouldn't have left with Jason."

"But, Mrs. Cameron, she doesn't love him. She loves me and I love her. Tawny had to know this!" He pointed out to Reba that it was only for Tawny that he'd returned to Virginia.

"Bart, I'm a very direct lady. I don't beat around the bush, shall we say. I come straight to the point, too. I have to be honest with you when I say that I thought it was you Tawny loved. Her announcement to marry Jason and leave so hastily came as a surprise to me. But he asked her to marry him. Did you?"

"I didn't realize that marriage was so important to Tawny until day before yesterday. I realize now that it must have been," Bart confessed to her.

"And you know why, Bart?"

"I guess I didn't."

"Then I guess I'm going to have to be the one to tell you that she was expecting a baby—your baby, Bart!"

If she'd given him a shock before, she really devastated him by this revelation. He sat there dumbfounded.

Now he understood so many things and the reason

342

Tawny had acted as she had when she'd come to the inn and why she'd been so bold when the two of them were in the garden. Tawny was desperate yesterday!

He'd never thought about the possibility that she might be carrying his child, and he should have, he realized now as he sat with Reba Cameron. After all the times they'd enjoyed the paradise of passion and the moments of rapture, he should have realized this was a possibility. After all, he was more experienced than Tawny and he should have let her know that she had no worry if this happened. Oh, what an absolute fool he'd been!

Now he had probably lost her, and he had no one to blame but himself!

"Tell me again, Mrs. Cameron—they aren't married yet? Is that right?"

That Bart was a distraught man was obvious to Reba. "No, they did not marry before they left. They were going to marry when they got to England."

"Well, that won't happen if I can help it. Tawny should have told me she carried my child!"

"Tawny had her pride, too, Bart. She wanted you to ask her to marry you because you loved her and not because she was carrying your child."

"I deserve that, and I also understand now. But I would not have hesitated a minute if only she'd come to me and told me."

"She could not have known that, though," Reba pointed out to him.

"Well, I've plans to make, Mrs. Cameron, so I bid you farewell. The sooner I can get back to England, the sooner all this will be straightened out. Jason Hamilton will not play the role of father to my child. My woman will not be his wife, either," Bart declared with firm determination.

"Good luck to you, Bart. I hope that everything works out. All I wish is Tawny's happiness," Reba said as he turned to leave.

Privately, she thought that he better get on a ship sailing for England as soon as possible if he expected to stop

343

Tawny's wedding from taking place.

She found herself feeling sorry for the young man who'd just left her parlor. She only wished that Tawny had not have acted so impulsively.

She silently prayed that Bart did get back to England in time to stop the wedding so she could marry the man she truly loved. Bart was that man!

Part Four

Timeless Love

Chapter 46

As soon as Bart Montgomery could pack up his belongings at the inn, he departed to ride to Chesapeake. By late afternoon he was at the outskirts of the port town. He did not make for the hotel in the main part of town, but instead, he went down to the wharf to inquire of the dockhands still working if there were any ships leaving for England. He was not too particular about what ship it was. The accommodations were not important to him at this point — he just wanted to leave as soon as he could.

One of the dockhands scratched his head as he thought about it before he called to one of his fellow workers, "Hey, Cal — ain't there a freighter shipping out of here this evening for England?"

"Yeah, the *Iron Lady* is leavin' anytime," the dockhand yelled back.

"You lookin' for passage, mister?"

"That's right," Bart told him anxiously.

"Can't say if old Barney will take on any passenger on his freighter, but over there is where you'll find him."

Bart thanked him and rushed to the small tavern where the man had indicated that he'd find Barney, the captain of the freighter.

He walked into the dimly lit smoke-filled cubbyhole of a tavern. Since he didn't know what Barney looked like, he asked the first fellow he ran into, figuring he might know the man.

Bart looked out of place in his fine-tailored pants and clean white linen shirt amid this gathering of seamen in their faded clothing. From the fetid body odor coming to Bart's nose all

347

of them appeared to be in need of a shave and a bath, but this didn't matter to him, either.

Barney was sitting at the back table with a couple of his buddies. Bart marched directly to the table.

"Are you Captain Barney?" Bart inquired as he came up to the table.

"That's me! Now, don't tell me you want to sign on the *Iron Lady*." He gave out a boisterous laugh. His two friends broke into laughter, too, as they looked up at the Englishman.

Bart gave a laugh of his own. "No, I fear I'd not be hired. It's passage I'd like to buy to get back to England as fast as I can. Just got the news that my mother is dying," he lied. The hardest-hearted man had a tender spot inside him for his mother.

The three exchanged glances as Bart continued to tell the captain that he didn't want to delay his return by waiting around in Chesapeake for another ship since he'd learned that the *Iron Lady* was leaving tonight.

"Ain't got passenger cabins, fellow. A freighter ain't a fancy ship, you understand?"

"I'm aware of it, but comfort isn't my concern right now," Bart replied.

"Well, there ain't no fancy meals — just plain seamen's fare. You'll be taking your meals with the rest of us fellows." He quoted the fee Bart would have to pay.

"I told you, Captain Barney, that I'm only interested in getting back to England, so I'll pay your price."

Barney told one of the men to take Bart on to the *Iron Lady*. "We're shipping out within the hour." As he was ordered, the seaman got out on his chair to follow his captain's orders. "Put him in with Disney, Pat."

The seaman nodded his head and urged Bart to come with him, and Bart went along with the short, lean fellow whose skin looked like tanned leather from all the years at sea.

As they walked down the wharf, Pat turned to him. "Didn't catch your name back there."

"Bart Montgomery," he told him and inquired as to his.

"Pat O'Roarke."

348

"A good Irish name, isn't it?"

"That's right. My pa came over here over thirty years ago."

"How long will it take us to cross?"

Pat told him he could not say, that it all depended on the weather. It could be as soon as two weeks or linger into three weeks.

When they stopped on to the deck, the crew was already preparing for the departure, and Pat suggested that he stay put in Disney's small quarters once he got him there. Bart was already seeing enough of the freighter to know that it was hardly the sleek-lined ship of Jason's or the fine ship, the *Caprice*.

Once he entered the small cubicle where he would be living for the next several days, he was doing well to stand up, for the ceiling was very low. Bart was hoping this fellow Disney was not a big man, or the two of them were going to have trouble moving around the quarters at the same time.

Once Pat got him to the cabin, he left immediately. Bart sought a corner to see his luggage down and out of the way.

Bart surveyed the meager surroundings. One bunk was placed against each wall of the cabin, and less than six feet of floor space divided them. The pad of the bunks was about two inches thick with a folded blanket lying at the foot of the bunk. Sheets were not snowy white, nor did they smell fresh.

He used one of the pegs on the door to hang up his coat. He found the small quarters stuffy and warm, so he unbuttoned the collar of his shirt and rolled up his sleeves.

He had already concluded that this was not going to be a pleasurable experience, and it could end up being a very dangerous one. He thought about the heavy roll of money and the expensive ring he was carrying with him that he'd not got the chance to give to Tawny. He was glad for the small hand pistol he had in his luggage, for it might come in handy before this trip was over.

While he was alone in the cabin, he changed his luggage over in the corner and slipped it snugly in a concealed, empty space under his bunk. It was obvious which bunk was used by this Disney, for the blanket was flung carelessly over the other bunk.

Captain Barney was not lying when he said that they would be leaving within the hour, for Bart felt the surging motions of the ship as it was leaving Chesapeake while he sat there on the bed.

A few minutes later he was to meet Disney, and he was pleased to see that he was as thin as a reed. After the two had introduced themselves, Bart learned that he was the ship's cook and that was the reason he'd come to the cabin carrying a covered platter of the bread he'd baked and some slices of a roasted hen he'd prepared in his galley earlier.

"Always bring myself a fine helping to my cabin to enjoy alone, but I'll be happy to share it with you," he told Bart. It tasted good to Bart along with the steaming cup of strong, hot coffee. After they'd talked a while as they ate, Bart learned that Disney was from Liverpool. He was glad that he was going to be sharing the time with someone like Disney instead of one of the sailors he'd seen when he came aboard. They had looked like an unsavory lot.

"The rest of the meat and bread are yours to enjoy 'cause I got to get back to my galley. Theres a lot of coffee to be brewed and a lot of pots and pans to get clean for in the morning before I can call it a night. I'll try to come in quiet in case you're asleep," Disney told him as he prepared to leave the cabin.

Bart considered he was lucky he had drawn Disney, for he seemed like a friendly fellow and looked rather out of place here. But then a cook didn't have to be a robust, rugged individual like the sailors.

With Disney as his cabin mate, Bart relaxed about the money and the ring in his possession. He got out of his clothes to stretch his long body on the bunk, which was miserably hard and uncomfortable. But the comforting thought was that he was on his way to England, and he was only two days behind Jason and Tawny. But he also knew the speed of Jason's *Sea Princess*.

There was one tormenting thought stabbing at him as he lay on that hard bunk, and that was the fear Tawny was sharing Jason's bed with him in his cabin. Damned if he wouldn't feel like killing Hamilton if he was lying with the woman he loved!

He told himself that he could not keep thinking about this or he'd go crazy. He mustered all his strong, determined will to believe that Tawny might have promised Jason that she'd marry him and even left to return to England, but she could never bring herself to make love with him. He had to believe this, for this was the one thing that would keep him sane.

Besides, he thought to himself, the baby she carried was his, not Jason's. That would surely stop her!

It was this thought that allowed him to finally fall asleep. He didn't know when Disney slipped into the cabin and exhaustedly sank down on his bunk to fall asleep immediately.

During the next few days, Bart and Disney developed a pleasant camaraderie, and it helped the time pass for Bart. The young man was a very good cook and Captain Barney was lucky to have him aboard his freighter, Montgomery considered.

Bart's hearty appetite was sated because Disney was always bringing extra food to the cabin for late-night snacks or a midday lunch. So Bart did not have a need to take some meals with the rest of the crew nor did he mingle with many of them when he left the cabin. He often talked to Pat O'Roarke when he strolled the deck, but some of the others had left a foul taste in Bart's mouth. He figured that the less he had to do with them, the better.

"How'd you happen to be a galley cook on the *Iron Lady?*" he asked Disney when he felt they had become good friends. Bart had decided that Disney was about his age.

"Worked for Uncle in his pub in Liverpool after I went to live with him and my auntie Tess. Had to cook the meals after my auntie got ill and helped my uncle in the pub in the evenings. That paid for my room and board with them. Captain Barney came into the pub one night and he got so drunk he couldn't stand up, so I took him home and took care of him. He was beholden to me and offered me this job. I thought I ought to take it."

"So you've been with him ever since?"

"That was five years ago. I figured that it relieved my uncle and aunt of me. I found a job to support myself. Now I save my money and I have hopes of having myself a little country inn on the outskirts of the city. I have it all here in my mind how I'd like it."

"And how is that, Disney?"

"Well, it'll be pleasant and cozy. I'd like to think people would enjoy the serenity my inn would provide and come to the dining room to savor my tasty foods and wine. Does that sound crazy?"

"Not at all. It sounds like a place where I'd like to spend a few days. I'll be the first to tell you that you are a magnificent cook," Bart assured the young man.

"Well, I appreciate that, Bart, for I sensed the minute we met that you are a gentleman of quality. I knew you had to be a desperate man to pick a freighter like the *Iron Lady* to get back to England."

"Yes, Disney — I'll admit to you that I am indeed desperate to get back to England as soon as I can."

Bart had Disney to thank that his first week aboard the freighter went by as fast as it did, and it also helped him to keep the troubling thoughts about Tawny off his mind.

Before this voyage was over, Bart Montgomery had decided that he would help this young man realize his dream. He knew of a place on the outskirts of London that would be ideal for Disney's inn. The last he'd heard, the owners were wanting to sell the few acres of property. Bart knew that the little two-story stone house would easily convert into the small inn Disney wished to own.

But he had plenty of time left before he said anything. How well he knew that you could be fooled by people! He had been played for a fool by the man he'd thought was his best friend. Never would he have believed that Jason would do what he did!

He'd never seen that side of Jason Hamilton before!

Chapter 47

A week at sea was enough to convince Tawny that she'd never love the sea as Jason did. It was the land she loved, and the times she enjoyed the most aboard the *Sea Princess* were when she was allowed to go down in the hold to pet and talk to Coco, as she had done with Diablo.

Impatiently, she counted off the days when she could finally put her feet on the ground or ride Coco in the countryside at Jason's home.

But while she'd dare not let Jason know how she was feeling, Tawny was questioning her impetuous act in agreeing to leave Cameron Farms to come to England with him. She was not forced to do this. Reba would have stayed at her side if she had had no father for her child. She was not forced to choose either Englishman—Jason or Bart. Now, she was questioning her wisdom. Had she acted too impulsively out of desperation? She feared that she had!

She had also had time to realize that she was glad that Jason had insisted in putting up the hammock. She wasn't sure she could have welcomed Jason to her bed. This was enough to really frighten her, for what was she to do when they arrived in England and he would be claiming her as his bride?

Oh, what a horrible mess she found herself in! She should never have left Cameron Farms and Reba!

By the time the second week of their voyage across the Atlantic Ocean had gone by, Jason was sensing that Tawny might be having some misgivings about her decision to come with him. He blamed himself for rushing her into it. So he decided that he'd certainly not rush her into marrying him once they arrived in England. But he said nothing about this to Tawny when they were together.

Something else was troubling Jason: he was convinced that Tawny was never going to love the sea as he did, and so how could he expect her to understand the grand exultation he felt about his ship and the sea?

With Bart, she could enjoy the thrill of his fine Arabian, Diablo, and the lovely English countryside. Had he been wrong? Should he never have appointed himself Tawny's protector?

Well, it was too late to ponder the right or wrong of his actions. Tawny had sailed away with him, and he would honor the vow to marry her even though he was wondering if she would ever love him as she had Bart Montgomery. But he was beginning to question if he could take a bride who loved another man.

He was glad the voyage was coming to an end soon, for the last two days he could feel the colder winds gusting across the deck of his ship and the waters were rough and choppy.

Jason did not relish sailing the Atlantic Ocean for the next several weeks, so he was anxious to make the most of the next few days to cover the distance to the coast of England.

Tawny spent most of her time in his cabin. Some days she didn't even want to take a stroll along the deck. He knew little about ladies when they were expecting a baby, but he assumed that the swaying effect of the ship urged her to stay in the cabin. He also noticed that she was often mending her gowns, and she finally confessed that she was letting out the seams so they would fit comfortably.

"You don't look a bit bigger to me, Tawny," Jason told her.

"Well, believe me, Jason—believe me, I am," she laughed lightly.

"But you've never looked more radiant and beautiful. I can tell you that we're not too far now from England, and I know that will be welcome news to you. I know how days at sea don't put you in the best of moods," he added grinning.

"I can't help it, Jason. Just to see all that endless gray-green water gives me a desolate feeling."

"There are seas that have the most beautiful azure-blue wa-

354

ters you can imagine, Tawny."

"At least, that would be nicer to see when you stood at the railing," she replied.

When Jason left the cabin to go up on deck, he knew there was no hope that Tawny would ever want to share the time on his ship as he'd like a wife to enjoy with him as he made his trips to various places around the world. Should they marry, she would prefer to remain back in England and he'd be forced to sail off alone.

As he roamed across the deck, he recalled what his mother had said once about how she had sailed many times with his father when they were younger because she did not believe that absence made the heart grow fonder. He thought she was absolutely right. But then his mother loved the sea, for she came from a seafaring family in Ireland.

The first few days after Tawny left, Reba found time hanging heavily on her hands, and the spacious house seemed empty and lonely. Perhaps it was this that urged her to visit Roberta Thacher daily, and Roberta found herself looking forward to those visits. The two of them always had a lot to talk about because of their mutual love for Tawny.

At Reba's insistence, Roberta finally agreed to go out to the farm to spend a few days. "You aren't able to cook or clean for yourself, Roberta, so a few days at my place would be good for you and you'd get well a lot sooner. Besides, I'm in need of some company with Tawny gone."

"Oh, I'm sure you are, Reba. That child always brought such a joy to my life, so I can understand how you feel," Roberta declared.

"And to mine and Bill's, I can assure you. But I have no one now and neither do you, so why shouldn't we enjoy each other's company for a while?"

"Guess that is right, isn't it? Yes, I'll come to your place for a few days." she told Reba. "It's mighty nice of you to invite me."

That afternoon Roberta accompanied Reba Cameron back to the farm, and when they arrived, Reba had Aurelia prepare the downstairs bedroom so Roberta would not have to tax herself climbing the stairs.

That short visit extended to the next three weeks. Each time Roberta would say something about it being time for her to return to her cottage, Reba would urge her to stay for a few more days. Roberta would always agree, for the truth was she was enjoying the time here on the farm. It was such a serene, peaceful place, and from any window she looked out of, she could see the beautiful countryside.

It was obvious that Roberta had gained strength, and Aurelia's good meals had to be credited for that. Aurelia warmed immediately to Roberta Thacher, and often when Reba was attending to the business of the farm, the two women would sit in the kitchen having a friendly chat.

It was at the end of the third week that Reba decided to approach Roberta with the idea she'd been mulling around in her mind for the last few days.

That night, as they sat in the parlor, Reba told her what had been on her mind. "Lord knows, I'm never going to marry again, and I venture to say the same is true for you. We're both here in Longcreek with no relatives and kin. I've got more house than I need and we seem to get along just fine. So why don't we share this place and keep each other company."

Roberta gasped, dropping the piece she was embroidering. "Oh, Reba, I don't know what to say," she stammered, for she could not believe the generous heart of this lady.

"Don't say anything tonight, Roberta. But think about it and you'll see that it could be the best thing for the two of us old ladies. Why pay that old landlord of yours all that money when you could be living here with me?"

The next day Roberta accepted Reba Cameron's generous offer, and the following days hired hands at the farm had all of Roberta's possessions moved out to the farm.

Life was strange, Roberta Thacher thought as she settled into her new home. How would she ever have imagined that she would be taking up residence at Cameron Farms as the winter approached the Virginia countryside?

Was it only last spring that young Tawny had excitedly come rushing over to her small cottage to tell her about this nice lady, Reba Cameron, and how she'd been invited to Cameron Farms? Now it seemed that destiny had brought her here to Cameron Farms!

But then she thought about Tawny and the turn of events that had taken place in her young life since the springtime when Maybelle was killed and Tawny's whole life changed.

Roberta could not dismiss the fact that there was a link binding their lives—hers and Tawny's with the Camerons. Ah, yes, it was strange!

One night, as she and Reba sat in the parlor sipping Reba's favorite sherry, Reba confided in Roberta that her husband Bill had been Tawny's father.

Roberta listened but said nothing about Tawny already telling her this. All she did say was that now that she knew that Bill was Tawny's father, she could certainly see a resemblance between the two of them.

"Oh, so could I, Roberta. I think I saw it from the first time I looked into Tawny's beautiful face. You know, Roberta—I think Tawny would be happy to know that the two of us are together now. She loves both of us so much."

Roberta smiled. "I think you are right, Reba. I think she would be pleased. We'll have to write her, won't we?"

"She'll be glad to know the two of us are so happy. Now we shall both pray that our dear little Tawny will find happiness," Reba said.

"She will. I have great faith in Tawny," Roberta declared in a very cheerful voice.

As they had done nightly, they left the parlor together to walk down the hallway. Roberta went to her bedroom and Reba mounted the stairway to go to her own room. Both were feeling a peace and tranquility that was comforting to two ladies of this age.

Both of them knew that it was young Tawny Blair who'd drawn them together. That was the way it had always been

357

with Tawny as long as either of them could remember, for she brought happiness into the lives of people she touched.

But two young men were feeling the torment of loving Tawny.

Chapter 48

Tawny knew that they were nearing land when she chanced to gaze out the small window of Jason's cabin to see the wide-winged bird taking a deep swoop down out of the sky. She felt her spirits mount with anticipation. Her dainty feet itched to touch the ground again after the weeks at sea.

A short time later, Jason came breezing through the cabin door. "We're home, Tawny!" he announced to her, lifting her up in his arms and swinging her around. His black eyes were gleaming as bright as coals as he looked into her eyes. He gave her a hasty kiss on the lips before he set her back down.

She knew that he was anxious to get back to England as she was to step foot on the ground again. As if she were a child, he cautioned her to have her cape ready to wear when she left the cabin. "There's a bone-chilling mist falling, honey."

She knew that she was to stay in the cabin until he came for her. She changed into the long-sleeved gold woolen gown trimmed with black braid. In readiness, she placed the cape Jason's mother had given to her across the bunk.

When the motion of the ship finally came to an abrupt stop, she was dressed and her valises were packed and she was ready to depart the cabin with Jason. Tawny prayed that she would not be sequestered to another ship's cabin for a long, long time.

Jason managed to get Coco up out of the hold of his ship and secured behind the carriage that would take them to his home. Then he went to the cabin to get Tawny.

The two of them walked across the deck of his ship with the misting rains pelting down on them, but Tawny broke away from Jason long enough to give young Rudy a farewell embrace before she went back to join Jason.

The mist came down all the way out of London as they traveled to the country estate of the Hamiltons. Tawny snuggled close to Jason and his arm rested around her shoulder. He was thinking it was going to be a bitterly cold winter from the way November was starting out.

The sight of the two-story stone house on the incline of the rolling English countryside, with smoke circling up to the sky from the many chimneys, was a welcome sight to both Jason and Tawny.

The carriage rolled up the long drive lined with tall, slender poplars, and the young stableboy was already rushing to greet the carriage. By the time Jason and Tawny got down from the carriage, the front door was opened and the manservant, Otis, was there to greet them. "Welcome home, Mr. Jason and Miss Tawny!"

Tawny eagerly stepped into the warmth of the hallway. Jason followed behind her, returning Otis's greeting. This time Tawny didn't feel nervous about Jason's family. Rushing down the hallway came the excited Joy, her face gleaming with delight at the sight of Tawny. "You did come back, Tawny! You did!" She grabbed Tawny in a warm, affectionate hug.

Jason laughed. "Joy, I leave Tawny in your hands while I see to getting Coco in the stable and out of this miserable weather."

He left the two of them in the hallway to go back out the front door.

When Jason had Coco cozily comfortable in a stall, he joined his family who were gathered in the warm comfort of his mother's garden room, a roaring fire blazing in the fireplace.

All he had to so was look at all their faces to know how delighted they were by the return of Tawny Blair to their home.

"Ah, Jason—it is so good to have you home, Son!" Lady Sheila declared as she rose to greet her son. He took his diminutive mother in his arms for a hug and kiss on her cheek.

She stood there looking up at Jason. "I don't have to tell you how happy we all are to have our little Tawny back," she said.

Jason grinned. "I rather had that suspicion."

"You didn't get back any too soon. I was hoping that you'd arrive before another week or two went by," his father declared as Jason sat down beside Tawny on the settee.

After all of them had enjoyed a cup of hot tea and cinnamon cakes, Lady Sheila suggested that she show Tawny to her room. "I'm sure you'd enjoy a nice rest, wouldn't you, dear?"

"I'm sure I'd be much better company after I've rested for a while," Tawny admitted to her.

"We'll allow you to do just that, won't we, Joy?" She lightheartedly teased Joy because she knew she was so thrilled to have Tawny back.

"I promise, Mother," Joy sighed, shrugging her shoulders as she glanced toward Jason who was grinning at his younger sister.

When Lady Sheila and Joy escorted Tawny to the same bedroom she'd been in when she was last here, Lady Sheila exclaimed how wonderful it was that she was back in time for Angela's wedding, then as they left Tawny to go back downstairs, Joy excitedly remarked, "Do you think they will announce that *they* are going to get married, Mother?"

Her mother gave her a soft laugh. "Wouldn't surprise me at all!"

"Oh, I hope so, Mother. I want Jason to marry Tawny."

A few hours later as the family assembled in the massive dining room aglow with candlelight, all the Hamilton family was filled with the expectation that Jason would stand up after dinner to make his announcement. All of them were especially impressed by the beautiful vision of Tawny that evening in her shimmering brown silk gown that served as a dazzling backdrop for the exquisite topaz teardrop earrings and matching topaz and diamond ring.

Lady Sheila was curious to know if Jason had purchased the jewelry for her and could not resist commenting on it.

"Your earrings are beautiful, Tawny, and I don't recall you wearing them before," she remarked.

"Oh, yes—I'm so proud of them. Mrs. Cameron gave them to me for my birthday just before I left," Tawny told her.

"And when was your birthday, dear?"

"October the fourteenth. It was my eighteenth birthday," she said, laughing.

"Ah, and it's such a special birthday," Sheila Hamilton told her. "I know it was for Jane and Angela."

The delicious roast duck was served with a divine orange sauce along with other tasty side dishes. But even when dessert was served, Jason still did not approach the subject all of them were anticipating. Finally Lord Addison made his move to leave the dining room to go to his study to enjoy his pipe and Jason accompanied his mother, sisters, and Tawny into the parlor.

Joy played the organ and sang some new songs she'd learned since Tawny had left a few months ago. As she sang, she observed Jason sitting there beside Tawny, holding her hand in his. This delighted her so much that she was encouraged to sing another song or two before she finally took her bow.

But there was no formal announcement about any wedding.

Finally, the only ones left in the parlor were Jason and Tawny. Jason had never seen her look as beautiful as she did tonight, and it was the first time he'd ever seen her wear jewelry. Tawny had suddenly realized after she'd dressed this evening that it was the very gown she'd picked to look her most attractive for Bart when he'd come to dinner at the farm. That was a time when she was still dwelling in the foolish fancy that he was going to propose to her.

"Well, Tawny—here we are back in England and I must tell you I was happy to get us here," he said as he ambled over to the liquor chest to get himself another glass of the red wine in the cut-crystal decanter.

"I was happy, too, Jason, and it is nice to be in a house again instead of a cabin."

Walking over to sit down beside her, he gazed tenderly at her. "I've never seen you look so lovely as you do tonight. You'd make any man feel proud to claim you as his bride and I rather suspect that my family was expecting me to make that announcement tonight. But I thought I'd wait until I'd had a chance to talk to you about that, so I remained silent."

She looked at him, thinking that no woman should feel as proud as she that such a man as Jason Hamilton had asked her to marry him. "I shall leave that up to you, Jason."

"All right, Tawny. I have a few things to attend to the next day or two. I've got to go back to London tomorrow and see to some business concerning the *Sea Princess*. I figure you will find plenty to do to keep you occupied, with Coco out in the stable and Joy underfoot."

"I'm sure I'll not be bored, Jason. It will be heaven to me to just wander around your mother's beautiful gardens."

When he walked her to her bedroom, he planted a gentle kiss on her cheek and bid her good night. "See you tomorrow, Princess," he said as she slipped through the door.

But as she was safely inside her room, the smile on her face faded as she gave way to a look of puzzlement.

What was it about Jason's kiss that made it seem like no lover's kiss? She had only to recall the fire of Bart's lips on hers to know the difference.

Chapter 49

Tawny slowly asked herself is she was just imagining certain things. She should be the happiest girl in the world, she reminded herself. The Hamilton family had lovingly welcomed her back and she should be happy to be so adored by them.

As she sat down in the gold gilt dressing table to remove her earrings, she gazed in the mirror and chided herself for all this discontent throbbing within her. She thought to herself that she'd never expected to be surrounded by such luxury and wonderful people like the Hamiltons a year ago but here she was in this palatial country estate, ready to marry the Hamiltons' son.

Moving away from the dressing table, she slowly undressed, her thoughts on Jason. She had to admit that she had expected him to tell his family about their plans to marry, but he hadn't. She was now wondering what they were thinking about her returning with him. But there were other things bothering her about tonight. When all the rest of the family had gone upstairs and they were left alone, would not two young lovers who planned to marry have eagerly stolen a kiss or two? When he told her good night at her bedroom door, would he not also have taken her in his arms to hold and kiss her for one brief moment?

A voice came to her in the room to remind her that Bart Montgomery certainly would have taken advantage of their privacy. His arms would have greedily claimed her and he would have taken her anxious lips in a kiss.

But then she could not lie to herself, either, for she had not been that anxious for Jason to kiss her. She was content for their moment of talking, since it was the first time they'd been alone since arriving this afternoon.

But was this the way she should be feeling? *Oh, Tawny,* she told herself, *you don't love Jason as you should love a husband. You love Jason more like a brother!*

She sat down on the bed, a look of dejection on her face. What had she done to herself and Jason? How could she undo what was already done, she wondered?

As she crawled under the coverlet, she was glad now that Jason had not said anything to his family. Like a bolt of lightning it struck her that Jason was suddenly realizing the same thing she was: he realized that he loved her like a sister and not like a woman.

Maybe he didn't know how to tell her how he was now feeling and he didn't want to hurt her feelings.

Tawny was finally able to go to sleep after she had decided that somehow everything would work out. Jason was so understanding and she loved him so dearly in a special way, so neither of them would hurt each other.

She decided that time would surely give them the answer to the situation.

Long before Tawny awakened, Jason had already left the house. Lord Addison decided to accompany his son into London this morning. Lady Sheila and her oldest daughter, Jane, had gone to the sitting room after they'd had breakfast. Jane was helping her water all the exotic plants and greenery in the bright sunny room.

"I know I'm always considered the strange, reserved one in the family, Mother, but I think Jason has acted very strangely since he arrived. Now, here he is leaving bright and early this morning to go back to that ship of his. I wonder what poor Tawny is thinking?" Jane declared as she moved down the long table which held several clay pots.

Sheila Hamilton quickly corrected her daughter. "Now, Jane, there is not a soul in this family who thinks you're strange. Reserved you are, sometimes. But I have no answer for the rest of your questions, dear. Most young ladies have resented Jason's obsession with his ship, so maybe that's why he's never gotten seriously involved with any of them."

"So you think Tawny is more understanding about it?"

"I can't say that."

"Well, she hates the sea. She told me that, and we know that Jason loves it. If they do marry, I can't see how it's going to be a very happy life for her because he'll always be gone."

Lady Sheila pointed out to her that Jason might not wish to be gone so much after he married Tawny. Jane gave a soft little giggle. "Oh, Mother—you don't believe that, do you? I don't. I think Jason will roam the sea as long as he can captain the *Sea Princess*."

Lady Sheila busied herself with the trimming of some dead leaves from one of the plants. She knew that her daughter spoke the truth.

"Well, Jason will be a fool to tarry too long away from Tawny. She is too beautiful to be left alone. Jason will be stupid if he does that."

Lady Sheila agreed with her daughter on that score, too. Neither of them heard young Joy enter the room, nor did they know she'd been standing there listening to their conversation.

As she marched over to where they were puttering around the table, she questioned the two women. "Did I hear right that Jason has chased back to that ship already, leaving Tawny here the first day? Well, I think that was really thoughtless of him. I think I'll just have to have a talk with my older brother the first chance I get. I know a handsome young man who might just take our pretty Tawny away from him if he's not careful!" She wore a smug look on her face as her mother and older sister exchanged glances wondering what Joy was talking about.

"And what handsome young man is that, honey?" Sheila asked her youngest.

"The handsome man I've had a crush on since I was twelve years old."

Jane knew exactly who she was talking about. It was Jason's best friend, Bart Montgomery, and Joy had never made any secret about it for a minute.

"So you think Bart might just ride up and take Tawny away from Jason? Now why would you say that, dear?" Lady Hamilton found herself very curious about her daughter's statement.

"Because I know something that neither of you knows. I know that the morning Jason took Tawny to board the *Caprice* to sail back to Virginia, Bart came over here to see Tawny, and he was stunned to learn that she was gone. In fact, I gathered that he was pretty angry with Jason for not letting him know. I was moping around because I was so lonely that morning, but Bart promised that he'd bring her back."

"He told you that, did he?" her mother quizzed.

"He certainly did, and I don't think a man would go all the way to Virginia if he didn't care an awful lot for a lady. I heard that is exactly what he did about a week after we talked."

Lady Hamilton did not take lightly what her daughter had just revealed. She had only to recall that Bart had made the return voyage home along with Jason and Tawny when he'd gotten that Arabian horse for his stables. From what Joy had just said, he must have become as charmed as Jason by Tawny Blair.

"Have you told Tawny about this, Joy?"

"No, I haven't had a chance. Maybe I won't if Jason tells us that the two of them are to be married. But then, as I told you yesterday, Mother, why would she have brought her horse?"

"Well, Joy—I guess we're all just going to have to wait and see what will happen. By the way, do you know if Tawny is still sleeping?"

"She was when I came down. I thought I'd see if she'd like to go for a ride and give Coco a little run. I was going to ride Prince if that is all right."

"As long as you think you are up to handling him. Did you have a problem last week when you and Sally went on your ride, Joy?"

"Not a one, Mother."

"Then I suppose it will be all right. Your father is not here for you to ask. He went into London with your brother."

Joy gave them a hasty farewell to go see if Tawny was awake yet. If she was, then she was going to invite her to go for a ride.

Tawny was just coming out of her bedroom door dressed in her bottle-green riding outfit, for she was planning on taking Coco for a ride over the countryside since Jason had told her last night that he would be gone all day.

"Well, if this isn't perfect. I was just coming upstairs to see if you were awake and invite you to go for a ride with me and Prince. Here you are already dressed to go riding," Joy said, giggling.

Exuberantly, Joy suggested that she could be changed by the time Tawny finished having breakfast. "I'll meet you downstairs in just a few minutes, Tawny. All right?"

"All right!" Tawny declared as Joy dashed on down the hall.

A short time later, they were trotting down the long drive of the estate. They made a handsome pair—Tawny on her chocolate-brown mare and Joy on the huge black Thoroughbred stallion.

Tawny allowed Joy to guide the direction they would ride. The weather was perfect for their trek over the countryside. While there was a chill to the November air, the sun was shining bright.

Tawny did not realize that Joy was taking a lane that led to the back of the Montgomery estate. It was not until she saw the stone outbuilding and the huge fence adjoining the long stable and barn that she called out to Joy riding slightly ahead of her. "Where are you taking me, Joy?"

"Montgomery Stables! Thought you might enjoy seeing Diablo again."

Tawny's fist clenched the reins and she was ready to protest when she saw a familiar figure in the paddock, and he also saw her. Harvey Green recognized the beautiful Tawny Blair the minute his eyes beheld her, but then what man could possibly ever forget Tawny? He was a little surprised to see her back here in England without Bart by her side. He'd expected that the two of them would return together, but here she was, and Montgomery was still away.

He came rushing up to the railing and straddled it as Tawny reined Coco beside it. "Well, if you aren't a sight for these eyes to see, Tawny!"

"Harvey, it is good to see you again," she told him as she reached out her hand to meet his. Now it was Joy who was a little dumbfounded until Tawny introduced her to Montgomery's horse trainer and explained how they'd met aboard Jason's ship.

"How is that rascal, Diablo?" she asked him.

"Well, I'll just let you see for yourself, Tawny. Just a minute," he said as he leaped off the top railing to rush into the stable. A few minutes later, the majestic black beast came prancing proudly out of the stables with his head held high and his black, silky tail swishing.

The sight of him took Tawny's breath away. "Oh, you beautiful thing!" she sighed. Before Joy knew what she was about, Tawny had leaped off Coco and was swinging her legs over the high, tiered railings.

"Diablo!" she called out to him, and he came toward her with his head nodding up and down as his thick mane flowed against his fine-arched neck. Her hands went up to rub his mane and broad forehead as his nose nuzzled the side of her face and hair. "Oh, you beauty! It's good to see you again!" she whispered to him. Once again, Harvey Green observed these two together and found himself as amazed as he had been in the hold of the ship when she had calmed this raging animal so easily. They were a regal pair—both were a rare breed!

Two other pairs of eyes were observing this scene. Two other people were having similar thoughts as they looked out the window!

Chapter 50

Lady Montgomery had been sitting in the dining room enjoying the light lunch Hattie had served her when they'd spied the two young attractive ladies riding up to the fence surrounding the stables. Lady Montgomery did not recognize either of them so she'd gotten out of her chair and gone to the double window to take a better look. Hattie stood behind her.

"Mercy me! Did you see what I saw, Lady Montgomery?" Hattie exclaimed as she watched the dark-haired young lady climb over the fence to greet Bart's prized Arabian as if they were old friends. There was not enough money in the whole world that would have urged Hattie to walk inside the fence with that fiery stallion.

Both of them stood there mesmerized by the sight of Tawny affectionately patting Diablo. Bart's stately mother was impressed by the regal grace of the young lady. She was like some beautiful princess of yesteryears.

"I don't know who she is, Hattie, but I certainly intend to find out. Obviously, from the way they greeted each other, Harvey knows her, so I will have no trouble finding out. I know one thing—she is the most stunning young lady I've ever seen!"

"Oh, she certainly is, and the bravest! Why, she could have that animal trotting after her without a rein on him, I'd swear!"

The two women stood at the window and watched until the young ladies rode away. Tawny turned to wave back at Harvey, and it gave Hattie and Lady Montgomery a full view of her lovely face.

"Lordy, that's a pretty little thing!" Hattie declared.

Lady Montgomery did not say anything but she was thinking exactly the same thing. She had forgotten all about the lunch Hattie had just served to her, and by the time she and Hattie moved away from the window, she wasn't hungry. But she took a few nibbles of the food and finished the cup of hot tea.

When she prepared to leave the table, she told Hattie that she'd be in the study working. "Send a message out to the stables for Harvey to come talk to me," she asked.

"Yes, ma'am. I'll do that," Hattie replied as she watched her walk out of the dining room. It sure was a different Lady Montgomery from the one she'd seen and served for so many years. A smile lit Hattie's face as she thought about the return of the young lord. That Scamp was going to be in for a shock when he got back! Why, she'd probably start bossing him around. Hattie chuckled when she thought about that happening!

Just the sight of Diablo and being there with him for a few brief moments were enough to brighten Tawny's day and lift her spirits. She was glad that Joy had taken her to see the stallion. But it was enough to bring back the bittersweet memories of Bart Montgomery and that ecstasy she'd shared with him. She knew that she'd probably never know such bliss again, but at least, she told herself, she'd known it once. Maybe some ladies never even known it once in their lifetime.

Joy was feeling elated that she'd had the brilliant idea to take Tawny over to the Montgomery estates to see Diablo. The look on Tawny's face when she'd seen that black stallion come out of the stables was a sight Joy would never forget. Her face had glowed radiantly and the way she'd climbed over that fence to go to the Arabian was something to see. She couldn't wait to tell her mother.

Tawny would never glow like that at any old ship Jason would ever own, Joy knew. Later, when she was in her room alone and Tawny had gone to her room, Joy had some very personal thoughts she'd never tell anyone. She'd certainly

371

dare not tell them to her mother! But she could not stop them from coming even if she'd wanted to.

If they had never gone by the Montgomery's stables, she realized, she might not have come to these conclusions. But they had, and Joy knew that Tawny shared something with Bart Montgomery that she could never share with her brother. Their mutual love of horses and land was enough to bind them together, so Joy realized that Tawny would be much happier married to Bart Montgomery than she ever would if she married Jason. Until today, she'd wanted nothing more than for Jason to take Tawny as his bride.

The more she thought about it the rest of the afternoon and as she was getting ready for dinner that evening, she envisioned the beautiful Tawny with her dark looks coupled with the dashing, handsome Bart Montgomery with his fair hair and brilliant blue eyes. Oh, they would surely be a most striking pair!

While Joy still considered him the handsomest man she knew, she'd forgotten about that crush she'd had on him. She knew that Bart looked upon her as Jason's bratty young sister. She'd accepted that he was just trying to be nice to her over two years ago when he'd playfully teased her to hurry and grow up so he could marry her.

It was someone like Tawny Blair who'd be able to conquer his reckless, restless heart, Joy realized. It would have to be a very unusual lady capable of holding Bart Montgomery's interest. But she figured that Tawny had already done that if Bart had been willing to travel all the way to Virginia to bring her back here, as he'd told her he would do.

But now, what the curious Joy was asking was why Tawny had returned with Jason instead of Bart and what was detaining Bart back in Virginia?

She'd overheard Harvey Green ask Tawny an interesting question as they stood at the stables and Tawny affectionately patted the stallion. "Did you get to see Bart before you left Virginia," he'd asked. "He's still not back yet."

"I saw him, Harvey, and as far as I know, he's still there," she told him. She'd seemed so casual when she spoke it was

372

enough to make Harvey question what had gone wrong between the two. He would have sworn that they were madly in love with each other as he'd observed them together on the crossing of the *Sea Princess*. He'd been so sure of it that he would have bet good money on it.

As Joy put the finishing touches to her hair, she wondered about this evening as the family gathered around the table for their evening meal. Would Jason remain silent again tonight about his future plans for Tawny?

Right down the hall from Joy's room, Tawny sat at her dressing table having similar thoughts. Somehow, she did not think he would say anything again tonight and she hoped that he didn't.

She dressed in a simple gown and wore no jewels, but she did tie back her hair with a pale-pink ribbon to match the color of her gown.

In the privacy of their bedroom, Lady Sheila Hamilton was quizzing her husband about his trip into the city and about their son. "Did he say anything to you today while the two of you were alone on the ride into London, Addison?"

"Not a word, dear. I had thought maybe he might, but that wasn't the topic of Jason's conversation."

"I adore that boy, but he also perplexes me at times, Addison. He must know that we are wondering what is going on when he brings this girl home with him. I'm getting a little vexed with him to say the least!"

A slow smile came to Addison's face as he taunted her, "Not you, Sheila—not where your adored son is concerned!"

Her dark eyes flashed and she gave him one of those particular Irish smiles of hers. "Ah, but I can also get riled just as easily when this temper of mine gives way. You know that, Addison!"

"Oh, I should after all these years, but just simmer down and maybe we'll learn something tonight," he consoled her and helped himself to a light kiss of her cheek. He thought she looked very attractive tonight in a rich purple gown with her amethyst brooch pinned at the high neckline.

He offered her his arm. "Shall we go downstairs, my pet, and await our brood to join us?"

When they arrived in the parlor, they were surprised to find Jason already sitting there. It was most unusual for him to be down for dinner so early. They gave each other a fleeting glance as they wondered if he was going to have something to say to them before the others gathered.

Lady Hamilton thought she detected an anxious expression on Jason's face, as though he was eager to say something.

"Well, Jason — you look very handsome tonight," his mother told him.

"And you look beautiful as always, Mother. I've . . . I've something I need your opinion on before Tawny comes down. I got her something today while I was in London and I remembered something you'd said quite often. Here, look at this and see what you think." He took a case from the inside pocket of his coat and handed it to his mother.

She opened the case and wound the single strand of pearls around her finger. "Look, Addison — aren't they exquisite?" In the case was also a pair of small, dainty single matching pearl earrings.

"You think Tawny will like them? I remembered you told me that pearls were always the perfect jewel to please anyone. I had to agree with you last night about jewelry looking so flattering on her. I'd never seen Tawny wearing any kind of jewelry until last night."

"You made the perfect selection, dear, and I'm sure that she will be very pleased," his mother assured him. "And you'll find out soon enough, for I think I hear her and Joy coming right now." Sheila smiled.

The two young ladies came gaily into the parlor. Sheila watched them enter and thought how pretty they both looked. Joy had always looked lovely in the shade of lavender she wore tonight with that silky jet-black hair of hers. Tawny looked so delicate and dainty in her pale-pink gown, and the simplicity of it was so flattering to her sensual figure. She could not have worn a more perfect frock to enhance the pearls that Jason was going to give to her tonight.

Sheila was very encouraged when she watched Jason walk over to Tawny, plant a kiss on her cheek, and tell her how lovely she looked. She noticed that Tawny was taken a little by surprise that he'd been so amorous in front of his family. Now his mother was just assured he was going to make the grand announcement!

Sheila was reminded of Jason as a young lad when he told Joy to shut her eyes and not open them until he told her to. There was that same look of mischief she'd seen so many times when he'd played his boyish tricks on her, Lady Sheila recalled. She'd always said to Addison that it was one thing to have three daughters, but a son was a completely different challenge. Oh, how often he had tried her patience to the limit! But he was so utterly adorable she could never stay mad at him too long.

Tawny went along with his suggestion good-naturedly as she closed her eyes wondering what in the world he was up to.

Jason took the one strand of pearls out of the case and admonished his sister Joy to say nothing as he fastened them around Tawny's graceful neck. The earrings were too complicated for him to attach.

"All right, Tawny—you can open your eyes," he told her as he took her hand in his to place the case with the earrings in her hand.

The Hamilton family stood awaiting Tawny's reaction when she saw Jason's gift to her.

Her thick long lashes fluttered and opened and she'd felt Jason's fingers at the back of her neck. Her eyes immediately went to the lustrous strand of pearls around her throat. When she could pull her gaze away from them, she looked into the case to see the matching pearl earrings. Her fingers caressed the two perfectly matched pearls as she looked up at Jason. She smiled and leaned over to kiss him on the cheek. "You have to be the sweetest man I know, Jason Hamilton." She felt no embarrassment to be so affectionate with his family there. The Hamilton family didn't make her feel restrained.

Jason laughed. "You heard that, didn't you, Mother? Tawny thinks I'm sweet."

Lady Sheila laughed. "I heard, Jason."

"But Tawny doesn't know you as well as we all do, Jason," Joy chimed in to taunt her older brother.

In the meantime, Tawny had managed to put her new earrings on her ears. Lady Sheila glanced over to notice the loveliness of her, that vision in pink. "You remind me of the lovely pink blossoms I see on my cherry trees in my garden, Tawny. It makes me wish for spring to come and this miserable winter to be over."

Lord Addison told her she would have to endure the next few months whether she liked it or not.

The mood of this gathering was festive and gay. Everyone seemed happy as they strolled into the dining room to enjoy dinner.

All of that was to change when Joy innocently mentioned the delightful time she and Tawny had enjoyed this afternoon.

"I took her to the Montgomery Stables to see Diablo. I've never seen anything like her with that Arabian. He was like a tabby cat with Tawny!"

She was talking to her parents, so she did not see the look on her brother's face when she mentioned the Montgomerys. She had no inkling of the black mood she'd sent her brother into by that mere mention.

Tawny was feeling so lighthearted that she had not looked in Jason's direction, either, but Lady Sheila had.

She didn't like what she saw on that handsome face that had been so happy just a moment ago! She now knew that there was friction between Jason and his best friend, Bart. She also knew the reason for this friction: it was the beautiful Tawny Blair!

What a cruel trick fate had played on them by deeming that they should both fall in love with the same young lady!

Chapter 51

Lady Sheila Hamilton wondered if Addison was aware of the change in Jason's mood. She certainly was, for it was a sullen, reserved look that came over him.

Joy and Tawny were not allowing it to affect them. The two of them were still in a frivolous mood. Only Jason had withdrawn from the rest of them. She felt sorry for her son for whatever was troubling him so, but for the life of her she could not figure out why he should be so upset over the fact that Joy had taken Tawny to see the Arabian she was so fond of.

By the time the meal was over, Jason's mother had guessed what was troubling her son. It had nothing to do with the prized Arabian, it had to do with Bart Montgomery!

For the first time in her life, Sheila Hamilton was seeing her easygoing son suffering from jealousy. She shrugged it aside, for no young person could escape it. Addison had exploded with fits of jealousy on several occasions when he was courting her. She, too, had felt jealousy a few times when she'd seen a pretty lady flirting boldly with him, and she could remember just how miserable she'd been.

She was tempted to tell Jason, when they had a private moment together, that if this was the way he was feeling, then he'd better waste no time formally announcing his plans to the world. She knew young Montgomery well enough to know he would not stay away too long from his home and stables, for Bart did not have the wanderlust that possessed Jason. He loved his land and horses passionately.

After the meal was over, Jason did not seek to join his family in the parlor. Instead, he suggested to Tawny that they take a stroll in the garden. She accepted his invitation but waited in the hall to talk to Joy while he dashed up the steps to get a shawl for her to drape over her shoulders.

"You may find it a little too chilly out there, Tawny. Don't let him keep you too long," Joy called to her as they were moving through the front door. Jason cast her a piercing look to tell her to mind her own business. She was still his bratty youngest sister, Jason thought as he took Tawny's arm.

"She can be a bossy little monkey sometimes," Jason grumbled.

Tawny just laughed. "But she means well, Jason."

After they'd gone a short distance and Jason had casually talked about various things, he asked Tawny the question on his mind. "Did you also meet Lady Montgomery? She lives there."

"No, I didn't. I guess you are speaking about Bart's mother?"

"Yes, I was speaking about Bart's mother," he said.

Tawny asked Jason about her.

"Well, I found her a rather reserved woman," Jason said. "Quite different from my own mother. She is a tall, very aristocratic-looking lady. I always got the impression when Bart and I were growing up that he was much closer to his father than he was to his mother." He suddenly realized that the entire conversation was dwelling on Bart Montgomery, and he damned well didn't wish it to continue.

So he changed the subject to tell her again how beautiful she looked tonight and how happy he'd been that she liked the pearls.

She laughed softly. "They're so lovely, Jason. For someone who had not one piece of jewelry over a month ago, I've suddenly gotten some beautiful things lately. I find myself appreciating gems and jewels more and more."

"I hear that can happen very easily with young ladies. I know my mother and Angela adore jewelry, and I suppose Joy will be the same. Jane is the exception. She'd far rather have a fine leatherbound book or a porcelain figurine . . . Are you getting too cold, Tawny?" he added in concern.

"No, Jason—I'm fine."

"Then we can sit down over there on that bench? I feel we haven't had a minute alone since we got here. As large as that house is, there always seems to be someone around." He led her over to the iron bench next to the ancient, wide-trunked tree. "I miss those times we had back in my cabin on the ship."

"Sometimes, I do, too, Jason," she honestly confessed to him.

"Do you really, Tawny?"

"I wouldn't have said it if I didn't mean it. You know me well enough to know I say exactly what's on my mind, Jason."

It was true that he knew of no one more honest than Tawny Blair, but he could not resist pointing out to her that he knew she certainly didn't miss the sea.

"No, I can't lie about that. I can do without the sight of it for a long, long time."

Could she possibly know what she was saying and how this would forever divide them when they were married? Jason was as honest as Tawny, and he knew that as much as he cared for her, he could never stay away from the sea or his ship. It was as necessary to him as breathing!

"Well, before I take you out of this cold and back to the house, I was going to ask you if you would enjoy a trip into the city to see the sights of London with your soon-to-be-husband. I thought it might be fun for the two of us. Joy is not included." He laughed. "She can sulk all she wants, but I'm selfish enough to want a little time with you."

"Oh, I'd love to Jason. That sounds like great fun!"

"Then we shall do it tomorrow. We will leave late morning and I'll take you to this little place for lunch before we tour the city," Jason told her.

Tawny's dark eyes sparkled with anticipation, for she'd never seen London, and Joy had talked about all the marvelous places and sights.

She was already planning what she'd wear as they walked back through the gardens toward the house. When she told Jason good night and went to her bedroom, she opened the armoire to get out the light woolen gold-colored gown that matched the gold cape. The gold velvet reticule made it a perfect outfit for her tour of London. She only wished that she had a perky bonnet to match the reticule.

She was too excited to go to sleep when she first went to bed, but finally she relaxed enough to drift off.

When the first rays of the morning sun came flowing through the bedroom window, Tawny leaped out of bed and immediately began to get dressed for her grand adventure with Jason. She wanted to look her very best for Jason in case they might encounter any of his friends.

She put on his pearls after she'd slipped into the gold wool gown, and the tiny, dainty earrings were fastened securely on her ears. The pearls gave an elegant touch to the gown.

She didn't want to wear her long wavy hair loose. She pulled it back severely, arranging small wisps by her temples. Copying Jason's mother's hairstyle, she tried to pin the thick mane of hair to the back of her head. Then she took up the hand mirror to see how it looked from the sides and the back. It was very attractive, and she felt that it gave her a more sophisticated air.

Now she was ready to go downstairs for a cup of coffee. She was too excited to eat a thing and Jason had mentioned that he was going to take her to a special place for lunch.

Tawny, Jason, and Lady Sheila were the only ones who enjoyed coffee in the morning. The rest of the Hamilton family had tea. But she could not eat the large breakfast that the family ate. The hot porridge and thick cream followed by eggs and sausage were just too much for her in the morning.

When she arrived in the dining room, she found Lady Sheila and Jason already at the table.

"How regal you look this morning, my dear!" Lady Sheila said. "Jason has just told me that you are going to see our city today. I think this will be a marvelous day for you. London is most fascinating."

"I was so excited I could hardly sleep last night," Tawny confessed.

"Well, dear, you sit down here and have your coffee. I'll be back in just a moment. I've something to get for you upstairs before you leave," Lady Hamilton told her.

Tawny was assisted into her chair by Jason, his dark eyes dancing over her. He was impressed by a different Tawny, who was still as strikingly beautiful as she'd been last night. He had to admit that this little backwoods girl from Virginia never ceased to amaze him.

He remembered that it was in a lighthearted, gay mood that he'd first called her princess the night she'd worn the dress given to her by his cabin boy, Rudy. But as he had observed her more and more the last several weeks, he realized she could have been a real princess. Tawny had been born with a certain dignity and charm that money or position could not buy.

He was also admiring the exquisite pearls he'd given her draped around the high neckline of her gold gown. She looked elegant, and he was going to be proud to escort her around London.

Lady Sheila came back to the dining room with a gold velvet bonnet in one hand and a rich brown fur muff in the other.

"This will go perfectly with your gown, Tawny. I thought you would find the muff comforting to slip your hands into as you and Jason ride in the carriage."

"Oh, Lady Sheila, you are so good to me!" Tawny exclaimed as she saw the fetching little bonnet. It was so perfect!

"It is my pleasure, Tawny dear. You make people want to do things for you, for you are so nice," she told Tawny. Those same words had been spoken to Tawny a long time ago by another lady, Roberta Thacher. An ocean might have separated them, but Tawny was thinking now of Roberta. She was carried back in time to when she was about nine years old and she'd asked Roberta why everyone was always so nice to her. "Because Tawny, honey—*you're* nice," Mrs. Thacher had quickly told her.

Tawny had wondered why those same people were never as nice to her mother, Maybelle. The answer never came until the year before Maybelle was killed and Tawny began to question such things as her mother stumbling into the cabin beaten and bruised, reeking of liquor.

Now once again, she asked herself why life could not have been kinder to Maybelle. A multitude of thoughts paraded through Tawny's mind.

"Come, dear, let's try this on." Lady Sheila beckoned to her. Tawny left the table to go to Jason's mother. She placed the bonnet on Tawny's head and tied a saucy bow at the side. A pleased smile came on Sheila Hamilton's face as she viewed the enchanting loveliness of Tawny's face framed by the golden velvet of the bonnet.

"Ah, Jason—is she not divine?"

"Absolutely gorgeous! I swear I don't know whether I dare venture out on the streets of London with her, Mother," he said laughing.

"Oh, you two!" Tawny giggled. But when she saw her reflection in the mirror, she had to admit that she did look grand. And when she touched the luxurious softness of the fur muff, she felt like a princess!

Jason announced that he was ready to go whenever she

was. She told him that she just had to go upstairs to get her cape and reticule.

A few minutes later, Lady Hamilton watched the young couple mount the carriage to go to London.

She thought they made a very handsome pair. But that Irish instinct of hers cautioned her to not count on Tawny's ever becoming Jason's wife. She could not shake the foreboding she had. Addison was always teasing her about this habit of hers and he had all the years they'd been married, but she knew that most of her foreboding had come to pass.

Lady Hamilton could not dismiss the vision haunting her—the vision of Bart Montgomery!

good hot bath to wash away those days on the
freighter," he remarked. "How about you?"

Chapter 52

Jason Hamilton had never yearned to be anything but
a seaman and captain of his own ship. However, today
he would have liked to have been an artist so he could
have captured forever the stunning beauty of Tawny
Blair. His mother's velvet bonnet so perfectly framed her
face as she sat there in the carriage draped in the gold
wool cape with her hands snug and warm in the fur
muff. She looked like the lovely ladies Jason had seen in
the paintings.

The ride from Jason's home to the city was a short
one, and Jason directed the driver to take them to the
Carlton Inn. For Tawny, the inn was a divine experience.
She loved the rustic atmosphere of the place and she ate
foods that she'd never tasted before. She thoroughly enjoyed the thin-sliced salmon served with a brown bread.
Jason insisted that she try the Yorkshire pudding.

After the leisurely lunch at the Inn, they got back into
the carriage and Jason instructed the driver to go to the
special places he wished to show Tawny. They went past
St. James's Park and Green Park, which lay between St.
James's and Piccadilly, and he told her some of the his-
tory of the parks.

Tawny was to see with her own eyes the impressive
Kensington Palace and Westminster Abbey. Their carriage
rolled around Trafalgar Square and she admired the magnificent statue of Lord Nelson there. What a letter she
could write to Reba Cameron and her dear Roberta Thacher!

There was so much to see that Jason told her they'd have to take several trips to London for him to show her everything.

"You've only had a small dose of our England today, Tawny, but there will be other days, and we shall see it all before we're through," he promised her.

"Oh, Jason, I don't know when I've had a nicer day than this. I've never seen a city like London before. It was thrilling!"

Jason and Tawny were amazed that the sun was setting low in the west by the time their carriage was heading to the outskirts of the city and homeward.

Tawny suddenly found herself very tired. She welcomed the comfort of the carriage and being able to lean back against the softness of its seat.

Jason saw how exhausted she was, and he wondered if he'd made it too long a day for them. But she had seemed to be enjoying herself so much that he hesitated to call an end to it. The hours had passed so swiftly.

The carriage swayed back and forth as it rolled along the countryside road. Jason watched Tawny's long, thick lashes flutter and close, and grinned as he realized that she was going to sleep.

Tawny was not the only one who'd enjoyed the day. He couldn't recall when he'd taken the time to go all over the city as he had today. It was fun with someone like Tawny to share it with.

In the quiet of the carriage, with Tawny peacefully sleeping, Jason was asking himself if he could find more contentment than he'd thought was possible if he stayed here in London instead of always shipping out somewhere in his ship.

Maybe he could, with Tawny by his side as she had been today!

As twilight descended over the countryside he was almost sorry to see the house come in view because he would have to wake Tawny up.

Something else invaded Jason's thoughts as the carriage passed Montgomerys' estate and he saw the lights gleaming through the windows. He wondered if Bart had arrived back in England. He doubted it, for passage out of Chesapeake was not that easily obtained on short notice. Bart might have to stay there longer than he would want.

Thinking of Bart and his impatient nature brought a smile to Jason's face as he thought about his old friend who always wanted things to happen at his own convenience.

He did not attempt to awaken Tawny until the carriage had arrived at the front entrance. She roused, feeling embarrassed that she had drifted off to sleep.

"I think I made it too long a day, Tawny," Jason apologized to her.

"But I loved every minute of it, Jason. I truly did," she assured him.

But he could tell when he helped her down from the carriage that she was very weary. Tawny realized it, too, as she walked up the steps and through the front door. She reminded herself that she was at least nine weeks pregnant by now, so maybe that explained her fatigue.

By the time they entered the house, Tawny turned to Jason. "Would I be terribly rude if I didn't join your family for dinner, Jason?" she asked. "I just feel like a warm bath and bed."

"Honey, never you fret about that! Take a bath and get propped up in your bed and I will see a dinner tray is served to you in the comfort of your room."

"Oh, thank you, Jason!"

When they reached Tawny's door, he gave her a quick peck of a kiss on her cheek, and as he ambled back down the hallway, he realized that he'd have to remember from now on that Tawny was expecting a child. It was hard for him to accept this, for he saw no change in her. Pregnancy had only enhanced her sensual curves, but he knew that changes did take place in a woman when she was expecting. Some had had strange cravings for foods at odd hours of the day and night. He knew about the queasy feelings an expectant mother experienced, but he had been too young to recall when his own mother was expecting his youngest sister, Joy.

When he encountered his mother in the hallway as he went downstairs, he told her that Tawny was exhausted so she would not be dining with them tonight. "I am the one at fault. I tried to take her too many places. But we were having such a good time."

"I'm sure the two of you had a very exciting day!" Lady Sheila laughed. "We'll have a tray sent up to her, dear, and she can just rest."

An hour later, Jason went downstairs to join his family for dinner, but it seemed strange not to see Tawny there.

After dinner, he joined his father in a chess game, which he had not done for a long time.

Joy found herself very bored by listening to all of Angela's talk about her wedding, so she quietly left the parlor to go up to her room.

All the pomp and pageantry the family was planning for Angela's wedding was not for her. She wanted something sweet and simple when she married.

She was tempted to look in on Tawny, but she restrained herself from going on down the hall to knock on her door.

A brutal storm moved in over the Channel the next morning as the Hamilton household roused up and began to greet the new day. Rain pelting against windows woke Jason up. Winter was here, he thought as he leaped out of bed to rush over to the window.

He stood there watching the branches of the trees blow furiously back and forth. He was thinking how treacherous it would have been if he had been trying to guide the *Sea Princess* to the coast of England. He was glad that he had arrived when he had. This was not the time to be plowing the Atlantic.

Addison had also been awakened by the pelting rains and he, too, got up to go to the windows to look out, recalling the fury of a blasting storm like this when he was a much younger man. He'd ridden out many storms on the high sea when he sailed his ship. Jason had inherited his love of the sea and fine ships. Ah, that was a grand and glorious time and he wished he could live it all over again!

He thought about his one and only son, Jason. Never had Sheila realized how excited he had been when she bore him a son after they had had their two daughters. Then after Jason, there had been the blessing of Joy. But Jason had been that wonderful blend of Addison's English heritage and Sheila's Irish heritage. He saw that in none of his other children unless possibly his youngest daughter, Joy.

Addison took a special pride that his son could carry on the shipping dynasty that he'd created years ago. His only fear was that Jason would not wish to spend time in London at the offices which would be necessary one of these days. That one was thing he'd always admired about young Montgomery when he'd taken over his father's estate. All things considered, Bart had assumed the tremendous undertaking at an early age. From everything Addison had heard, he'd done a remarkable job and was already respected for his expertise as a breeder of fine Thoroughbreds. Addison had not had the opportunity to see that black Arabian he'd heard so much talk about, but he intended to do so before too long.

Looking out his window now, he knew that this wasn't a day to do anything much but stay inside. Maybe he'd talk Jason into a game of chess or cards to pass this miserable day. He doubted that Jason would be making any trips today.

He turned away from the window to go into his dressing room, moving quietly as he went by the bed where his wife lay still sleeping. When he was dressed, she still slept peacefully. Rain always had that effect on her, he knew. She found the sound of it soothing, and she was never put in a gloomy mood by a cloudy, rainy day as he was.

He smiled as he ambled on through the doorway looking back over at the bed. There had to be a grain of truth to the saying that opposites attract, for he had been attracted to the beautiful Sheila O'Grady the first time he saw her, and they were as opposite as day is to night.

But they'd had a good life and a happy marriage!

Chapter 53

For over an hour, Bart had observed the lantern swaying back and forth in the small cabin. When he looked out the small portal, he could see nothing but steady streams of rain beating against it. When he left the cabin to walk toward the deck of the ship, he found it difficult to walk steadily. While he was not a seaman, he knew it must be a rough, angry sea out there.

As he reached the top of the steps and was about to step out on deck, one of the crew clad in a slicker stopped and warned Montgomery. "I'd advise you to go back where you came from, fellow. You ain't got no business on this bloody deck right now."

Bart saw what he meant when he noticed the raging stream of water flowing across the deck of the ship and the seamen scurrying back and forth. He figured the sailor had given him good advice, so he turned around to go back down the steps.

When he entered the cabin, Disney was there. "Lord, don't tell me you've been out in this?"

"No, I was just going up to see what was going on, but I saw pretty quick that I didn't need to be up there and one of the crew told me just that," Bart informed him.

"It's a bad one out there tonight, I can tell you. A fellow could get blown right off that deck into the sea on a night like this," Disney told him. "I saw it happen on one trip."

"You've convinced me, Disney. I've no wish to be buried at sea. I want to be buried in the ground." Bart gave a laugh.

"Well, how about some coffee while we ride this thing out, for I'm going to be putting in a long night in my galley, I figure. There are going to be many pots of coffee to brew and I'll have a lot of tired hungry sailors to feed as they take their breaks. This is going to be a long, long night."

Bart welcomed the cup of coffee he poured for him, but what was more tempting to Bart's eye was the generous piece of fruit pie. Disney was always bringing an extra helping of food to their cabin as he took a break from his galley. Montgomery was certain that he was going to arrive back in England several pounds heavier due to Disney's generous snacks. The two of them sat there eating the pie and drinking the coffee as the ship swayed back and forth, and the awesome wailing winds could be heard along with the torrents of rain falling.

"Well, I must leave you and you may not see me until tomorrow, Bart. Stay here, for you are safer here than anywhere," the cook told him.

"Rest assured, I will!"

The young man left the cabin to put in a long tour of duty.

Since he had nothing to do, Bart figured he might as well crawl into the bunk and try to go to sleep. Maybe when he woke up in the morning this storm would be over. But after he'd removed his clothes and got in the bunk with the blanket tucked around him, the rocking and swaying of the ship seemed to be worse. He realized that sleep was not going to come too easily.

He found himself pitying those poor men out there on that rainswept deck. At least Disney had it a little safer in the galley. Since sleep seemed to be out of the question, Bart lay there thinking about Tawny and praying that she had not married Jason yet. Those were agonizing thoughts! He thought about this young man, Disney. He had made this voyage more pleasant for Bart than it might have been had he been quartered with some of those other sailors. After all the days and nights they'd spent together, Bart considered that Disney deserved a chance to do something with his life instead of being a galley cook on this old freighter, and he could help him do it.

He'd decided to give this young Englishman a chance to have his dream of owning a country inn. Before they docked in London, Bart intended to offer the opportunity to him.

If Disney were successful and the inn prospered, then he could start repaying Bart. And if it didn't, then Bart figured he had at least given the young man a chance to chase a dream. Bart Montgomery knew the magic of a dream and he had always been lucky. Some might have thought him foolish to travel all the way to Virginia to acquire his black Arabian. This did not matter to Bart.

Most would have surely called it foolish folly that he'd rushed back to Virginia to claim the woman he loved but he had no regrets about that either. What he did regret was that he'd been so reluctant and stubborn about asking Tawny to marry him, for never had he considered Tawny to be his mistress or courtesan.

Bart knew that there was no other woman who could make him feel as he did about Tawny. If only he could get back to England before she married Jason, he'd convince her of his love for her. Since Reba Cameron had told him about Tawny carrying his baby, he'd had a lot of time to think. The thought of his own son or daughter had begun to excite him. There was no way he was going to allow Jason Hamilton to lay claim to the role of father to his child!

Finally, sleep did come for Montgomery, and when he woke up, Disney was just coming to the cabin to fall exhaustedly into his bunk. "It's over! We're through it, Bart!" That was all he could manage to mumble before he collapsed on the bunk.

Bart got out of his bunk and dressed. Quietly, he left the cabin, knowing Disney was in need of sleep. He figured that it would be safe for him to go up on the deck.

Bart encountered Captain Barney up on the deck and he had only to look on the captain's weathered face to know he'd had little sleep, if any at all.

"Well, Bart Montgomery—if we don't have any more nights like last night, you will be back in London by tomorrow," Captain Barney told him.

"That's the best news I could possibly hear, Captain! And yes, it was a rough night from all I heard."

"Such is the way of a seaman, Montgomery. That is what intrigues a certain breed of men—like me. The sea is like a woman, unpredictable and tempestuous, but that is what makes her so exciting and challenging."

"Is that what is it all about, Captain Barney? You see, I have a good friend who is a sea captain and I've always sworn that his passion was for his ship and the sea instead of a woman."

A slow smiled creased the old sea captain's face as he answered Bart. "Well, it's pretty close. There might be an exception once in a while, but not too often."

Bart grinned, but made no comment. Silently, he was thinking that obviously Tawny Blair had been that rare exception.

When he went back to the cabin, Disney was still sleeping soundly, so he tried to be very quiet as he went to sit down on his hard bunk. Bart decided one thing and that was if he got back to the shores of England, he didn't give a damn if he ever left them again for a long, long time. He was ready to put his feet on the ground and walk on the earth. The sea was not for him! He was ready to mount Diablo and ride over the countryside. There was only one other thing that he needed to make his happiness complete and that was to win Tawny's love.

With her by his side, Bart knew the future he wanted for himself and the son or daughter that she was carrying in her petite body. He would not accept for a minute that fate would be that cruel to him to deny him this right. He had to believe that he would arrive in time to prevent this from happening.

Later that day, Bart figured it was the right time to tell Disney about his offer to purchase the old house on the outskirt of the city. "The captain tells me we are to be in London very soon now and I wanted to give you some time to think about it before we land. I applaud you as a cook, Disney, and if you are willing to gamble, then I am."

The young man from Liverpool was flabbergasted.

Bart realized that he had put the young man in a state of shock, so he allowed him a while to absorb what he'd said.

"Well, Bart," Disney finally stammered, "if you have that kind of faith in me, I've got the faith that I could make it work." His voice was cracking from deep emotion.

"If I didn't think you could do it, Disney, I would not have made the offer. I'm a very shrewd businessman. I never waste my time or money on anything I'm unsure of. I think your inn would be successful because you are a fantastic cook."

"I think it could be, too. I appreciate your faith in me, Bart," Disney told him.

It took Disney a long time to come out of the daze Bart's startling offer had put him. From their many conversations, Disney had gathered that Bart was a man of wealth, because it took a great deal of money to be a breeder of Thoroughbreds—and Bart had told him about his prized black Arabian.

Bart did not need the captain or Disney to tell him the next morning that they were approaching the English Channel, for he saw the birds soaring high in the sky. It was a most welcome sight to him, for he was more than ready to be leaving this freighter.

Sometime he was going to tell Miss Tawny Blair just how anxious he was to get to her that he'd sought passage on this miserable freighter to get back to England as soon as he could.

Something deep inside him told him that he was going to get back before any wedding had taken place. He was certain she could not forget that wild, wonderful passion they'd shared each time his arms had held her.

That would be enough to stop her from marrying Jason and becoming his wife, Bart was sure! He had to believe this.

Chapter 54

The downpour of rain lasted until late in the afternoon, and all of the Hamilton family remained inside the house. The fireplaces blazed with a cozy warmth, for there was a chilly dampness inside with the winds blowing and the rains falling.

Tawny did not make any effort to go out to the stable to look in on Coco for fear she might slip and fall with all the water standing in puddles.

Jason and his father spent the rainy day playing chess. Lady Sheila and Jane enjoyed each other's company in her sitting room while the two of them knitted. Joy was the nervous one who could not seem to find anything to do to occupy her time.

After lunch, Tawny decided it was a good afternoon to finish the two letters she'd started but never finished to Reba and Roberta.

Angela's young man had braved the rains to come over to spend the afternoon with her, so they occupied the parlor. Joy found no contentment anywhere. She made frequent trips to the kitchen to help herself to snacks. The cook was finding her to be a pest by midafternoon while she was preparing for the evening meal.

"You're going to be so full, Miss Joy, that you're not going to have any room for this leg of lamb I'm trying to fix for your dinner," the cook, Cotilda, told her.

"Oh, yes I will. You didn't tell me that was what you were fixing," Joy remarked, for that was one of her favorite meals.

"I've hardly had a chance to tell you anything. You've run in and back out too fast."

"I promise, Cotilda, I won't come back in here and bother you any more the rest of the afternoon," Joy said as she skipped out of the kitchen.

She went down the long hallway, which seemed unusually dark because of the overcast, cloudy day. It was then she noticed the shadowy figure coming to their front door through the wide glass pane. She went to the door to see who might be coming to call.

A young man in his teens stood there with water streaming down the rim of his hat and running off his slicker. "A message for Miss Tawny Blair." He handed the message to Joy. Joy's curious nature was whetted to a keen point as to who might be sending a message to Tawny. At least it gave her the excuse to go to her room, so she turned to go swiftly up the steps to the second landing.

When she got to the bedroom door, she knocked and called out to Tawny. Tawny had been wondering just how long it would be before Joy came up to visit.

"Joy, come on in." Tawny called.

"This was just delivered to be given to you." She handed the message to Tawny.

"To me? But who . . . ?" Tawny was as puzzled as Joy had been.

"Well, open it, and then we'll both know!" Joy urged her.

Tawny laughed. "I guess that would be the best way, wouldn't it?" She opened the piece of paper to read the message and she was still perplexed. It was from Lady Montgomery requesting that she join her for tea tomorrow afternoon. She handed the letter to Joy as she stammered, "But I . . . I don't know her. I've never met her, so why would she want me to come to tea?"

Joy gave a very simple answer. "Perhaps that is the

reason for inviting you to tea, Tawny. Maybe she wishes to meet you."

"But how would she have known my name?"

"Well, Bart certainly knows your name, and there is Harvey Green who you talked to the other day. Perhaps he told her."

"Oh, goodness, Joy—what shall I do?"

"What do you mean, Tawny?"

"Well, I don't know her. It is a little frightening to me, I guess."

"Oh, I think you should go. Lady Montgomery is a nice lady. I've known her all my life. Everything will be just fine," Joy assured her.

"Oh, Joy, what would I do without you!" Tawny declared.

"Well, I'm sure you would do just fine, but I thank you for your kind words. Now, let's see which of your gowns would be just right for your tea with Lady Montgomery," she suggested to Tawny.

Tawny followed her over to the armoire. Both of them were of the opinion that the gold wool would be the one to wear. Joy rushed to her room to get a white lace collar she thought would go perfectly around the high-necked gown. When she returned with it, Tawny had to agree that it did give a very elegant touch to the gown.

"Wait until I tell Mother that Lady Montgomery has invited you to tea, Tawny," Joy exclaimed with a big smile on her face. "In fact, I'm going to go downstairs right now and tell her!"

Before Tawny could say anything, Joy rushed out the door. She was left there to ponder why Bart's mother had invited her to have tea. The truth was, she could not stand tea, but she must try to have one cup, she supposed, and be gracious to the lady.

As the afternoon went on, she found herself thinking more and more about the meeting with Bart's mother.

How would she respond to her? Would there be that instant warmth she'd felt when she'd met Jason's mother? She hardly expected that.

But by the time she was starting to dress to go down to the evening meal, she was feeling an air of excitement and anticipation about meeting Bart's mother.

When she entered the parlor, Angela and her husband-to-be were already there with Lord and Lady Hamilton. So were Jane and Joy. Only Jason was not downstairs yet.

Shortly after she'd entered the parlor, Jason made his appearance. He came immediately to Tawny's side and took her arm to escort her in to dinner.

He leaned over to whisper in her ear that she looked very beautiful. She rewarded him with a warm smile. Lady Sheila watched the young couple out of the corner of her eye, for she was wondering how Jason was going to take this news that Lady Montgomery had invited Tawny to have tea with her tomorrow. She had not mentioned it to him after Joy had rushed into her sitting room to tell her and Jane about the invitation.

She had told Addison when the two of them were in their bedroom dressing for dinner. "Only Tawny?" he commented. "You were not included?"

"No, dear, I was not invited—only Tawny."

"Hmm, I find that interesting, I must say."

"So do I, Addison."

"And am I to assume that she is going to go?"

"From what Joy tells me she is, and they have already picked out what she will wear. Joy finds it all very exciting that Tawny got such an invitation."

During dinner, as they were all enjoying the delicious leg of lamb with the special mint sauce, Joy announced that Tawny was going to the Montgomerys' for tea.

A sudden silence fell around the table as Addison looked over at his wife and Jason turned in Tawny's direction. Jason's sister Angela casually remarked, "Oh,

399

good, Tawny. The Montgomerys are very nice."

But the older Hamiltons both saw the disapproving look in their son's black eyes as he glared at Tawny. They heard the tone in his voice as he spoke to her, too. "You had not mentioned this to me," he said. Tawny also sensed that Jason did not seem to greet the news as pleasantly as Joy had.

"I'd not had a chance to mention it to you, Jason." she told him. Her eyes darted over to Lady Montgomery and she was suddenly feeling embarrassed that she and Jason seemed to be the center of attention. She just wished that the adorable Joy had kept her mouth shut!

"I didn't know that you knew Lady Montgomery," he declared. His black eyes darted over to his mother. "I guess you were invited too, eh, Mother?"

"As a matter of fact, I wasn't, dear," she answered him. "But I think that it was very gracious of Bart's mother to invite Tawny. Your sisters and I have gone there many times during the years. Of course, I'll admit that it has been a while now."

"Then you'd think she would have included you, too." He insisted on pursuing the subject.

"Well, Jason dear—it does not matter to me so it should not disturb you," Lady Sheila gently admonished her displeased son. She prayed this would end the issue.

He sank into a quiet mood and nibbled at the remainder of the pie on his plate, but it was obvious to everyone at the table that Jason was not happy about Tawny going to the Montgomery estate. Some of them couldn't imagine why and others thought they knew the reason.

Tawny made no effort to question him and decided to ignore his black moodiness the rest of the evening. She was also beginning to realize as she was around him more and more that Jason was not so easy to understand.

She was glad she was seeing this side of him before any wedding took place!

Lord Addison turned to his youngest daughter as they were departing the dining room. "How about some dominoes, Joy?" he asked her.

"I suppose so, Father."

When the two of them were seated at the small square game table, he made a point of telling his always talkative daughter, "It would have been better, my pet, if you'd have allowed Tawny to tell Jason about her invitation."

"Well, believe me—I know that now! But I can't see why Jason was acting so funny about it. Mercy, you'd think that the Montgomery family were our mortal enemies, the way he acted. He surprises me sometimes."

Addison found it impossible to get too angry with his perky little Joy and laughed. "I am often surprised by my family, but to tell you the truth, I agree with you. There was no cause for Jason to act the way he did."

"Well, I'm glad you feel that way, too, Father. I felt kind of sorry for poor Tawny. I think she was startled by his manner."

"Well, then, aren't you glad I invited you to join me in here? We'll just let your mother and Tawny attend to Jason. She can always manage to get him into a good mood, so Tawny will not be left alone to deal with him," he told Joy, giving her hand an affectionate pat before he placed the dominoes on the board to begin their game.

Her dark eyes looked at him as she remarked in a very serious voice, "I'll tell you what I think, Father. Between you and me, I think Jason is jealous of Bart Montgomery and that is why he's irked that Bart's mother invited her over for tea."

"Well then, dear, why don't you just keep this between you and me for a little while?"

"I will."

"Good girl! Now let's play and forget about Jason," Lord Addison urged her.

Joy sat there very thoughtfully for a moment then turned to her father. "Love is a very complicated thing, isn't it, Father?" she declared. "It makes people do a lot of crazy things, I'm beginning to think."

Lord Addison broke into a laugh. "Oh, Joy—life and love are both very complicated at times. You'll see for yourself as you get older."

He didn't have to convince her that he spoke the truth, for she believed him!

Chapter 55

Their domino game lasted much later than Joy had expected, and when she left her father's study, she took the time to look in the parlor, but everyone had gone upstairs and only one lamp was still dimly lit.

Lord Addison had remained in his study to read as he often did at night. A lot of evenings it was well after midnight before he left his study to go upstairs. Lady Sheila did not stay up so late and he enjoyed the quiet of his study so as not to disturb her with the lamp on in their bedroom.

But Joy saw Tawny's lights still gleaming under the threshold of her door as she went by. Everyone else's seemed to be dark, even Jason's room.

She could not resist giving a soft rap on Tawny's door and calling her name softly. Quickly, the door was opened and Tawny greeted her.

"I'll only stay a minute, for it is late," Joy answered. "I . . . I just wanted to tell you I'm sorry about what happened because of me talking when I should have kept quiet. Father is always telling me I talk too much. I guess he's right."

Tawny patted her shoulder. "You have nothing to be sorry about, Joy. Remarking about my invitation was no cause for any problem."

"Well, I sure didn't think so, but anyway I am glad you are so nice and understanding about my busy mouth," Joy said, laughing. "Now, I'm going to go to my own room."

After Tawny closed the door, she sat down on the bed and smiled, figuring that Lord Addison had probably said something to Joy when they were alone in his study. For a brief moment, Tawny was impatient with Joy for mentioning the invitation but it was utterly impossible to stay mad at her too long. She had certainly meant no harm. Quite the contrary, she had been excited about the invitation.

Tonight was the first time Tawny had ever seen Lady Sheila look at Jason with disfavor. Usually there was a warm glow shining in her dark eyes when she glanced in his direction. It had not been so tonight. Lady Sheila had turned a very cool shoulder to her son.

After he had left to go to his room, Lady Sheila moved over to sit on the settee with Tawny. "I guess it it always natural for a young man like Jason to get piqued," she told Tawny, in her very straightforward way, "but I sensed that you were embarrassed during the meal by the way he was acting, and you had every reason to feel that way. I trust you are not going to change your plans for tomorrow about going to the Montgomerys'?"

"No, Lady Sheila, I'm not! I intend to go."

"Good for you, dear. I'll see that the buggy is ready by three to take you over there."

Tawny smiled. "Well, I've never been to tea before, so this is a new experience for me."

"Well, I'm sure it will be a pleasant experience and you'll be just fine all on your own. I think it was a surprise to Jason that I was not included in the invitation."

"It was for me, since I've never met this lady."

Sheila smiled at Tawny. "I'm sure that Lady Montgomery had her reasons for it."

"Well, we'll find out tomorrow."

Tawny did not see Jason the next morning when she went downstairs. Joy explained that Jason and her father had left about an hour ago to go into London. Her mother had gone to visit an ailing friend. But Joy quickly assured Tawny that her mother had left orders for the buggy to be ready for her by three if she'd not returned home by then.

"In fact, it seems everyone has somewhere to go today except me and Jane. I'm thinking about going for a ride just to get out of the house for a while. I know that will delight Jane because she doesn't like me pestering her, as she says."

Tawny laughed. "You don't pester anyone, Joy."

"Oh, maybe not you, but Jane and Angela would not agree with that."

Tawny requested that she keep her company while she had coffee and one of the little iced rolls. Joy accompanied her into the vacant dining room and they chatted while Tawny had her morning coffee. When Tawny went back up the steps to prepare to dress, Joy left to go to the stables.

Tawny took a long warm bath scented with some of the perfumed oil Angela had given her. She dressed with very special care, for she wanted to look her best when she met Lady Montgomery for the first time. She fashioned her hair in a huge coil at the back of her head as she had the day she went to London with Jason. She planned to wear Lady Sheila's gold velvet bonnet again.

She looked at herself in the full-length mirror from all angles after she had fastened Jason's pearls around her neck and on her ears. Feeling quite satisfied and pleased with the way she looked with Lady Sheila's bonnet on and the satin ribbon tied to the side, she turned to go to the door. With the cape flung over her arm, she was ready to meet Bart Montgomery's mother.

As Lady Sheila had promised her, the buggy was waiting at the front entrance. The driver leaped down to assist her up into the buggy seat. A moment later they were rolling down the long drive to go to the country lane that led to the Montgomerys' estate. Tawny was glad the rains were over and the sun was back out.

When she arrived promptly at four, Tawny was met at the front door by one of the Montgomery servants and guided to the parlor.

Lady Montgomery rose to greet her. Tawny saw where Bart got his height from, for his mother was a tall, stately lady, elegantly dressed in a deep-blue gown trimmed with a white lace collar and cuffs. She wore no jewels. While Tawny noticed the very aristocratic air about her that reminded her of Bart, she could not see any resemblance between the two of them.

"Miss Blair, I am so pleased that you came. Please come over here and have a seat. Hattie will have our tea here shortly. I am so grateful that the weather improved."

Tawny took a seat. "Yesterday was a miserable day, so I, too, was very happy to see the sun out this morning."

The plump, matronly Hattie entered the parlor carrying the silver tray with the teapot and cups. Hattie's eyes were busily surveying the pretty young lady sitting with Lady Montgomery. She was just as beautiful today as she had been when she and her mistress saw her in the yards with Harvey Green, but she looked more sophisticated now than she had in her casual riding outfit.

"Please, Miss Blair—let Hattie take your cape," Lady Montgomery exclaimed after Hattie had served them.

Tawny smiled. "I forgot to give it to the servant

when I came in. I was so anxious to meet you, Lady Montgomery." Removing the gold cape, she handed it to Hattie. She gave Hattie such a lovely warm smile that the housekeeper decided that she could melt anyone's heart. As she returned to her kitchen, she was thinking to herself that this pretty creature could even melt that granite heart of the young lord. That Scamp wouldn't be able to resist this little lady. From what Hattie had observed the other day, she shared Bart's love of horses. What could be more perfect? Too bad he was gone and would miss meeting her.

Tawny sipped her tea very slowly so she would not be forced to have another cup. But she enjoyed the little white iced cakes on the tray.

"I guess I should tell you how this invitation came about, Miss Blair. I saw you through my window when you and the Hamiltons' daughter rode over the other day. Harvey Green told me who you were."

Tawny gave a soft laugh. "Now I understand. I have to admit I've been curious about your invitation."

"Well, now you know. I admired you in our yard with that highstrung Arabian of my son's. Most of my hired men shy away from him. Harvey and one other man are the only ones who dared go as close to him as you went. Since Bart and my husband Edward have bred and sold horses for years, I was amazed to see a petite lady charming Diablo so easily, so I summoned Harvey to find out who you were." Lady Montgomery smiled warmly.

"Well, I'm very happy you were curious and we got to meet. Please just call me Tawny. Everyone does."

"All right, dear. I must ask how you manage to have so much skill with horses. You are so young. Were your parents breeders and were you raised around them?"

"No, Lady Montgomery. I really wasn't around

407

horses until about a year ago." She told her about her first experience when she'd met the Camerons. Finding Lady Montgomery easy to talk to, she ended up telling her far more than she'd planned to, but Bart's mother found it very intriguing that she already met her son.

"My goodness, what a small world it is! It has been most interesting talking to you, Tawny. How fortunate the Hamiltons are to have you visiting in their home. I must get you to promise to come see me again."

"I would love to, Lady Montgomery."

"Then it is settled, and I just hope my wayward son will get home soon. I can't wait to tell him what he's missed by not being here today."

Tawny managed to give her a weak smile when she brought up the subject of her son. She thought to herself that he might not have found the meeting so pleasant. But she said nothing about this. What she did say was, "Now I know where Bart got his charm."

"Oh, no, Tawny—Bart is the image of his father, and his ways are more like his father's than mine, but you're very sweet to say that."

Tawny told her once again what a delightful time she'd had, and this wasn't just to be polite. She liked Lady Montgomery much better than she'd expected to.

Lady Montgomery walked to the front door with her, and once again suggested that she come again, and very soon. Tawny promised her she would.

"Tell Hattie her iced cakes were delicious! And give my regards to Harvey Green."

"I shall, dear, and you come see Diablo anytime you like."

"Oh, thank you very much, Lady Montgomery," Tawny said as she went down the steps to be helped into the buggy by the driver."

As the buggy rolled back down the road toward the Hamiltons', Tawny mused about the afternoon she'd spent with Bart's mother, the grandmother of the child she was now carrying. How could she possibly go through a marriage with Jason? As dear as he and all his family were to her, it wasn't right! It wasn't how it should be!

She would be living a lie if she allowed it to happen, and this was not her way. Somehow she had to find an answer to this devastating dilemma she found herself in.

The sun was sinking low by the time the little buggy pulled off the main road to go up the long drive.

What would Jason's mood be this evening when she came face-to-face with him? Would he be sullen again, knowing that she'd kept her appointment with Lady Montgomery? One thing in her favor was that his family did not pamper him last night. Quite the contrary, they seemed to sympathize with her!

But the way he acted last night was enough to convince Tawny that a marriage between the two of them would be a disaster. Jason could never forget that it was Bart's child and not his. There would be times when his resentment would lash out at her, and when the baby was born, he could also turn on it.

This Tawny would never tolerate!

Chapter 56

As she had promised Lady Hamilton before she left to go to the Montgomerys' estate, Tawny went directly to the sitting room to seek her out. But she heard her talking with her husband as she approached the door so she hesitated for a moment. What she heard Lord Addison telling his wife was enough to stop her from going into the room.

"He said he was going to spend the night on his ship, Sheila. Said he had some things to do. I didn't say anything, but I didn't believe him for a minute. Jason is a young man with something troubling him."

"Maybe a night on his *Sea Princess* will be good for him, Addison."

"Well, my patience is growing thin, I fear, concerning him and Tawny. Why did he bring her here if he didn't plan to marry her, and if that is so, then why does he not announce it?"

Tawny did not linger to hear what his wife would say. Cautiously, she moved back a few feet before she turned around to go toward the stairway. She mounted the stairs swiftly, praying that she'd not meet anyone before she could get to her room.

She only took time to remove the cape and bonnet before she sank down on the bed and gave way to the tears that wanted to flow. She lay there crying until she could not cry anymore. Only then did she sit up on the side of the bed and notice that there was a letter on

410

her nightstand. Her fingers trembled as she tried to open it, for she saw that it was from Reba Cameron.

She read the letter once, then read it a second time to be sure that she had understood its contents. Reba told her about Bart coming to the farm and that she got the impression he was devastated to find that she had already left with Jason. It stated that she only prayed that her letter reached England before Tawny married Jason. Reba expressed regrets that she had left so hastily with Jason.

But Reba's letter was not telling her anything that Tawny had not been saying to herself for a few days. She had acted impulsively because she'd been so hurt by Bart. Jason had just happened to appear in Longcreek at a moment when she was so in need of his comfort and company.

For whatever reason Jason had not urged them to rush into marriage as soon as they got here, she was glad now. Maybe fate had planned it this way.

But Tawny had decided after this afternoon and getting Reba's letter that she would not marry Jason even if Bart never asked her to marry him. Somehow, she felt like a heavy burden had been lifted off her dainty shoulders and she knew why.

Jason Hamilton deserved a young lady who would give her love as willingly and eagerly as she had to Bart. Tawny had realized more and more that she did not feel this kind of love for him. The kisses she enjoyed from Jason were the brotherly pecks on the forehead or cheek or the warm hug of his arm around her shoulder.

As she dressed for dinner, Tawny knew that she must tell this to Jason as soon as possible. Perhaps this would ease his troubled mind.

She managed to act gay and lighthearted when she met the rest of the Hamilton family for dinner, but it

411

was going to be hard to face them when the truth did come out. She was certain that all of them, especially young Joy, had been expecting her and Jason to be married.

Lady Sheila was her usual lively self as Tawny told her about the nice time she'd spent in the company of Lady Montgomery. "Oh, I'm so glad, dear! I felt you would."

"Well, Tawny—anyone would like you!" Joy chimed in.

All of them responded with a gale of laughter. Tawny sat there looking at Joy's radiant face and knew she must think of some way to make it easy for her to accept the fact that she could never be her sister-in-law. But there was no reason why they could not be friends forever. Somehow, Tawny knew that Lady Sheila would understand.

It turned out to be a pleasant evening, and everyone knew why. Jason's absence eased the intensity they'd endured the night before.

Tawny's sleep was peaceful, for she was no longer pulled in two directions. She knew which way she was going to go. Confusion no longer troubled her!

The late afternoon the freighter, the *Iron Lady,* docked in the harbor, the captain and his crew were greeted by perfect weather. The fierce storm was far back in the waters beyond the Channel Islands. The only thing that had Captain Barney in a fury was that he was going to lose his galley cook when they docked. Disney had told him the night before that he wasn't going to be shipping out on the *Iron Lady* again. He was going to remain in London. That was all he figured the captain needed to know. That he had accepted the deal Bart Montgomery had offered him was no

412

one's business but his and Montgomery's.

As soon as the ship docked, Disney wasted no time leaving the freighter, and he met Montgomery there on the wharf. Together, they boarded a carriage to go to Bart's townhouse. It had been so many months since Bart had spent time there and he was wondering if his manservant Wesley or Wesley's wife, his housekeeper, Thelma, would even recognize him.

He was going to give Disney lodging here until they could purchase the property for the inn. Disney was like a young child about the prospects of owning his own inn. He'd never met anyone like Bart Montgomery and he still could not believe his good fortune. Disney was willing to work hard to realize his dream.

About the time the carriage was pulling up to the side of the street lined with several townhouses similar to the one owned by Bart, a flurry of snowflakes began to fall.

Disney laughed. "I'd have sworn I saw the sun bright when we arrived."

"But the sun is down now, Disney, and I guess we have to say that it is winter we're facing now that we're back in England."

They got out of the carriage, each of them carrying their luggage as they mounted the steep steps leading to the front door of the townhouse. The short little manservant Wesley answered the rapping on the door and excitedly greeted Bart. "Lord Montgomery—how grand to see you!"

Bart laughed. "Happy to see you remember me, Wesley. Good to see you again." As the three of them walked into the black-and-white tiled foyer, he informed Wesley that Disney would be his guest at the townhouse. He instructed him which guest bedroom to take Disney's luggage to.

"Yes, Lord Montgomery!" The little manservant took

413

one valise in each hand after Bart told them they would be in his study for a while before they went to their rooms.

Before going upstairs to rid himself of the long days of travel on that freighter by having a bath before dinner Bart felt the need for a taste of his favorite brandy.

He figured that the announcement that he was here at the townhouse would send Wesley's wife Thelma into a frenzy. She was a delightful, excitable little woman and a fastidious housekeeper. She and Wesley certainly earned their wages. When he and Disney went into his study, Bart saw that all the furniture was highly polished and everything was in order as if he had been coming daily to inspect it.

His liquor chest was properly stocked as he always requested. He found it pleasant to be back and he also recalled just how many months it had been since he'd last spent any time here. As a matter of fact, Bart knew to precision the last night he'd spent here, because it was in this room that he'd approached Jason about taking him to Virginia to see if the fine Arabian was all that his father's devoted friend Jeffers had said it was. It was after the two of them had enjoyed some brandy in this same study that they'd mounted the carriage outside to go pick up the two ladies they were escorting to the theater.

That was a time when he and Jason could laugh and jest together about the ladyloves of their lives because the affairs were taken so lightly. In the time and space that it took Bart to pour a drink for him and Disney, he relived a number of memories involving Jason and him. There was no way he could ever forget that particular time of his life. It seemed like a lifetime ago now.

Fate had handed the two of them a cruel blow when they happened to fall in love with the same girl. Bart would never have expected something like that to hap-

414

pen to such good friends, but it had, and Bart regretted it. However, as much as he'd always valued Jason's friendship, his love for Tawny far surpassed that. Nothing was going to stop him from having Tawny!

He turned from the liquor chest to hand Disney the brandy he'd just poured. "Well, Disney—shall we drink to your future and mine?"

"I'll certainly drink to that," the young cook from Liverpool grinned. This one small room was the grandest he'd ever been in. Disney was awestruck by all that was happening to him, so very fast. He had noticed that the manservant had addressed Bart as Lord Montgomery, but he'd known him as just Bart. It would seem strange now to call him anything but that.

Bart took a seat in the overstuffed leather chair by the hearth and crossed his long legs as he took a sip of the brandy. "I'll be leaving in the morning, Disney, to go out to my place in the country. I'm sure I've got a pile of things waiting for my attention there after being gone several weeks. That's why I wanted to get you settled in here tonight before I left. Make yourself comfortable here, and Wesley and Thelma will take very good care of you while I'm gone. The carriage is at your disposal anytime you'd like to use it."

"Oh, Bart, you don't worry about me. Guess you have already figured out from our time on the freighter that I'm sort of a loner. I'd not mix or mingle much when I had any time to spare, but usually went to my cabin to read."

"Well, help yourself to any of the books in my shelves here."

Disney's eyes darted over to the one wall that was a complete shelves of books. "I'll have plenty to occupy my time, it looks like," he said, laughing.

Bart noticed that Disney's brandy was gone and so was his. "I'm ready to get upstairs and have myself a

415

good hot bath to wash away those days on the freighter," he remarked. "How about you?"

"That sounds like a good idea to me." Disney followed Bart out of the study and into the hallway.

The lanky young cook followed Bart up the steps and down the thick-carpeted hallway to the room he was led to. "I'll meet you in about an hour down in the parlor. Be prepared, 'cause Thelma is one bloody good cook." Bart grinned as the young man started to move inside the doorway.

During the next hour, Disney enjoyed a hot bath, shaved, and changed into the clean shirt and pants packed there in his bag. He had to admit that he was ready for that good meal Bart had spoken about. But he'd also had time to test the softness and comfort of the bed in the room and thought to himself of the good night's sleep he was sure to enjoy tonight after all the months of sleeping on that hard bunk on the freighter.

While he had never known the luxury of the rich, mahogany furnishings he saw all over this room, his eyes could certainly appreciate them. He could also appreciate the elegant taste of the decor. He was thinking of the inn Bart was going to purchase for him and that he was going to operate. Seeing Bart's fine townhouse had ignited many ideas for his inn. He wanted a touch of elegance. Right now, he was filled with new ideas.

He was so engrossed with his dreams of the future that it took Bart knocking and calling to him twice before Disney leaped off the bed to go to the door.

"Are you ready to eat?" Bart asked as Disney opened the door.

"Sure am!"

"Well, let's go! I'm famished!" Bart declared, and Disney did not hesitate a minute to leave the room.

They had only to start going down the stairs for Disney's nose to smell the delightful aroma of the food. He knew already that Bart had spoken the truth about his cook, Thelma.

Chapter 57

Disney was embarrassed when he finally woke up to see by the hands of the clock how late he'd slept, but he blamed it on the cozy comfort of the bed and the delicious meal he'd enjoyed the night before. It was a meal that he'd not had to cook and that alone was a pleasant treat for him.

He had no doubt that Bart was already gone to his country place when he finally dressed and went downstairs.

Wesley was in the hallway when he descended the stairway. "I trust you rested well, sir?"

"I certainly did. I've not been used to such a comfortable bed as the one I lay on last night, Wesley. Never have I enjoyed such a grand meal as I ate."

"Thelma will be pleased to hear that. Now, do you wish some breakfast or would it be lunch you're liking?"

"I don't think I'd like anything but a cup of tea, Wesley. Do you suppose Thelma would mind if I just sit in her kitchen to have it? I'm sure Bart is gone, isn't he?"

"Oh, yes, he's been gone for a few hours now. If you'd like to have your tea in the kitchen, Thelma would be pleased. She enjoys someone to talk to when she's working. Come this way." The short little Welsh servant urged him to follow him. Disney felt like a giant as he walked behind the small Wesley, but when he entered the kitchen and greeted Wesley's wife, he saw that she was even inches shorter than her husband. He doubted that she would reach five feet.

Disney spent a most enjoyable hour drinking tea and becoming acquainted with Thelma. They talked endlessly about food and the preparing of it. He found himself very interested in her use of the various herbs she grew outside the kitchen door.

Disney listened intensely, for he figured he might learn a lot from this middle-aged lady who had prepared such a superb meal the night before.

Thelma found their guest a most remarkable young man. She thoroughly enjoyed talking to him and was delighted that he seemed to enjoy her company. She had no way of knowing what his association was with Lord Montgomery, but knowing the young lord the way she did, she figured that he held him in high regard to have brought him here to his townhouse. Rarely had he brought anyone here to spend the night. The only gentleman who'd ever stayed here was Jason Hamilton.

When Bart Montgomery's carriage came rolling up the long drive, it was Harvey Green who first spied him as he was giving Diablo a workout in the fenced area around the stables.

The minute Bart leaped out of the carriage, he rushed over to the fence to savor the sight of his handsome black stallion. The pleased smile on his face told Harvey, as he reined the stallion over to the fence, that Bart was as entranced by Diablo as he had been a few weeks ago.

"Still think he's the king, Bart?"

"You know it, Harvey! There's no other like him!"

"I'll agree with that! It's good to have you back, Bart!"

"It's good to be back, and this time it's going to be for a long time. I've no desire to be on another bloody ship for a long, long time!" he said laughing. Telling Harvey that he would see him later, he turned on his booted heels to go toward the house.

When Bart entered the front door and started to walk down the hallway, the first sounds he heard were laughter coming from the direction of the kitchen. He turned to go in that direction instead of his mother's sitting room where he'd expected to find her at this time of the morning.

He was surprised to see Hattie and his mother sitting together, enjoying each other's company over a cup of tea.

"Well, Scamp—you're back!" Hattie greeted him as she spied him coming through the kitchen door.

"Bart! You're back!" his mother chimed in.

"I'm back! The two of you are a sight to see," he teased them as he came on into the kitchen. He gave his mother a warm embrace, as well as Hattie, but he graciously declined Hattie's offer of a cup of tea. After the hearty breakfast he'd enjoyed back at his townhouse, he didn't need anything.

Seeing his mother sitting with Hattie was his first surprise, but going to his study to see his deck cleared away was a delight, and he credited his aunt for the marvelous job she'd done while he was away.

But an hour later when he went back into the kitchen to find Hattie there alone, he was informed by her that his aunt had not been here for weeks. "Your mother's been doing it all, Scamp. Your aunt didn't stay here a week after you left."

"Are you telling me, Hattie, that my mother has been tending to everything?"

"I'm telling you just that, Scamp. I think you are going to be in for a lot of surprises now that you are home. I think you better keep yourself here a while now that you're finally back."

"Hattie, you're not being too nice to me on this first

day I've returned. I think you must be mad at me. Didn't you miss me?" he teased her.

"Well, maybe I am mad at you!"

Bart laughed as he gave her an affectionate pat on the back. "Well, I'll try to get back in your good graces, Hattie," he told her.

Hattie was not Bart's prime concern, and the good graces he was concerned about were Tawny Blair's. He had wasted all the time he intended to waste. He had Disney settled into his townhouse and everything seemed to be running smoothly here at his country place. Now, he was anxious to seek out Tawny and pray he wasn't too late. Reba Cameron's words had haunted him for weeks now and he was apprehensive about riding over to the Hamiltons'. If he was greeted with the news that Jason and Tawny were already married, he did not know what he would do or how he'd react.

He wasted no more time in going to the stable to have Diablo saddled up, and as soon as the fiery stallion was ready, he prepared to mount him. Diablo seemed to know that his master was back as he anxiously pranced back and forth. Hastily, Bart and Diablo galloped down the lane.

He never reached the long drive of the Hamiltons' country estate. When he would have reined Diablo into the long drive, his blue eyes caught the sight of the beautiful vision he'd dreamed about so many nights galloping up the country road astride her little brown mare, Coco.

He set out in hot pursuit of her. The little mare was a feisty one, and she galloped at a fast pace. He saw Tawny's long thick hair flowing as she rode the mare. He knew why she was the only woman who could thrill and bewitch him as she had as he watched her riding her mare. Tawny was like no other woman he'd ever known, and that was why she must be his!

He spurred Diablo to move faster to close the gap

that divided them. The Arabian moved swiftly to obey his master's command.

Tawny's keen ears heard the sound of pounding hooves behind her and she turned her head to look back. Her heart almost stopped when she spotted that magnificent black stallion galloping behind her, and the rider was the fair-haired Bart Montgomery! Her heart started pounding erratically. It was Bart! He was back!

She spurred Coco to move faster, but she knew that the little mare was no match for Diablo.

Bart had seen that beautiful head of hers turn around for one brief moment and he also saw how she was urging the little mare to go faster. She had to know that she wasn't going to outrun him so why was she trying to?

It really didn't matter to Bart, for he was going to catch her and he was going to make her listen to what he had to say whether she wanted to or not.

He was not going to allow that little minx to run away from him as she had in the gardens of the Greenfield Inn that day. He should have run after her, and he'd always regretted that he hadn't. If only he had, he could have saved both of them a lot of wasted time. No one realized that more than Bart. It was only after he'd had his talk with Reba Cameron that Bart had realized Tawny was as proud as he was. He respected that. She was just as headstrong and stubborn as he was, too.

She'd give him no quarter, but then Bart admired that, for he'd never found that quality in any other woman he'd ever known. Life with Tawny Blair would always be a challenge; he'd never be bored. Forever he would find her whetting his interest. Always he'd known that it would take such a woman to make him want to share his life with anyone.

The distance separating them now was less than a few yards. Bart's heart was pounding wildly as he got closer to her. Tawny was determined not to give way to the urge to pull up on the reins to make Coco stop, and she could not suppress an amused smile as she spurred Coco to go faster. There was a devious streak in her wanting to make Bart pursue her just a little longer. He deserved to be punished for the pain she'd felt that afternoon in the garden of the inn. But she also had to admit that Reba's letter had mellowed her heart about Bart. In fact, that letter had a very definite impact on Tawny when she coupled it with other things troubling her about the relationship with Jason.

But the chase could not last too long with Coco vying against the Arabian. Bart caught up with her, and his hand reached over to grab the reins as he grinned at her. Both the horses had slowed to a trot.

"Ah, Tawny—you're a beautiful sight to behold!" his deep voice told her as they came to a complete halt.

His brilliant blue eyes made love to her as he gazed at her lovely face so glowing and flushed. Remembering what Reba Cameron had told him about Tawny carrying his child, he thought she had never looked more beautiful than she did today.

For a brief moment no words were spoken between them as they eyes met. Bart took charge of both their horses as he led them off the road. When he found the spot he was looking for, he stopped and secured the horses to the trunk of a tree, then went around Coco's side to help Tawny down.

"Well, aren't you going to tell me you are glad to see me, Tawny love?" His hands firmly held her waist as he guided her down.

"I . . . I guess I'm a little startled at seeing you appear so suddenly, Bart. I had no way of knowing you were back." She knew that he had just arrived today, since she had visited his home yesterday.

By now she was standing in front of him with her deep brown eyes looking directly up at him, and he

423

bent his head down so he might meet those sweet lips so temptingly inviting his kiss. "Well, I'm back and I'll be damned if I'll let you run away from me again, Tawny Blair!" he muttered before his mouth captured hers.

As always, when their bodies pressed against each other, both were to feel that rampaging, untamed passion surging within them.

Tawny felt his strong arms encircling her, and did not try to fight it. Her pretty head was whirling with giddiness. Bart felt the sway of her body pressed against him and he reluctantly released her lips as his hands went under her knees so he could swing her up in his arms.

Walking a few feet away from where he'd tethered the two horses, he found a cozy spot that would conceal them from anyone riding down the country lane.

He lowered himself to the ground, still holding Tawny in his arms. He held her there on his lap as he planted gentle featherlike kisses around her face. "Now, young lady, we're going to pretend we are back in that garden at the inn and I'm going to do what I should have done that afternoon. I'm asking you to marry me, Tawny. I want you for my wife, for no other woman would do." He felt he could hardly breathe until she would ease the torment that she might have already married Jason. If she told him she was married to his friend, Bart wasn't sure what he would do.

She gave a sigh. "Oh, Bart! Dear God, Bart, why didn't you ask me to marry you back at Greenfield's?"

"A damned fool is all I can say. I honestly don't know, because I was crazy in love with you and I still am." Was she getting ready to tell him that she didn't think he loved her so she had married Jason as soon as they arrived back here in England?

A slow smile came to her face as she softly confessed to him. "Do you know how much I wanted to hear you

424

say this, that day in the garden?" Her small hand went up to caress his cheek as she told him, "Your love was all I ever wanted, Bart Montgomery—all I ever needed to be happy. And yes, I will marry you anytime you say."

"Oh, God!" Bart heaved a deep sigh. "The sooner the better, love! It can't be too soon for me."

She had no inkling how impatiently he had been waiting for her answer and how the heavy burden was lifted off his chest when he found out that he had gotten to her before she'd married Jason.

As far as Tawny was concerned, it couldn't be too soon for her, either.

Every fiber in Bart's body ached to make love to her right then and there, but his strong will made him deny himself the pleasure. Somehow it did not seem right to do that when this beautiful lady was carrying his child.

His next words endeared Bart to Tawny and convinced her of his sincere love for her. "I want to make love to you. God knows I've dreamed of it so many nights, but now I want to wait until you are truly my wife." He gave a devilish laugh. "So we're going to get married damned quick!"

"Well, if you're willing to wait, then I guess I must, too," she playfully teased him.

But that vow didn't keep him from taking his fill of kisses from the sweet nectar of her lips!

Chapter 58

Lord Bart Montgomery and the lady he was to marry were sitting on the ground on a country lane to make their plans for the very simple wedding they both wanted.

"You can understand why I can't show my face around the Hamilton estate right now, can't you? You know that Jason and I have been at odds since it was known to each of us that we were both trying to win your love."

"I understand, Bart, and you must understand that I owe Jason and his family so much. I . . . I just can't walk out of there and go with you, as much as I want to."

"And I'm not asking you to do that, Tawny. But since things are the way they are and you have no family here in England, I'd like to make the arrangements for us to be married in London at my townhouse. I don't want my mother to try to make it some big outlandish affair."

"I don't care if it is just the two of us," Tawny agreed. She felt it would be awkward for the Hamiltons to be present since she knew that they had been expecting her to marry Jason. "Why couldn't we just wait until we're married to tell everyone, Bart?"

"My sentiments exactly, love!"

When they had mounted their horses, all their plans were set. This time it was not painful for Bart to have to part company with her and watch her gallop up the drive leading to the Hamiltons' house. She would be coming to his townhouse in London at the end of the week. There they would be married, because it was there Bart wanted to live with Tawny. There she could be the mistress of their home. This could never be here on the country estate, for this was his mother's home and she was the mistress.

Bart was a very happy man as he rode Diablo back to his home, for he was sure Tawny did love him and destiny deemed that they not be denied this great love they shared.

His spirits were soaring as high as the sky by the time he reined Diablo up the long drive leading up to the house.

Tawny's whole world had turned completely around with the appearance of Bart Montgomery. Everything that was wrong yesterday was perfect now. What a difference a day could make!

The happiness she felt showed on her face as she approached the house and the stables. When she arrived at the gate of the yards around the stable, the young stableboy was there waiting to take charge of Coco.

Lady Sheila happened to be by the window in her bedroom. She'd heard a rider coming up the drive and thought it might be Jason returning from London, but it was Tawny.

It did not seem to be depressing Tawny that this was the second day Jason had not been home, and now she was wondering if he would be absent from the dining room again tonight. Such puzzling behavior for a young man who had a beautiful young lady with him! she thought to herself.

Someone else had been staring out her window, and longer than Lady Sheila! Joy had leaped out of her chair when she'd seen the magnificent sight of Bart Montgomery astride his black Arabian, riding side by side with Tawny on her little brown mare on the main country lane. She'd seen Bart lean over to take a kiss before he said good-bye and gallop on down the road as Tawny turned Coco into the drive.

Joy sank back down in her chair with a solemn look on her face. There would never be a wedding between Jason and Tawny, she just knew it! Bart was back!

But she couldn't blame Tawny, for how could anyone resist the handsome Bart Montgomery. She could not have if she had been in Tawny's shoes.

Like her mother, she wondered if Jason would be showing up for dinner tonight.

But as his family and Tawny would find out by the time they all gathered in the dining room, Jason was not going to be joining them. Lord Addison and his wife were pleased to see their little guest was in the best of spirits, but neither of them could say the same for themselves. Lady Sheila's Irish temper was ready to explode and her calmer English husband was out of patience with his son. Lord Addison considered Jason's behavior inexcusable, and he was going to tell him so when he did get home. That sweet little Tawny was too nice for Jason to treat her so shabbily.

When the dinner was over and the family gathered back in the parlor, Tawny was suddenly feeling that she was a stranger in their midst. Suddenly she felt the need to excuse herself, for her thoughts were wandering from the conversation.

When she did make her gracious exit, Lady Sheila and her husband assumed that it was because she was upset about Jason. Their sympathy went out to Tawny.

Joy did not think Tawny was upset at all. In fact, she suspected that Tawny was deliriously happy in her own little private world, a world that the Hamilton family played no role in. She would have liked to rush out of the parlor and follow Tawny to her room so they could talk, but she realized that Tawny was not ready to talk to her tonight. She was sure Tawny wanted to be by herself and dwell on her memories of the time she spent with Bart this afternoon. At least, this was what the young romantic Joy Hamilton surmised. She felt a deep sympathy for her brother right now.

When Bart returned home, he spent an hour in his study, and it was long enough to see that his mother had done a magnificent job while he'd been away. If Hattie had spoken the truth, and he knew she had, then all the credit went to Lady Laura and not his aunt Augusta. *He was delighted to see that she'd finally taken charge, as he'd wanted her to do. Whatever had brought about the change, he was happy about it.*

He was certainly going to make a point of telling her how much he appreciated finding his desk cleared away when he returned.

By the time he had gone to his room to change his clothes, it was getting close to the dinner hour, so he went back downstairs to join his mother in the parlor. He found her enjoying a glass of wine before dinner.

"Well, Mother—I must say you look awfully content. You also look very attractive tonight in that gown."

"Well, now, aren't you nice! Your father always liked me in this shade of wine. He said that it reminded him of the wild berries we used to pick when we strolled down the lanes of this countryside. Contrary to what you might have thought all your life, the two of us enjoyed the simple things. It is why we preferred this country estate instead of some fine house in London."

"There is a quiet and peace here that you can't find in the city," he agreed as he walked over to the liquor chest to pour himself a glass of wine.

429

But they had little time to engage in conversation before Hattie was announcing that dinner was ready. Bart did not need to be summoned a second time. But he did have to admit as they dined and talked casually, that things had certainly changed around here while he'd been away. He found that he was enjoying the evening in the company of his mother. She seemed more like Aunt Augusta.

Bart was relishing the last of the beef roast Hattie had fixed for them when his mother remarked that she had met a most interesting young lady the other day. "She was not only the most beautiful young lady I've seen in many a day," she praised, "but she seemed to have a level head on her shoulders, which is more than I can say for most of them these days."

Bart said nothing as he continued to eat the small roasted potato remaining on his plate, but he was thinking that he should have known all his mother's old ways had not changed. She had picked another young lady she wanted to match with him. He remembered the last two times this had happened and they had been disasters!

So he said nothing as she kept singing the praises of this particular young lady and how she'd invited her to tea.

"That was nice, Mother," he mumbled as he took a sip of the red wine and forked the small portion of beef left there on his plate.

"I thought so. I had wished you were home, dear, for you know her. It was Tawny Blair," she informed him. She was startled when she noticed her son seemed to be choking on his food. "Bart? Bart—are you all right?"

Clearing his throat and taking another gulp of the wine, he stammered, "You had Tawny here to tea?"

"Yes, dear. Was that wrong of me?" Lady Montgomery asked with a puzzled look on her face. "I found

430

her absolutely delightful.

Bart gained control of himself and questioned his mother, "How did you happen to invite Tawny to tea? Did she accompany Lady Hamilton?"

"As a matter of fact, I didn't include Lady Hamilton or any of her daughters. I just invited Tawny, and as to how it happened, it was quite by chance. A few days earlier as I was sitting right here in the dining room preparing to eat lunch, I was looking out the window when I saw two young ladies riding up by the stables. I recognized the Hamilton girl, but I did not recognize the other young lady. But the way she sat her horse was enough to make me get up from the table to go to the window."

A very pleased grin broke on Bart's face and he gave his mother his full attention.

"Hattie and I stood by the window and watched her swing over the fence and walk right up to that Arabian of yours. Why, she patted and rubbed him as if he were some gentle old mare. I couldn't believe it, and neither could Hattie."

She went on to tell him that she'd summoned Harvey to the house to find out who the girl was, because she knew he must know her from the way she observed them talking to each other.

"So Harvey told you who she was?"

"That's right, and I sent an invitation to her over at the Hamiltons' for her to have tea with me, and she came."

Bart found himself a little dazed that his mother had obviously been so taken with Tawny that she'd invited her to tea. He was hardly prepared for this news.

"Well, I'm glad you and Tawny had such a nice afternoon, Mother," he finally managed to say.

"Well, we did, and she has promised me to come back. I'm looking forward to see her again and hope you'll be here, dear, when she comes."

431

Bart could hardly restrain an amused laugh erupting, but he managed to keep a straight face as he assured her. "Oh, I'll make a point of it, Mother." Later he and his mother would share a few laughs about this night, but for now, he wanted to keep his plans secret.

"Now, Bart Montgomery—that is the kind of young lady you should pick as a wife," she told her son with motherly concern. "She has everything—beauty, brains, and such grace and charm."

Bart was finding it hard not to confess to her that Tawny *was* the woman he'd picked for his wife and very soon she was going to be his bride as well as the mother of his child.

"I'm sure Tawny would be very pleased to know you think so highly of her."

"She told me she knew you, and that the two of you had met when you were in Virginia to buy the Arabian. All I can say is that you must have been so entranced by that horse that you didn't notice Tawny and set your cap for her."

He gave out a laugh but said nothing.

Chapter 59

Bart did not linger in the country but one more day, for he had many things to attend to back in London. He was elated by Harvey Green's news that the mating of his Arabian with Sir George's mare was successful. The mare would have a foal sired by Diablo!

Before he went to his townhouse, he rode by the vacant old two-story stone house to see if anyone had purchased the property. It still stood empty, with more weeds growing around the grounds. Bart knew the solicitor handling the estate of this property and other homes in London, and knew the owners had died within months of one another. That had to have been over four years ago. So he rode directly to the office of Thomas Melton to make his bid on the place.

To his advantage, Bart found Melton was eager to dispose of the property at a reduced price, since it was the only one remaining unsold in the estate. He could finally close the books on it if Lord Montgomery bought it, so he greatly reduced it. Melton made himself a deal and Bart was pleased that he'd gotten Disney the inn he wanted. The rest was in Disney's hands.

Now he was ready to give this news to Disney and inform Thelma that there would be a wedding taking place in the townhouse at the end of the week. It might be a very private little wedding, but Bart intended that it was going to be a grand night, one that Tawny would always remember. Thelma was going to be a busy lady for the next few days preparing the special dinner he wished served after the ceremony. And there must be a wedding cake and champagne.

He already had a vision of the beautiful wedding gown he wished to see his lovely Tawny wear when she married him. Tomorrow, he would make a call on Madame Renée to see if she could possibly get something like that made in a few days' time. He didn't have to fret about purchasing a ring. For many weeks, he'd had the ring, but now it could finally go on Tawny's finger.

He was a man very pleased with himself as he rode up the street to his townhouse. Lady Luck was surely with him again. For a while, he was beginning to think that he'd been deserted, but now he was feeling more like the old Bart Montgomery again. Once again, he could say that he'd gotten what he'd set out to get. He had Tawny's love and he was sure of that!

No one knew when he arrived at the townhouse, and he decided not to announce his arrival and went directly to his room to enjoy a warm bath before dinner. He'd tell Disney his good news at dinner later. As he walked into his dressing room to pull out one of his linen shirts and take a pair of his fine-tailored pants from the rack, he was reminded of the meager wardrobe of his young friend, Disney. The young man could use a few things. Perhaps he should take Disney to his tailor, since he was also going to Madame Renée's salon tomorrow and the two shops were conveniently close to each other.

When he pulled on his fawn-colored pants and tucked his shirt inside, he forgot about a coat. It was a night to be casual in his own home and Disney would be wearing only a shirt and pants.

He found Disney already in the parlor, enjoying a glass of wine. "I see Wesley is taking good care of you, Disney," Bart greeted him.

"A fellow can get spoiled quickly with Wesley and Thelma around," Disney said, laughing. "I'm not used to being so lazy. I offered to help Thelma in the kitchen, but she shooed me out of there."

"Oh, I can believe that! Thelma even tosses Wesley out of the kitchen!"

Bart poured himself a brandy. He saw no reason to delay telling Disney his good news. "You won't be lazy long, Disney. I made the deal this afternoon on the old house I told you about. You've got a lot of weeds to cut down to get to the front door."

"Oh, that I'll gladly do! You really got it?"

"I got it, and for a cheaper price than I'd figured."

Now Disney's spirits were soaring as high as Bart's. By the time the two of them went into dinner they were in a very jovial mood.

That evening the atmosphere of the townhouse was one of gaiety and joy. No one was happier than Thelma when Bart Montgomery went to the kitchen after dinner to praise the excellent dinner she'd prepared. When he told her about the wedding he was planning for the end of the week, she was overjoyed.

"I knew that one day you'd come to me just as you have tonight and tell me you were going to be married, Lord Montgomery. No long, drawn-out affair for you!"

"You know me very well then, Thelma, and I want a magnificent wedding cake for me and my bride."

"You shall have it!" Thelma's eyes were sparkling, for she was so happy to hear that the young lord was finally taking himself a wife. She was curious to see this young lady who'd won Lord Montgomery's heart. She had to be a very lovely creature, Thelma knew!

Bart had a very busy day tomorrow, so he did not seek to linger downstairs long, for there were too many things to accomplish. His bride would be coming to him in just a few days!

Only one thing marred Tawny's ecstatic happiness

and that was the talk she knew she must have with Lady Sheila Hamilton and Jason when he returned home. She owed them so very much that the last thing in the world she wanted to do was hurt them. She dreaded this ordeal.

But it was Jason's mother who gave her the opportunity to say what she had to the next day. It was the perfect time, for all the Hamilton daughters were gone for the rehearsal of Angela's wedding. The spacious house was very quiet with no one there but Tawny, Lady Sheila, and Lord Addison.

Jason's mother had invited her to join her in her sitting room. Tawny knew that this was the right moment to have the confidential talk with her.

As soon as the two of them were seated in the bright sunny room Lady Sheila called her garden room, she immediately addressed the issue that was troubling her. "Tawny, it is good to have this time alone with you, for I have a great need to talk to you. It's against my Irish nature not to be truthful. I don't understand why Jason is staying away and I don't understand why he's acting the way he is."

Tawny reached over to pat her hand. "Don't be too harsh with Jason, for he is troubled, and I think I know why. I've felt this way for many days now, Lady Sheila. Like you, I don't like being dishonest, especially when your family has been so nice to me. The truth is, Jason doesn't love me the way a man should love the woman he wants to marry, and I don't love him the way a woman should love the man she marries. I think we both realized that after we arrived back here in England."

"Oh, Tawny—then that would explain so much!"

"That is why I said not to blame Jason. Jason is a most honorable man and he *had* asked me to marry him, but lately he's been tormented. I understood, for I suddenly realized that my love for him was deep but it was the love for a brother."

"Oh, Tawny dear—I always knew you were an exceptional young lady."

"When Jason returns home I am going to tell him I can't marry him. There is another man I love and Jason knows this. But there were reasons why he asked me to marry him. Jason always was protective of me. Maybe he felt about me like he did his three sisters. I think he realized that lately more and more."

Lady Sheila listened intently as Tawny spoke. She was very wise for one so young, Jason's mother thought.

"But you see, Lady Sheila, before we left Virginia and I accepted Jason's offer of marriage, I told him that I was expecting another man's baby. I could never have married Jason and let him think the child I'm carrying was his." Tawny anxiously waited to see how she would react to this revelation.

"The other man you love and whose child you are carrying is Bart Montgomery, isn't it, Tawny?" Lady Sheila calmly said without blinking an eyelash.

"Yes, ma'am, it is. It has always been Bart I loved with all my heart."

"Then it is Bart you should marry, Tawny dear, for it would not be fair to Jason or you if the two of you married."

"You can't know how much you're understanding means. The Hamilton family is very dear to me." Tawny heaved a deep sigh of relief. She felt she could begin to relax now that she'd made her confession to Lady Sheila. But there was still Jason she must face and, of course, there was Joy.

"Well, you know how dear you are to us, and just because you marry Bart doesn't change a thing for me. I'll be delighted to know that you will be living in England and we shall be able to see you from time to time."

"You can be sure that I will be calling on you very often."

Lady Sheila, with that Irish humor of hers, laughed. "The truth is, if you'd married Jason, he could have taken you to some faraway place. That young man will always have the wanderlust, I fear."

Tawny smiled. "Well, we'll just have to hope that he'll find some young girl who likes to wander like he does. Then he would have found himself the perfect wife. She must love the sea as he does."

"Yes, that would be the perfect mate for Jason, and until he finds her, I think my Jason should remain a bachelor."

Tawny went directly to her room, for she did not want to face all the Hamilton girls right now and they would be returning shortly. For now, she just wanted to be alone after the long talk she'd had with Lady Sheila.

Disney found Bart Montgomery to be a man of inexhaustible energy by the time he'd spent the entire day with him.

Their first stop at Levine's Tailor Shop had lasted over an hour, and when they left Disney was the proud owner of two pairs of pants and a half dozen white linen shirts. He wore the deep-blue woolen coat Bart purchased for him and it felt warm and comfortable, for there was a chill to the air today.

Bart left Disney at a tea room next to Madame Renée's Salon while he went to see about the wedding gown for Tawny. He wanted to do this without Disney's company. "I'll be back in a half hour, Disney."

As he entered the exclusive salon Bart was thinking that it had been a long time since he'd been here. He wondered if the feisty couturière, Renée Bourget, would remember him from the time when he accompanied Eliose Harcourt here. It was the first time he'd thought about the lovely Eliose and their torrid affair, which had lasted longer than most. But Bart had never for one minute thought of it as anything but an affair. Marriage had never entered his mind!

A fashionable young lady greeted him as he entered the salon.

"Would you tell Madame Renée that Lord Montgomery would like to speak to her," Bart told the young lady.

"Just a moment, monsieur." She hastily walked to the back of the salon and, as quickly, she returned to invite Bart to follow her. The tall, handsome, blond-haired Montgomery drew stares from the elegant ladies in the salon as he ambled toward Renée's private office in the back of her shop. Bart had been there before, too.

Renee ushered Bart into her office. "Well, Bart—you finally came to see me again!" A long cigarette dangled between ring-bedecked fingers. Her jet-black hair was pulled back into a severe coil atop her small head. Bart had never seen anyone with more piercing black eyes. Everything about this little woman was animated and dramatic. Each gesture of her graceful hands and each sway of her small body told what a vivacious person she was.

"But I'm here now, Renée, and for a very special reason. I want a wedding gown for my bride, and no one can do that for me but you!"

She gave out a gusty laugh. "Ah, others could, but it would not be as exquisite as Renée's. *Oui?*"

"Oui!"

She invited him to sit down and tell her about this special gown he wanted. When he had told her, she raised her fine-arched brow and asked, "Now tell me about this young lady who won the restless heart of Bart Montgomery."

Now it was Bart's turn to give a husky laugh. But he

439

did not hesitate to tell her about Tawny Blair, and he gave such a vivid description of the woman he loved that Renée Bourget smiled. "You know every delicate feature of this beautiful lady, eh? I can envision her myself."

"Well, will a few days give you enough time to make such a gown for Tawny?" Bart asked her.

"I don't have to make one, monsieur! I have one right now that I designed and just finished today to take out for approval. We have a young duchess about to be married so I made up three different styles. But if you like this one I speak about, then it is yours."

Renée summoned one of her seamstresses to bring the gown to her office. When the young lady carried the satin-and-lace gown into the office, Bart knew it was exactly what he wanted Tawny to wear the evening they were married.

Venice lace trimmed the Queen Anne neckline with the deep V cut, and the full, flowing skirt had tiers of Chantilly lace. The long Elizabethan sleeves of white satin were edged too, with Venice lace. Renée displayed the lovely lacy petticoats to be worn underneath the gown.

"Does this not please you?" She smiled, knowing already that it did.

"It does, Renée. Could you send it out to my townhouse? Tawny will be arriving there in a few days."

"It will be there when she arrives, Bart. Now, may I assist you with anything else?" With a teasing gleam in her black eyes, she told him she had a most exciting array of lingerie.

By the time Bart left Madame Renée's salon, he'd not only purchased a wedding gown and white satin slippers, but an assortment of lovely nightgowns and matching wrappers trimmed with lace in shades of coral, yellow, and robin's-egg blue, which Renée assured him would be perfect for the brown-haired temptress Bart had described.

Poor Disney had waited more than an hour for Bart to return to the tea room. But when he came into the tea room with his arms laden with packages, Disney understood why he'd been gone so long.

Disney figured that they would be going back to the townhouse now, but he quickly learned that their day was not over yet. Bart asked him, once they were in the carriage. "Well, Disney would you like to see this place that will be your inn?"

"Could we, Bart?" Disney's eyes came alive with excitement.

"Of course, we can!" Bart ordered his driver to take them to the outskirts of London where the old stone house was located.

"Shall we wade through the weeds and take a look around?" Bart asked when the carriage came to a halt.

Disney was more than willing to brave the waist-high weeds. When they went through the creaking front door, Disney realized that the house had not been occupied for a long time. To him, it was sad that such a nice house was empty of people and life. The outside structure of the two-story house looked fine and sturdy. Disney was more than impressed after they entered. He was a man with wondrous visions as he strolled through the downstairs rooms. He saw a cozy, inviting setting by the stone fireplace with pewter candleholders on the mantel brightening the room with its candlelight, giving a pleasant atmosphere to the room. Tables for couples wanting a very intimate setting would enjoy this setting. All he would have to do would be to tear out the wall to extend this room to make it a larger dining room to accommodate the larger groups. That left two rooms he would expand into his working kitchen.

Upstairs were four nice-size bedrooms. There would be no drastic changes to make to them. There would be a lot of work to put them in order, and furnishings to buy, but Disney didn't mind. One of the rooms would serve as his bedroom and the other three could be available for overnight lodgers. He could make it a prosperous inn, and he knew it!

"I'm ready to get started on it tomorrow, Bart!" he said as they walked back downstairs. Bart could see the excitement on his young face.

"Well, it's in your hands, Disney! I leave this up to you," Bart told him.

"I'm coming out here tomorrow and get all these weeds out of here."

"Well, you just ask Wesley for any tools you'll need to clear away the weeds. Now I've only one request to ask you. It's very special to me and a wedding present to my pretty bride."

"Anything, Bart! I can never repay you for what you've done for me."

"I'd like it to be called Blair's Inn," Bart declared.

"Blair's Inn it will be!"

Chapter 60

Jason left the *Sea Princess* and boarded the buggy to return home. He was prepared to face the disapproving look he'd see on his father's face this evening when he joined the family for dinner, but it was more than a displeased look he'd get from that Irish mother of his. She'd not hesitate a minute in giving him a good tonguelashing, for she had a fierce temper when she was angry.

He didn't even want to think about what he would see in Tawny's face. Perhaps she would be sadly disappointed in him, and he could hardly blame her for that. But he had to have these two days and nights away from her and his family to do some clear thinking.

For Jason, marriage was for a lifetime, so he had to think seriously about the proposal he'd made to Tawny. He'd been very sincere when he'd asked her to be his wife, but was he doing her any favor by marrying her just because he was willing to marry her and Bart wasn't. Was it better for her child to be illegitimate than for her to be married to him for the rest of her life when she loved another? Tawny was too honest to live a lie. It could destroy her!

These were things Jason had to think about and decide for both of them. Tawny was too dear to him for him to make the wrong move. One small baby could not decide the path of both their lives, Jason had finally concluded.

Now he knew he must get back home and have a talk

with Tawny as soon as possible. He urged the bay pulling his buggy to go faster as he traveled to the outskirts of London.

Suddenly his black eyes observed the fleeting sight of two men emerging from the old deserted two-story stone house that had stood vacant for the last few years. He turned around to glance back at the tall, fair-haired fellow he could have sworn was Bart Montgomery. But as he traveled on homeward he told himself that it couldn't be Bart, for he would not have had time to get back from Virginia where he and Tawny had left him a few weeks ago. Besides, he didn't recognize the young man with him. It surely couldn't be Bart.

Jason hoped he could manage to get inside the house and up to his room without encountering one of his family members or Tawny.

As he entered the front door and ambled down the hall to mount the stairs, he thought the house had an unusual quietness until he realized that it was late in the afternoon and everyone would be upstairs refreshing themselves before the evening meal. So he did manage to get to his room without meeting any of his family or Tawny.

He wasted no time in shaving his bearded face and taking a bath. When he was dressed in a clean white shirt and dark trousers, he took the brush to his thick hair. Now he looked more presentable to go to join his family and Tawny.

Across the hallway in their bedroom, Lord Addison was informing his wife, as she put the final touches to her hair, that their son had returned. "I saw his buggy arrive just a few minutes ago and I think I just heard him go to his room," he told her.

"Well, I think it's about time. But I have to admit that I don't feel so angry at Jason after my talk with Tawny this afternoon."

"Nor do I, dear, after you told me what Tawny had to

say. I admire that young lady even more now."

"I think we should allow the two young people to have their privacy in the parlor after dinner is over, Addison."

Lord Addison laughed. "Ah, but what about Joy?"

His wife rose from the stool, assuring him that she was going to go to Joy's room right now to have a little talk with their youngest daughter. "I'll be back shortly, Addison."

Lord Addison smiled and nodded his head.

Joy was surprised to see her mother coming to her room at this time of day. She was about to slip into her gown and Sheila obliged her by fastening the back buttons. "Your brother is home, Joy, and so he will be dining with us. Now, I am sure that he and Tawny will have some things to talk about in private. So this is why I came to talk to you before you went down to dinner."

"I promise to not say a word at dinner, Mother. Don't worry."

"That's fine, dear, but that's not all I have to speak to you about. Your father and I will not linger in the parlor after dinner, nor will you."

Joy gave the skirt of her gown a swish as she sat down to brush her long hair, which she was going to allow to flow around her shoulders unadorned without ribbons or combs. "So you wish me to come back to my room after dinner?"

"That's right, dear. I think we should all leave them alone tonight," Lady Sheila said, patting her daughter's shoulder as she turned to leave the room.

"Well, is Joy going to disappear upstairs with you and me, dear, after dinner?" Lord Addison asked when Lady Sheila returned to their room.

"She better, and I'm sure she will," Sheila told him. Now she was ready to accompany her husband downstairs to wait for Tawny and Jason to join them.

Tawny had no inkling that Jason had arrived back home until she left her room and was walking down the carpeted hallway toward the stairway. Jason just happened to be coming out of his room and was greeted by the sight of Tawny who stood there with a surprised look on her face.

"Jason! I didn't know you were back!" she greeted him as he took her arm and they moved down the steps together. He told her that he had arrived just a short time ago.

"Hope you're not angry at me for being away for a couple of days, Tawny, but I just needed to tend to some things," he lied a little.

"Why should I be? I'd find it hard to get angry at you." She gave a soft little laugh and patted his arm warmly.

Neither Jason nor Tawny had not felt so at ease as they both did this evening when they entered the parlor arm in arm. They were looking at each other with smiles on their faces. It was Lord Addison and Lady Sheila who were in for a surprise to see the two of them entering, with Tawny holding his arm. She looked very radiant and glowing in the pale-pink gown and her long dark-brown hair tied back with a pink satin ribbon.

Joy was the last to appear, and it was a very merry group she found gathered in the parlor. The festive air continued throughout the evening meal. She was thinking what a shame it was that it should not continue after the meal when everyone seemed so happy, but she'd dare not do what her mother had forbidden. She did notice, though, that everyone lingered longer than usual after the dessert was enjoyed and the servant had cleared away the dishes.

Finally, Lord Addison announced his intentions of going to his study to look over some papers and he got up from his chair, which was the cue for the others to rise.

"Jason, dear—I must leave you to entertain Tawny. Joy and I have the gown that she is to wear for Angela's wedding to check over. It must be taken back to the dressmaker tomorrow. I'm sure you will excuse us, Tawny?" Lady Sheila declared as she took Joy by the arm to guide her along with her. She was not leaving anything to chance that her daughter might get busy talking to Tawny and forget everything she'd told her earlier.

Joy went along with her mother, giving no protest. Tawny smiled because she knew why Lady Sheila was staging this little disappearing ruse. Jason had also figured it out, too. When the two of them went into the parlor, he laughed. "Ah, my adorable family! I got the idea that they want us to be alone tonight, Tawny."

"One could get that idea." She smiled at him as they went on into the parlor.

After Tawny was seated, Jason went to the liquor chest to pour himself a brandy and a glass of sherry for Tawny.

Tawny was glad for the opportunity to have Jason to herself, and she knew that Lady Sheila had cleverly manipulated this so she could have her talk with Jason as she had told Lady Sheila she was going to do.

After the two of them had enjoyed a few sips of their drinks, Tawny saw no reason to prolong what she must say to Jason. She knew that she was right in the decision she'd come to about her and Jason. He had not even kissed her when they'd met there on the second landing. That was not the way of a man romantically in love with a lady. Jason was not in love with her any more than she was in love with him. They were friends—the best of friends! But that was all it was or ever could be.

"Jason, I've something to tell you, and I've thought about it for days now. I rather suspect that you have, too. I can't marry you, even though I promised to. We

447

don't love each other as a couple should."

A slow smile came to his face and her declaration took a tremendous burden off him. "I know, Tawny, and I've been bothered about that a lot lately. I didn't want to hurt you, but I've had a terrible itch for a little over a week now to be back on that ship of mine to be going somewhere. It's as I told you, I never linger here in London too long. A few weeks and I'm ready to seek new horizons."

She laughed. "Well, now you can feel free to seek them out, Jason. I'll be leaving here in a couple of days—or maybe sooner now."

"Wha—what are you talking about, Tawny? You're not going back across that Atlantic at this time of the year, are you?" His black brow arched in disapproval.

She laughed. "No, Jason, I'm not about to board another ship for a long, long time, I hope. I'm going to Bart. He's back, Jason, and he does want to marry me."

"He's back! So that *was* Bart I saw today," he drawled slowly.

"You saw Bart today?"

"I saw him and some other man at this old vacant house at the edge of the city. At least, I thought it was him, but then, I couldn't figure out how he got back here so quickly. Now, I know that I was right."

Tawny told him that she would be going to Bart at his townhouse in London. "I will take you to Bart, Tawny," Jason quickly responded. "I'll take you to his townhouse. After all, I took you away from him back in Virginia so it only seems right that I return you to him."

"Yes, Jason—I would like for you to take me there," she declared. If Jason took her to the townhouse, maybe the two men would mend the friendship that had been broken because of her—a friendship that had endured too many years for the two of them to be enemies.

So it was settled that Jason would take her to London when she wished to go. Together, they left the parlor and went up the steps. When Jason walked her to her bedroom door, Tawny was so happy that she and Jason had come to terms about their true feelings for each other. Theirs was a friendship that would last for the rest of their lives and they both knew it.

As much as she loved Bart Montgomery, there would be a special place in her heart for Jason Hamilton as long as she lived.

Chapter 61

When she went to bed, Tawny knew that there was nothing left to delay her from going to London and Bart. Her departure would be with no hard feelings. She'd had her talk with Lady Sheila and the woman had understood. She and Jason had made a wise decision not to get married as they'd planned. She was so happy that they could still be the dearest friends.

Just the thought of being with Bart tomorrow night was enough to make her happy. Finally all her dreams were coming true. The man she loved was going to marry her, and he loved her as she loved him. She wanted nothing more! She was not going to end up like her mother, Maybelle.

She realized that Bart did not know about the baby, for she had not mentioned that to him. Would he be happy or would he be displeased? She prayed that he'd be happy about it. Tawny found out that overwhelming happiness could keep her as wide-eyed as troubling thoughts as she lay there sleepless for the longest time.

Down the hallway, Jason enjoyed the best sleep he'd had in many a night. He had only to look at the glow on Tawny's face when she mentioned Bart's name to know how happy she was. He was glad that things had worked out as they had for all three of them. Bart should be Tawny's husband and father to his own child. And now Jason could return to his happy-go-lucky days, free to sail his seas. When the young right lady came into his life, then he might think about marriage. Until then he could continue his life of freedom.

Jason questioned only one thing about Bart's arrangements, and that was why he was having her meet him at the townhouse instead of the country place. Why was he not coming to their home to pick her up? Jason was going to personally escort her to the townhouse, but this would be the last time he would play the role of Tawny's protector.

Tawny didn't have to tell him that she wanted to go to London tomorrow. He sensed it as they talked. She was eager to go to Bart as soon as she could.

Jason's sleep was deep and he didn't awaken until very late the next morning.

The rest of the Hamilton family were up long before Jason finally came downstairs. Tawny already had talked to Joy and told her she would be leaving this afternoon to go to London to join Bart at his townhouse.

Of course, Joy had a million questions to ask her, and Tawny tried to answer as many of them as she could, but she didn't know what Bart's plans were. He was taking charge of the private wedding ceremony, she told Joy.

She smiled at Tawny. "Well, we can still be good friends now that you aren't going to be my sister-in-law."

"I think maybe that could even be nicer, Joy."

"It might just be," she declared. "You can tell Bart that since it's you he's marrying I'll forgive him for not keeping his promise to me when I was twelve to wait for me to grow up so he could marry me," she giggled.

When Tawny left Joy to go upstairs to pack her belongings, she told Joy she'd like to talk to Jason.

"I'll tell him, Tawny, if the sleepyhead ever gets up."

Tawny could not hold back the tears flowing down her cheeks when she said good-bye to the Hamiltons. It was not a final good-bye, but nevertheless, Tawny could not help shedding a tear or two as she hugged Lady Sheila and Joy. They had become her family in the last few weeks.

451

The more reserved Lord Addison patted her shoulder and gave her a kiss on the cheek. "Tawny, this is your home, for we adopted you in our hearts," he declared. "Come back to see us anytime you want."

"Oh, I shall, Lord Addison. You aren't rid of me yet." She smiled through the tears. "I'll . . . I'll make arrangements to get Coco in the next day or two."

"Don't worry your pretty head about that, dear. Your little Coco is welcome here, too, just as long as you want," he assured Tawny.

Finally, she turned to allow Jason to help her up in the carriage and Addison Hamilton realized the deep impact Tawny Blair had had on the family. When or if Jason ever brought another young lady home, she would have to be an outstanding young miss to impress his family as Tawny had done. He might never find such a woman!

A late autumn twilight descended over the countryside as their carriage traveled down the country road. The cozy warmth of the fur muff felt good as Tawny burrowed her hands inside it. Lady Sheila had insisted that she have the muff and gold velvet bonnet when she left.

Jason was thinking about how Bart Montgomery might react when he appeared with Tawny at the townhouse. No one had to tell him what an explosive temper his old friend could have. But he guessed that he'd just have to take his chances on that.

He didn't have long to wait to find out because the trip into London took less than a half hour.

As they pulled up in front of the stone townhouse, Jason asked Tawny if Bart knew she would be arriving this evening.

"No, I had no way to let him know," Tawny told him.

The carriage halted, and Jason leaped down to assist Tawny out the door. For a brief moment he was carried back in time to the first time he'd seen the barefooted Tawny when Reba Cameron had introduced her to him when the two Englishmen had come to the farm to inspect the black Arabian. It amazed him how much she'd changed since that day. There was an air of sophistication about her now that had not been there that day. But forever he would remember that innocent girl he'd met in the springtime in Virginia.

Together they walked up the steps, and it was Wesley who opened the door. He recognized Jason Hamilton immediately.

"What a pleasure to see you, sir. It has been a long time," Wesley greeted Jason as he and Tawny entered the tiled hallway.

"Good to see you again, Wesley, and it *has* been a long time. Is Bart here?" Jason asked him.

"Yes, sir—he's in his study."

"Would you tell him I've brought a young lady with me?"

Wesley was a little distracted by the beautiful lady holding on to Jason Hamilton's arm as they moved inside the door. Wesley's eyes were appraising her rare loveliness as he ushered them into the parlor while he went to the study to announce their arrival to Lord Montgomery.

After Wesley left, Jason smiled at Tawny. "Well, Tawny—what do you think of your new home?" he asked her. "Bart does things in a grand way, doesn't he?" Jason had never sought out a townhouse for himself like many wealthy young bachelors, for he spent his time aboard the *Sea Princess* when he was not at his family's estate.

Bart was taken by surprise when Wesley announced to him that Jason Hamilton and a young lady awaited him in his parlor. The first thing Bart thought was Jason was playing some kind of dirty trickery on him, for he knew the young lady with Jason had to be Tawny.

"Thank you, Wesley. Bring some of that white wine to the parlor," Bart requested as he rose from the desk where he'd been going over some papers before he had dinner alone. Thelma had packed Disney's dinner in a basket so he could spend the evening at the new inn.

His white shirt was opened at the neck and he tucked it inside the waistline of his tailored pants as he ambled out of the room to go greet Jason and Tawny. Many thoughts paraded through his mind. After all his plans for his wedding to Tawny, was something going to change all that? Was the purchase of Tawny's wedding gown and the many things he'd done so that their wedding could take place in two days going to be for naught?

Today Wesley had purchased all the various foods Thelma had listed as necessary for her to prepare the wedding dinner Bart had requested. Everything was ready for that grand and glorious night. But it was an apprehensive Bart Montgomery marching toward his parlor to greet Jason and face what he must.

He loved Tawny Blair more than anything else in the world, but if she had allowed Jason to change her mind or influence her to not marry him, then he would never forgive her or Jason as long as he lived.

When he entered the room to see Tawny sitting in the gold-colored woolen gown and her lovely face framed with the gold velvet bonnet, he forgot about everything except rushing to take her in his arms. "You came, love, and two days earlier than I'd expected," he declared. "Nothing could delight me more." He held her close to him.

It was only then that his blue eyes darted over in Jason's direction to see a slow grin coming to Jason's face. Tawny smiled up at Bart. "Of course, I came. You knew that I would. Jason offered to bring me." Her eyes turned in Jason's direction.

"I took her away, Bart, I thought it was only fitting that I bring her back to you," Jason told his old friend. Bart realized that it was Jason's way of telling him he was hoping to mend the wound of their friendship.

Bart tightened his arm around Tawny's waist and smiled at Jason. "Well, now that I've got this little miss back, I'll never let her out of my sight again. She's too hard to keep track of. I thank you, Jason, for bringing her back. The three of us are here together again and I think the occasion calls for champagne. What about it, Jase?" Jason

454

knew that this was Bart's way of telling him that he also wanted the two of them to forget their differences of the past and be friends again.

"I'd say that was a splendid idea, Bart," Jason eagerly agreed.

The three of them sat in Bart's parlor and enjoyed the champagne. Jason toasted his two friends, wishing them all the happiness in the world in their lives and marriage.

Bart had insisted that Jason stay and join them for dinner. At first Jason was reluctant to accept until Tawny urged, "Oh, please Jason! I wish you would," and Jason found himself helpless to refuse her request.

When Bart left the room to inform Thelma that there would be two more at the table, Tawny told Jason, "It is wonderful to see you and Bart on friendly terms again. It reminds me of the time when we were all aboard the *Sea Princess*. That seems like a lifetime ago now."

"You're right, Princess. We all have lived a little since that time, I guess," Jason remarked as he took the last sip of his champagne.

Bart stood in the doorway listening to Tawny and Jason and was glad the evening had turned out as it had.

Tonight seemed like the right time to present Tawny with the magnificent diamond ring he had bought for her so many long weeks ago.

After they had dined on the delicious meal Thelma had prepared and returned to the parlor, neither man had to ask Tawny if it would bother her if they indulged themselves in one of the cheroots they both enjoyed smoking, as they had nightly aboard the *Sea Princess*.

Bart poured each of them another glass of champagne. He served Tawny her glass, but along with it he lifted the small velvet case out of his pocket and handed it to her. "See if this pleases you, love," he said, grinning.

He stood there with Jason, waiting to see her reaction when she opened the case.

A brilliant sparkling star nestled in the black velvet-lined case. "Oh, it's . . . it's the most beautiful thing I've ever seen in my life, Bart!" She stretched up on tiptoe to kiss him. But when she tried to slip the ring on her finger, her hand was trembling so she couldn't, so Bart slipped it on her finger.

"That ring's waited a long time to get right here on your finger, Tawny my love. I'm happy to see it's finally there."

When the three of them had taken a seat and Tawny had finally begun to calm from the excitement of Bart's sparkling diamond, she found herself offended by the obnoxious odor of the cheroots. She could not imagine why, for it had never bothered her when they'd all sat around in Jason's cabin in the evenings.

Suddenly she realized that she had not been pregnant then as she was now. But the longer they puffed, the more miserable she felt. Jason noticed that she was very quiet and looked weary, so he decided it was time that he tell the two of them goodnight and start for home.

Shaking Bart's hand and giving Tawny a peck of a kiss on the cheek, he said good night. "I imagine the next time I see you two, you'll be married."

"We will, if I have anything to say about it," Bart replied.

"Good night, Jason, and thank you for bringing me to Bart," Tawny said as she stood by Bart's side.

Jason just smiled and gave her a nod of his black head as he turned to go out the door. Boarding his carriage, he felt in the highest of spirits even though he sat without Tawny by his side. She was by the side of the man she loved and that was all that mattered.

It was good to have Bart Montgomery as his friend again!

Chapter 62

It was not until Wesley and his wife Thelma were in their own private quarters on the first landing at the back of the townhouse that they discussed the arrival of the new young mistress.

"Pretty little thing, isn't she, Wesley?" Thelma remarked as she let her thick coil down so she could brush her hair.

"Pretty, and very nice is my opinion, Thelma. I think she'll make the perfect mate for Lord Montgomery. Never seen him have a happier face than when he saw her."

When she finished brushing her hair, Thelma wasted no time getting into her comfortable nightgown and crawling into bed. She noticed that Wesley was still not undressed. "Aren't you coming to bed, Wesley? Aren't all your duties through for the night. Lord Montgomery and his lady have gone on upstairs, and didn't I hear you let Disney in just a while ago?"

"Yes, but the young man was starved so I fixed him a small feast and I was going to check on everything before I came to bed."

"I'll say one thing for that lad—he's not afraid to work."

Wesley agreed with his wife. As long as there was light, Disney had told him he'd worked to rid the grounds of all the high weeds and grass. After dark, he'd lit a lantern and worked on the two front rooms, wiping down all the cobwebs from the walls and the ceiling. Before he'd finally left the old house, he'd cleaned out all the old ashes in the hearth and swept the floors of the two rooms.

"He's got many a day of hard work ahead of him just to

get the place cleaned. There's six more rooms to go over," Wesley told his wife.

"Well, he's a young, healthy lad, and I don't think he's lived an easy life from what he's told me while we've chatted in my kitchen. Loves to talk cooking, he does!" Thelma commented.

"Dim your lamp. Thelma, and get your rest. I'll be back shortly," Wesley urged her.

Thelma did not have to be urged to do just that. The next few days were going to be busy with two extra people here and a wedding taking place.

Bart was escorting Tawny to the guest room across the hall from his master suite. With a devilish glint in his blue eyes, he told her, "Damned if I know why I made the stupid vow not to make love to you until we were married! But I'll bloody well keep it if it kills me. So kiss me, love, and then get inside that door quickly before I make myself a liar."

She laughed as she arched up so his lips could meet hers in a good-night kiss. "I know why you made that vow, Bart Montgomery," she murmured softly after he released lips as sweet as the wine they'd drank at dinner.

He arched a brow and quizzed her. "Oh, you think you know?"

"I do, and I love you all the more for it," she replied as she gave him a tantalizing smile and swayed through the door leaving him in the hall as she closed the door.

It was not until he had gone to his own room that he realized that he'd not told her about Disney living here and had not had a chance to speak to Disney since he was not here when Tawny and Jason had unexpectedly arrived.

But when he left his room to go down the hallway to check to see if he'd returned to the house, he found that Disney was still not in his room.

So Bart returned to his room and prepared for bed. Sleep was not going to come easy for him knowing that Tawny was right across the hall in his guest bedroom.

But Wesley had informed Disney that Lord Montgomery's lady had arrived so when he went up the steps and moved down the hallway, he tried not to make a sound as he went to his own room.

What kind of young lady would she be, Disney wondered? He found himself most curious about the woman Bart would pick to be his wife. He knew she would have to be an outstanding lady to have attracted such a man as Bart.

Tomorrow he would be seeing this Miss Tawny Blair. Tonight his body ached with tiredness, and the comfort of his bed lulled him to sleep quickly.

The townhouse was a beehive of activity the next day. It began with the arrival of Tawny's wedding gown from Madame Renée's Salon. Renée Bourget, along with her driver, arrived at the townhouse just before noon. Wesley had ushered them into the parlor while he summoned Bart.

But Tawny had not come downstairs yet, and Bart wasn't sure she was awake. He'd not expected the madame to be coming to the house to personally deliver the gown.

He went upstairs to knock on Tawny's door and she opened it, still looking sleepy. He noticed that she was without her shoes. "Good morning, love. Are you awake enough to try on your wedding gown. Madame Renée is here to see to the fitting."

"My wedding gown, Bart?" she stammered.

"My bride has to have a beautiful wedding gown, doesn't she?" He grinned, letting his hands snake around her waist.

Tawny raised up her hands to clasp them around his neck. "How could I have ever doubted that you loved me, Bart?"

"Damned if I know. I thought I told you in a million ways, you little minx! Now, may I send Madame Renée up?"

"Yes, Bart—along with some coffee, too."

"Already sounding like the wife, aren't you, Tawny Blair?" He laughed as he turned to go back down the stairs.

A few minutes later, Madame Renée was to meet the barefoot goddess standing there in her pale-yellow gown when

Tawny greeted her at the door. "Good morning, Madame Renée. I understand I've a wedding gown to try on." Her dark eyes had already seen the flowing folds of white satin and lace lying across the lady's arm.

"You have, and the gorgeous gown should be absolutely stunning on you. In fact, I am now wondering if I didn't create this gown for you, madamoiselle even though I didn't know it at the time."

Tawny smiled at the tiny lady carrying the huge mass of satin and lace. "Would you like to lie it there on the bed, Madame Renée? By the way, my name is Tawny Blair."

"Tawny . . . Tawny Blair. The perfect name for you, mademoiselle." She immediately started assisting Tawny out of her yellow gown so she could try on the wedding gown.

Amazingly, there was not one seam to be taken out, and Madame Renée was astounded to see that it fit with perfection. She was now convinced that this gown was surely meant for Tawny Blair. Madame Renée was only sorry that it was to be a private wedding so that her creation could not be gloriously seen by all society on Tawny's sensuous figure. But Madame Renée knew there was the future, and as the wife of Lord Bart Montgomery, London was going to know the beauty of Tawny Blair. If she was lucky, it would be her gowns the young wife of Bart Montgomery would be wearing when she attended the social affairs in the city.

With great pleasure, she announced to Bart waiting downstairs that the gown was a perfect fit so she did not have to take it back to her salon.

"She is absolutely enchanting, Lord Montgomery. I must ask where you found such a divine lady?"

"In Virginia, Madame Renée. Virginia has the most beautiful ladies and the finest horses in the world," he declared with a grin on his handsome face.

"You've convinced me, monsieur! Anytime I can serve you again, just call on me. It will be my pleasure," she told him as she prepared to leave with her driver.

Bart laughed. "Now that I will have a beautiful wife, I'm sure I'll be in need of your services quite often, Madame

Renée."

"Especially when one is as breathtakingly beautiful as Mademoiselle Tawny." Renée gave him a soft laugh and a wink of her eye as she went on down the steps of his townhouse to the street below, where her driver awaited to help her into the carriage.

When Bart went back inside and was preparing to mount the steps to go upstairs to Tawny's room, he stopped to listen to the laughter coming from the kitchen. He realized that it was Tawny's lilting laughter mingling with Thelma's. He grinned as he changed his direction. It would seem that the little minx was making herself very much at home.

Sitting there at the small kitchen table was not only Tawny but his friend Disney having themselves a cup of coffee as Thelma puttered around. As Bart went into join them, he learned that the subject of their amused laughter was that Tawny had absentmindedly forgotten her slippers when she'd come downstairs after Madame Renée left.

"Tawny is guilty of that quite often, aren't you love?" Bart declared to all of them.

"I plead guilty," she smiled up at him.

"I see that I've no reason to introduce you to Disney," he remarked as he took the vacant chair.

"No, Disney and I introduced ourselves, didn't we, Disney?"

"Yes, ma'am, we did," Disney replied as he rose from the table to leave the townhouse to put in another day's work out at the old house. Only today he was getting a much later start due to sleeping so long.

All Bart had to do was notice the warm, friendly atmosphere of the room when he'd walked in to know how his enchanting little Tawny was going to be able to wind everyone around her little finger. All he had to do was see Thelma and Disney's faces when they looked at her.

Later, Bart told her about Disney and how he happened to be here at the house. Tawny found herself admiring Bart tremendously for his generosity, which brought to mind the generous hearts of Reba and Bill Cameron.

"You are a wonderful man, Bart Montgomery! I'm finding that out more and more all the time," she lovingly declared to him.

"I kept trying to tell you this. You were just hard to convince," he teased her lightheartedly.

"Oh, I wasn't that hard at all and you know it, Bart!" Her dark eyes looked at him, and Bart saw the love reflected there. He could not imagine how it would feel to be any happier than he was today with Tawny sitting there with him in her dainty bare feet.

He thought that there was no reason to delay their wedding an extra day. The wedding gown was delivered and it fit, so there was no problem there. Besides, impatience was gnawing at him fiercely. To endure another day was too long to wait and now that she was here with him. He knew the vicar would be pleased to perform the ceremony tomorrow night instead of the next night.

When he approached Tawny about his change of plans, she was more than agreeable. He was delighted to hear her say that. He was not prepared to hear her say her next words. "I think, Bart, there is only one thing I'd like to make it the perfect wedding I'd always remember."

"Anything you wish, love. You know that."

"I'd like to have your mother and the Hamiltons here to see us married. That is the way it is done back in Virginia. The Hamiltons are the closest thing I have to a family here in England."

For a minute, Bart sat speechless. Finally, he grinned. "Well, if this is the way you want it, I'll ride out this afternoon to invite them."

"Thank you, Bart. Every girl has her dreams of her wedding day, and mine will be complete to have people I love sharing the happy occasion. There will only be one wedding ceremony for me, Bart, and that is the one I have when I marry you."

"Oh, love! You can't know what a happy man you've made me. I guess I was too selfish wanting not to share it with anyone. But I'm very greedy where you're concerned.

462

But a lady who's going to be so beautiful as you in that wedding gown should be seen." He kissed her passionately, wishing that he never had to let her go out of his arms.

Because of these new plans, he had things to accomplish before the afternoon was over, so he left Tawny's side to go to the vicarage. From there he went to tell his mother about his plans and on to the Hamiltons.

Dusk was gathering around the countryside by the time Bart traveled back toward the city. He was glad that Tawny had insisted that they invite the Hamiltons and his mother to their wedding, and they were all elated to get the invitation.

After he'd arrived back in the townhouse, he sought out Thelma to alert her to the additional guests they would be having tomorrow night. "I know, Lord Montgomery," she quickly informed him, "the little mistress has already told me about them and that it will be tomorrow night instead of the following night. So I got started on my baking this afternoon."

Bart ambled out of the kitchen thinking to himself that it was no little helpless miss he was marrying. He would never have to concern himself about Tawny taking charge as the mistress of her house. She was already doing it!

He found himself admiring this air about her. But then there was always that fire and spirit about Tawny Blair, and it was one of the reasons he'd fallen so desperately in love with her.

There was a mystique about Tawny that would forever thrill and interest him!

Chapter 63

As they sat at the table that evening, Bart admired his beautiful bride-to-be looking so regal and elegant in her brown silk gown and the lovely topaz teardrop earrings dangling from her ears. On her left hand she wore Reba's topaz ring, and her right she wore his magnificent diamond. She looked absolutely striking.

It was only he and Jason who remembered this sophisticated lady as the little backwoods beauty they'd both first seen at Cameron Farms the day Bart had gone to see the Arabian. But there were some things about Tawny that would forever remain the same, Bart knew. Like no other woman he'd ever known, there would always be the challenge she'd give him, for there was an unpredictable air about her.

When they had finished Thelma's delectable dinner and were enjoying the dessert, Tawny announced to him that she would not be seeing him tomorrow until they met for the wedding ceremony at six in the evening.

Bart bristled and insisted on knowing just where she would be. She gave a soft laugh. "I shall be here, my darling," she told him. "Right here in the house! But it is bad luck for the groom to see his bride on their wedding day, and I will not chance bad luck, Bart."

He saw how serious she was so he did not dare try to change her mind. "Very well, I'll not bother you all day. I'll not come to your room, but may I send up a tray for you so you won't be starved when you come down to marry me?"

A slow smile came to her face and she gave him a nod of her head. Disney was sitting there with amusement playing

464

on his face as he watched the two of them. He had the greatest admiration for Bart Montgomery for all the things he'd done for him, and in the very brief time he had known Miss Tawny, he found himself admiring her as well. For the two of them, he had to make his inn a success. One day Blair's Inn would be the talk of London and that would be his tribute to the two people who had been so kind to him.

He'd persuaded Thelma to allow him to help her in her kitchen tomorrow night in preparing some of the delicacies. He wanted to contribute something to the occasion tomorrow night.

Already, the atmosphere of the townhouse was a very festive one. Bart, Disney, and Tawny left the dining room to go to the parlor. But as it had been the night before when Bart and Jason lit up their cheroots, the same effect washed over Tawny as the aroma permeated the parlor.

The solution was for her to make a quick exit, she decided, so she graciously bid the two men good night, telling them, "A lady must have her beauty sleep the night before she is to be married."

Bart rose up out of his chair to escort her to the base of the stairs. "Go back and talk with Disney, Bart. I can find my room," she assured him. But he insisted on going up the stairs with her and rewarding himself with a kiss before she moved through the door.

In the solitude of the room, Tawny could not believe how wonderful life had been to her as she sank down on her bed to remove her slippers. Tomorrow she was to marry Bart. This lavish townhouse was to be her home, and she could not help thinking of the humble cottage which had been her home the first sixteen years of her life. She thought about the expensive, elegant wedding gown she would be wearing tomorrow night when she married Bart, and she recalled the ragged frocks she used to wear. There on her hands were the exquisite rings. Why had fate been so kind to her and so cruel to poor Maybelle, her mother? She knew that she'd probably never know, but she did prod tonight for the answer.

She got undressed and slipped on the nightgown and robe. Sitting at the dressing table, she began to stroke her thick brown hair. When she looked into the mirror and saw her reflection, she was bothered. But did she dare chance destroying everything if she told Bart before the wedding that she was carrying his baby? Would he want to call off the wedding because he would feel that she had played him false?

As perfect as everything was, did she dare chance telling him before their wedding? Dear God, she wanted nothing to ruin tomorrow!

She knew not how long she'd sat there at her dressing table dwelling in her private musings when she heard Bart going into his room. The little clock on the chest in her room was chiming ten.

Getting up from the dressing table, she tied the sash of her pink robe that had been hanging loose around her waist. Tomorrow could not begin with any lies or secrets. She had to be honest with Bart before she married him. If he loved her enough, as she felt he did, it would make no difference that she was carrying his child.

She opened the door and quietly walked across the hall. Softly rapping on the door, she called out to him.

Bart had been in the process of undressing when he heard her soft voice calling his name. He hastily rushed across the room to open the door to see her standing there in her nightgown and robe.

"Something wrong, love?" he asked her, taking her by the arm to lead her into the room. Her brown doelike eyes looked so serious, and her thick mane of dark hair flowed around her shoulders. Bart saw the tempting swells of her breasts in her diaphanous pink gown and wrapper as she followed him into his room.

"Everything is so wonderful, Bart, and that is the trouble. That is what is bothering me. I had to come to you and talk about it. I want everything to be perfect and it can't be."

"Now, why can't it be, Tawny?"

466

"Because of something I should have told you a long time ago."

It was hard for him to suppress the amusement playing on his face, for he had wondered why she had yet to tell him what Reba had confided in him back in Virginia. He had figured it to be her pride. But this had not mattered to Bart.

"How long ago should you have told me, Tawny love?"

"I should have told you the day we were walking in that garden at Greenfield's. But I didn't."

"Neither did I ask you to marry me that day, Tawny, and I should have. So we both made a mistake."

Tawny could hardly breathe. "I am carrying your child, Bart," she managed to tell him. "I've been carrying it for almost three months now. I . . . I couldn't marry you tomorrow without telling you this tonight."

His arms went around her lovingly and his blue eyes danced adoringly over her face. "My sweet Tawny, I've known this since the day I talked with Reba Cameron, and it's made me love you all the more. Why do you think I was so eager to get to you that I took passage on a damned freighter to get to England? I could not be happier about it. I just didn't want you marrying Jason instead of me."

He didn't give her a chance to reply, for his lips had joined with hers in a kiss to assure her he meant every word he'd said. Right then he didn't give a damn about any vow he'd made, for her soft, supple body was pressed against him and he was only human. He could not fight the overwhelming passion he could not tame or control.

He felt the sweet surrender of Tawny as she pressed closer to his bare chest, and he knew she was as hungry for his love as he was for hers. He was not going to deny either of them so he laid her back on his bed and his fingers started untying the sash of her robe. Just as quickly her gown was lowered so his lips could caress her satiny flesh and he felt her arch boldly against him. "Oh, love—how I've yearned to feel the sweet touch of you against me like this!" his deep, husky voice whispered in her ear.

"Oh, Bart," she moaned softly.

He felt the softness of her thighs pressed against his as he lowered himself down. He looked upon her face, which was radiant with the sensuous flush of passion, and he listened to her kittenlike sounds of delight as his strong forceful body pressed more powerfully to join with her.

His fevered lips teased the rosy tips of her breasts as her undulating body made his passion mount higher and higher.

His hands felt the sudden quakes of her body as he touched her and she felt the ripples of his firm muscles as her hands clasped his back tighter, as though she would never let him be free of her again. Bart was caught up in a frenzy of passion. Eagerly and untamed, Tawny soared to that peak of ecstasy with him. In that private paradise known only to lovers, they dwelled for many golden, precious moments.

Afterward, they breathlessly clung together wanting to hold on to this moment of splendor, for they both knew now that their love was forever and ever. Nothing would ever separate them again!

Bart was not too sure of how long they lay in each other's arms, serenely quiet and calm. He almost wished time could stand still at this moment except that he had yet to make this adorable little minx his wife tomorrow. There were no doubts in his mind that he and Tawny would have many such nights of delight and pleasure.

Besides, he heard the chiming of the clock and he recalled that Tawny had told him it could be bad luck if he saw his bride on their wedding day. He didn't want to take any chances about that.

She was so quiet that he wondered if she'd fallen asleep in his arms. Gently, he nudged her. "Love, are you awake?"

"Barely. Oh, Bart — it was so wonderful to have you love me again like that. It . . . it had been so long," she softly murmured.

"Well, it won't ever be that long again, love. Now Tawny, my sweet — I've got to ask you to leave my bed so we won't have that bad luck you spoke about. In thirty minutes it will be our wedding day."

"It will? Oh, mercy!" She jerked up to free herself from Bart's encircling arms.

It was this delightful childlike simplicity of Tawny that made her so divine. Her long thick hair was tousled and she was still naked. An amused grin was on Bart's face as his eyes devoured her for a moment. He told her, "Get your gown on, you wicked little vixen, and get to your own bed!"

She gave out a giggle as she looked over at him. "Tomorrow night you won't be telling me that, Bart Montgomery!" She had a most provocative look in her dark brown eyes as she reached for her gown and pulled it over her head.

He laughed huskily, "No, I can assure you that we'll never have separate bedrooms as some couples I've heard about."

Dressed again in her gown and wrapper, she languorously strolled toward the door. Bart moved around the bed to give her one last kiss before she left the room.

"Until tomorrow, love. Sweet dreams," he said as he released her arms and watched her move through the door of the guest room.

Tawny now had everything to make her happiness complete. Bart was happy about the baby. There was nothing standing in the way of their wedding or their happiness now.

She just knew it was going to be a glorious day tomorrow. If she could have had one more wish it would have been that Reba and Roberta could have attended her wedding, but she knew life had been too kind to her already.

She could ask for no more!

Chapter 64

Tawny awakened late in the morning of her wedding day. She lay in bed for a long time, remembering Bart's fierce lovemaking. She was completely happy.

She looked out her window up into a bright, clear blue sky. She was pleased that it was not one of those gray, gloomy days with a damp dismal rain falling.

When she saw that she had slept half the day away, she ordered a light lunch tray along with a carafe of coffee sent to her room, for she was determined that Bart would not see her for the next six or seven hours.

But she saw him down below as he went out of the townhouse to board his carriage.

She knew that the next few hours would seem endless, but she had two pleasant surprises. First, Thelma came with the lunch tray, and along with her lunch there on the tray was a faded blue satin garter. "It was mine, Miss Tawny, so I give it to you now to wear when you wed Lord Montgomery. Lord only knows, it's old and blue." Thelma smiled. "We'll say you borrowed it from me."

Tawny reached over to kiss her cheek. "This is awfully sweet of you, Thelma."

"Well, we want you to have all the lucky charms for this evening. I knew that was why you were staying up in your room today, but Lord Montgomery has gone out to fetch his mother so he'll be away for awhile."

A short time later, Tawny heard another knock on her door. Madame Renée was the last person she expected to see. She stood there holding an exquisite headpiece with white satin ribbons and delicate white blossoms.

"I made you a headband with orange blossoms. In France, it is the custom that the bride must wear orange blossoms for good luck and happiness.

"You are so sweet and thoughtful. And how should I wear it, Madame Renée?" Tawny asked.

"May I suggest that you pull all your lovely hair back with soft curls hanging down your back and little wisps curled at your temples. The headband will make a lovely crown over the top of your head. It will be *magnifique!* Let me show you."

She pulled Tawny's hair back from her face, placed the headband, and pulled out a small wisp of hair at the temple, curling it around her finger. "You see what I mean? Is that not attractive?"

"Oh, yes — I like that!"

"I am now pleased and I shall not take up any more of your time. It is a hectic time when one is to be married, but I wish you great happiness, *ma petite.*"

"And I thank you so very much for being so good to me, Madame Renée," she said as she walked to the door with the couturière.

"It was my pleasure, and I tell you one more thing, Tawny Blair. Stay always as you are now, for you, too, are good as well as beautiful!" Madame Renée smiled as she turned to leave. Rarely had she met a stunningly lovely lady like Tawny who was not smug and conceited. That was what set Tawny apart from most of the gorgeous lovelies Renée Bourget encountered in her salon.

Bart and his mother returned to the townhouse about four in the afternoon. Tawny was glad she had insisted that he invite Lady Montgomery and the Hamiltons to the wedding.

A short time later, as she was preparing to step into the tub filled with sweet, perfumed oils and warm water, there was a knock on her door. Hastily, she pulled on her wrapper. She was surprised to see Bart's mother standing at the door.

"Oh, Lady Montgomery — please come in."

Lady Montgomery sighed warmly as she embraced the girl standing there. "Oh, Tawny, I can't tell you how happy I am that Bart is marrying you." She was not a woman who gave vent to her emotions too often, but Tawny saw the mist of tears in her eyes now. "I think Bart is a very lucky young man.

"I think we're both lucky to have found each other, Lady Montgomery."

"Well, dear, I'm not going to linger, for I see your bath is ready, but I had to give you this before you came down." She handed Tawny a velvet pouch. Inside was a bracelet of sapphires and diamonds. "It was my mother's, Tawny, and I wore it the day I married Edward, so I wanted you to wear it when you married Bart."

"Oh, Lady Montgomery!" Now it was Tawny who had tears in her ears for she could not believe how kind people were. She had been blessed and she only wished that such generous hearts could have been known by Maybelle. Maybe her whole life might have been different.

Many things paraded through Tawny's mind as she took her leisurely bath after Lady Montgomery left the room. She lived her whole life in those few brief moments and knew that everything had led her to this moment when she would become Bart Montgomery's wife.

After she had bathed and put on the lovely white satin wedding gown, she sat at the dressing table and looked at herself in the mirror. She knew she'd probably never look this beautiful again. But for this one night, she felt like a queen.

As she arranged her hair so that she might place the headband on properly, she heard a familiar voice calling her name just outside the door. Tawny smiled for she knew who the voice belonged to.

And indeed standing there was her little friend, Joy. "Oh, I just couldn't resist sneaking up here to see you before the ceremony, Tawny! I twisted Bart's arm and he told me which guest room you were in."

"I'm glad you did, Joy."

"I . . . I have something to give you, Tawny," Joy said as she handed her friend a delicate lace-edged handkerchief. "I thought you could carry it when the tears of joy start to flow."

"Oh, Joy—dear, dear Joy! What would I ever have done without you! Tawny embraced her.

Joy gave out a soft little laugh. "Well, that's why I came up, so I could escort you down the steps to the parlor. It's time, Tawny. Shall we go?"

"I'm ready," Tawny told her as she started toward the door.

Tawny and Bart took their wedding vows in the candelit parlor of Bart's townhouse, a most romantic setting, with lavish bouquets of flowers decorating the room. Everyone had to admit that none of them had ever seen a more beautiful bride than Tawny. Lord Addison knew he would be seeing his own daughter, Angela, being married very shortly, but she could not possibly be more radiantly beautiful than Tawny looked tonight.

Jason sat awestruck as he watched Tawny standing by Bart's side. He knew why he'd called her "princess" when she was on his ship so long ago, for a princess she surely was!

All were having their own private musings during the ceremony. Lady Montgomery was thinking what absolutely beautiful grandchildren these two were going to present to her. Lady Sheila Hamilton was hoping that someday Jason would find a bride as beautiful and sweet as Tawny. Secretly, Joy was glad it had been Bart who Tawny had married instead of Jason because her friend would be happier.

Disney should have felt out of place at this elegant gathering of two wealthy English families, but he didn't, as strange as it might seem. There was a young lady in the gathering who had captured his eye the minute she entered the parlor. She seemed so shy and reserved, but something about her attracted Disney. He could not help staring at her across the room during the ceremony and Jane noticed him looking in her direction and smiled. Disney was elated!

Lord Addison was finding himself to be more sentimental in his old age. Wedding ceremonies were very draining emotionally, and so he was prepared for the exhausting ordeal Angela's would be with all its pomp and splendor. It was not going to be a simple affair like Bart's. But he would have to get used to all the hustle and bustle, for he and Sheila would be going through weddings for Joy, Jane, and Jason.

When the ceremony was over and Bart kissed his bride, he softly whispered for her ears only, "You are the most beautiful woman in the whole world and now you are mine forever!"

While Tawny and Bart began to circulate among their guests, Wesley and Thelma served the group from silver trays lined with glasses of champagne. As they moved from one group to another, Bart told his bride that Coco was now stabled with Diablo. He'd seen to that when he went out to get his mother to bring her back to the townhouse.

She smiled at her new husband sweetly, and murmured softly, "Everything and everyone seems to be where they belong, Bart."

The party of eight went into the elegant dining room to enjoy the wedding dinner Thelma had prepared along with Disney's help, and it was a most scrumptious feast. The spacious room was flourishing with cut-crystal vases filled with arrays of pastel blossoms and the brilliance of candlelight.

By the time the Hamiltons' carriage pulled away from the townhouse it was almost midnight. They took Lady Montgomery back to her home. All of them knew it was a night they would remember with the fondest of memories for a long time to come.

Disney excused himself from the newlyweds to go up to his room. He certainly felt that it had been a special night for him, since he'd just met a young lady he was very attracted to!

Bart and his bride shared one last glass of champagne before he dimmed the parlor lights and they went upstairs. He lifted his glass to toast his bride. "A more beautiful bride does not exist, Tawny my love. Destiny led me to you in Virginia. When I think that I went there seeking out a black Arabian, and I found you! God, I bless that day!"

"Oh, Bart—it was the most wonderful wedding any girl could ever dream about, and I love you for making it so. Every girlish daydream I ever had has come true."

"Ah, Tawny—we've only begun. There are so many wonderful dreams we're going to see come true. Just believe me, for it will be!"

He had not noticed that she had taken off the little white satin slippers and had her feet tucked up on the settee. "With all the good luck charms I had on tonight, we are bound to have a wonderful life! Joy gave me a handkerchief, Madame Renée made me this beautiful headband with orange blossoms, which she told me were good luck in France, Thelma gave me her blue garter, and your mother gave me the bracelet which both she and your grandmother wore on their wedding days." She laughed lightheartedly.

He made one swooping motion to take her up in his arms, and it was then that he noticed that she already had shed her slippers. He could not resist laughing at the sight of her dainty bare feet as he carried her out of the parlor and mounted the steps.

"Ah, Tawny—I'll always think of you as my little barefoot goddess, and I want you to promise me that you'll never change, love!"

"That is exactly what Madame Renée said to me this afternoon," Tawny told him as they came to the second landing.

"Madame Renée is a very wise lady!" Bart knew exactly what Renée Bourget was saying to Tawny whether she realized it or not. Tawny was that rare individual who was able to spellbind the people she met with an irresistible power she was not aware of.

Bart had laid out on his bed the sheer coral nightgown

he'd purchased at Madame Renée's when Tawny spied it, she picked it up in delight. "Oh, this is almost too beautiful to wear, Bart!" she declared.

A devious grin broke on his face. "That's your choice, love."

"Well, I've just got to try it on if you'll help me get out of this gown," she taunted, a gleam of mischief in her dark eyes.

He was more than willing to oblige her. He wondered if his young bride realized the sweet, tormenting agony she could stir within him as she sensuously taunted him in the translucent folds of coral and lace. There was a time when she might not have known, but now she sensed it from the look in his blue eyes, gleaming brighter when he was stimulated.

"You like it, Bart?" she asked, playing the coquette.

"Oh, God, Tawny!" he managed to stammer as his arms reached out to enclose her and his lips took hers in a long, loving kiss.

The rapture they'd found last night was to be theirs again on their wedding night.

Tawny knew that this all-consuming passion she felt for Bart would always make her feel fulfilled and happy.

Bart was convinced that his bride was the only woman who could hold his love all the days of his life!

Epilogue

Six years later, Bart Montgomery was as passionately in love with his wife as he'd been the day he'd married her. Having his two sons and one daughter had only enhanced the sensuousness of her lovely figure, it seemed to him.

Their first son was named William Edward to honor his father and Bill Cameron. Their second son was named Jason. When the third baby arrived, both of them were delighted to have a daughter. Bart eyes misted every time he looked at her, for he knew that this must have been the way Tawny looked as a babe, with big brown eyes and brown curls. This child was named Joy, for she was the joy of their life. The Hamiltons could not have been more pleased that Bart and Tawny had named two of their children Jason and Joy. The bond of the two families was forever united.

Blair's Inn was a most prosperous venture, and when Disney had established himself and felt he was wealthy enough to call on Jane Hamilton, he did court and win her heart. By the time they were married, the two-story stone house had doubled in size. Jane loved the life she shared with Disney, helping him run the quaint little inn.

One year of living at the townhouse was enough to convince Tawny that she wanted to raise her family in the country, so she urged Bart to leave the townhouse in the care of Wesley and Thelma.

Lady Montgomery could not have been happier to have the spacious house filled with the adorable children. She was eager to turn over the role of mistress to Tawny.

Tawny was content, for she could see Coco and Diablo daily and go for a ride around the beautiful English countryside anytime she wished. By now, the magnificent Arabian had sired many foals and Tawny had met royalty from various countries who'd visited Montgomery Stables wishing to breed their mares with the black beauty, Diablo.

On their fifth anniversary, Bart had purchased a special gift for Tawny—a feisty little mare sired by Diablo some four years ago. He'd also purchased from Madame Renée a magnificent black velvet cape trimmed in ermine.

When Tawny received her two gifts, she was elated by both of them. When Bart asked her what she was going to name her Arabian mare, she did not hesitate for a minute. "She shall be called Velvet," she told her husband. "She is as black and glossy as my beautiful cape."

Tawny couldn't imagine how she could be a happier lady as the spring approached, for she was finally to have a visit from her dear Reba Cameron.

Bart knew how excited Tawny was about Reba's visit to England, but the last several weeks he'd also noticed a special glow on her face.

That night when he took her in his arms and his lips tenderly kissed her, he asked, "Well, Tawny love, what will this one be—a son or a daughter?"

He felt her stiffen in his arms. "Now, how did you know that, Bart Montgomery?"

He gave a robust laugh. "Ah, when you love a woman like I love you, there are no secrets. I've known for a few weeks that you were expecting another babe. So tell me, love—is it a son or a daughter we will be having?" There was an amused grin on his handsome face.

In a firm, assured voice that he had to believe, she told him that it would be a daughter. "And she shall be called Reba," she added giving a girlish giggle as she snuggled closer in his arms and pressed against his broad chest. As it always had been when he held Tawny in his arms, he gave way to the wild, untamed passion she seemed to ignite in him.

The little backwoods girl from Virginia had the power to bewitch and enchant him after all this time. She still in-

478

trigued him as no other woman ever could, and he swore she still did not realize the charms she possessed.

But Tawny did know, and she'd known for a long time!